The Old Soul

BY

Kenneth J. M. MacLean

TheOld Soul

ISBN: 978-0-9996724-1-9 (eBook), 978-0-9996724-2-6 (paperback)

Cover Image Credits:

Homo Ergaster, José Luis Filpo Cabana, Wikimedia Commons

Kheops Pyramid, Nina Aldin Thune, Wikimedia Commons

License: https://creativecommons.org/licenses/by-sa/3.0/deed.en

Contents

Acknowledgments

Thank you to Kurt Rosenwinkel, Mark Turner, Taylor Eigsti and Eric Harland, and all of the great musicians out there for the beautiful music that was my inspiration for writing this book.

Thanks also to Lee Carroll and Kryon for their great vision of humanity's future.

"Dear reader, traditional human power structures and their reign of darkness are about to be rendered obsolete."

— Buckminster Fuller, from *Cosmography: A Posthumous Scenario for the Future of Humanity*

Part I

CHAPTER **1**

200,000 years ago. Rügen, island off the coast of Germany

The hominid walked upon the barren plain, searching for food. It was cold. It wore a crude, patchwork fur made from the various animals it had caught. Its feet were encased in fur; the soles were of tough tree bark.

The hominid was lonely. The females in this area had already been taken. This meant he only had to hunt for one, but the desire for procreation was strong within him.

The creatures were all in their burrows or dens today. He had spotted a fox over a mile away, hunting, but it had run off. Like the fox, he would probably go hungry today unless he could catch a fish. There were tubers and nuts he had stored for the winter in a small cave but his body demanded protein.

His cave was only a quarter mile from the Atlantic Ocean. He walked down to the beach and checked his crude nets. A fish was struggling. Despite the bitter cold he waded in and bashed it on the head with his flint axe. He would not starve today.

He walked back to the cave, gathering sticks for his fire. The hominid knew about flint and fire; he knew about nets for fishing and the construction of the spear with its shaped head of flint from the limestone cliffs on the island. He did not know how he knew this; it was simply a part of his knowledge base. Fire had been a part of human consciousness for hundreds of thousands of years, as had the construction of axes and spears. He went to his small cave and pushed aside a wall of carefully constructed brush that shielded him from the wind and cold. Painstakingly he constructed a fire and cooked his fish. He ate everything, including the scales.

When the sun went down he pushed aside the brush and looked at the rapidly diminishing light in the sky. His instinct told him it would be cold but sunny tomorrow. Creatures would be about, the hunting might be good. The light vanished from the sky; small lights appeared in the darkened sky. The hominid did not wonder about what the lights were or where they came from. They were just there. He accepted them.

The hominid let his fire burn down in its small pit. He placed tinder and sticks within easy reach. With his axe he had already cut wood. Tomorrow he would need to rebind the axe head to the wood. He placed his body down on top of the warmth from the fire and slept.

The hominid lived approximately 23 years. He never found a mate on that lonely island. One night after an unsuccessful hunt he lay down upon the cave floor and expired.

Marian

The hominid saw a tunnel of light. As he flew through the tunnel he began to remember things. His life had been simple: the hunt, the eating, the search for a mate. During his life he thought of nothing else, did not desire anything else. Now he felt his awareness expanding. It was very confusing. He arrived in a cave, but this was a funny cave. It had a multicolored light that soothed him. The light was accompanied by music. Music? Such a thing was unknown. But it pleased him. Someone came up to him. "This is the cave of creation. Here there is nothing lacking, dear one. When your confusion is gone someone will come for you."

This communication was strange. For almost his entire life on earth he had been silent. But now there was understanding. The hominid began to think. There was the birthing, the life on the planet...suddenly he remembered. The energy test! Yes, the soul splitting, the short life span. What was it for?

His body was now light, it did not need tending. He began to think some more.

He saw how pointless his life was. He had not mated, had not increased the species count. But yet his life had been important. Somehow his life had been necessary.

After a time in the cave (there was no diminishment of the multicolored light or the soft music) the memories of his life on earth began to fade. He felt himself reuniting with pieces and parts of himself he didn't know he had.

Someone came for him. He entered a gigantic hall, lined with people he had never seen on earth. But he knew each one. They were his dear friends. A great celebration was in progress. Wa-hee realized it was for him! His name was sung in light and song. The entirety of the Great Central Source knew him. He was loved beyond measure. It was a feeling he could never have remotely experienced on earth. Wa-hee was Home.

"Dear One, look," the voices were singing. Wa-Hee looked at his light body and saw that he had earned another stripe. His light body was magnificent; so brilliant and complex he could barely contemplate the beauty of himself. All of his lives were displayed before him; each stripe he had earned representing his service to the All-That-Is and the wonderful souls who were raising the All to higher and higher vibrations.

He was again a fully integrated being of light and song, linked with the Great Central Source. He saw the other souls who were part of the great experiment on earth. Everyone celebrated the magnificence of the earth, the life on it, and themselves.

Wa-Hee went into his personal temple. It was a magnificent multidimensional structure that represented the entirety of his experiences on the earth since he/she became aware. Wa-hee went to the "rooms" he had created for each lifetime on earth. He saw that he had already lived 136 lifetimes. He was one of the original souls of earth. More souls would come, much later.

He created another room from the light substance that surrounded him. Wa-hee placed there an axe, a spear, a piece of flint, and other memorabilia from his past life on Rügen.

He knew now what he had been sent to do. Each time he had gone hunting he had contemplated how best to accomplish his task. He had organized his simple life as best as he could. He had begun the very first vibrational resonances that would lead to the Seeding – the uplifting of human DNA from hominid to human being. This could not be accomplished by the low consciousness which presently existed on the planet. It must come from a Graduate planet. The Uplift of humanity would come from the stars.

Wa-hee began to get excited as he saw the potentials for his next life. He reviewed them with the entity(ies) who called themselves Marian.

Marian was a group consciousness, and the soul manager for earth. It was the soul manager's job to prepare souls for incarnation on earth, and to reorient them after they died.

"Look Wa-hee," Marian said. "Your next life will be in a much warmer climate, in Africa.

Wa-hee saw the potentials for himself and the planet. The life he had lived in northern Europe had been bleak and without pleasure; a struggle merely to survive. He had been sent there to walk the earth and seed a potential energy in a place that would not have significance for almost 200,000 years. Now it was his time to relax a little.

"Your goal is to raise consciousness in Africa as much as you can, in the heart chakra of the earth. You will incarnate as the son of a king." Wa-hee and the soul manager saw that the king had taken on an aggressive aspect and was busy trying to conquer his neighbors. "Your job is to mitigate this destructive tendency. Try to create as much compassion as you can."

Wa-hee nodded. The life in many ways would be pleasant. But he would have a soul responsibility. "It is your gift," Marian said. "For the first time on the earth an incarnated soul will have an inkling of the other side. But only for an instant." Wa-hee saw a crucial incident in which he confronted his father as he was about to go off to war.

"Your action here will determine the success of your life."

Wa-hee saw that it would be almost impossible to deflect his father from his campaign of aggression. "Your job, Wa-hee, is simply to plant a seed in the heart of your father. A suggestion that compassion might be a better solution. If you are successful the soul of your father will have advanced slightly in consciousness. It will be of great value in his next lifetime."

Wa-hee knew that the odds of success were slim.

"You will be allowed only a glimpse of your soul mission. As your father's loyal son the situation will call for your unqualified support for your father. To not do so would be an act of treason."

Wa-hee saw how the low consciousness of the hominids on earth prevented anything more. He saw what a huge climb it was to raise the consciousness of an entire planet. He began to feel a sort of soul hopelessness and depression.

Marian spoke quickly. "See the potentials for 200,000 years down the road."

Wa-hee saw that the population of the earth, if all went well after the Seeding, would eventually increase. Peace on earth was the ultimate objective.

"No, not the ultimate objective," Marian said. "Peace on earth is merely the beginning point of a true civilization."

Wa-hee saw it. Lifetime after lifetime must be lived. The vibration of the earth would, hopefully, be raised painstakingly, one lifetime at a time. There would be many setbacks. The potential for multiple extinction events for humanity was high. Many planets like earth never made it, sinking into degeneracy and internal conflicts.

"Why go through all of this work?" Wa-hee asked. "I see thousands of lifetimes. The potential for much suffering. Why do this when we are already in the arms of God?"

Marian saw the great plan of the Creator. But this young soul was not yet ready for the complete vision. The soul manager showed Wa-hee how the Uplifting of the earth benefitted the entire galaxy, and in turn the universe. Wa-hee became inspired at his level of soul knowledge and understanding.

"Now it is time for the wind of birth. Are you ready?"

Wa-hee prepared (him)self. He would be a male again. In order to "fit" his consciousness into the hominid body almost all of his soul would have to stay on this side. He would essentially be, as in his previous life, a walking collection of protoplasm with no awareness of Self. He would have one brief chance in the life to make a difference. He hoped he would be able to recognize it.

"Wa-hee. Do you give your permission to incarnate on the planet, despite the difficult life facing you?" Marian asked.

Wa-hee was warming up to the challenge. He was an adventurous soul, like all the others who participated in the Great Experiment. "Yes. I am ready."

Wa-hee entered the birth vortex. He felt pieces of himself being stripped away, preparing his lowered consciousness for insertion into the primitive (but now uplifted) human body. At one point he almost backed out, but then his awareness became so limited he didn't remember what he was doing. Suddenly he felt himself associated with the body. This feeling was familiar to Wa-hee after 136 lifetimes on the earth.

"A son!" cried the Chief of the little tribe. He grabbed the squealing infant from the breast of his mother and held him up in the air. "A brave warrior! An intrepid hunter! So shall you be."

The Chief tossed the infant onto his mother's stomach. He spoke in a primitive *Ursprache*, or proto-language. "Take good care of my son, woman."

Son of Chief grew to manhood. The climate at that time was warm, during the middle of an inter-glacial period. Game was plentiful. Son of Chief learned how to hunt and found a mate. The little hunter-gatherer tribe was able to hold a wide swath of territory and became powerful. When he was 17 his father heard of a great treasure held by another tribe to the east. Son of Chief was dimly aware that his father was motivated only by greed and ego, and did not give a thought to his people.

The Chief gathered his warriors and hunters together. "Now is the time to strike! We will leave tonight and arrive before dawn." Here was Son of Chief's moment. For an instant his soul mission appeared in his consciousness. But Son of Chief was excited about the coming battle. The moment passed.

The next day the Chief took a spear to the heart. Son of Chief died when a huge warrior split his head with a crude stone axe. Both souls transitioned.

Marian

The soul manager had little to do. At this time the population of the earth was about 300,000. Approximately 100 souls died each day, replaced by about 100 others.

Chief and Son of Chief arrived back at the cave of creation. Wa-hee had lived less than 18 years. His memory returned much quicker than Chief. Soon they were both again in front of the soul manager.

"Do you see why your life was terminated?" Marian asked Wa-hee.

"Yes. To live after the moment passed would have been pointless. The consciousness raising, as trivial as it was, failed. I could not see past the current life. I was too excited about the battle."

"Yes dear one. Lives are short because the level of consciousness is so low. The veil is thick; usually allowing only one fleeting opportunity per lifetime." They both reviewed Wa-hee's life as Son of Chief.

"What would have happened if I had been successful?" Wa-hee asked.

Marian showed the potentials. "Chief's proposal would have been rejected by the tribe to the east. A conflict would have resulted in a short time; both of you would have been killed."

"The same result. It is sad."

"This will change, Wa-hee. The Seeders from the Seven Sisters have come to this planet. Your DNA, and all who incarnate after, have been enhanced. You will have a chance for more rapid advancement."

Wa-hee could see that the human race had almost no chance to evolve unless it was uplifted. If evolution were to take its natural course, trial and error *might* raise the primitive hominids of earth to an intelligent civilization. More than likely it would not. The odds of advancement to a true civilization, even after millions of years, were slim if changes to the biology were not made.

Wa-hee had a thousand questions. "How did the Seeders get here? What have they done?"

Marian smiled. "That is something you will experience during several hundred more lifetimes dear one. After the Seeding there will be a long period of very slow advancement. A test of energy will begin 150,000 years from now in Lemuria. But that is a long way off."

Wa-hee incarnated once more. And again. And again, and again...

CHAPTER 2

The Seeders. Merope, the Pleiades, 1,000,000 years ago

Hummhum-Ha was flying over the ocean, which separated two huge land masses that covered the planet's surface. His mission was to get at least one of his three missiles into the enemy's main launching platform at Bummipatrum.

As he looked out the cockpit of his modified boomerang he saw the snow falling in huge flakes, obscuring his vision. He tinted the viewing window, flying by electronic guidance only. He saw on his scope that he had attracted two bogeys. They were locked on to him now. Hummhum-Ha slowed slightly and lifted his boomerang, allowing the bogeys to pass underneath. He quickly turned over, flying upside down. The g-force crushed the air out of his lungs, but he had trained for that. He un-opaqued his cockpit and saw the startled glances of the two pilots as he accelerated, flying over them. Hummhum-Ha waved. He fired his laser cannon in two short bursts directly at their quantum ramjet engines, crippling both bogeys enough for him to make his escape. The precious aircraft were so valuable it was unthinkable to destroy them. On Merope it was a crime whose punishment was instant execution.

Hummhum-Ha saw land ahead. Huge snow-covered mountains raised their rocky points five miles above the planet's surface. He raised his boomerang to an insane altitude of thirteen miles. Four of the Seven Sisters were visible above the curve of the globe. He would be almost invisible here. If he could remain undetected for thirty more minutes he could reach the enemy station. Suddenly brightly colored tractor beams began to penetrate the ionosphere. Hummhum-Ha set his guidance system to random. Now it was the electronics of his craft versus the electronics of the enemy. If he were caught he would be tortured and the precious mission data extracted from his mind as his consciousness left the body.

Hummhum-Ha reached the middle of the continent and loosed his missiles at the enemy launching pad. Four enemy craft were flying toward him now. As he was surrounded, a tractor beam grabbed his craft. He only had a second before the tractor would paralyze his biology. He pushed the button that would destroy the data center of his craft. As he lost motor control of his body he grinned broadly. Mission completed! His name would be sung in light in the Heroes Chamber back home in the Humm Confederacy.

25,000 years later a descendant of Hummhum-Ha flew in a survey craft over a devastated planet, imaging the destruction. Huge craters were visible over both ice and snow-covered continents. All major cities had been destroyed. The planet's population had been reduced to 5,000 shivering souls. The Bumm and the Humm had been forced to make a truce after 25 millennia of continuous war. It was either that or racial and planetary suicide.

1,000 years later the Bumm and the Humm were still in desultory negotiations about how to share the limited resources offered by their planet. They were stuck. A tension-filled peace had existed between the two sides as the population of Merope gradually increased. It had been agreed that technology was a path to species suicide. Over the centuries Merope had begun to recover from millennia of war. The planet had become pastoral and tribal; the climate had warmed. Each tribe within the Bumm and the Humm was fiercely proud of its traditions, and of their faction.

Bummmamanipum-Bu spoke to his counterpart at the negotiating table in the capital city, which was located in a legally autonomous region that had no association with either faction. It had been agreed that at least one member from each faction would be present at the table at all times. Those who became angry or frustrated were encouraged to leave and clear their heads.

"During the past century no progress has been made. The issues are well known, but 25,000 years of war have hardened attitudes."

Hummhum-Li agreed. "I am afraid that war will break out once again."

"If this happens we will destroy ourselves and this planet."

Bummmamanipum-Bu agreed. "The situation is desperate. Hope is gone. We must ask for assistance."

Hummhum-Li made a suggestion. "Let us gather the entire Council of Negotiators. You and I will read the statement we have both prepared."

-Bu called for a Messenger. "Assemble your team and bring all negotiators to the Hall of Audiences."

The Messenger ran off.

Gradually the members, 50 on each side, began to appear in the great auditorium, which was only used for the most important occasions. The Pleiadians are 12-foot tall humanoids with two arms, two legs and a head, as is all intelligent life in Desiree, the Pleiadian name for the Milky Way galaxy. They have thick, deep blue leathery skin that protects them from the planet's weather. Merope was a smaller planet than earth, and colder, with much less biomass and bio-diversity.

The Negotiators filed into the great hall. The colors of the Humm were black and each wore a black robe and a hat. The colors of the Bumm were red. Each also wore ceremonial robes and red headgear. Much grumbling and grousing was heard. Several members on each side spoke sharply to one another. One of the Humm threw off his cloak, shouting. A Bumm removed his cloak. A fight broke out.

Bummamanipum-Bu and Hummhum-Li sat at the head of a large circular dais, slightly raised from the floor. Hummhum-Li banged three times on a gong with the *balal*, a seasoned and engraved piece of wood that was over 1,000 years old. The two combatants were separated. All of the delegates quieted. The ceremonial gong had not been used in over two decades. Whatever announcement was to be made, it had planetary importance.

The auditorium gradually quieted.

Bummamanipum-Bu, the Bumm's best orator, began to read from a piece of parchment. "Myself and Hummhum-Li have agreed on the following statement:

> Delegates to the planetary council, it is time for our species to face reality. War
> is inevitable.

At this pandemonium broke out. Another fight began. The ceremonial gong was sounded once again.

Bummamanipum-Bu continued.

> War is inevitable. For 25 millennia we have fought. Three times have we almost
> wiped ourselves out, and the planet as well. For almost 1,000 years we have been
> trying to negotiate a final peace settlement. We have not been successful and
> we will never be successful. Let us admit to ourselves that our species is insane.
> Without help we are sure to destroy ourselves once more.

The delegates grumbled. There were some angry shouts. But all present understood that the speaker spoke truth that had never been uttered before. Hummhum-Li continued with the statement.

> -Bu and myself have agreed: We must ask for outside help. This help must come
> from entities with a higher consciousness. Legend has it that our planet was
> seeded by a Graduate life form, a species that has attained a higher conscious-
> ness. Despite 26 millennia we have not been able to live peacefully together.

Therefore, we must engage in a planet-wide meditation, something that has never before been attempted. We must call upon the Old Ones to help us. Without intervention we will annihilate our species and our planet in a final Armageddon.

None of the delegates had to be reminded of the meaning of the word. On earth Armageddon is a place. On Merope it was a state of mind, a sort of berserker frenzy that could only be expunged in killing and death. Bummamanipum-Bu continued.

Both –Li and myself agree that unanimity is the only way this can work. Therefore we must send out the Messengers to every hamlet, city, and village on Merope. On the agreed-upon date, which shall be set unanimously by the Council, all Bumm and Humm will ask for assistance from the ethers. The enlightened ones, if they still exist, will have permission to intervene and save our civilization and our planet.

A babble of excited voices was heard. Surprisingly, all 100 delegates agreed. For the first time in centuries of negotiation there was no debate or rancor.

"Finally," a delegate was heard to say. "Finally, someone has told the unvarnished truth."

At this all of the delegates laughed nervously.

Hummhum-Li concluded the statement.

The theme of the meditation will be as follows: Dear Enlightened Ones, we beseech your assistance. After thousands of years of war and destruction, we as a species admit that we will destroy ourselves unless help from outside comes forth. We hereby give permission for intervention and ask for your aid.

"Of course this wording is not set in stone," Hummhumm-Li said. "But the intention is clear. This will work only if every individual on Merope gives their consent."

Again there was no dissent among the delegates. A few smiles were seen. This proposal was regarded by all delegates as an unprecedented and wonderful omen. Bummamanipum-Bu and Hummhum-Li sealed the agreement. Both embraced each other on the dais and proclaimed that they would die rather than raise weapons against each other, or fight physically or verbally.

Most of the delegates could not see their way to do this with their neighbors, but the necessity for such an action was recognized.

"Why have we not seen this solution before?" a Bumm asked.

One of the Humm shrugged. "Desperate times call for desperate measures. Always before solutions involved conflict. Now, perhaps, it is time for true peace."

The delegates could agree on this.

"Must every individual on the planet agree to participate?" a Humm asked.

Bummamanipum-Bu and Hummhum-Li both bowed and took the hands of each other. Already the atmosphere in the Hall had lightened considerably as the two chief negotiators demonstrated a feeling of trust between them. Both spoke as one. "Yes. All must agree or the exercise is pointless."

Everyone in the room felt the force of this proclamation.

"How shall we proceed?" someone asked.

Hummhum-Li responded. "First, the formal votes of all present in Council must be recorded. The process must begin with us. Then we will, only for this special occasion, make a planetary broadcast using the crystal apparatus."

This provoked some comment, for this apparatus – a huge geometric array of tuned crystals – was not only a communications device, but a weapon of frightening power. It was kept within the Council chambers and guarded.

"The broadcast will only use the lower frequencies, ensuring that no harm can come to any. Then, the Messengers will be summoned. The votes of all 100,000 of the People across the planet will be recorded. If even one is against, the project will be terminated."

There was much debate on this issue. But a new harmony had been established. After two days of intense consultation and discussion it was agreed. A formal document was drawn up, signed by all 100 members of the Council.

One of the Bumm spoke. "I'm afraid that although this project is a wonderful idea, it will be hopeless. To get the agreement of every citizen on Merope? It is a fruitless task."

Many agreed. Yet it had been established that unanimity was the only way. For thousands of years the People had learned to solve their problems using force and conflict. The new proposal was such a radical departure there were yet no contrary memes associated with it. Therefore all remaining objections were resolved. The aye votes of all 100 Council members were formally recorded.

The broadcast was made. The Messengers were summoned. They would travel the length and breadth of Merope and speak personally to each village, city, and hamlet dweller.

The date for the meditation was set for one half of a planetary orbit from the day of the broadcast, to give time for all votes to be counted. The votes would be recorded using the recording crystals. On Merope these communication devices were similar to today's mobile phones. All citizens had one for their personal use. The votes would be gathered from all 60 regions of the planet.

Each vote would be recorded in the presence of a Messenger. This led to a solemnity befitting the magnitude of the undertaking.

Each Citizen felt that he or she was participating in a planet-wide event.

A second broadcast would be given in six months, announcing the results. The votes of every citizen would be announced, along with their name and location. To ensure fairness the votes would not be tallied until all 100,000 votes from each recording crystal had been personally deposited within the planetary council chamber by the Messenger assigned to that region.

The Messengers were sent forth across the planet.

The Council stayed in session, hearing progress reports. The mood of the Council had turned glum after the original excitement wore off. Yet unanimous agreement was still present. It was clear that only a completely new and radical approach stood a chance of success. Planetary and species destruction was inevitable otherwise. Twenty-five centuries of hatred would see to that.

"What is the sentiment of Region 17?" Bummamanipum-Bu asked one of the regional Messengers when he reported in with his tally crystal.

"Remarkable," was the reply. "The idea of consulting everyone and reaching unanimous agreement on the entire planet was so radical that citizens couldn't believe it. At first there was shock, then disbelief. Then, as the implications sunk in of the magnitude of the experiment, the People seemed enthusiastic."

Bummamanipum-Bu sighed. "Yet it will only take one vote to scuttle the process."

The Messenger shrugged. "Everyone I saw recorded their vote with the utmost seriousness. There was almost a sacredness surrounding the voting process."

In five months all of Merope had been surveyed. A month later all 60 recording crystals from each region of the planet, with their tallies, were deposited within the Council chambers. It would be the Council's duty to count the votes. As part of the proclamation it had been agreed that votes would be announced live, as the information from each of the 60 tally crystals were opened. Even if negative votes were recorded the counting would continue until the final vote. Fifty Bumm would count votes from the 23 Humm regions. Fifty Humm would count votes from the 37 Bumm regions.

The vote counting began.

"Bamapartham-Bumm, from region 1, votes affirmative." This was a good start. Most of the Council members smiled. "Lualanamum-Hu, from region 1, votes affirmative...." And so it went. Because every vote was so important, each one was announced without haste. For the first time in 26,000 years every one of the People were being consulted.

Citizens went about their daily tasks. Even those warriors preparing for conflict kept their broadcast crystals tuned to the Council vote count. A sort of camaraderie was building up in every population center. The curious tuned in to see who voted no.

At the end of the voting over 99% of the population had voted yes. There were only 737 negative votes, but each one had been like a dagger thrust into the belly of the process.

The Council spokesperson made an announcement. "Because unanimity has not been achieved, the experiment cannot proceed."

At the Council chambers all was gloom. The agreement was that war would ignite somewhere on the planet. It would spread to engulf everyone.

Bummamanipum-Bu was devastated. His first reaction was to accuse his friend Hummhum-Li. It was ingrained in the confrontational consciousness of Merope. Almost all of the "Nay" votes were from the minority Humm faction.

At that moment a messenger arrived, breathless, with a new recording crystal. "All 57 Nay voters in Region 11 have changed their vote to Aye."

Everyone on the council was hoarse. Each had taken turns announcing the tally.

"What difference does it make now?" someone remarked.

Bummamanipum-Bu rose. "I shall personally make the announcement of the vote reversal in Region 11 using the crystal apparatus." As he did so he felt the defeated atmosphere in Council lift a little.

All across the planet citizens were debating. Regional communication stations were humming with discussion. Several local skirmishes broke out. Before Bummamanipum-Bu had a chance to make his announcement, a regional leader of the Bumm made the accusation that would ignite the war. "It is always the Humm who impede progress!" he broadcast. "The Nay votes of the citizens from Region 11 have destroyed hope for all of Merope!"

The citizens of Region 11 (a region in the Humm Confederacy) began to pick up arms as their spokesman accused the Bumm (as always) of using their majority to run roughshod over the Humm minority. "Good citizens of Region 11! The fascists in Region 40 are inciting their population for another pogrom! Take up your arms before they attack, as these treacherous snakes always do!" Region 40, a Bumm area, and Region 11, shared a border along a narrow river. As warriors from both sides were about to fall upon each other one of the Humm heard the announcement of the voting switch from Region 11 on his communication crystal. "You snakes!" he shouted across the river to the Bumm. "Have you heard the declaration of the Council concerning our vote reversal?"

On the Bumm side all was confusion. Their leader had made the accusation knowing that all in Region 40 had voted "Aye." He halted their advance and held a parley with his forces at the river's edge, twenty feet from the Bumm forces.

"If it is confirmed that all of your scum have voted as true citizens should, you will be spared," he shouted.

"You dare to call us scum! You malignants!"

This peroration almost caused the forces to clash. At the last moment the Region 40 leader gave the order. "Stand down! If these...citizens...have changed their minds, we must not sully our honor by attacking true men."

"Humm reprobates!" several shouted, grabbing their weapons. But the Bumm regional leader was a recognized authority. "Stand down I say! We are not murderers. We fight only for our honor." The Bumm warriors reluctantly put down their arms, grumbling.

The Humm contingent on the other side of the river heard these exchanges. Their leader relaxed, as did their men. "If this is more Bumm treachery, you will feel our wrath!" he shouted. But he withdrew his forces a few paces.

The Region 40 leader also withdrew his forces a few paces back, to precisely match the distance of the Humm across the river. "We will stay here until this...development...has been confirmed."

"I will send one of our men as a hostage," the Region 11 commander shouted. "Do you also send us one of yours. We will both independently confirm this new occurrence."

It was agreed.

The Region 11 commander was secretly pleased that his citizens had changed their votes. The 57 "Nay" votes from his region had been a grave disappointment to him. He discussed it with the others.

"Do we trust these Bumm?" he asked his fighters.

"Of course not," one of his men said. "But what can we do? If a war starts here it will engulf all of Merope. I do not wish to be responsible for that."

Another fighter agreed. "It would be an indelible stain on our honor and on our souls."

The Humm leader felt the hatred all of his men felt toward the Bumm; a hatred combined with hopelessness. "That is so. This must stop somewhere. Ours must not be the conflict that ignites the end of our species."

His second in command agreed. "We are helpless against our own karma. Somewhere out there are the Enlightened Ones. We must ask for their help. All of us, even these Bumm."

On the Bumm side there was heated discussion among the fighters. "If the Humm votes from Region 11 have indeed been reversed, we will lay down our arms," the Bumm leader announced.

As the hostages were being exchanged, all of the Humm recognized the opportunity brought by the announcement from the Council. The Bumm across the river recognized it as well, but were suspicious. Both sides agreed merely to temporarily postpone the conflict while the Messengers from each group communicated with the Council Messengers in the capital city.

The vote change was confirmed by both sides.

The tenseness in both camps calmed. It was agreed that each side would send a small floating platform to the middle of the shallow river. There, a formal peace treaty was signed between Region 11 and Region 40.

When this was reported to the Council the members expressed joy. The announcement of the treaty was broadcast, as well as a statement from the two regional leaders expressing their hope that planetary agreement was still possible.

After that Messengers began to arrive to the Council chambers with more tally changes. Within three months the entire planet had agreed to the global meditation. Tensions were still high, for failure to attract the needed help would send Merope back into conflict. The old hatreds simmered strongly beneath the surface.

On the appointed date when the sun was highest over the capital city, all 100,000 citizens of Merope, in their own way, beseeched the Enlightened Ones (or any Graduate race) for help, giving permission to any with loving hearts to come forward and save their species.

Within minutes of the completion of the global event, great beings of light were seen in every city, village, and hamlet. They arrived without the aid of technology, using the power of the merkaba, the vehicle of consciousness, to project their consciousness through the ethers.

All citizens at first bowed low in worship. But the great beings, who said they were from the star system of Arcturus, said this: "Dear Ones, get off your knees. It is time to find the God within. You have asked for help and we are here to grant your request. Your courageous action has started your race on the path to Graduate status. And so it is."

On Merope citizens learned of the society of races that had evolved to find the Creative Source. The light beings announced that a great celebration was now underway in the rest of the galaxy among all Graduate planets. The monumental accomplishment in the Pleiades was being recognized. Each citizen was made to feel that their actions to avoid war and embrace peace were part of a seminal event for the entire galaxy. Each citizen felt an overwhelming joy and sense of satisfaction from the great beings.

With agreement from the collective on Merope, the Arcturans announced that the eons-old karma on Merope could be dissolved completely. This had never even occurred to any of the Bumm and the Humm.

In another planetary meditation each citizen agreed unanimously that old hatreds would be forgiven and forgotten.

The great beings of light smiled. "From now on the road will get easier and easier. Within a hundred generations there will be true peace here. We will remain to oversee your development, and to teach you about the higher realms of consciousness. But remember dear ones, you will have to do the heavy lifting yourselves. We will guide, but you must do the work. If you are successful, we look forward to eventually admitting you to the society of Graduate planets."

After the second meditation all citizens experienced a feeling of lightness and well being. This was a new feeling after millennia of war and conflict.

"Do not despair if you take a step backward for every two steps forward dear ones. We are here to aid you whenever you wish." The great beings from Arcturus – whose bodies were only two feet tall but who shined brighter than the sun of Merope – showed the citizens the merkaba and its potentials. The Teaching began.

And so it was that in the Pleiades, the source of consciousness and the connection to the Creative Source was discovered. After a further 900,000 years of development Merope, and all planets in that sector, attained Graduate status and joined the community of civilizations able to communicate and travel along the multi-dimensional pathways using the merkaba.

The Arcturans impressed upon the Pleiadians the necessity for continuation of the process of upliftment. As a requirement of Graduate status, the beings on Merope had to find another planet and uplift the beings there.

Earth, 210,000 years ago

Hammarumum-Ho and his Graduate group scoured the local star systems, looking for a planet to seed. Like their planet of Merope, it had to be an obscure planet, off the galactic trade routes. Hammarumum-Ho's group did not travel in spacecraft. After a million years of evolution, they simply sent their consciousness remotely into the galactic substrate, and were able to perceive far better than any instrumentation. This is one of the benefits of attaining Graduate status and higher consciousness.

Hammarumum-Ho and his group flew by a brilliant Type B binary star with seven planets at the edge of the Taurus cluster. They discussed their objectives.

"Let us find a planet with a warmer climate and a more resource-rich biosphere," -Ha suggested. During these discussions the familiar was used. All beings in this consciousness group are part of the HummarBummum, the integrated consciousness of the stellar systems in the Pleiades.

"Agreed," said –Lu. "Our planet was so cold it bred contention and warlike behavior."

"The planet should have an abundance of water." –Wu said. "Water is calming and soothing. It breeds greater contentment. Life can thrive there."

These suggestions were unanimously approved.

"Of the approximately 200 billion star systems in our current catalogue, only two percent of the planets have attained graduate status," –Li said. "This is unacceptable."

"The lack of advancement in the galaxy is puzzling. Why are so many planets mired in conflict and war?" said –Hi.

A slight reactivation of old hatreds was felt within the group as everyone remembered the eons old conflict on Merope.

"The goal is to raise the spiritual evolution of the galaxy, -Hu said. "We can all agree on that."

"Let us return to our inspection," –Wa stated.

The group calmed and regained their composure.

Some time later the group was passing over a planetary system with a single sun, a G2V type star, a yellow dwarf on the main sequence. The stellar system appeared to be in a backwater and was hidden quite nicely.

"Look at that." –Hi pointed to the third planet, a blue jewel with a huge expanse of ocean and four continental land masses. The planet's ecosystem was biologically diverse. The HummarBummum accessed its history grids and discovered that temperature was the planet's mechanism for sustaining and maintaining itself. The group discovered that periodic cooling was intermixed with periods of warming.

"Enhanced life forms could grow and expand here during the periods of warmth," –Hi remarked.

"The planet already has indigenous hominid life forms that could be uplifted through genetic enhancement," –Wu observed.

"This place is perfect," –Lu said enviously, thinking about the harsh environment of Merope. "The path of these beings could be accelerated."

"We must make sure," -Ha said. "How did this planet with but a single sun develop intelligent life? This is an anomaly."

The group again studied the planet's esoteric history grids.

"4.5 billion local years ago a binary system developed," -Wu said. "Two stars orbited in ellipses around a common center of mass and ten planets formed."

"That is typical," –Li remarked. "Almost all planets that develop intelligent life revolve around binary star systems."

"Yes, but look what happened next," -Lu said. "Four billion years ago, Sol's stellar companion was hit by a gigantic meteor that plunged into its heart, destroying it. A gigantic ejection of hot gases seared the first planet and turned it into a roasted husk. Then, shock waves traveled into the heliosphere, arresting development on all ten planets. Over the next 3 billion years, the orbits of the planets slowly adjusted to the single star."

"This solar system is an outlier," –Xi said.

"Yes," -Ha said. "Despite all odds the third planet from Sol begins to develop an atmosphere with an oxygen content that could support life. Periodically, life on the planet is wiped out by magnetic pole shifts, severe ice ages, tectonic plate movement, asteroid strikes, volcanic eruptions, and coronal mass ejections from its single sun."

"This world is unique in the galaxy to my knowledge," -Su said. He was the group's geologist and climatologist. "After another billion years of volatility the planet finally begins to settle down, even though periodic ice ages occur every 100,000 years or so. Intelligent life does not appear until the very last second of its existence."

"How could a world with so much volatility develop intelligent life?" -Wu said. "It defies the laws of planetary evolution."

All agreed that the blue planet was a miracle.

"This world has been stable now for almost a million local years," -Su said. "A complex ecosystem has evolved. The ice comes and goes, refreshing the oceans and the life there, making it possible for an expansion of life on the land masses for long periods of time."

-Hu noticed something. "This is peculiar. See how the planet wobbles on its axis like a top losing momentum?"

"A wobble like this does not occur on any planet in our catalog," -Li said. "Another sign that this world is unique."

"How long does it take for the planet to complete one wobble on its axis?" –Xi asked.

"Approximately 26,000 local years," –Su said.

It was a huge omen. Merope itself had 26 millennia of conflict before stability had been assured.

The group considered. Should they resume their search for a more stable planet? The Pleiadians looked at the beauty of the world and were reluctant to let it go. Finally –Hu spoke for them all. "It is well. Let us recommend to the Council that this obscure planet be given the gift of Light and Dark. After the hominids here are genetically enhanced, this beautiful place will be a planet of free choice."

Each of the Seeders had already gone through the process on Merope and the other planets in the Pleiadian sector. These were not theoreticians sitting in an ivory tower. They had experienced it all, both bad and good.

The group pondered their personal memories and experiences.

"Free choice means that the humans here cannot be judged for their choices," -Hi said. "But each one must experience the consequences of their choices."

Everyone knew that the potential also included great suffering, brutality, and misery, as had occurred on Merope. The possibility that the uplifted race would choose the darkness and destroy itself was strong. The group contemplated the potentials for the new species. Would the earth planet do better than the Seeders themselves had done on Merope? That was the hope.

The Duality

About 200,000 years ago the Pleiadian seeders altered the DNA of the indigenous hominids on earth. Part of the Seeding was the laying on of the Template of God within human DNA, which is an esoteric, multi-dimensional gateway to higher consciousness. During this process the 24 human chromosome pairs became 23.

Much later, science would give a purely physical explanation for this, observing that the genes on human chromosome 2 are divided across two chromosomes in chimps and in other hominids. Science would call the fusion of chromosome 2 a mere chromosomal abnormality; an evolutionary accident. But the chromosome fusion event could not have been a random physical abnormality because it created a viable and completely separate species. Homo sapiens is different from all other hominidae on the planet, which have 24 chromosome pairs.

The Uplift is part of a galactic program of advancement, where Graduate races with high consciousness seed young, indigenous races. It would (hopefully) transform a race of hominids very quickly (in evolutionary terms) to a race of human beings that could potentially reach a higher consciousness. Thus would the resonance of the galaxy also be enhanced via the cosmic web – the implicate order – which connects all things.

After the Uplift human DNA had a physical and an esoteric component. However, the esoteric ("God") component would be invisible to the five human senses and, much later, to scientific instruments. A great test or experiment would be possible. Would human beings, with free choice, discover the link to their Higher Selves and find the Creator? Or would humanity remain mired in a "prove it" materialism, competition, skepticism, and survival concepts that only involved the body? If the latter, homo sapiens would remain stuck in low consciousness, barbarism, and endless war, despite the genetic enhancement.

Free choice is the only way a species can advance to higher consciousness. However, the test couldn't truly begin until humanity's biology had advanced in evolution enough so that free choice could operate. If there is no awareness of Self, there is no conscious choice; just primitive instinct. The Uplift was just the starting point. A long, slow, evolutionary process of the biology of the new human species would be necessary to make the test of free choice possible.

Over the course of the next 80,000 years all human sub-species died out, unable to compete with the enhanced awareness of the uplifted homo sapiens.

The Seeders stayed on earth to watch over their young brothers and sisters. They did everything they could to ensure success for the new species.

"The rule is, we can help but not interfere," –Bu said. "Otherwise the test is invalidated."

"Even after the Uplift evolutionary progress is very slow," –Su said. There was an element of frustration.

-Hi nodded. "We are beginning to understand the difficulty of our mission."

"The path to Graduate status must be walked through experience," -Wu said. "It cannot be gifted. Otherwise the participants cannot evolve in knowledge and wisdom and the experiment is worthless."

"The test is difficult," -Bu acknowledged. "Within the uplifted, esoteric DNA are the instruction sets for galactic and multi-dimensional communication and travel. But these instruction sets are esoteric, and therefore hidden as part of the test!"

"It is almost unfair," -Su said. "Look how much difficulty we had on Merope."

-Hi recognized this. "We must do as the enlightened ones did for us, the great beings from Arcturus. Their instructions were explicit."

The group moped a little about their mission. "The difficulty of the Uplift is probably why only 2% of the planets in this galaxy make it," -Bu said. "The rest are mired in mediocrity or barbarism."

Even the enlightened Pleiadians did not know why this was. "Perhaps after we complete our mission we will discover why the test must be so hard," -Hi said.

"And so long," -Bu said. "It requires great patience on our part."

"Yes! The little humans only live for a few years. For them it is over quickly. We who are enlightened essentially live forever. It is harder for us."

-Bu was philosophical. "It takes time. We have plenty of that."

The group recognized that the hard way was the only way to soul advancement, both for them and the new species of humans.

"The earth experiment is still in its beginning stages," -Bu said. "Homo sapiens will need another 70,000 years or so for the consciousness of the new species to gradually rise far enough to participate in the test of free choice."

This was agreed to by all of the group.

The test would then begin with a perfect 50-50 balance between the light and the dark. The Seeders had already picked out a "Garden of Eden," an isolated continent in the middle of a vast ocean that would later be called the Pacific.

CHAPTER **3**

75,000 years ago

Over 100,000 years of evolution had advanced the biology and the consciousness of the original hominids, thanks to original souls like Wa-hee. After over a thousand incarnations Wa-hee was now an old soul on earth. We follow Wa-hee's next lifetime, which began as a female 75,000 years ago in China.

When (she) entered the vortex of birth she experienced a stronger connection to the other side within the human body she was to occupy than when (he) was Son of Chief 125,000 years ago. Wa-hee felt that her soul mission had a better chance of success. The goal was to instill compassion in her mate, an influential hunter and warrior.

When Wa-hee was 15, one morning before dawn on the day of an important hunt, she arose and looked at the stars. She wondered: What are the lights? Where do they come from? Wa-hee had a vague feeling that there was something more. She had the feeling she had to do something important.

The men were gathering for a pow-wow. Several miles to the north an acquisitive tribe had accumulated a great store of four-legged animals they used in the hunt. T'shok, Wa-hee's mate, had first seen these *horses* used during the spring of the year, when game was plentiful. The hunters had chased and then surrounded a giant bear with these animals, subduing it with their spears. T'shok had tasted bear meat, and liked it. The plan was to invade the tribe to the north and take their horses.

Wa-hee (who did not have a name in the tribe, being merely the woman of T'shok) spoke. "Would it not be better to ask these hunters how they gathered and utilized the creatures? Instead of fighting our two tribes could share knowledge and resources, thus making us stronger. You would be the leader of an expanded tribe with greater influence."

T'shok was about to dismiss the female's comments, and raised his hand to silence her. But something held him back. T'shok considered the new idea. Could cooperation lead to more power? Perhaps.

Wa-hee saw that she had gotten through to the male. Something inside her leaped with joy. Without knowing it in her conscious understanding, she had accomplished her life's mission.

After a few moments T'shok dismissed the idea of his mate. He wanted no dealings with another tribe. He would steal their horses and use them to his advantage. Then he would scatter the tribe to the north and take their lands.

The next spring Wa-hee died in childbirth, presenting her mate with a son. T'shok was saddened for a moment at the passing of Wa-hee. The woman had strange ideas but had been loyal. She had given him two sons, one of whom had already died from the claws of a fanged cat.

Life went on. T'shok found a new mate after Wa-hee transitioned.

Marian

When Wa-hee's soul came back to the other side she was not surprised. The process of death was now as familiar to her as breathing had been to her physical body. Again her life had been short. But this time both she and the soul manager were very pleased.

"Your suggestion to T'shok was not immediately rejected," Marian said. "It was considered carefully."

Marian showed Wa-hee how T'shok's moment of contemplation had penetrated the planetary grids of subtle energy. "This was a seminal moment dear one. It set up a slight resonance toward cooperation that someone else may tap into."

Wa-hee stayed on the other side until T'shok's death. Both she and Marian saw how T'shok had twice more thought carefully before going to war. "The balance between the male and female energies is unbalanced," Marian said. "Male energy has predominated for over 100,000 years. When the balance between male and female is equalized, peace on earth will be established."

"It is much harder to be a woman," Wa-hee said.

"But women have a greater connection to the Great Central Source, even in primitive societies."

Wa-hee contemplated her lifetimes as a woman and as a man.

"That is so. I feel more content as a woman."

"Your gender will not change for the next 50 incarnations," Marian said. The soul manager showed Wa-hee the changes on the planet since the Pleiadian uplift. "Progress will be faster now, but it is still very slow. Changes will occur from generation to generation."

At that time the population of earth was less than one million. Human populations still consisted almost entirely of non-sedentary hunter-gatherers. Marian showed Wa-hee the potentials for the earth.

"The planet's climate is about to undergo a dramatic change. Look."

The scene shifted to what is the site of present-day Lake Toba in Sumatra, Indonesia. "A gigantic super volcano will erupt. This event will cause a global volcanic winter of six to ten years and a 1,000-year-long cooling episode.[1] It will send 2,800 cubic centimeters of ash and dust into the atmosphere." Wa-hee saw that the eruption would drop over 2 1/2 inches of ash over what is now South Asia, the Indian Ocean, and the Arabian and South China Sea.

"See how this sediment in the atmosphere will dim the sun, disrupt seasonal rains, choke off streams, and deposit cubic miles of hot ash across acres and acres of plants. Berries, fruits, trees, and African game will become scarce. Human populations are concentrated in Africa. Many will transition. The earth will get colder and more inhospitable. The population of earth will plummet."

Wa-hee was shown how the average temperature would drop 20 degrees in some areas. All of what is now China would be very cold. Wa-hee did not want to go back there.

"The grassy plains of Africa will shrink back significantly. The small bands of humans left will be hungry for thousands more years."[2]

Wa-hee became angry. "I have lived over 1,000 lifetimes! All of it for nothing! Is all our work to be senselessly destroyed?"

Marian smiled. "Relax dear one." The soul manager showed Wa-hee the state of the earth's grids of subtle energy. He/she had not seen this before.

"These grids were placed here by the Pleiadians just after the Uplift for precisely this reason."

Marian showed how all of Wa-hee's work (and the work of the other "original" souls of earth) had been recorded and stored.

"The coming climate change will merely postpone the progress of human life on earth for several thousand years," Marian said. "But now, because of the grids, consciousness will be able to resume from its former state."

Wa-hee was mollified.

"The task of keeping humanity on the planet during these years is not your work, dear one. Survival specialists who revel in these situations will keep the human population from disappearing."

"All right."

"It is time for a rest dear one. You have been working very hard. Stay with us in timelessness and in the glory of God."

Wa-hee was able to adopt the perspective of her/his soul, most of which always stayed on the other side. It was blissful here. He/she would play in his temple, compare notes with the others in the Great Earth Experiment, and take his/her attention off physical things.

Wa-hee stayed on the other side for over 6,000 revolutions of the planet. The he/she began another long cycle of incarnations, readying the earth, and slowly evolving human biology for the Lemurian age.

Lemuria, 52,000 years ago

After 150,000 years of painstaking evolution since the Uplift, homo sapiens was ready. The test of free choice could begin. In Lemuria, the Seeders set up homo sapiens with a 50-50 balance between dark and light, as measured from the earth's esoteric grids of subtle energy. These grids interfaced directly with human consciousness all over the planet and were connected to the earth's magnetic field. Therefore the test involved humanity and Gaia in a cooperative experiment.[3] What happened in Lemuria would esoterically affect the rest of the earth via the grids, and vice-versa.

Lemuria was chosen because it was isolated by hundreds of miles of ocean and was therefore protected from invasion by barbarians and raiders. The Pleiadians set the length of the Lemurian experiment for precisely one precession of the equinoxes, or just under 26,000 years. Unless something went wrong of course.

"On this isolated continent a peaceful, pastoral society can develop," -Li said.

'We are cheating a little bit, are we not?" -Bu replied. "The rest of the planet consists of hunter-gatherers who often compete and fight each other for resources. We are getting ahead of ourselves."

-Li shrugged. "We have merely chosen an ideal spot for the beginning of the test. There are no predators on the Lemurian continent; no animals that could be mobilized for war. Food is abundant. The struggle to survive will be minimal. We will start here with a fresh slate. The higher vibrations will be accessible. What the humans do here is a true test of free will, unimpeded by outside forces."

"What happens if the Lemurians choose the dark side?" –Li asked.

"That is unthinkable," –Bu replied.

-Li laughed. "Even uplifted planets don't make it. If we fail here we will have to start over again somewhere else."

"Then we had better be good teachers and mentors," –Bu said.

"We can teach but not interfere with the free choice of the humans."

"That is understood."

Wa-hee

Wa-hee came before the soul manager before her next incarnation. "Welcome back Wayshower!" said Marian enthusiastically. This was the soul manager's term for original souls who had been on the planet even before the Uplift.

"Wayshower indeed!" Wa-hee responded. He/she now had almost 1,500 incarnations on the earth.

In Lemuria every human would feel the connection to God. But only so much as to establish free will choice with no bias either way.

Marian and Wa-hee were excited. Wa-hee incarnated as Ona.

The Geology of Lemuria

Geologically, Hawaii is a unique place. Lemuria (the remnants of which are the Hawaiian Islands) was formed from a hot spot. There are only a few hot spots on Earth. The one under Hawaii is right in the middle of the Pacific Plate, one of the largest crustal plates on Earth. A hot spot is an area in the middle of a crustal plate with volcanic activity. Molten magma breaks through the crustal plate to create a land mass. In Lemuria this occurred because a thin part of the Pacific Plate allowed magma to build up, spread out, and cool. 52,000 years ago Lemuria was a small continent, much bigger than the islands of Hawaii. It was essentially built upon a crustal bubble. In the middle of Lemuria a towering mountain, which was called Mu, rose almost 20,000 feet.

According to ice core data from the polar regions over the past million years, the earth has gone through natural cycles of warming and cooling with attendant changes in sea level. Although water vapor and clouds are the primary contributor to the greenhouse effect, carbon dioxide and methane levels in the earth's atmosphere correlate very strongly with temperature. Today, carbon dioxide levels are at 379 parts per million. In Lemuria carbon dioxide levels were only 200 ppm. Methane levels also strongly correlate with temperature. Methane concentration is now at 1750 parts per billion. In Lemuria, 52,000 years ago, methane levels in the atmosphere were about 450 parts per billion.

At the time of Lemuria the earth was cooler than it is now, and sea levels were lower, thus exposing much more of the land.

Ona

Ona's first life in Lemuria was pleasant. The population at the beginning of the Test was 100,000 and would eventually grow to 150,000. Even though cooler and drier than the tropical Hawaii of today, there was much abundance. Various species of the *Arecaceae* family of plants were plentiful. These plants provide coconuts, bananas, betel nuts, dates, and acai fruit. Little time need be spent on life's necessities. Ona felt contentment.

In Lemuria at this time life resembled the metaphorical biblical descriptions of a Garden of Eden. While most of the planet was in survival mode, Ona experienced a strong connection with the higher vibrations. This was part of the test. War was unheard of.

When Ona approached her 30th birthday a vague memory stirred within her. She became very sick and visited a healer.

The healer read Ona's Akash, the record of her lives on earth. "Ona, this sickness is not physical. It is a remnant from your previous lives. Always before you died young. What you are experiencing is a shadow death."

Ona recovered. As she grew older she expected death to come at any moment. But after her 100th birthday she no longer thought of it.

Her lifetime in Lemuria was uneventful and lasted almost 150 years. One day she was walking along a wooded trail to a lake with a beach, where she liked to sun herself. As she lay down on the warm sand Ona felt a pleasant lethargy. She knew it was her time. There was no pain or discomfort, only joy. As she took her last breath she realized it was the first time she had ever lived and died without conflict and struggle.

Marian

When Wa-hee/Ona returned she was ecstatic. There was no need for adjustment; she was brought forth immediately before the soul manager. "Oh Marian, this is more like it! I wish to live forever in Lemuria."

"Dear One, that is not possible. You will only have two lifetimes there, at the beginning and then at the end."

Ona/Wa-hee was crushed. "Do you mean that this paradise will be destroyed?"

Marian was silent. How much should this soul be told? The soul manager had the long view. Marian saw how the earth, with its 4.5-billion year history, was a blink in the cosmic eye of Brahma. Souls like Wa-hee were specialists, action-oriented beings who reveled in the physical experience. The soul manager paused for a moment and contemplated the vastness of the Creation. There were levels beyond even his/her/their understanding, but it was magnificent. Marian felt something he/she/they had never felt before: a tug that spoke of Creations beyond this one, of unthinkable joy and love.... "I am sorry dear one," Marian said. "I was contemplating."

For an instant Wa-hee had felt something wonderful, well beyond her understanding. Wa-hee realized dimly that evolution proceeded far beyond her little adventures on this planet.

Marian answered. "The potentials are for Lemuria to last for one wobble of the earth, 26,000 orbits. Dear one, your life in Lemuria was a setup. For 500 years your Akash soaked up the higher vibrations of that wonderful place. Now it is your mission to incarnate all over the earth, preparing the way for the Great Migration that will take place after Lemuria is no more."

Wa-hee understood. "I am a Wayshower."

Marian smiled in love. "Precisely, dear one. No matter where you go now, male or female, the energy of Lemuria will be a part of you."

The soul manager showed Wa-hee the potentials for his/her lives along the timeline. "You will be seen as different," Marian said. "This is because you hold the sacred energy of the light. You are already an old soul. As you walk the earth you will spread your light wherever you go. You will have choices where to incarnate."

Marian showed Wa-hee that all of the old souls from Lemuria would have similar life missions. They would only live one or two lifetimes on the continent, then incarnate elsewhere. She saw how, during the coming millennia, these Lemurian souls, lifetime after lifetime, would send light into the grids all across the earth. This light could then be (potentially, with free choice) picked up by others.

Wa-hee was awed. "This is what it means to be a Wayshower."

Marian beamed. "Yes dear one. All 150,000 of you will live somewhat isolated lives. You will be the shamans, the healers, and later the writers and musicians who will inspire the people and raise the consciousness of humanity."

Wa-hee saw it. How the Seeding created the foundation for advancement. "But why must we go through all this? Would it not be better for all to live like we have in Lemuria?"

Marian showed Wa-hee various planets where this had been tried. After several thousands or even hundreds of thousands of years, these societies eventually stagnated, falling into a sort of pointless mediocrity. Wa-hee laughed. "Who would want to incarnate there?"

At this the soul manager belly-laughed (even though he/she/they did not have a body). "Ha! Dear one, you have struck the flint at the right spot! Societies like Lemuria eventually die because they are too...boring. They provide no impetus for evolution and advancement."

In a blaze of profound understanding Wa-hee understood. "So THAT'S why I had to go through all that SHIT!"

Marian laughed again. "Yes dear one, and you will go through more of that shite. But you will enjoy it immensely at the soul level, even if there is temporary suffering in the body."

For once Wa-hee was speechless. He/she realized that she had made a great leap forward in wisdom.

After a moment Wa-hee spoke. "Yes. I see it now. The body is a temporary vehicle for soul advancement. This planet is also a huge gameboard, a playing field whose purpose is soul advancement."

Marian beamed. The little soul was growing quickly. "This planet, dear one, is a great galactic catalyst for soul evolution for the entire galaxy. The greatest that has ever been. And you are a part of it."

The soul manager showed Wa-hee the possibilities for the next incarnation. "Eventually you will touch all of the major population centers – and sacred places – on the earth." Wa-hee was given her choice of northern Africa, China, the sub-continent, or the life of an indigenous in Australia.

"Let me ease back into this," Wa-hee said. "I choose Australia."

Marian smiled. "You have chosen the most difficult place."

"I have? How?"

"To divulge that information would spoil the test. Is this your decision?"

Wa-hee looked at the environment. The area was cooler than it is today but nothing like the life he had lived in Rügen. Wa-hee vowed never again to choose such a cold place. "Yes. I am ready."

As she had done so many times before, Wa-hee entered the birth vortex. She felt herself shedding awareness as her consciousness was truncated to "fit" inside the low energy of the physical container. Then she landed in the body of an infant female.

The birth vortex disappeared. Before Wa-hee entered the body she knew she was to be a shaman and medicine woman to the people. She was in one of the northern coastal areas of what is presently New South Wales in Australia, approximately 340 miles northeast of present day Sydney. This area included what the Bundjalung people called the Wollumbin, the rainmaker, a sacred mountain. Today this area is in the Bundjalung National Park.

From the first the parents of "medicine girl" knew she was different. The little girl was immensely curious, inspecting the trees and the plants. She often looked toward the rainmaker, where the spirits of wounded warriors are present within the mountain. The injuries of these warriors manifested themselves as scars on the mountainside. The thunderstorms in the mountains, she was told by medicine woman, are memories of the sounds of those warriors' battles. When viewed from the north, the face of the chief warrior was visible from the shape of the mountain's rocks.[4]

Medicine girl often walked to this place and stared at the mountain. Even the medicine woman, steeped in spiritual knowledge, criticized her for this. "You are wasting time, medicine girl. Time which could be spent learning the medicinal plants and herbs that can cure the people of their illnesses."

Medicine girl shrugged. "With your help I have already learned these things. More important is to learn the magic-that-heals."

This was a sore spot with medicine woman. The old lady was skilled in the healing arts using herbs and plants, but had never mastered magic.

"That is but on old woman's tale," she said. "Only the great medicine man Mukwa has ever been able to do it, and he lived long ago."

"I can do it," medicine girl said.

Medicine woman was startled. "You speak boastfully, girl. This attitude is not helpful."

Medicine girl was contrite. She did not want to upset her teacher. "Perhaps you are right. I will strive for greater modesty."

Medicine woman was mollified.

Medicine girl's spirit soared as she grew older. She became what we know as a tomboy. She insisted on learning to play the instruments. Her friend, a young man, taught her to play the gum leaf, a leaf from a tree of the Eucalyptus family. He showed her how to hold the leaf against her lips and blow to make bird-calls. Within days medicine girl was using the leaf as a musical instrument. Members of the tribe shook their heads. "Either medicine girl is a great shaman, or she is insane," they said. She learned to play the bullroarer, a long elliptical piece of wood tied to a string used to communicate over long distances. She became an expert.

"Why do you waste time with things that are for men?" the women of the village asked her one day when they were gathering plants and herbs. "Are you possessed by an evil demon?"

Medicine girl laughed and bowed. "That is for you to judge."

31

Medicine girl also excelled on her clap stick during the tribe's sacred ceremonies and rain-making ceremonies. The clap stick is a percussion instrument whose pitch and tone can be varied. But when medicine girl decided to pursue the *didjeridu*, the bamboo trumpet, she was severely chastised by the chief and the village council. "Woman, stick to your herbs and your poultices," she was told.

The tribe's chief, a great hunter, was secretly pleased with medicine girl's great spirit. He wanted to take her for his mate, for she was almost 13. But it was forbidden. Clearly this woman would become a great shaman and be a great boon to the village.

Medicine girl wanted to compete with the men in the upcoming foot race. It was scandalous, but allowed by the chief. He had seen her running after an insect a month ago and was amazed by her quickness. Before the contest he made a bet with the other members of the village council. "I place one emu skin on medicine girl in the speed race."

The men of the council exploded in anger.

"It is not a woman's place to race with men!" one shouted.

"Let the woman tend to her pots!" cried another.

After the babble died down the chief spoke softly. "Our young men are afraid to compete against medicine girl." He smiled. "And so are you."

Another explosion. "Don't be crazy!" one of the elders said. "It is unprecedented."

The chief was a wise chief. "Certainly it is. But the spirit of medicine girl must not be dampened. It is obvious that one day she will be a great healer, and one like Mukwa who can use the magic."

At this the men quieted. One of the elders smiled and spoke. "I will match your emu skin and throw in my best clapper."

The aboriginal people understand the connection to the earth and to the Great Spirit. In some areas of the earth their history goes back, unbroken, for over 30,000 years.

The betting was on. The men emerged from the council; the chief made an announcement that night after the night meal had been eaten and the women had cleaned up.

"Tomorrow is the great race," the chief said. All of the young men swelled with pride. Each had their own bets, either on themselves or on their favorite racer.

"Medicine girl has entered the contest. The Council has approved."

The young men burst out into heated objections. The rest of the council members took their seats around the fire. Several of the women moved away from medicine girl, contemptuous. The men turned angrily to the girl, shouting the usual objections. The chief said nothing, but stood before the people with a smile on his face. His tribe was growing; he was pleased to see the animated conversation. The dispute did not bother him.

After several minutes the chief spoke to the racers, his voice dripping with scorn. "You object because you are afraid," he said softly.

All conversation halted immediately. The young men looked at each other. They could find no real objection. One of the contestants spoke. "It is not right that women should race against men."

"Why not?" said the chief. "Be not afraid to speak."

The man opened his mouth and closed it.

The chief smiled. "It is settled then. Tomorrow medicine girl shall race against you." The chief walked away to his personal hut just beyond the fire.

The men grumbled. Medicine girl's friend laughed. "Watch out! Medicine girl has powerful magic."

This made the men grumble even more, for this statement had been accepted as truth. "The girl is possessed," someone said. This statement was echoed by a few of the women, who sat on the opposite side of the fire.

The friend of medicine girl defused the tension. "The chief himself has bet on the girl. An emu skin."

Medicine girl was shocked, as was everyone else. One of the men laughed. "You had better win, medicine girl, or the honor of the chief will be sullied."

The statement was so absurd that everyone began to laugh. Soon the entire village had calmed, and talk turned to the great competition and the new entrant. The woman who had objected loudest to medicine girl's entry placed her best gum leaf on the ground. "Medicine girl will win," she said, recording her bet. "Women have pride too. We too have honor." Most of the women were shocked. But the force of this assertion was felt by all. Soon the other women were also placing bets.

On the morning of the race, which would be held just after dawn, the entire village gathered. Ten men and one girl would race. There were two contests, a speed race and a mile race (or its equivalent in Bundjalung). The speed race was first, the equivalent of the modern 100-yard dash. The contestants lined up next to a small Eucalyptus tree. The women saw that medicine girl had been given the most disadvantageous position. She was crowded against the bark of the tree as the men all moved to cut off her progress. The women noticed this but said nothing. The chief smiled.

Just as he was about to begin the race the chief met the eyes of medicine girl. In his gaze was a thought: "For the good of village harmony you cannot win the race, even though I know you are the fastest."

Medicine girl understood immediately and nodded. One of the elders picked up on this. So did several of the women. "What did the chief mean with that glance?" they asked each other.

The race began. In his eagerness, one of the young men bounded from the starting line before the chief gave the signal. The chief frowned and pointed at the young offender. "You are disqualified," he said censoriously. The young man was ashamed and withdrew.

The racers lined up. With his foot the chief scuffed a line in the dirt. One of the men was over the line; the chief motioned him to step back. Then he gave the signal. Medicine girl was ready. She was eager to test her skill against the others. She bounded off the line so quickly that she was a pace ahead of the others after only three steps had been taken. As she flew across the dirt she gloried in her physical ability. She would never have children, but this once she would revel in her body. After the race was three quarters complete she was still two paces ahead of everyone else. She was going to win!

Just then she remembered the chief's request. She was almost at the finish. The women were screaming with pleasure. The men were angry. Medicine girl saw a small rock ten feet from a large tree that served as the finish line. Her toe caught upon the rock. She plunged forward to the ground, one foot short of the finish. The men all passed her. She finished last.

The women looked at each other. "So that was what Chief told medicine girl."

The others nodded. "The chief is wise. But she would have won!"

Two of the women were contemptuous. "A ridiculous spectacle. Look at her, covered with dirt."

But medicine girl did not look ridiculous at all. The girl had a natural dignity and athletic grace. Her male friend helped her up and embraced her. "You would have won," he said.

Medicine girl smiled. "I think I will stick to my herbs and medicines from now on," she announced to the gathering. She had proven herself.

The women were satisfied, even those who had criticized her.

Medicine girl found her place in the tribe. When medicine woman died she took her hut on the outskirts of the village, away from the others. She tended to the physical needs of the tribe, but did no magic. She used use the resin from the trunk of eucalyptus gum trees to treat burns, wounds, and diarrhea. Medicine woman used tea tree leaves to treat wounds, infections, coughs, colds, sore throats, and skin ailments. She began the tradition of inhaling the oils from crushed leaves to enhance treatment. When she discovered how to use the oil from emu skins, all of the hunters were grateful. Medicine woman massaged the oil into the skin to promote wound healing and to alleviate pain and disability from musculo-skeletal disorders. She collected the oil by hanging the emu skin from a tree. Sometimes she wrapped it around the affected area and allowed the heat of the sun to liquefy the emu fat to enhance absorption or penetration into the skin. Medicine woman discovered uses for every plant and herb. She was celebrated but remained apart. Many of the villagers felt a latent power from her that frightened them.

Drought

One evening during a drought medicine woman saw the spirit of Mukwa appear before her. Mukwa told her about his sacred ceremony for bringing the rain. "First you must climb the great mountain," the spirit said. "Then pray to the spirit of Wollumbin in this manner." Mukwa showed her how to activate the rain-making templates that were inherent in all weather systems. "This is wonderful!" she cried. Medicine woman thanked Mukwa. She gave thanks to the spirit of the mountain and to the warriors who had died. She prayed to the divas in the soil and asked permission from the mountain to utilize its healing powers for the land.

The next day a hot, dry sun rose on a baked landscape. There was no game. Plants were dying; trees and shrubs were shriveling. The chief came to see medicine woman.

"If you know magic, now is the time to use it," he said. Medicine woman was finely made now, and beautiful. He desired her, as he always did when he saw her. It was well that she lived outside the village.

"I have had a vision," she said. She told the chief about her visit from the spirit of Mukwa. "I know what to do."

The chief nodded and stepped aside. The mountain was but a mile distant. Medicine woman began walking, carrying several tokens, including her sacred circle of beads which she placed around her neck. As medicine woman walked away the chief saw the sway of her hips and heard the rattling of the beads. The woman had filled out. It was a waste to have her living without a mate. He strode toward her, intending to take her where she stood.

Medicine woman heard footsteps behind her and knew what it meant. She silently summoned the spirit of Mukwa, asking for his intervention.

The chief was dazzled by the beauty of medicine woman. But as he reached for her he felt a presence. His head cleared. The chief growled. "Do as you must, woman."

Medicine woman walked to the mountain and did as Mukwa taught her.

Within several hours dark clouds appeared on the horizon. An hour later a soaking rain fell. The rain lasted for two days and two nights, causing a muddy mess around the huts of the villagers. But the ground eagerly soaked in the water. Waterholes became filled once more. Game reappeared.

After this the chief turned against medicine woman and her great magic. The villagers also turned against her. They used her services when they had to. Medicine woman lived an isolated, lonely life. But a long one.

One day a young hunter came to her hut, looking for a salve for his wound. The old woman was dead. She was still beautiful, the young man thought, as he observed her body lying on the ground. The old woman's face was creased in a smile. She had died content. He saw a small bottle he recognized as the salve medicine woman used. He took the bottle and walked back to the council hut, informing the elders that another medicine man must be chosen.

Wa-hee

When Wa-hee transitioned it took a while for her to adjust. She had been living alone for several decades. It was a shock to be reunited with the parts of her soul that had to be left behind. But Wa-hee came back from the Cave of Creation refreshed and exhilarated. After the ceremony of celebration, where her name was sung in light once again, the soul manager was there to greet her.

Marian was ecstatic as they went over Wa-hee's previous life. "Look at the energies before and after your life." Wa-hee saw that the grids in the area had been infused with Lemurian energy. The esoteric resonances of Wollumbin had been activated from her rituals. Millennia in the future, the area would be recognized as sacred and a national park built around it in Australia.

As before, Wa-hee and the soul manager discussed the potentials for the next life.

It is of course impossible to detail every life of Wa-hee. Incarnation after incarnation, lifetime after lifetime, the soul grew in experience, knowledge, and wisdom. Each time Wa-hee was able to carry slightly more of his/her soul into the body than the last time. Wa-hee was a warrior in India, China, and Mesopotamia; a tribal queen in Africa, Indonesia, and Tibet. He was a king, a doctor, a scientist, an accountant, an astronomer, a surveyor, a temple worker, a builder; several times a householder and several times a slave. She was a mother who wept when her sons died in battle, a wife of a rich man and a freeholder, and many times a slave. He was a monk and a guru, a courtier and a spy. She was a prostitute, a farmer's wife, and a wet nurse. During the next planetary wobble Wa-hee experienced all there was to experience on planet earth.

Wa-hee averaged two to three lifetimes every century. In 26,000 years he/she had experienced an additional 720 lifetimes. When she passed the 2,000 mark a special celebration was held. Her stripes, the multi-colored badges of honor that marked each lifetime on earth, shone brilliantly. Wa-hee, along with the 50,000 other original souls who had incarnated into the first hominid bodies, were now regarded with awe by the others in the human soul family.

Wa-hee's Akash, the record of his/her physical experiences, grew. Before his next incarnation Marian gave him some information. "Every soul's Akash is stored in a special, multi-dimensional area inaccessible to human beings." Wa-hee was shown this area. It was not a space as we understand it, or a container, but a template outside, or beyond, three dimensions. "Your Akash is picked up by your soul when you incarnate, and it is released when the body terminates and the soul transitions."

Wa-hee was confused. "Why keep a record of all the bad stuff? Why not keep a record of only the good bits? Then we could all advance much quicker."

Marian smiled. "Because that would invalidate the test of energy. What would happen if you were playing a ball game on earth and only counted when you hit the target and ignored the misses?"

Wa-hee saw it. "But...I have killed people, committed murder. Early in my 'career,' if you can call it that, I was a thief, a con-man, an assassin, a traitor. I have betrayed my colleagues and have abandoned my family. I have also suffered at the hands of those who see my light as dangerous. I have myself been murdered, betrayed, conned, shunned, isolated.... This has been happening more and more. What is the point of all this suffering and misery?"

This soul had progressed immensely in knowledge and wisdom during the previous cycle. Therefore an enhancement of soul knowledge was also called for. Marian showed Wa-hee the energy balance on the planet.

"Despite the work of the Lemurian souls, humanity has begun to explore the dark side," Marian said. "The potentials are that this development will continue for tens of thousands of years. The balance is now in favor of the dark."

Wa-hee understood that his own choices had contributed to the trend toward the dark side. He thought of the other souls now on the planet. "Has everyone else been doing what I have done?"

"I am afraid so," Marian said. He showed Wa-hee the energy balance in the Akash all of the souls now associated with the earth project. "Observe how free choice mingles with previous actions, or karma."

Wa-hee had never seen this, because when he incarnated he lost awareness.

"There is no karma on our side of the veil," Marian said. "Karma, negative energy, is strictly a phenomenon of earth. It is part of the test."

"Then there is no free will," Wa-hee said. "After karma builds up too much, actions are proscribed in only one direction. It looks as if that direction is toward the dark. And destruction."

Marian was sad. "That is correct – in one sense. Despite the present karmic balance toward the dark, free will is always in operation. Karma – the Akash – is just a life setup. You always have the choice to go to the light or to the dark."

Wa-hee was appalled. "But why did I not know of this before? I might have changed my actions."

"No dear one, the test must be fair. The level of consciousness of the whole is established by its parts. These decisions must be free of taint. Those who participate must make free will choices and then abide by those decisions."

Marian showed Wa-hee how karmic buildup had led to the rise and fall of many cultures during the previous cycle. "But humanity always restarts afresh, for souls return Home and are ready to renew the challenge."

The soul manager examined the multi-dimensional geometry of time and space of the planet, and the potentials for it. To three-dimensional eyes it would appear as a gigantic ring with no beginning and no ending, for that is the property of the circle. The worm ouroboros. Past, present, and future are connected in a seamless whole. Every action on the ring affects every other. The potentials were constantly changing, the display a tapestry of interacting energies. We will refer to this multi-dimensional construct as the Ring of Potential. Marian showed Wa-hee what was about to happen in Lemuria, where the great experiment had begun.

Marian examined the grids around the Lemurian continent, and the level of consciousness on the earth. Although Lemuria itself had remained pure, the pressure from millennia of planetary karma was to flow toward that beautiful paradise. The potential was for destruction of the beautiful continent.

There was still hope however. All of the original souls of earth were to be sent to Lemuria for their next lifetime in an attempt to stave off disaster.

Wa-hee felt a sudden urgency. "I think it would be best for me to return immediately," she said. Wa-hee had a longing to return to Lemuria once again. It had been by far her most pleasant lifetime on earth.

As if completing a cycle, Wa-hee would again incarnate as Ona. She was to be a messenger this time around, with access to the top of Mu, the sacred mountain.

Ona's Return to Lemuria, 26,000 Years Ago

Kulani, Iolana, and Ona walked slowly up the mountain trail to the Elders Complex. The three women were messengers, delivering requests and information back and forth from dwellers in the lowlands and those on the sacred mountain. They were constantly cold at the higher elevations. Their feet were hardened by walking on the rough mountain trail. Their footwear often wore out and needed repair or replacement.

As they walked Ona saw a figure about twelve feet high on the trail several hundred feet in front of them. "Look!"

Kulani, Iolana, and Ona immediately fell to their knees in the cold dirt as the figure approached. They lowered their heads.

"Rise, children," the figure said. The three women got to their feet.

"It is Bummamunum-Bu," Iolana said with awe. "One of the visitors."

Kulani noticed that the figure shimmered in the cold afternoon light. She could see part of the trail through the figure's body.

"I have important messages for the Elders," the figure said.

Ona, their leader, held out her hand. "We live to serve," she said.

Bummamunum-Bu smiled. He glowed. The three women felt a wave of serenity and contentment. Bummamunum-Bu handed Ona several cuneiform scrolls. "Deliver these to Elder Akamu. He will know what to do with the information."

Ona bowed. Bummamunum-Bu smiled once more and the women again felt a benign energy emanate from the great being.

The figure of Bummamunum-Bu became filled with light and then disappeared.

The three women looked at the scrolls, which were written on a kind of parchment they had never seen before. Thin and perfectly smooth, the paper contained symbols that leapt off the paper when gazed upon.

"The scrolls are sacred," Iolana said. "We should hurry to deliver them before sunset."

The messengers walked swiftly up the path.

When the three messengers reached the Elders Complex Ona went directly into the main council chamber, which was next to a molten pool of lava. At intervals along the mountain, molten pools of magma from the hot spot that had formed the mountain also provided heat. At the higher elevations, and at the very top of the mountain where the observatories were, these heat sources were essential. Ona took her time, enjoying the warmth as she approached a large stone table. Elder Akamu and Elder Keao were drinking *kola,* a beverage made from plant roots.

Iolana and Kulani went inside the healing chamber. Their usual task as messengers was to deliver requests from lowland dwellers for sacred ceremonies to be performed at the top of the mountain. Each of the messengers carried several scrolls of parchment for this purpose, which they delivered to the functionary in the healing chamber. Other messengers would take them up to the top, in stages.

Ona walked up to Elder Akamu and silently handed him the sacred scrolls. It was permitted for messengers to sit by the heat source and warm their bodies before departing to their sleeping quarters or continuing their journey up the mountain path. Ona gratefully sat down, reveling in the intense heat.

Elder Akamu observed the seal on the sacred scroll. It consisted of a series of concentric pentagons, which when observed expanded in the observer's eye so that he or she became immersed in an energy of benevolence. This knowledge had been delivered to the Council by the visitors. Akamu knew that the pentagon was sacred, consisting entirely of golden ratios, the representation of perfect mathematical harmony. When Akamu looked at the seal he felt an almost overpowering wave of love that made him weep. The Seal of the Visitors was the undeniable representation of universal truth. Akamu reluctantly removed his attention from the symbol. This scroll was genuine. Akamu verified the other scrolls and nodded to Ona, the messenger.

Akamu handed one of the scrolls to Keao, who prepared her mind for the presentation. When Keao fixed her attention on the hieroglyphics, the symbols on the page combined in her mind to form a multimedia video presentation. She saw how volcanic activity on the hot spot of the Pacific Plate had formed the small continent. Fascinated and horrified, she saw that the majority of the Lemurian land mass was actually a crustal bubble. Sometime during the next 50 years, that bubble would collapse and her homeland would sink into the sea.

Keao, shocked, let the scroll drop to the table top. She picked up the second scroll, which showed the building of seaworthy craft to sail the oceans. The Visitors showed her people sailing south to the islands of the Southern Pacific and east to Australia and New Zealand. The plan was for others to sail west to North and South America, and some to the east, to what is now China, Japan, and the Philippines. From there they would travel to Africa, the sub-continent, and Mesopotamia, and later, Europe. Keao knew that many would die on the journeys.

The scroll depicted, in picture form, the Lemurian's knowledge of healing and their connection to the Source being transferred across the planet. The plan was that her people would be responsible for enlightening the entire world about compassion and the love of the Creator.

One of Elder Akamu's scrolls showed how to construct vessels that would carry his people across the Pacific Ocean. It showed how to navigate by the stars, and what would be necessary to take with them on their journeys.

Keao and Akamu talked through the night as food was brought to them. The two summarized, correlated, and categorized the information in their minds. Then they went to bed and slept until the sun was overhead. That night a meeting of the entire Council was called.

Ona continued her life as a messenger. As she grew in experience she was given more important duties. At the top of the mountain, at almost 20,000 feet, the most important healing center was maintained. Those who had the greatest spiritual insight stayed here and meditated. Research was also conducted by the continent's best minds. The top of the mountain was the most sacred place on the planet. All here were attuned to the higher vibrations and knew about the grids of the earth. Their job was to channel this higher energy into the earth.

Ona's job was sometimes menial and sometimes sacred. Often she simply transported materials that were used for writing, and requests for sacred ceremonies by the lowland dwellers. Mostly she was a messenger for communications between those who lived and worked on the mountain. Ona was cold a lot, especially when her duties took her to the top of the mountain.

Ona lived for the moments when she participated in the sacred rituals. At these times all present on the mountain top gathered together. They chanted, they sung, they invoked the Great Central Source, led by the holy ones. Ona's messenger duties often took her to the bottom of the mountain. At these times she rested and talked with family, or strolled leisurely in the forests or along the trails.

For two years plans were made and thousands of trees were planted. In two decades the construction of the boats could begin. A poll was taken of the citizens and a tally of those who were going where. The Lemurians knew where the landmasses were, courtesy of the visitors. Bummamunum-Bu prepared several more scrolls for the Council, which showed distances, weather, and what might be expected on the journeys off the small continent. There was great sadness when the announcements from the Council were made.

Yet for the first two decades no discernible sinking of the land was noticed. Most of the Lemurians relaxed, for life there was pleasant and without stress. Things returned to normal.

After the announcement of the Council Ona asked to become a healer. She was shown by one of the priests how to counsel the people, and how to interface with the healing energies. At that time in Lemuria the dark-light balance was much more favorable than on the rest of the planet. Human DNA functioned at a much higher level. Those who were trained could access and become a conduit for the higher energies.

In her new life Ona saw many of the people. She assisted at births (all births in Lemuria were water births, the baby going from the fluid in the mother to the fluid of Gaia). She prepared potions from the herbs and plants in the area. Her main work was energetic. She would simply ask permission and then give intent for the body to be healed. Ona knew that there was no such thing as "healing." A helper assisted a person to find the energetic balance necessary to activate the healing templates in the other's merkaba. Ona enjoyed her work immensely. She did not find a mate or have children.

During the next decade fifty feet of land on the coastal areas at the south side of the continent disappeared. Several earthquakes shook the land, spurring a mild panic and a re-commitment to the evacuation program. The population of Lemuria at that time was about 150,000. Approximately 500 seaworthy vessels would be needed to transfer the entire population off the island. A few of the vessels were constructed and, following the directions of Bummamunum-Bu, practice runs of several hundred miles were undertaken in all directions. Some brave souls decided to depart early. These sailed south and east into the areas now known as Micronesia, Melanesia, and Polynesia.

For the next 10 years the land remained stable and the urgency retreated, despite repeated warnings from the Visitors and proclamations of the Council of Elders. Then, during the fifth decade after the announcement, steady sinking of the continent was noticed as the crustal bubble slowly collapsed. A frantic push to construct more of the vessels was undertaken. The Visitors advised the Elders to remove themselves from the mountain. The Council chambers were hurriedly transferred to the lowlands.

Then the mountain began to rapidly sink into the ocean. There were no more ships to launch. The land quickly flooded and sunk into the Pacific. A few desperate souls tried to escape the maelstrom in canoes, but these were quickly sucked down into the ocean by the collapsing land mass. Everyone perished.

Present day Hawaii is just a series of small islands; essentially the exposed peaks of a great undersea mountain range now known as the Hawaiian–Emperor seamount chain.[5] The continent of Lemuria, which had formerly been a continuous land mass stretching over 1,000 miles north from modern day Hawaii, was almost completely submerged.

The Lemurian language was simple and based on the speech of the Visitors during their interactions with the people. Life there did not in any way resemble our modern technological society. It was more like the indigenous who live in warmer areas of the planet. On the Hawaiian islands no relics, no monuments or statues, no roads, no technology of any kind will ever be found of the Lemurian civilization. When the continent of Lemuria disappeared, it lived on only in the Akash and in the soul memories of those who had lived there. There were no "adventures" there as we know them today (except at the very end), or conflicts, or war. In Lemuria, life was truly a Garden of Eden. It was a perfect setup for the start of the great test of energy.

The civilization there had provided a powerful engine of light, which balanced the energies on the rest of the planet. The original plan of the Seeders was for Lemurians to gradually spread out over the earth during the next precession cycle, bringing light and higher consciousness to the other continents, and creating a planetary civilization.

But it was not to be.

When the continent sunk, the Akash of all Lemurians contained a huge engram filled with sadness, fear, and death. The fall of Lemuria would affect the future evolution of earth for the next 26,000 years.

After the destruction of Lemuria the visitors from Merope tested the energy of the planet. What was the ratio between light and dark? The collective choices of the human race across the earth were recorded in an esoteric grid set up by the visitors; a sort of etheric hard drive. The 26,000-year period of the Lemurian experiment had not been enough to prevent an overall shift toward the dark over the rest of the planet. There was much sadness, for the same trend had happened on Merope.

Millennia later, the descendants of those who had managed to escape Lemuria before it sunk rode the Pacific in their canoes, travelling from island to island in what is now Micronesia, Polynesia, and Melanesia. These navigators had knowledge of the islands from Easter Island in the west to Palau in the east, a distance of 8,000 miles; and from Hawaii in the north to New Zealand in the south, a distance of 4,600 miles. They were able to navigate at night using the position and motion of specific stars and where they would rise on the horizon of the ocean. They knew about the weather in the Pacific and around the various islands at various times of the year. They knew the best and worst times to travel. They knew which wildlife species congregate in particular areas. They used the direction of swells on the ocean and the "feel" of their ships through the water to guide their vessels. They knew how the colors of sea and sky indicated weather and land masses. They understood how clouds would cluster at the locations of some of the islands, and the best angles for approaching harbors.

When these intrepid sailors approached Hawaii for the first time they became overwhelmed with emotion. Something in their Akash said that here was home.

On January 18, 1778, the English explorer Captain James Cook sailed past the island of Oahu. When the white man began to settle the island it was warm and tropical compared to when Ona and the old souls of Lemuria perished there 26,000 years ago.

CHAPTER 4

Marian

Wa-hee and almost 150,000 other original and old souls transitioned at the same time from Lemuria. The beginning of the free choice experiment in the Garden of Eden had ended in a catastrophe.

The soul manager was pleased with the overall result however. For 26,000 years Lemuria had soaked the earth in the higher vibrations. Yet, at the end, karma had balanced across the planet. Common sense says that the collapse of the hot spot under the continent was a simple result of geological activity. But there was an esoteric component as well. The collective actions of humanity affect Gaia, for the consciousness of earth and the consciousness of humanity are linked.

The soul manager had much to do. Although all souls completely release their attachment to the body and to the Akash after transitioning out of the physical, Wa-hee/Ona remembered what had happened to her beautiful land at the soul level. The death of an entire continent! Some of the Lemurians were eager to go back to the earth, and did; but many did not. Almost 4,000 years would pass before Wa-hee went back to the planet.

A new civilization had arisen in Atlantis.

Atlantis, 22,000 years ago

Wa-hee would reincarnate as Teir-Rea in Atlantis, a small continent between Europe and North America in the Atlantic Ocean. Another original soul, Tuamit-Ra, would also incarnate there. 12,000 years in the future Wa-hee and Tuamit-Ra would be best friends in Egypt.

The soul manager went over the soul mission for Wa-hee's life. "Observe how many Lemurians have tried to recreate in Atlantis the higher vibrations of Lemuria."

"It is not working," Wa-hee said. "In Atlantis the society is much more materialistic than that of Lemuria."

"Yes. The duality has increased so that two classes of humans are fighting one another."

"The struggle is for power and influence. The ego, once an assist to the heart and mind in Lemuria, has now gained precedence in Atlantis."

"That is correct. Humanity has continued to explore the dark side." Marian sighed. "Do what you can. Your job will be to soften the heart of Reit-Aluna, of the Haramun, the ruling class."

Wa-hee saw the potentials. "It is an impossible task."

"Perhaps. Do what is possible. Carry your light. What occurred in Lemuria must not recur on yet a second continent."

Wa-hee saw that another such mass engram would throw the collective Akash of humanity into emotional turmoil.

Wa-hee found his way through the birth vortex into the body of Teir-Rea.

Teir-Rea

Reit-Aluna was angry. The slave should have cleaned the laboratory without disturbing the positions of the crystals. The fool had altered the geometry of his carefully arranged matrix. He called Teir-Rea, his assistant.

"Rearrange the matrix according to our experimental data," he ordered.

Teir-Rea bowed. "I am scheduled for a session with the healers. I will attend to this as soon as I have returned."

"You will attend to it now. Your problems are none of my concern."

Teir-Rea tried to conceal his fury with another bow. "Yes, *duma*." Duma was the Atlantean term for master. Teir-Rea walked slowly over to the array, seething. He was dressed in white cloth, the garb of the technician. Reit-Aluna wore a beautiful red tunic with black stripes at the collar and down front and back. His shoes were dyed black and his head dress, which indicated his rank, was red with several black ribbons circling it. Red and black were the colors of the ruling class in Atlantis.

Teir-Rea knew the crystal array by heart and began to restore the geometry of the matrix. He would have a word with the slave who had caused him to incur the disapproval of the master. In his heart Wa-hee/Teir-Rea recalled his soul mission: to soften the heart of Reit-Aluna. But when he thought of the arrogant, pretentious, and cold *duma*, his heart hardened. In that moment Teir-Rea knew he was not strong enough to overcome his own karma and his conditioning in Atlantean society. Revenge was his motivation. To return the slights and insults of the ruling class, to give them a dose of the cruelty they administered to all beneath them.

Reit-Aluna was muttering to himself. As Teir-Rea worked he looked around the laboratory, which was built from native stone. It was situated just outside the principal city on a level plain of hardened dirt.

Salat-Ra had discovered, several hundred years ago, the power of crystal matrices to generate energy pulses and resonances. Here at Nahar-Mit they were working on resonant frequencies. Salat-Ra had discovered that every object, whether living or dead, has a resonant frequency. This is the vibration which would cause the molecular structure of the object to internally vibrate. It was possible to tune this frequency and amplify it so that the object would either explode, disperse, or melt into a pile of goo. In the healing centers this idea was used to destroy pathogens and other harmful invaders in the body.

Teir-Rea had an idea. In his spare time he had built what he called a "disruptor" that would, theoretically, be tuned to the resonant frequency of any object, including a human body. He called in a slave.

"Go to the healing center. Obtain the resonant frequencies of the major organs in the human body."

The slave nodded and left. In Atlantis disease was almost unknown. Invaders and pathogens that attacked the body were eliminated by finding their resonant frequencies and destroying them. Fortunately the resonant frequencies of the human body were far above those of the attacking entities, so the process was at worst harmless. But what would happen if a crystal matrix could be built to vibrate at the exact frequency of the body? Teir-Rea would experiment on the arrogant and cruel Reit-Aluna and his ilk in the ruling classes. Then, perhaps, social equality would finally come to the most advanced civilization on earth.

There were three classes in Atlantis: the ruling caste, the technicians, and the slaves.

The Haramun were only 15% of the population but controlled the technology and were the keepers of knowledge.

The technicians were simply workmen who built, operated, and maintained devices. These devices were not machinery as we understand them. The physics in Atlantis was different from the fossil fuel economy of today. For example, to move large boulders and stones in construction projects, crystal matrices were used, along with sound and geometry, to levitate large masses and to machine materials. There were no washing machines in Atlantis; no cranes, no automobiles or electronic devices like mobile phones and computers. There were no oil refineries or electrical generation plants. Energy was obtained using what Nikola Tesla called the "cosmic energy." Tesla was an Atlantean. Atlanteans knew how to access this energy, just as we know how to build electrical generation plants and electrical grids.

Slaves were the third class in Atlantis, around 70% of the population. These men and women farmed and harvested, did construction work, cleaned houses, washed clothes, and waited on the other two classes. Despite an advanced knowledge of physics, Atlantean society was rigidly hierarchical.

The slave returned, citing from memory the resonant frequencies of the main organs of the human body. Teir-Rea dismissed her.

Reit-Aluna saw this exchange and strode forward. "What is the meaning of this?" he demanded. The slave froze.

Teir-Rea bowed. "Merely informational. This slave retrieved valuable data necessary to the success of our project."

Reit-Aluna's aristocratic face hardened. "In future, request permission before undertaking actions that affect our work."

"Yes, duma."

The slave was terrified. Knowledge of any kind was zealously guarded by the aristocracy. Slaves were only given information necessary to perform their tasks. It was similar to the compartmentalized special access programs within the bowels of today's intelligence agencies.

Reit-Aluna looked at the female slave with contempt. "Be gone, slave." She left hurriedly.

Teir-Rea kept his expression completely bland, so as not to incur censure from the hard-hearted duma.

"Your conduct is becoming unpredictable," Reit-Aluna said, making it clear his disdain for a mere technician. "Henceforth you shall not have access to messenger slaves. All requests for information will go through me."

"Yes, duma."

Reit-Aluna went back to his station. Teir-Rea decided that when his disruptor was perfected, the first person to die would be the coldly arrogant and patronizing Reit-Aluna.

That evening Teir-Rea went to a meeting of technicians at one of the public halls. He was the first to speak.

"If society is to change, we must initiate that change. The slaves are helpless. The Haramun are incorrigible and will never give up their power. It is up to us."

"You speak foolishness, Teir-Rea," said Arun-Mao/Tuamit-Ra, a technician who worked in one of the city's healing stations. "Any action on our part will be immediately reported to the authorities. Including this meeting."

There was a lot of nervousness as the technicians, almost three dozen, looked around the huge meeting area with its arches and stone columns. Scribes and hawkers of goods lined one side of the public place. Other groups were meeting and talking in every area of the structure. Their voices would hopefully go unnoticed in the babble of conversation.

"You have not seen this," Teir-Rea responded. He brought out his disrupter from a large carrying case. "Here is the programming array, and the amplifier matrix. Observe." Teir-Rea walked over to a huge boulder sitting outside the thick stone walls of the meeting area. He scraped off a few shavings with a sharpened knife. He placed the shavings within the programming array of crystals. He set the disruptor on the ground about fifty feet from the big rock. "Now, watch this." Teir-Rea pursed his lips and whistled into the amplifier matrix, activating the disruptor. The boulder disintegrated silently, becoming a pile of grayish silicon, aluminum, and iron.

The technicians were shocked. "You have used resonant frequencies for destruction," Arun-Mao accused.

"I have. What's more, I have programmed this device to do the same to human beings. Or shall we say, the Haramun. I have also catalogued the resonant frequencies of the continent itself."

The implications were not lost on the group.

"You have created a doomsday weapon," said Tahit-Alun. Tahit-Alun was known to work for Salat-Toor, a malicious and vindictive aristocrat who routinely beat his technicians and brutalized his slaves.

Teir-Rea nodded. "Now, my friends, we must decide what to do with this knowledge."

The group engaged in animated conversation until everyone else had left the public hall and gone to their dwellings. The consensus was that the Haramun would not listen to reason. Even many of those opposed to violence understood that force would be required. However, the technicians who worked in the healing stations, including Arun-Mao/Tuamit-Ra, would have no part in murder and death. It was agreed that the healing stations and their workers must remain intact and functioning in case of injuries to technicians and slaves. The healers would be neutral and exempt from participation in the class struggle.

"The Haramun, they will be killed for the good of society," Teir-Rea said. "Then we can start over."

When Teir-Rea got home he thought for hours about his campaign against the aristocracy. Murder was unknown, although class tensions had been rising for several decades. To deliberately kill another human being would be a crime against humanity. He went to sleep consoled by the knowledge that he could fight back against the tyranny of the Haramun. He decided not to engage in criminal behavior unless something egregious occurred. He would bide his time. The ruling classes would decide their fate by their own behavior.

Teir-Rea endured the cruel and arrogant behavior of Reit-Aluna for another three weeks. He seethed but did nothing. Something inside him, a distant memory, told him that compassion was the only solution.

The next day Reit-Aluna used the stick of discipline, bruising his arm for a mistake he made in his work. When he got home that evening his arm had swollen and he was in pain. He went to a healing center for treatment where he saw his friend Arun-Mao. "Tomorrow shall be the reckoning for Reit-Aluna," he told the healer. "By his actions shall I judge all the Haramun."

The following morning Teir-Rea brought his disruptor and placed it in a hidden compartment by his workstation. During the day Reit-Aluna was his usual demanding and dismissive self. A slave was beaten for poor performance, for something that was easily corrected. When Teir-Rea objected, he too felt the duma's wrath. Bleeding and angry, he went back to his station and brought out the disruptor. He took a little blood from his bleeding shoulder, programming the device's crystal array. Human bodies were different, but the resonance frequencies of human organs were within a small tolerance. The vibration of his human blood would set the vibrational baseline for his device.

Teir-Rea walked over to Reit-Aluna's station carrying the disruptor. The duma heard his footsteps and turned around.

"I did not give you permission to approach me."

"Why did you beat me? Why did you beat the slave?"

"Malcontent, get back to your business and stay out of matters that don't concern you!"

Teir-Rea pointed to his bleeding shoulder, which had stained his tunic red. "*This* concerns me. You arrogant, stupid fool."

Reit-Aluna's face began to turn crimson in anger. He reached for a solid piece of wood about the size of a baseball bat. "Ingrate, your insolence will be punished!"

As the duma raised his arm to strike, Teir-Rea activated his disruptor. Almost at once the Haruman's face contorted and his body began to shake. The stick of discipline fell from his hand, clattering on the pounded dirt floor. A slave entered the premises, watching. Reit-Aluna's blood literally began to boil and he fell lifeless to the floor. The slave approached, the one who had been beaten earlier. Teir-Rea's eyes met those of the slave. Reit-Aluna's beautiful cloak was smudged with dirt. His headdress lay several feet from the body.

"What shall we do with Reit-Aluna?" the slave asked.

"Leave him. It has begun now. Tell your fellows to be ready. It won't take long for the Haramun to understand what happened here." Teir-Rea stripped the aristocrat and put on his clothing. All of the technicians and slaves abandoned the facility and went to their homes.

Teir-Rea was right. When the authorities came to examine the facility, which had not reported in three days, reaction was swift. The disrupted body of Reit-Aluna provoked outrage amongst the Haramun. Teir-Rea had been the chief technician at the facility. The call for his death went out to all the ruling class.

Most of the technicians (those not in the healing centers) supported the death of Reit-Aluna. An example had to be set. Most of the slaves who did not work in the healing centers were also with the technicians. Disruptors were quickly built; the technology was the same as used in the healing centers.

The Haramun, incensed by the murder, refused to give up an iota of their power. The continent became divided into two armed camps. The technicians, led by Teir-Rea, and the slaves and technicians who did not work in the healing complexes, began a guerilla assault on the aristocracy, killing as many as they could. The Haramun responded. A cold war of hostilities broke out. The Haramun, although a tiny minority, yet found plenty of slaves and technicians willing to support their side in exchange for the comforts of life. The population was fairly evenly divided. The Haramun and their allies occupied the north side of the continent. The rebel slaves and technicians, along with a dozen or so Haramun who had defected, occupied the south.

Over the decades, attitudes hardened further.

One day the technicians in the south received notice that the Haramun were about to launch a massive attack. Several gigantic disruptors had been built on the north side of the continent, tuned to the resonance frequencies of the earth under the enemy territory in the south. The attack was successful, almost completely wiping out the opposition. A great celebration was held by the aristocracy.

Then disaster several months later. The continental land mass, weakened by seismic ruptures in the south, began to perforate and collapse.

Like Lemuria, Atlantis disappeared into the ocean. Even so, there were several thousand survivors. At that time glaciers covered much of Europe and Canada, and parts of the United States. These massive sheets of ice locked away water, lowering the sea level in the Atlantic, exposing continental shelves, joining land masses together, and creating extensive coastal plains.[6] Sea levels at the time of the fall of Atlantis were up to 400 feet lower than they are now. Land bridges were open to Europe. Europe was too cold to be comfortable and some Atlantean knowledge eventually traveled to Mesopotamia, northern Africa, Asia, and the subcontinent.

Marian

When Teir-Rea/Wa-hee transitioned he was totally confused. It required some time before he could fully integrate with his soul. When he met the soul manager Wa-hee was very disappointed.

"I have lived so many lifetimes and have grown in wisdom. But now I have been responsible for the deaths of tens of thousands of souls. I have helped to destroy an entire continent."

On the other side of the veil negative emotion is unknown. But Wa-hee, with so much experience on earth, knew what bitterness was.

Marian was optimistic. "Yes Wa-hee. From now on your incarnations will become more difficult. This engram in your Akash will require many lifetimes to purge." The soul manager and Wa-hee knew that he could not stay on the other side as he had done after Lemuria, for his actions in Atlantis had created karma for himself and many others. That karma would have to be resolved as quickly as possible.

Wa-hee was frustrated at the soul level. "It will take many lifetimes just to work off my karma. Instead of helping the planet I will be like a man running in place."

The soul manager gave the equivalent of a shrug. "It is part of the test of free will. You and all who participated in Atlantis have grown greatly in wisdom. You have experienced first-hand that violence and retribution can never be solutions."

Marian and Wa-hee looked at the Ring of Potential for earth. The Ring was Wa-hee's name for an esoteric tool the soul manager used to evaluate the potentials for humanity's future. Imagine a calculator that can keep track of the interactions of every human being on earth, and then make flawless predictions based on their past and current actions. To human eyes this calculator would look like a gigantic Ring that displays past, present, and future like a constantly changing 3D movie.

Wa-hee saw that the trend on the planet was for more suffering, conflict, and war. This would continue until the end of the second 26,000-year cycle. At the end of that cycle was the potential for humanity to annihilate itself as well as the earth.

Marian showed Wa-hee the weather patterns for the next 20,000 years. "As you know and have experienced, Gaia breathes and refreshes herself via temperature changes, which result from the planet's changing orbit around the sun, solar activity, ocean flow, and changes in the magnetic field. Observe how the planet's weather will slowly warm. At the midway point of the current 26,000-year cycle, the earth will have warmed to the point where sea levels will rise. Conditions for the expansion of life will become much more benign. The potential is for a huge population increase."

Wa-hee saw this. "Yes. But if events continue along their present course, the destruction of the human race is inevitable at the end of the current precession of the equinoxes."

"Correct. Human DNA is now functioning at only 40% instead of 50% as it was in Lemuria. Awareness of the divinity, of the soul, and the Creative Source is at its lowest point since the test began. Materialism is beginning to assert itself as human beings lose sight of their higher potential. If the percentage falls to 30% the entire human race will wipe itself out. This beautiful jewel with its tremendous biodiversity will be a barren husk, for all life will slowly die off."

Wa-hee saw the unleashing of the energy of the atom in the last century before the end. Yet there was still time to avoid the Great War that would result in an extinction event.

Wa-hee was a Wayshower, an adventurer. He/she loved Gaia and all of the souls who worked the puzzle on earth. Wa-hee was determined to access the energy of Lemuria, to shine his light, and to help others whenever he could. Even if it meant his own death, over and over.

The Seeders measured the energy of the planet after the fall of Atlantis. The collapse of Atlantis just four millennia after Lemuria had created a further engram in the Akash of all souls who incarnated there, many of whom were Lemurians, and in the planetary grids, where the memory of all activity on Gaia is stored. This meant that even in many of the old souls the dark energy had power.

The Light was beginning to fade from the planet.

Chapter 5

10,000 years ago. Beginning of Neolithic Subpluvial[7]

After Atlantis, Wa-hee and his fellow Lemurians lived lifetime after lifetime, all over the planet. He was a king, an advisor, an artisan, a householder, a priest, a philosopher, and a slave. She was a mate, a prostitute, a householder, a shaman, a healer, and a slave. Wa-hee worked off his karma. Anywhere he could be of service he/she went. Wa-hee grew in wisdom. His connection with the other side while on earth strengthened. The veil between the physical and the other side was thick; yet in his/her physical lifetimes he/she began to know what would work and what would not; what was best to be done and what should not be done. Wa-hee was awakening to his soul mission at an early age. Thus did the experiences in Wa-hee's Akash for 200,000 years, both good and bad, begin to "leak" into his physical incarnations and give him/her the wisdom of an old soul.

During this period the planet gradually warmed, the ice melted, and the oceans rose. The consciousness of humanity fell further. Problem resolution through conflict and war was now the norm. The balance between male and female energy was tilted significantly to the male. The heart of humanity had hardened. Gaia cooperated by spreading disease and pandemics at occasional intervals. Lifespans shortened.

All of the original souls and old souls gathered for a big meeting with the soul manager.

"It is necessary to make two changes in the plan," Marian said before they all incarnated back on earth. "One will be esoteric and the other will be physical. First, let us create a small army of advisors and helpers for each human being. These angels and guides will be the parts of the incarnated soul that reside here on the other side. They will be, in essence, the Higher Self of the human being. These assistants will follow the human being wherever he or she goes, holding out their hands if the incarnated soul should request assistance."

All agreed that this was a brilliant idea.

"Free will must be respected or the integrity of the test will be violated," the soul manager said. "Therefore, the soul helpers must never initiate contact. They may only respond if the human being makes a conscious request for help."

It was agreed.

"The distance in awareness between the human being and the soul helpers will grow wider and wider if the trend toward materialism and the dark side continues," Wa-hee remarked. "It may not matter."

"That is why we need the second extension to our plan of graduation," the soul manager said. "Physical markers must be built that can capture and distribute light from the cosmic web to the grids of Gaia."

The soul manager showed everyone how the presence of old souls spreading their light and wisdom would not be enough to prevent an extinction event at the end of the second 26,000-year cycle. "The buildup of karma after the destruction of two continental land masses has severely set back the progress of humanity, and the earth."

Everyone saw it. Wa-hee was sad (as sad as anyone can be who is on the other side, and connected to the Creative Source).

"Do not despair dear one," Marian said. "Here is the plan for physical enhancement." To explain this, the soul manager gave a little class in arithmetic, geometry, and cartography.

"A central point for the access of cosmic energy will be established. Here, at Giza in what will become known as Egypt. Three pyramid structures will be built there, anchored by the Great Pyramid. This will be the energetic base point for a series of pyramids, monuments, and mounds on the earth."

Marian showed them a grid based on latitude and longitude, with pyramids in Mesopotamia, China, North and South America, Central America, and other points in Asia. "This grid will stabilize the energy on the planet and give humanity a chance. Otherwise, if current trends continue, the show will be over."

"How is this to be done?" Wa-hee asked.

"Through free will of course." Marian looked at the 50,000 original souls. "All of you will be sent to different areas of the earth with the knowledge I will give you. You will have a strong motivation to construct these holders-of-energy. How successful we are depends on you."

Marian began the lesson.

"These structures must be built to last for at least 10,000 more orbits of the planet, until the critical time at the very end of the current 26,000-year cycle. Their design must capture and amplify the cosmic energy and transmit it into the earth. The design must also be so clever that the construction and the location of the structure should indicate its purpose and its function. For this reason we have to use obvious universal metrics and constants. When the structures are observed thousands of years later, even if consciousness has lowered further, they can be decoded."

All nodded in agreement.

"The basic structure will be a four-sided pyramid, square at the base, and tapering to a capstone at the top. When constructed properly, these pyramids will trap and distribute life-giving cosmic energy into the grids of the earth. Other designs will also be used. But the pyramid will be the baseline construction. Wa-hee, you have been chosen to direct the construction of the Great Pyramid, if you so choose."

Wa-hee felt eagerness and excitement. He was to be the primary Wayshower!

"What is the simplest, most elegant form in the universe?" Marian asked.

"The circle," Tuamit-Ra replied. This entity had been a priest or a scientist in many of his incarnations.

"Correct! Our great pyramid will be based on the circle." Marian drew a circle with a horizontal line connecting both sides of the circle. "What is the relationship between the circumference of a circle and its diameter?"

Shara-Li responded. "Even I know that." Everyone laughed. Shara-Li was as interested in math as a cat taking a bath. "The ratio known on earth as Pi."

Marian smiled lovingly. "Correct. Can anyone guess the dimensions of our pyramid? We know it must be a square at the base, so each side at the bottom will have equal length." Marian showed a picture of a pyramid. "Each of the sides will be a triangle, by definition. But how high will the structure be? What will be the apex angle? The slope angle? How will we make it so that, just by observation, it will transmit important information?"

Tuamit-Ra answered. "The structure must be based around the simplest and most obvious constant in nature: Pi."

'What would happen if we made the slope angle Pi?" Marian asked.

"Pi is only 3.14159," Shara-Li said. "It would be almost flat, and not a pyramid at all."

"If we made the apex angle Pi, it would look like a needle," Wa-hee said.

"Correct. So how do we use Pi to make a useful pyramid?"

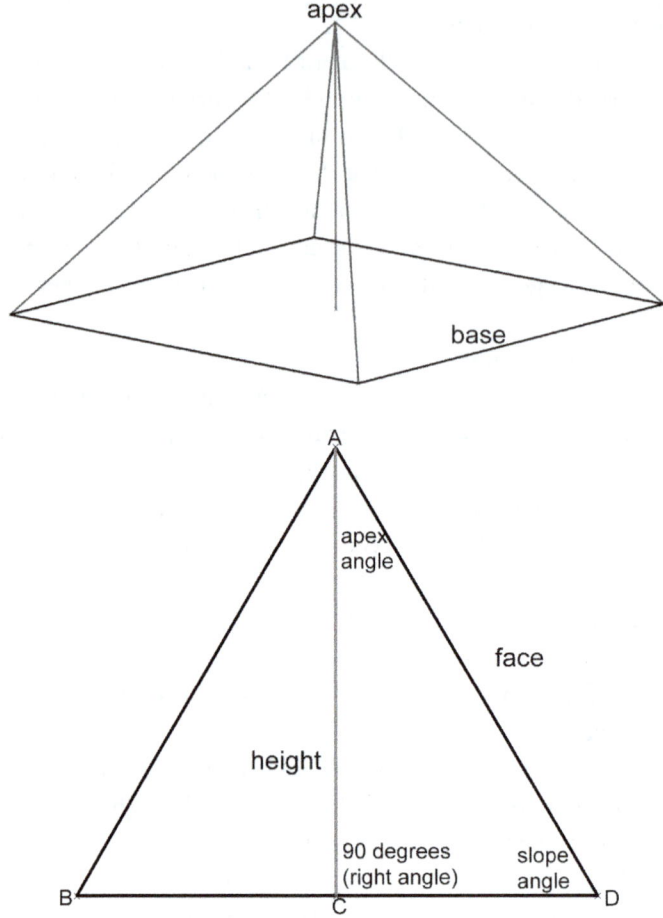

"It has to be something really simple," Shara-Li said. "Something anyone with only a little knowledge of numbers could decipher."

"I have it," Tuamit-Ra said. "We divide Pi by 4, because there are 4 sides to the pyramid. We use the tangent of that number to get the angle. Tangents are based on the circle."

"Excellent," Marian said. "The knowledge of simple arithmetic based on the circle has been kept by the priests and the mystery schools since the fall of Atlantis."

Wa-hee began to calculate. "The pyramid has 4 corners, so we divide Pi by 4 and get 0.785398. Now, what number of degrees has 0.785398 as its tangent? That will give us a working pyramid."

Tuamit-Ra looked to Shara-Li (math is a lot easier when you are on the other side). She did some rapid calculations. "The number that has this tangent is 38.146026 degrees. I see! We use that as our apex angle. This will make a nice looking pyramid."

"OK, so our slope angle must then be 51.8539736 degrees because the other angle is 90 degrees," Wa-hee said. "Everything has to add up to 180 degrees in a right triangle."

Shara-Li laughed. "When we are on earth we will have to keep things simpler. Let us make our slope angle 52 degrees and our apex angle 38 degrees."

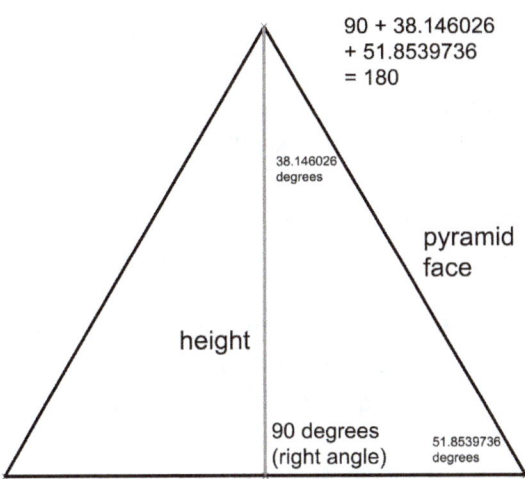

90 + 38.146026
+ 51.8539736
= 180

38.146026 degrees

pyramid face

height

90 degrees (right angle)

51.8539736 degrees

"That is wise," Marian said. "Now, what should the height of our pyramid be? We must incorporate Pi into the entire structure."

Tuamit-Ra thought for a moment. "A circle has 360 degrees. Let us add a simple ratio like one-third or two-thirds of Pi to the 360 of the circle. Let's see, two-thirds of Pi is 120 degrees, and one-third of the way around a circle. If we add 360 to 120 we get 480. That is simple arithmetic, and a good height for our pyramid."[8]

"Speak for yourself," Wa-hee said. He was thinking about how he was going to build this thing. "That's a lot of stones to make and haul up to the top."

Tuamit-Ra spoke a bit smugly. "Well, it is you who wanted to be in charge of this project."

Wa-hee was about to respond when Marian broke in. "Yes, but Tuamit-Ra, you will be the chief architect. Wa-hee is a very good organizer, but we need your architectural and arithmetic skills. "

Tuamit-Ra began to get excited. "All right, I accept. Now, if we multiply the height of the pyramid by twice Pi, we get the total circumference of the four sides of the structure at its base."

Shara-Li did some arithmetic. "The height of the pyramid is 480. Multiply that by twice Pi and you get...3,016 for the total distance around the base of the pyramid. The base of the pyramid is a simple square. So each side of the four sides is 3,016 divided by 4, or 754."

"Excellent!" Marian said. "We have incorporated the circle, and Pi, in our pyramid. The next question is, what metric do we use? How large is each of our numbers?"

Wa-hee thought for a moment. "We can use the length of the human foot. It varies in size from person to person, but a standard measure can easily be decided on."[9]

Each of them imagined the size of this pyramid, at 480 feet high and 754 feet on each side. "It will be very, very large," Wa-hee said. "Perhaps we can make it smaller and save a lot of work."

"It must be large enough to have significance all over the planet," Marian said. "It must be a marker for all generations to come, for the next 10,000 years. It must be *the* energetic marker for Gaia."

"Very well," Tuamit-Ra said, accepting this. "But where precisely should it be located? The location should also transmit information."

"Can we use our circle and Pi to find the exact latitude on the earth?" Marian asked.

Wa-hee did some calculations. "The planet has a tilt of about 23 degrees. The tilt moves of course over the millennia, but let's draw the longest line through the center of the earth's land mass." After this was done, the apex of the great pyramid would be centered at precisely 29°58'51" latitude.

"What about the longitude?"

Marian spoke. "I can be of help here. At the time of the end of the wobble, 10,000 years into the future, the zero meridian line will be here, in what will be known as Greenwich. What would happen if you took the slope angle of the pyramid itself and used that as the longitude from Greenwich?"

Tuamit-Ra looked at a longitude and latitude grid superimposed over the earth. He noticed where the latitude and longitude lines met. "51.839 degrees is the slope angle. This translates to 51°51'14.30. That is our longitude."

"A prime location indeed," Marian said. "This spot is the precise center of the land masses on earth, if you project a line upward from the center of the planet."[10] [11] The two lines met by the Nile.

"In later years the land surrounding the Nile will all become a desert. But the ground is now solid."

"That is all well," Wa-hee said. "But how shall we arrange it so that millions

Image credit: Helena Lehman, http://pillar-of-enoch.com/author/

of stones averaging one to four tons in weight are situated so that the apex of the pyramid, 480 feet high, is precisely located over the center of the pyramid? And how shall we raise the stones?"

"Simple," said Shara-Li. "We employ the technology of Atlantis. We use tuned crystals, geometry, and sound to levitate and machine the huge stones."

Marian smiled. "Dear one, that is not possible. That knowledge was lost with the fall of Atlantis."

Shara-Li understood. "This is why we are getting a lesson in arithmetic."

"Correct! So how can the stones be machined and raised using only the knowledge available to humanity?"

Tuamit-Ra thought for a moment. "Tracks and rope pulleys."

Wa-hee understood. "Brilliant! The quarries for the stones are about 900 feet from the pyramid site, about 50 feet or so uphill. The workers walk downhill on the track or beside the track using the rope pulleys, thus lifting the stones upward or moving them forward. If necessary, counterweights that exactly balance the weight of the stones to be moved are placed on the other side of the track."

Shara-Li understood. "The greater the incline, the easier it is to walk downhill. Pulley stations should exist every 200 feet or so." Shara-Li beamed. "I understand this very well. I wish also to be a part of the project."

Marian smiled. "How would you like to have a project of your own?"

Shara-Li was eager. "I would!"

"Then you shall have it. It shall be called, in later years, Stonehenge. It will also be based on Pi in a most obvious fashion."

Shara-Li clapped metaphorical hands. "Let us go over the construction. In this male dominated society I will probably have to be a man to have the social recognition to get anything done."

"Indeed you will. It is time you switched genders."

Shara-Li reluctantly agreed. She loved being a woman. "All right."

Wa-hee and Tuamit-Ra were curious as Marian explained the construction to Shara-Li.

"The site will consist of 60 stones in a circle," Marian said. "60 is one-sixth of a circle, a simple fraction. In the middle, a series of larger stones placed in a semi-circle, also representing the circle. How will the stones lay upon one another?"

"Pi!" they all shouted.

"Pi it is. Two upright pillars, one lintel above, around in a circle. Stonehenge shall be a monument to Pi, and thus to the circle, which represents eternity and the Central Source from which all life comes. Now let us look at the latitude. There are 360 degrees in a circle. The 60 stones * 360 = 21,600. What latitude would exactly equal 21,600?" Marian asked.

Tuamit-Ra was first with the answer. "51 degrees, 10 minutes, 42.35294 seconds of arc."

"I see," Wa-hee said. "Multiply 51 by 10 to get 510. Multiply 510 by 42.35294 to get 21,600!"[12]

Shara-Li was delighted. "I understand everything so far. 51 degrees north. I will be cold. But where on this circle of latitude at 51 degrees will I built the monument?"

Marian had the answer. "A thousand years or so before the end of the 26,000-year period this little island will be called England." Marian indicated the spot on the three-dimensional model of earth floating before them. "It will become the most powerful country in the world, and give the planet a new form of government. It will need balance."

The Ring of Potential showed three great confrontations between dark and light at the very end of the cycle. In the second of these great wars, the little island would be attacked viciously by evil forces. Destructive objects would be hurled at it by vimanas from the sky. Almost the entire world would be involved in the conflict. Then, the third and final war...

Shara-Li shivered. "It is appalling."

Marian looked at Shara-Li. "You will help to provide balance. Go and build Stonehenge."

The soul manager had a private consultation with Wa-hee.

"You will be given a special dispensation of knowledge, Wa-hee. You will also have the ability to access your merkaba for a brief time, for reasons which I cannot tell you now."

"The task would be much simpler if I and Tuamit-Ra could employ the ancient technology of Atlantis to raise and shape the stones, as Shara-Li said. Tuamit-Ra and I were there you know."

Marian shook his head metaphorically. "That is not permitted. Since Lemuria, consciousness and knowledge has decreased. The knowledge of the levitation of heavy objects via geometry, sound, and the placement of resonant crystals has been forgotten. You must work to build your pyramids only with the materials and the knowledge available."

Wa-hee sighed. "Sometimes this test, and all of our work, seems silly."

But when Marian showed him the scope of the project and the engineering and organizational skills required, Wa-hee became less despondent. "It is a considerable challenge."

The soul manager smiled. "It can be done and you and Tuamit-Ra can do it. The pyramid builders will all remember these simple arithmetic calculations. The Giza pyramid project will become known throughout the world."

Marian and Wa-hee looked at the most probable timeline for his next life as Thoth, and the potentials for the great undertaking. Wa-hee and Tuamit-Ra became more and more animated as they saw how important the work was. They were both grateful to be given enhanced insight and abilities.

All 50,000 original souls incarnated as pyramid builders. Many went to Egypt and North Africa, some to China, many more to Central America. You can draw a line, with the planet tilted, and find many of the great pyramids on the earth on or close to it.[13]

Marian hoped it would be enough.

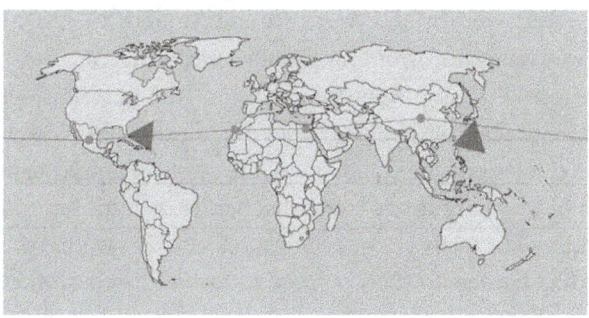

Image credit: https://www.mysterypile.com/connecting-pyramids.php

The Pyramid Builders[14]

Wa-hee incarnated as Tahuti, a great priest. Tahuti, or Thoth as the Greeks would later call him, was the god of wisdom, knowledge, and science. The country of Egypt was but a potential at this time, but hominids and men had existed here for at least 200,000 years. Tahuti was given great wisdom for the time. His stature as an original soul of earth made him different from all others in the area. His assistant Tuamit-Ra, known as Shahir, was also like Tahuti. Together they commanded great respect among the people.

Thoth and Shahir first identified the quarries where the stones would be mined. Shahir oversaw this process personally. The bulk of the stones would come from limestone quarries on the Giza plateau itself, which were a few hundred feet south from the site. These stones were gray-yellow nummulite limestone. Shahir discovered that the area where the pyramid was to be built had useful quarrying stones. Thoth designed a wooden gauge that would be a guide for indenting the outer casing stones to 52 degrees, the slope angle of the pyramid.

Shahir would use stones of different sizes and heights for the layers. The stones must be very large in the lower layers. These foundational stones were about 3 feet by 7.5 feet and 3 to 4.5 feet high. Each of these massive stones weighed between 6 and 10 tons. Shahir would use smaller stones for the higher-up layers. These were about 3 feet by 3 feet and about 1.5 feet high.

Shahir/Tuamit-Ra remembered that because the pyramid would be tilted, some of the weight of the stones would transfer sideways. Therefore the foundation track and the foundation stones would be cut at an inward angle to account for this.

White limestone would be needed for the outer stones – the shinier and harder facade that would literally glow when the sun struck them. (These stones would later be removed by the Arabs in and around 800 AD, to build their mosques.) They would come from the Tura quarries upriver.

Shahir was very pleased when he found the Tura quarries south of Cairo on the eastern shore of the Nile, about 10 to 12 miles from Giza. With his quarrymen he inspected the limestone there and found it to be of very high quality: white, very fine-grained, not very porous and somewhat harder than the limestone from Giza. "This limestone will be easily be cut and formed." Shahir saw that the outer layer of the limestone had hardened when exposed to the air. "See how the sun shines on the limestone and makes it glitter." The quarrymen were pleased that their master took a personal interest in their work. The next step was to choose the ground for the pyramid. Shahir and Thoth discussed this.

"Such a massive structure must have firm ground underneath it," Shahir said. "How do we determine this?"

"Let me do a survey of the ground around the Giza plateau. Do you identify the proper quarries and the proper stone to use for each part of the pyramid."

While Shahir was traveling with his quarrymen, Thoth began his geological survey by using a long metal spike that he and his workers pounded into the soft ground at various places. Thoth also used his intuition – a dispensation granted to him by the soul manager – and chose the best ground existing on the Giza plateau, on top of a rock core which goes down to at least 24 feet under the pyramid.

Thoth also designed the interior of the pyramid. He had in mind a sacred King's chamber, a Queen's chamber and a gallery. Inside was a space approximately 100 feet long in the middle of the pyramid. This chamber would magnify and focus the cosmic energies gathered by the structure.

Shahir planned to use granite stones for the interior chambers. These would come all the way from Aswan, several hundred miles downriver to the south.

A double series of pulley blocks, aided by water, would be used to transport the blocks up the side of the pyramid. These would be constructed so that workers could walk downhill on the side of the pyramid while the stones were pulled upward.[15]

When all was settled and construction was ready to begin, hundreds of workers and craftsmen had already showed up. Workers from everywhere around the Mediterranean knew of the gigantic undertaking. Already it was said to be the greatest construction project in the world. Nubians from central and southern Africa also arrived. Shahir did not turn anyone away.

Thoth gave a speech to all those engaged in the project.

"Men, we are building the greatest monument the world has ever seen or will see. I cannot emphasize to you how important this project is. This structure will have magical and esoteric properties that will help keep the land fertile, the Nile flowing, and even energize the atmosphere around it. It will be here ten thousand years after we, you and I, build it."[16]

Thoth was a commanding figure as he stood on the first stone deposited from the quarry. His eyes seemed to blaze with a cold blue fire; an aura of light appeared to surround his head. Men turned to each other, nodding. This was to be sacred work. And a leader worthy to direct it. All were satisfied.

Almost everyone associated with the project was enthusiastic, although the work was hard and difficult. Thoth saw to it, through his leadership, that the men disciplined themselves. Each workman was allowed to inscribe his personal mark on the interior of the stones, along with a short message. Women and families were allowed on site, boosting morale. Despite the good start, however, malcontents and saboteurs were identified. At first these men were beaten to death with chisels or hammers by the others. Their bodies were thrown under the stones of the pyramid.

One day after the cornerstones had been carefully laid and the first row of massive foundation stones meticulously put in place, Thoth heard an argument. A Nubian worker was being attacked by several men from the north. Thoth recognized these workers as coming from Damascus. (At this time the great city was in its infancy, but the people there had a distinctive culture.)

Thoth strode over to the workmen. "Hear now, what is this? Identify yourselves."

The Nubian wiped blood from his forehead. "I am Wazir, from the Kingdom of Kartoom to the south." Thoth and the other men were able to understand his speech. "My king sent me to participate in the sacred project. I am skilled in the cutting and placing of large stones." The man spoke bitterly. "Here I am attacked by savages."

This provoked outrage from the Damascus workmen. "I am Fulud," said a brawny man with a large black beard. "This man Wazir was attempting to sabotage the cornerstone!" His two companions concurred.

"He was attacking the stone with a chisel!" said Hamal. "Is that not right Abdur?"

Abdur nodded his agreement. It was he who had first accused the Nubian.

Thoth said nothing, but regarded the men. Gradually tempers calmed. "Let us look at the stone in question. If there is mischief, Wazir will be dismissed. If all is well, you three will be disciplined."

The men from Damascus nodded. Wazir bowed. "It is fitting."

Thoth and the men walked over to the stone. Fulud pointed to one of the all-important cornerstones. "This man was cutting into the stone, disturbing its placement relative to the two stones adjacent to it."

Thoth saw the situation immediately.

"Explain yourself," he said to Wazir.

The Nubian bent down, pointing to the corner stone. He placed a wooden template beside the massive block. "This corner angle on this stone is too large. If the angle on the cornerstone is not precise, error in the slope angle will destabilize the structure."

All of the men understood this. The cornerstones would have to support and absorb much of the pyramid's enormous weight that pressed down and sideways. These critical blocks had a special shape and were very massive.

Wazir straightened. "The outer stones must all be very precisely cut, because here the angle of inclination of the pyramid is defined. The angle of the corner is very difficult to achieve. High precision in workmanship is required."

The men from Damascus bristled. "Are you suggesting that this stone is improperly cut?" Hamal asked.

Wazir spoke with dignity. "See for yourself."

By this time a crowd of men had gathered.

Fulud was suspicious. "Who is this Nubian who speaks so precisely and who understands the arithmetic of stone cutting?" Fulud pointed to the template. "What is this and who designed it?"

Fulud's companions supported him. "This is a trick," Hamal said.

"Wazir promotes mischief and disturbs the harmony of our work," Abdur asserted. "He should be dismissed."

Thoth smiled. He himself had constructed a similar device. "The difficulty is easily remedied." He pointed to Wazir. "Did you construct this template?"

"I did."

Thoth took the template and examined it. He held it out to Fulud. The men from Damascus inspected it critically. Fulud measured the angle and found it to be correct. He placed it on the corner stone. The angle of the cornerstone as it was cut was seen to be slightly too large.

Fulud grunted. "I can find nothing wrong with this," he admitted reluctantly. "The stone will have to be shaved slightly to get the correct angle."

Both of Fulud's companions were mollified. "It is ingenious," Hamal concluded. Abdur, who had accused Wazir, looked at the Nubian. "I retract my previous statement. This will save us time and effort."

The men looked to Thoth. "What say you?" Wazir asked.

Thoth smiled. "It is well. The One smiles upon us today. He has brought us a master craftsman."

The men were curious about this phrase. "The One?" Fulud asked.

"The higher power, that which represents unity in diversity. The infinite creator."

The men looked at each other curiously. "I do not understand these words," Wazir said, speaking for all four. "There are many gods."

"All is well my friends," Thoth replied. The tension had now disappeared. "By the time this project is completed I am sure you will have a greater understanding."

Fulud looked at his men and then at Wazir. All four shrugged. "We will see, o Thoth."

The men were about to get back to work when Wazir spoke. "We have forgotten something."

Fulud and his men stopped. Thoth smiled.

"There is the matter of punishment." Wazir was testing Thoth. He wanted to see how the leader would handle the men from Damascus.

Thoth spoke to Fulud. "What say you? It has been agreed that punishment should be meted out for your assault on Wazir."

All could see the dried blood now caking upon the Nubian's forehead. A trickle of it dripped to the ground.

Fulud looked to his companions and spoke. "Our punishment will be to work under Wazir. He shall be our superior."

"You are wise, Fulud," Thoth replied. "Wazir, please see Shahir. He will place you where your skills can be best utilized." Thoth turned to Wazir. "These are now your men to command."

Wazir bowed to Thoth and to Fulud, Abdur, and Hamal. "Come with me, men. We shall see Shahir together."

The crowd of men dispersed. From that moment a calmer atmosphere pervaded the work site. Thoth was grateful. Such discordances were not in harmony with the sacred undertaking.

After this incident discipline was only occasionally necessary. Tracks and rope pulley stations were constructed along the route where the stones would be quarried to the building site. Using trial and error, Shahir soon found the optimum number of pulley stations and their placement along the track. To haul stones up the pyramid itself, he thought, a dual-pulley system would be required, for the angle of inclination of the side surfaces is 52°. Pullers would walk downhill, raising the blocks to the proper place on the pyramid. A special track system was built for the heavy granite blocks. A counterweight would be employed at the top of the ramp to help the workmen, thus reducing the amount of human effort to slide it upward.

Quarrymen soon devised the optimum methods for cutting the stones, which were always done at the quarry site. Stones that would be laid down next to each other at the site were broken next to each other in the quarry. This would ensure that they were the same height and fit to each other exactly along the line of breakage. Master stone men such as Wazir and his crew of Damascus men checked the longitudinal side of each block and saw to it that the line of breakage actually fitted to each other. If the stones didn't fit well when placed on the pyramid, workers had to correct the fit with their hammers and chisels. At first this caused great discord between the quarrymen and the stone fitters. Several fights broke out, and a man died when his head hit a stone after being shoved by another workman.

Whenever a fight broke out Thoth was there to ease tensions. Soon the inexperienced or incompetent quarrymen were weeded out and work proceeded apace. These, however, always demanded some kind of job at the site, even if it was to be one of the laborers who lifted and pulled the stones into place. All who worked there became proud of their association with the project.

Shahir appeared every day to supervise the work. Thoth himself came regularly to inspire the men and examine the progress of the structure. He himself would sometimes inspect the stones, and took measurements everywhere. Sometimes stones would have to be moved slightly to conform with the arithmetic of the structure. For this Wazir and his men were employed. Uppermost in the thoughts of Thoth was that the pyramid adhere precisely to the blueprint in his mind. Shahir and Thoth worked together almost without friction. This set an example to the workers, who tried to emulate their masters.

The number of workers on the pyramid project varied between 6,000 and 7,000 at any one time, including the quarrymen and those who moved and placed the stones. Hundreds more provided and distributed food. Domiciles were built to house the workers, for the project would last almost two decades. A city grew upon the spot, which is now called Giza, the third largest city in Egypt.[17]

One day after their labor was complete Wazir and Fulud were inspecting the work at the pyramid. It had rained that day, soaking the quarry sites. Fortunately the pyramid itself was above hard rock, but drainage for rainfall had to be provided.

Wazir looked out over the lush plain. The greenery was now over two feet high. "It is said in the legends of my people that the entirety of North Africa was once a desert."

Fulud laughed. "You must be joking," he said, pointing to the grasses and flowers growing everywhere.

"This is before the melting of the ice, when the earth was colder. Here, and in my country, the weather was very dry. These lands were barren."

Fulud shook his head. "It is a thing hard to believe."

As they walked in the fading light Fulud pointed past the huts of the workers to a campground where dozens of men were building fires.

Wazir groaned. "More men looking for work."

"We already have more than we need."

Wazir looked closer. "These are not workers. This is a party of war."

The clank of metal on metal was heard. Fulud thought he heard swords being withdrawn from scabbards, and the clank of sword on shield.

Fulud was alarmed. "We are helpless!"

"Let us scout around the camp and see how many warriors are present."

Fulud wanted to go back for his two companions Hamal and Abdur, but they were probably already at their domiciles on the other side of the pyramid. Wazir circled around to the west, Fulud walked warily to the east. Both men were unarmed. They had not even thought of battle for almost a year, their minds occupied with stonemasonry.

Fulud crept up to the camp. Sentries were posted. He heard shouts and talk. Fulud recognized these men. They were from the north and west of here, barbarians. Their coarse speech and their talk of murder and plunder disgusted him. He estimated a force of several dozen. The men seemed to be well armed.

"Who goes there?" Someone shouted in his direction.

Fulud did not run, but moved slowly and silently away from the fires. The darkness enveloped the land. He would remain unseen if he moved quietly.

He met Wazir several minutes later. "It is a considerable force. Barbarians from the lands to the west of here."

Wazir nodded. "Three dozen men I would estimate. But what could they want here?"

Fulud snorted with disgust. "Word has spread of the project. These fools think there is treasure here, or valuables. They come to prey on the workers and steal what they have."

"And to kill for the sake of killing."

Fulud and Wazir headed toward the dwelling of Shahir, who was always present on site unless inspecting one of the quarries.

Wazir and Fulud reported their observations, and that the force was hostile.

"Do you have any idea if and when they will attack?" Shahir asked.

"They will attack, certainly," Wazir said.

"My guess is just after sunrise," Fulud said. "These barbarians are afraid of the dark. This is why they wail and drink and keep fires until the rising of the sun."

During the night the workers could hear shouting coming from the camp. Everyone was nervous. Men brought out their weapons and sent their wives and children scurrying across the plain to a small city five miles to the northeast, the site of present day Cairo.

Shahir, Wazir, and Fulud, along with Abdur and Hamal, went to the dwellings of the workers, trying to calm them. "Are there any military men among you?" they asked.

A dozen men with military experience were identified. Several knew of the tactics of the invaders. "These barbarians merely gather together and charge wildly. Usually they are inebriated. Their goal is plunder and blood."

Shahir smiled. "Then let us surround them. Move all of the men out of their tents to the perimeter of the area. Leave fires burning and all possessions as they are. Move silently and swiftly. Carry only your sword, if you have one."

Fulud and Wazir grinned. The five men left and the evacuation began, under the guidance of Shahir and the military men. Before dawn almost everyone was several hundred feet outside the small makeshift city, in a semicircle. The night was cool.

Just before dawn Thoth arrived on the scene. He had just returned from a long journey to Aswan, inspecting granite stones to be used for the interior of the pyramid. He heard the shouting and the carousing from the armed camp. He was pleased to see that Shahir had evacuated the area.

Thoth sat down on a stone and meditated for several minutes. No one saw him. If someone had been there to observe, they may have seen an aura of blue fire around his body.

Thoth began walking toward the armed camp. It was growing lighter. He saw some of the workers with their swords, talking nervously. Shahir had everything in hand, it seemed.

Thoth continued walking. The light grew brighter. After ten minutes he was approximately 100 feet from the first campfire. Men began to stir. Many of them were intoxicated. Swords were unsheathed, shields were being strapped to arms. Coarse shouting came from the back of the camp.

Thoth was noticed. One of the sentries and several of the men laughed and drew their swords. The other men were massing behind for a charge on the city of pyramid workers. The lead group was now almost close enough to strike Thoth with their weapons.

Just as the charge was about to begin Thoth held up his hand. A blue fire around his body grew more intense. A white sphere of light came forth from his hand. "Barbarians, halt!" The lead group, through their drunken stupor, felt a powerful force and shrank back. Some of the men behind stumbled and fell, causing angry shouting.

"I am that I am," Thoth intoned. His voice was not loud but could be heard above the noise of cursing and shouting. The light from his hand became brighter. "In the Name of the One, the Creator, the All-Powerful, I command you to withdraw."

The invaders were stunned. They had never heard such speech before, and were confused. Some of them felt the power of the light emanating from Thoth and dropped their weapons. The others behind them charged, holding their swords outstretched and piercing the bodies of the men in front of them.

Several hundred feet away the workers watched silently, barely able to breathe. When the charging men were almost ready to hack him down, Thoth stepped back and repeated his performance. His voice now became like thunder and the light around his body glowed brilliantly.

"Barbarians! If you do not withdraw this instant, I shall strike you down!" Another sphere of white light came forth from his hand, enveloping the men in front, who collapsed to the ground. Curiously, none of the invaders were hurt and looked as if they were sleeping quietly.

But the invaders became terrified. Instantly they halted and the shouting stopped. When the light from Thoth was gone, the sleeping men got up groggily.

"Take your weapons, turn around, and go back to the west. If ever you should set foot upon this soil again, bolts of lightning shall pour forth from the skies, destroying you and all you possess."

The aspect of Thoth was so frightening to the invaders that they turned and ran. Many of them dropped their weapons and their shields. The ragtag force fled to the west and was never seen again.

Thus was the legend of Thoth born. When the attackers reached their lands they spread the story of the great and terrifying wizard to the south and east. Workers from the pyramid project who went back to their lands around the Mediterranean spread the story far and wide. It became embellished, of course. Who knows whether white light actually came forth from the hands of Thoth? But certainly the formidable presence of Thoth/Wa-hee was enough to frighten the low-consciousness barbarians. As a science fiction writer would say, thousands of years later, 'the force has a strong influence on the weak-minded.'

Soon the name of Thoth and his strange speech about the One Creator, the All-Powerful, became known even to those tribes in China and on the subcontinent. Many puzzled over these words, for were there not multiple gods? The god of war, the god of thunder, the weather spirits, the god of the earth, and many others.

The words of Thoth were taken seriously because of the miracles he had performed. Therefore the idea of the One God, for the first time since the fall of Lemuria, entered the consciousness of humanity.

Twenty years later

Thoth, Shahir, Wazir, Fulud, and his two companions Abdur and Hamal gazed up at the magnificent structure. The work had been completed. The sun glinted brilliantly off the casing stones, sending light everywhere. The pyramid was visible for dozens of miles around. Word of its completion was spreading throughout the known world.

When the capstone was put on, Thoth felt a great disturbance in the ethers. This pyramid was funneling a tremendous amount of energy into the ground, anchoring the structure to the earth. His work was not done, however. Two smaller pyramids, but still huge structures later known as the Chephren and the Mycerinus, must also be built. Other pyramids were also being built around the world. Even Thoth did not know the connection between them. All he knew was that this one was the anchoring structure for the entire grid of pyramids and monuments that were being built across the planet.

Marian

When Wa-hee transitioned this time he hardly noticed. In order to do his pyramid work he had been granted a special dispensation: a powerful connection to his soul on the other side. After only a very short time he came before Marian after leaving the Cave of Creation, where the soul energy from his last life had been deposited. Wa-hee was looked upon by the soul manager with awe.

"You, along with Tuamit-Ra, were magnificent."

Just then Shara-Li showed up from her/his excursion on the island in the north Atlantic.

"How did it go?" Wa-hee asked.

"Oh my, I was cold most of the time. I didn't think I would ever get used to it."

Wa-hee thought of his time on Rügen, and his/her messenger duties on Lemuria as Ona. "We go where we are needed, I suppose."

Shara-Li was able to see the lifetime of Wa-hee by his stripes, and Wa-hee saw Shara-Li's.

"I would like to make love with you if we meet on earth," Shara-Li suggested.

"I would like that," Wa-hee said. "Perhaps we could be mates. Have a little fun."

Marian smiled at this colloquy. "It shall be done. You both completed huge tasks for the planet and for humanity."

"I would also like to be with Tuamit-Ra," Wa-hee offered. "In my physical incarnation I grew to love him as a brother."

"Tuamit-Ra still has work to do on the planet," Marian said. "He has to oversee the construction of Chephren and the Mycerinus pyramids. He will live to a very old age. But if he desires it, he can be your child."

Both Wa-hee and Shara-Li laughed. "Could we handle him, do you think?" Wa-hee asked.

"He is very powerful, but I would like to try. As long as –Ra does not have an important soul mission. I think all three of us should have a relaxing life."

Wa-hee smiled. "Well then, I would like to have as my friends Wazir and Fulud. Please, make them male. I do not want any temptation."

Shara-Li smiled. "Oh Wa-hee, when you see me you will have eyes for no other." Shara-Li sent him a mental picture of her in the next life.

"Wow! Will I be able to handle you? You are magnificent."

"As long as you have that attitude we shall get along fine," Shara-Li said.

Wa-hee laughed. "Good! Do you have friends you would like to have as well?"

Shara-Li considered. "No. The men I worked with were surly, and so was I. Although we all felt the magnificence of the construction at Stonehenge, we were too cold to enjoy much of anything. My previous lives were not of a nature to meet good companions." Shara-Li smiled. "But I have grown. I have learned responsibility."

"So you have." Marian laughed, a little wistfully, at this exchange. No part of his soul had ever split and had a lifetime on earth. It never would. He/she was a helper. Always safe and snug within the arms of the Creator, but never would he have the adventures of these two on earth. He gazed at their "stripes," the soul record of their incarnations. These original souls were awe-inspiring. Wherever they went on this side they were engaged by the other souls coming to earth. Marian felt almost envious. But then he remembered his own experiences on other planets before this one. It was enough.

Wa-hee, Shara-Li, and the soul manager planned their next lifetime. Tuamit-Ra would return first, then Wazir and Fulud, who were with him, shortly after. There was not much life planning to do, for these souls would take a "vacation" during their next expression.

Now Wa-hee and Shara-Li were shown how the other original souls were doing. "Look at the structures here in Mexico and in Central America," Marian said. They were shown how all of the major pyramids and monuments were located on specially designed grid points. The world's original Prime Meridian is the latitude and longitude at the Great Pyramid in Giza. All of the major high-rise pyramids in the world encode Pi and the 360-base system of the circle. Therefore, with knowledge of this, every pyramid in the world could be located on a grid.

"Even though the pyramids in Mexico and Central America look slightly different," Marian said, "they all encode Pi and the circle."

The two were shown the pyramids at Teotihuacan in Mexico, the Sun pyramid, the Moon pyramid, and the Quetzalcoatal complex. "Do you notice anything?"

Shara-Li saw it. "The layout of these three pyramids is exactly the same as the three at Giza!"

Wa-hee was amazed.

"The Sun pyramid also encodes Pi," Marian remarked. "This complex in Mexico balances the complex at Giza. Over the centuries more pyramids and mounds will be built. These will all be strategically placed on the grid to hold things together energetically."

Marian showed them the potentials by displaying the Ring of Potential, which showed the past, present, and future of earth from its beginning as a cloud of galactic dust, until its end when the sun eventually novaed 2 billion years from the present. Shara-Li recognized that the gases from the sun would explode into the galaxy, creating the material for a new solar system. "Astronomers on earth have it wrong," she said. "Stars begin as red giants, collections of stellar material, and then evolve to white-hot stars that spew out that material again in a recycling fashion."[18]

Wa-hee was impressed. "You are rapidly gaining in wisdom and maturity," he said. "I would like to make love to you now."

"We can meld together. But it will be nothing like on earth."

Wa-hee agreed. "Let us leave now." He turned to Marian. "Make sure all is arranged."

Marian laughed. "Thoth, you had better watch that tone with Shara-Li. She will quickly put you in your place."

Wa-hee laughed. "I can't wait for that."

Marian saw them both into the birth vortex. They would incarnate in Central America to a peaceful tribe in what would later become the lands of the Maya. Wa-hee would be a householder, Shara-Li his wife. There would be no difficulty.

Tuamit-Ra, Wazir, and Fulud died within a year of each other. They had lived very long eventful lives and were exhausted after their labors on earth. It took each of them some time before they exited the Cave of Creation and integrated fully with their souls.

The soul manager met them, of course, after the celebration of their lives on earth. He told all three of the plans of Wa-hee and Shara-Li. When Tuamit-Ra saw that Wa-hee had beaten him to the punch with Shara-Li, he was a little jealous. When he saw the expression of Shara-Li, he was even more miffed. He spoke a bit petulantly (for a soul in the arms of the Creative Source). "It is Thoth who always gets the prize," he said. Wazir and Fulud laughed. But they were also a bit envious, for Shara-Li was one of the most popular old souls. To incarnate with her, regardless of gender, was a treat.

"Never fear dear ones. Like Shara-Li and Wa-hee, you are also ready for a break." Marian explained to them the plans of Shara-Li and Wa-hee.

"Oh ho, Wa-hee!" Tuamit-Ra cried. He looked at his dear friends Wazir and Fulud. "Let us cross them up a little," he said mischievously.

Marian was a bit concerned until Tuamit-Ra explained. "Our friends Wa-hee and Shara-Li cannot abide too much contentment. A life of complete calm is not what they want."

Marian smiled. "Explain your plan."

Tuamit-Ra consulted with Fulud and Wazir, who were known on the other side as Pele-Khan and Mutu-Boran. But we will continue to refer to them by their names on earth when the two were involved with the construction of the earth's greatest monument. (Actually these were not their names at all, because on the other side they were composed of light and song. These are their truncated equivalents in English.)

Wazir spoke. "I am ready for a gender change, I have been a man too long. I wish to incarnate as the daughter of Wa-hee."

The soul manager smiled. "Wa-hee is wanting sons."

"But Shara-Li wants daughters."

Wazir looked at Fulud. They both broke out laughing.

"I am afraid those two are going to have a harder time of it than they expected," Fulud said. "I shall incarnate as Wa-hee's son."

Wazir laughed. "I shall be a very strange daughter to Shara-Li, for she will want me to be soft and feminine like her. But I am not familiar with the feminine energy. My Akash is composed mostly of masculine energy." Wazir smiled. "I am afraid I will be a great trial to her."

Now it was Fulud's turn to laugh. "And mine is composed mostly of feminine energy. I will be the daughter in a male body that Shara-Li wants. Wazir will be the son in a female body that Wa-hee wants."

The two began laughing so loudly that Marian was afraid Wa-hee and Shara-Li would hear it on the planet.

Once again the soul manager became slightly envious. Oh, to play these fun games with each other! Many of these physical expressions were rough ones, but there were also some delightful ones.

Tuamit-Ra now spoke. "I shall incarnate as the beautiful daughter of the chief. My Akash is perfectly balanced between male and female, so I am comfortable with both genders. Shara-Li will look at my beauty and be jealous, for I shall be 15 years younger. Fulud and Wazir will be torn. As a male, Fulud will be attracted to me. But so will Wazir as the daughter of Shara-Li, for Wazir's Akash is mostly male. There will be some sexual tension. Oh, it will be delicious!"

Marian shook his/her head. These old souls can get very complicated.

"All right. Tuamit-Ra and Fulud will incarnate now. A year from now, Wazir will enter as the daughter of Shara-Li and brother to Fulud, the son of Wa-hee." Marian paused. "Are you sure you three want to do this? Poor Wa-hee and Shara-Li need a break."

Fulud, Tuamit-Ra, and Wazir all scoffed. "Poor Wa-hee indeed!" Tuamit-Ra said. "My life was much more difficult than Thoth's. I had to work much harder and had greater responsibilities. I want some fun!"

Marian saw the truth of this. Fulud and Wazir felt the same. "We will all show them a grand time," Wazir said to Fulud.

Marian saw Tuamit-Ra and Fulud to the birth vortex. As the soul splitting process began the soul manager heard them both laughing as they entered their bodies. A year later on earth (there is no time on the other side) Wazir entered as the daughter of the chief. Marian shook his metaphoric head. Nothing would go wrong this time around except a little game-playing.

Not too much need be said about this lifetime of the five friends. It passed just as Wazir, Fulud, and Tuamit-Ra planned it. Wa-hee and Shara-Li did have a wonderful time and lived (mostly) happily until a ripe old age.

Soul families

The soul manager was planning ahead As more souls came to the earth during the Great Experiment the population would increase rapidly during the final millennium, and would explode during the last century. Not even the Ring of Potential could predict what would happen then. Marian's job was to get humanity through to the final decades of the cycle without an extinction event. It would then be up to the free will choice of humanity whether the final war destroyed the earth.

The souls of earth had already divided themselves into soul families. These families could be large or small, like the five friends Wa-hee, Shara-Li, Fulud, Wazir, and Tuamit-Ra. The soul families consisted of the scientists and technicians, the managers/executives (this sector, in business and commerce, would grow rapidly in the final millennium), the priests and those involved with religion, a very large family of musicians/artists/architects/builders, and the politicians/rulers/aristocracy.

Marian noticed a disturbing trend: a very small but determined percentage of souls who were embracing the dark side. In any group of any size, there would be at least one. These dark side souls seemed to relish karma and thought little of doing child abuse, murder, and destruction while on earth.

On this side these souls were beautiful, but when they incarnated their Akash would bias them to evil. Then there were the star seeds, who were coming early to balance the dark side souls. These came from various graduate planets who had already made it.

The most numerous soul group would cross boundaries. These were the new souls who would come into the planet during the last 70 years of the cycle. They were by far the most numerous and would incarnate in every country and ethnic group. These would be the "swing" energy on the earth: those who had no prior experience here, no Akash. They would have no preference either way as to the direction the planet would take. They would not know enough about how earth worked to even notice. They would be the unattached souls who would act as a buffer between those who were more highly motivated on either side. The soul manager's plan was for the karma of humanity to be diluted by a huge influx of newbie souls with no earth karma, somewhat like an insurance pool, where the cost of accident-prone people would be paid by the vast majority who were more careful.

But that was a long way off yet.

A very tiny but influential soul group are the Ascended Masters and those who would evolve to Ascended Masters. There were already a few in the making, such as Wa-hee/Thoth. In the future these would come in during crisis situations, in an attempt to turn the tide. Marian saw these masters coming in during the time of the Buddha, Christ, and afterward. But again, this was several millennia down the road.

Marian

Wa-hee/Thoth returned from an incarnation in Patagonia, at the tip of South America. Marian had sent him and Tuamit-Ra there to work with the whales. These great creatures carried a "backup" copy of the imprints of humanity's Akash, across the oceans. Shara-Li, Fulud, and Wazir had returned from incarnations in China, attempting to spread compassion there.

The five friends were reunited once more. Shara-Li had balanced her Akash somewhat by becoming male for several dozen incarnations. Wazir had done the same as a female. Each had become the other's mates, children, grandchildren, parents, and grandparents. These five, over the millennia, were one of the very few soul groupings without karma between them. They were a small but formidable team. Marian decided that they must return to North Africa.

The soul manager showed the five the Ring of Potential, and the potential for their coming lives. The five would incarnate as a family. In the area, a band of warriors had just learned to train the horse for war.

"This is a development that can lead the earth further into darkness," Wa-hee said.

Fulud and Wazir agreed. "If the horse becomes militarized, the likelihood of war increases as those who desire power see a way to overwhelm their enemies."

Tuamit-Ra was disturbed by this. "What can be done?"

"See here." Marian showed the five a potential confrontation between a family and a band of raiders. "This incident could be the first on the earth between war-riors who train the horse for war, and peaceful human beings. It is a test. We will send you five, original souls, to the planet to balance the energy of war with that of peace. The result will be a good indicator of what is likely to happen in the future."

All five saw it. The Ring of Potential had pinpointed the crucial moment in linear time when the decisions of a group of human beings would affect the entirety of human consciousness. From this seed event a potential would be manifested. The grids of Gaia would see this and be guided by it. To a casual observer it would mean nothing; just another interaction out of millions on the planet. But this would be a seminal moment in history, unrecorded in the history books. Each knew the importance of the coming lifetime.

Shara-Li and Wa-hee were briefed and entered the birth vortex. As had hap-pened before, Tuamit-Ra, Fulud, and Wazir would come in later as the children. The crucial event sequence was set for 27 years in the future along the earth's time-line.

Another soul group would participate, but Marian did not tell this to the five. The old soul Darshook and his six warrior friends, who had no karma between them, would also have an assignment.

CHAPTER **6**

6,000 years ago. The 5.9 kiloyear event

Shara-Li, Tuamit-Ra, Fulud, Wazir, and Wa-hee were a family again, this time in modern-day Somalia, on the Gulf of Aden. The small tribe kept sheep and pigs and used the camelid (the dromedary) for travel. Wa-hee and his eldest son Fulud also hunted.

One day Shara-Li came to the tent and spoke to her husband. "This morning I saw something unusual," she said to Wa-hee. "Just after dawn."

"Speak."

"A band of nomads, traveling upon the backs of swift creatures. They were carrying swords and wore clothing to protect their bodies."

Wa-hee was alarmed. "We know of these *hamaj*. They come from the north, from the lands near the great sea. What are they doing down here?"

Shara-Li had no answer. Just then Fulud and Wazir, her two sons, ran into the tent, which was a portable structure made from animal skins. When the little family needed to move, they walked and carried their possessions in the tent, which was placed on the back of the camelid.

"Where is Tuamit-Ra?" Shara-Li asked.

"I don't know," Fulud said.

Wazir shook his head.

"I will find her," Wa-hee said. "Stay in the tent."

Wa-hee walked a hundred feet to a small grouping of trees. Tuamit-Ra was on her knees, inspecting a brightly colored beetle crawling on a rock. Wa-hee thought he spotted something from the corners of his eyes, in the far distance. "Come daughter, it is time to go back to the tent."

"I'm having fun here. Father, what is this creature?" Tuamit-Ra picked up the beetle, which had a bright blue carapace.

"I know not daughter. Come, there may be danger."

Wa-hee grabbed his daughter and carried her back to the tent.

Wa-hee built a small fire and roasted some meat which had been carefully wrapped in leaves and buried in the ground. The family ate quickly.

"I will take our eldest son Fulud and scout the area. Do you stay in the tent Shara-Li, with our youngest son Wazir, and Tuamit-Ra."

Shara-Li was frightened. A small tribe to the north had been butchered and their animals stolen just a few weeks ago. "Perhaps we should move further south."

Wa-hee shrugged. "Fulud and I will determine the best course. Come, son."

Fulud was pleased to be called beside his father. It was warrior's work. The young man and his father walked upon the open plain, which was mostly green. Small shrubs and plants grew; small groups of trees could be seen in scattered clumps. Wa-hee taught his son how to scan the plain, first going to the long distance and coming forward. Fulud often turned backward and to the side, scanning in a 360 degree circle. This was a thing taught to him by Wa-hee.

"Down," Wa-hee said suddenly. He placed his hand on his son's back. Forcing him to the ground. "Lie still."

"I don't understand father."

"Turn your head very slowly to the left. Focus on the far distance."

Fulud saw it. A faint dust rose in the air. There was movement.

"The hamaj. No doubt the same barbarians who ran off our friends to the north."

"They come nearer."

Wa-hee observed closely. Were these men coming with a purpose, or were their movements random? He saw the creatures upon which they rode. They moved swiftly, as Shara-Li said. This band could swoop down and quickly overwhelm their little camp.

"The men are forming a line now," Fulud said. It was clear the riders had spotted their tent and the animals, which had been let loose to graze on the green of the plain. The hamaj began to move slowly toward them.

Wa-hee made up his mind. "Let us walk back to the tent. Do not run. Above all do not show fear."

Father and son were half a mile from their encampment. "The barbarians are several miles in the distance," Fulud said.

Wa-hee looked backward out of the corner of his eye. "They come more swiftly now. Walk faster, but do not run."

Wa-hee and Fulud reached the tent. Wa-hee sent Fulud inside. "Get our spears. Bring the bow and arrows."

Fulud reappeared with the weapons. Wa-hee made sure the bowstring was taut. He placed his precious arrows in a little pouch that hung from his shoulder. Wa-hee had devised this weapon four summers ago, to help in the hunting and for defense. He was expert in its use.

Fulud and Wa-hee watched as the hamaj came galloping up to their encampment. Despite himself Fulud was excited and impressed with the horses. "What beasts are these?" he asked the leader of the band.

The man was dressed in a fur and wore skins on his feet, for the weather was cool. He carried a spear and rode like a man accustomed to the back of a horse. He laughed. "These be horses. Strange but powerful creatures."

The men behind him silently sat their beasts, who snorted and moved sideways on their feet. All were armed.

The band had the look of being well fed. Wa-hee relaxed a little. Something very important was about to happen, but he didn't know what it was.

The leader pointed to his bow and arrow. "What be that device?"

In answer Wa-hee quickly grabbed an arrow, notched it, and let fly. The arrow buried itself in the trunk of one of the trees Tuamit-Ra had been playing at an hour ago.

The leader and his men cried out. "A bolt of lightning, swiftly raised!" The leader and his men were all astonished and excited. "How is this device constructed?" The leader got off his horse and approached. Wa-hee showed no fear. He would be a friendly warrior, talking as one who had superior knowledge. In this way the confrontation could be defused and peace would result. In the back of his mind he knew he had done something like this before.

The leader pointed proudly to himself. "I am Darshook. These are my men." The warriors behind him straightened in their seats. Wa-hee smiled. "A formidable band I see. You have trained these amazing animals very well."

Darshook swelled with pride. "It is a thing unknown in these parts." He pointed to the bow and arrow. "As is that."

Wa-hee assessed the situation. He would show Darshook how to make the bow and arrow, even though it might eventually be to the family's detriment. Wa-hee would move quickly out of this place. To the south, as Shara-Li had suggested, further into the continent.

"Come Darshook. I will explain how I made this device."

Darshook nodded. He motioned to his men, who got off their mounts and stood silently beside them, holding their heads.

"Your men are well-trained," Wa-hee acknowledged.

Darshook grunted and motioned to the bow. "Show me how to construct this device which throws bolts of destruction so swiftly."

Wa-hee spent an hour showing Darshook the bow and arrow, and the materials he used to make it. As he did so he became worried. Darshook's men were also looking closely. They had the demeanor of men who had plans.

Wa-hee did not offer refreshment. At the end Darshook's attitude turned more hostile. He looked around at their camp. Darshook then mounted his horse and grunted. He and his men moved off, riding fast. Soon their shouts were inaudible as Wa-hee's keen eyes lost the mounted band in the distance.

"You did well son," Wa-hee said to Fulud. He was 14 now, a man. His son had not spoken a word the entire time. He had observed and listened, he had shown no fear. It was something for a father to be proud of.

Shara-Li came out of the tent. "You did well," Wa-hee said to her. "Not a sound from inside. That was well done."

Shara-Li beamed. She loved it when her husband praised her.

"Pack up everything and place it on the camelid," Wa-hee instructed Shara-Li and Tuamit-Ra. "Sons, gather the animals. We move now."

Wa-hee knew their progress would be slow. They would lose most of their sheep and pigs, which would run off. But it was necessary.

Two weeks later the family was fifty miles to the south, on the coast. They had found a good spot but would have to start over. Two sheep and three pigs had followed them loyally. It was enough. Wa-hee set up his tent beside a small forest of trees. Perhaps they could supplement their diet with fish.

Three weeks later the family was settled. One night Wa-hee heard pounding and shouts. Arrows flew through their tent, impaling Shara-Li and Wazir, their youngest son. Wa-hee and Fulud grabbed their bows and arrows. Wa-hee had taught his son and they were both armed. They came out of the hut to see Darshook and his men riding up, all carrying their bows. Their force had been augmented with more warriors.

Wa-hee remembered something...something about Thoth. He held up his hand. For some reason he knew peace must be maintained. "Turn away Darshook. You have killed my wife and son."

Nothing extraordinary happened. Wa-hee shook his head. It must have been a dream. He began to get very angry.

Darshook laughed. Wa-hee grabbed, notched, and let fly from his little store of arrows so swiftly that five of Darshook's men cried out and fell to the ground. Their eyes had been pierced by arrows, which had killed them instantly, penetrating directly to the brain. The invaders were not yet proficient with the new weapon, and their arrows were poorly made. They fumbled with their bows and arrows.

Darshook was amazed and incensed. Fulud was notching and firing his arrows at the hearts of the invaders. These arrows penetrated the thick skins that covered their torsos, penetrating to the heart. Wa-hee's and Fulud's arrows had killed six of Darshook's original band, but seemed not to impede the charge of the remaining bandits. "I'm sorry father," Fulud said as Wa-hee watched his son get hacked to pieces. Wa-hee fired the last of his arrows at Darshook, hitting him in the left eye. Darshook fell to the ground, screaming his death song. The last thing Wa-hee saw before he died from a blow to the skull was his daughter Tuamit-Ra being placed on the back of a horse.

Years later a cold, dry windswept the plains of the Sahara. The green of the plain disappeared. Trees and shrubbery shriveled and died. Within a decade the entirety of North Africa had turned into an almost lifeless desert. When the occasional rains came a few oases still survived.

Across the planet the weather also turned much harsher. Many died. The population of North Africa, which had been almost five million, shrank to about 300,000. Much knowledge was lost as societies disintegrated. Gaia was cooperating with the direction of human consciousness.

Marian

Wa-hee, Shara-Li, Fulud, and Wazir transitioned. It took them a while to reorient.

"I failed," Wa-hee said. "I could not stand still when my family was murdered." Wa-hee looked lovingly at Shara-Li and Wazir. "I now see I was wrong."

Marian interjected. "Never that dear ones! There is no wrong or right. Only free choice. It is part of the test."

"Yet the consciousness of the planet lowers," Fulud said.

"Sadly, this is true," Marian responded.

They all looked at the Ring of Potential. The confrontation with Darshook would henceforth act as an attractor for all incidents of this kind. Some conflicts could be defused, as Wa-hee had done at first. But more would end up in killing. Marian and the four soul friends noted that Wa-hee had deflected Darshook and his band temporarily, but only through the invention of a new instrument of war, which eventually had been used against the peaceful family.

"This test is senseless," Wa-hee concluded. "As an original soul on the planet I should have a say in how it is conducted. We are doing so much work but it seems all is for naught! I say we should allow a dispensation of light to all who come from now on."

The other three soul friends agreed.

Marian smiled. "Dear one, you know this is not possible. This is not a test of souls, or even of humanity. It is a test of energy: does the light win, or the dark? Your suggestion biases the test."

Wa-hee frowned. "But why? There is so much suffering, so much time spent, and no result!"

Marian felt deep compassion and love for these developing souls. Were they ready to be given the greater, galactic perspective? No, not yet. "Dear one, the test is not over. There are thousands of years remaining before the critical century."

Wa-hee acknowledged this. It was difficult to feel negative on this side of the veil. The strongest memories were always the excitement of the physical challenges, and the good times. Wa-hee smiled. "I do not like to die in this way, watching my entire family get slaughtered by barbarians of low consciousness."

Marian affirmed this. "But the system ensures that what occurs on earth stays on earth. The soul comes in pure, picking up the Akash just before incarnation, then depositing the life activity within the soul crystals in the Cave of Creation at the time of death. It was agreed at the beginning. All souls are pure."

Wazir laughed. "Wa-hee, you would not have exchanged your last lifetime for anything."

Wa-hee started to object, then he smiled. "That is true now that I am here. There was much to be liked in that life." He smiled at Shara-Li.

"I am glad I had you for a mate, Wa-hee. To think of what women are going through! It surpasses the imagination."

Marian also acknowledged this. "The earth is sliding further into imbalance. However, there is still time to turn it around."

Fulud, Wazir, Shara-Li, and Wa-hee agreed with this.

"Where is Tuamit-Ra?" Wa-hee asked.

"She is still on the planet."

The four went to the Ring of Potential. They saw that Tuamit-Ra had been taken by what remained of Darshook's men, who had found a new leader. She had been forced to tend to them, and had been repeatedly raped. She would transition soon.

On the other side it is not possible to feel anything but compassion and love for the actors in the earth play. Yet something stirred inside all of them.

"This is not right," they all said at once.

"All endings are happy endings," Marian replied.

At this the four soul companions smiled.

"It is true," Fulud said. "The more gruesome the lifetime, the greater joy is there when the transition occurs."

"It is well-being and benevolence beyond imagining," Wazir said.

"Now we wait for our beloved Tuamit-Ra to come back to us."

The four asked the soul manager a question. "Is it better to always stay here, wrapped in love and light, or to experience these difficult physical lifetimes?"

Marian smiled. "That is for you to decide dear ones. You always have the choice to never return to earth."

At this all four experienced a shock. To never return! They looked at each other and laughed. Of course they would return, again and again, until the test was over. "Thank you for this lesson Marian," Wa-hee said, speaking for them all.

Shortly afterward Tuamit-Ra arrived. She left her Akash in the Cave of Creation and re-assimilated her soul energy. Soon the five were reunited. There was immense joy and great celebration.

"Our brother/sister Tuamit-Ra is here!" they all shouted. The friends melded their energies and discussed the last lifetime in great detail.

At this point Darshook and his original six men appeared before them. They too were original souls. Wa-hee gasped at their beauty. All of the human family did as well, for on the other side all were united in love.

The combatants on earth discussed the fateful incident. "We tried also and failed," Darshook told them, speaking for all his men. "I and my men were supposed to develop the horse for peaceful purposes. But we could not resist the urge for battle, and power."

The five family members, Darshook and his six warriors, all embraced. "Perhaps we will all be on another mission together," the 12 souls agreed.

"We now have interacted together and have karma that must be resolved," Darshook and his warriors said to the five. "We will undoubtedly interact again in future lives."

After the meeting with Darshook and his men, each felt motivated to push the test to a successful conclusion. Despite the outcome, all 12 souls celebrated their previous lives on earth.

After the celebration the soul manager conducted a briefing for all of the old souls and original souls.[19]

"Because of the change to a colder and drier climate, much of the population in North Africa is moving north to the Nile, and northeast into Mesopotamia," Marian said. "The situation again calls for original souls to incarnate with their wisdom."

"Cities of learning and knowledge must be established to guide the population to higher awareness," Wa-hee suggested.

"You have anticipated my briefing," Marian said. "Only 6,000 years remain until the end of the precession cycle. Conditions are not optimum. This process must be started now."

A great discussion ensued, in which the Ring of Potential was often referred to.

"The best place to establish centers of learning is in the Tigris and Euphrates valley, at the head of the Nile, and in the Indus valley," Marian concluded.

"Fortunately the Mehrgarh civilization is already well established," Shara-Li said. "The climate there and on the subcontinent is more favorable to the development of pastoral, and more peaceful, societies."

"Most of your work will be done at the head of the Nile and in Mesopotamia," Marian said.

And so it was that original souls incarnated within the various tribes on the move to the Nile and Mesopotamia. They worked, as priests or wise men and women, to establish a civilization with more light and knowledge that would propel human consciousness upward and halt the cycle of decline that had been ongoing since the fall of Lemuria.

The first to be successful were those who congregated in what is now southern Iraq. These old souls encouraged peaceful pursuits such as farming, tying the people to the land along the valleys of the Tigris and the Euphrates rivers. Wa-hee, Darshook, and over 20,000 of the original souls helped to develop the first proto-writing, and eventually cuneiform script. Lifetime after lifetime they slogged, with the occasional "vacation." Sometimes they were attacked by dark souls who saw them as threats; often they failed. Sometimes they made progress. After several centuries they were successful. A re-established society now existed in Uruk and the surrounding areas such as Eridu.

Sumeria, 4,000 BCE

Over the next 2,000 years the original souls incarnated over and over in Egypt, the Indus valley, in China, and in Mesopotamia. But progress in knowledge always led to an equal and opposite advance on the dark side of the duality. For example, in

Sumer they introduced wheeled vehicles in the mid 4th millennium BCE. This development came from the invention of the potter's wheel. This should have led to advancement in trade, transportation, and communication, and it did. Mill wheels were invented which made the processing of grain and food distribution much easier. Unfortunately the wheel was quickly militarized, and led to the creation of two- and four-wheeled chariots of war, drawn by Onagers (a species of the horse family). The advancement of military technology went right alongside the advancements in writing, mathematics, astronomy, and measurement.

The Sumerians mapped the stars into sets of constellations. They also invented military formations. Sumer had courts, jails, and government records, just like we do today. Sumerians developed the first known codified legal and administrative systems. But they also introduced the basic divisions in war between infantry, cavalry, and archers.

The first true city-states arose in Sumer. Unfortunately these city-states were in an almost constant state of war for 2,000 years.

The Sumerians used writing on clay tablets for debt and payment records and mail delivery, as well as inventory lists for business and commerce. They developed a very wide trade network, as far south as the Indus valley, for the Mesopotamian plain lacked trees and many other resources, which had to be imported. But they also invented the metal helmet for war, which covered the face and which came to a point in back.

The Sumerians established the first formal schools. Wa-hee and his team of original souls ensured that the schools were directed by the city-state's primary temple. They also introduced the phalanx formation in war, and the use of professional soldiers.

The Sumerians domesticated sheep and cattle and developed the world's first irrigation systems, which led to intensive agriculture that could support large populations. Sumerian city-states also had defensive walls and conducted constant siege warfare, which mitigated the benefits brought about by these advances.

At every turn the dark side of the duality countered the work of the original souls. It was a constant source of frustration for them, but they plugged away. The future of the planet was at stake.

In the Indus valley Wa-hee and his five friends had many incarnations. The development of this civilization paralleled in many ways what was going on in Mesopotamia. Having seen the constant warfare between Sumerian city-states, Wa-hee/Thoth and his group of original souls tried to develop a more heart-centered culture, attempting to establish religions that promoted peace and harmony. The Vedic culture eventually led to Hinduism and a recognition of the Central Source inside the human being, which would be exemplified by the master Gautama Siddhartha. Unfortunately this culture also fought amongst itself. Yet seeds were planted that would have a great influence during the last half of the last century before the end of the cycle, when Eastern wisdom would penetrate materialist Western culture.

As the Egyptian climate aridified, civilization there settled along a small strip by the Nile. In Egypt, Wa-hee/Thoth saw to the establishment of the great library at Alexandria.

2,000 BCE Marian

After 2,000 years of work, the old souls gathered for another consultation with the soul manager.

You might ask, "Is it possible to get soul-weary?" No. When on the other side all traces of the earth experience are gone. All of that goes into the Akash, which is part of the planet. The Akash only comes into play when in a physical incarnation. Therefore, between every lifetime there is complete soul reintegration. It's as if nothing ever happened, even if you spent your entire life in misery. You go back to complete joy and well-being. You are completely refreshed for the next time around. As a spiritual system it is benevolent, for there is no eternal punishment or damnation for playing the game of free choice on earth.

"Hello friends!" Wa-hee said as he saw Tuamit-Ra, Shara-Li, Fulud, and Wazir, and the other original souls. After so many incarnations the 50,000 original souls were intimately known to each other. They had planned their incarnations together. They had worked, sweated, and loved each other over thousands of years. Greetings, celebrations, and parties were held. These activities went on until every one of the original souls had returned from earth and fully reintegrated.

The soul manager called them all together.

By this time each of the original souls had over 4,000 incarnations. Their "stripes" of honor were so magnificent we might say that the soul manager felt gobsmacked.

"Observe what has been happening on the planet." The soul manager demonstrated what had occurred esoterically over the past several millennia using the Ring of Potential. These souls had been so busy on earth they hadn't had a comprehensive briefing in a long time.

"It is clear now that Gaia is cooperating with the free will decisions of humanity, just as the Seeders intended," Marian said.

Tuamit-Ra was concerned. "If humans continue to go to the dark, the earth will become more inhospitable. Disease will spread more rapidly. Weather patterns will become harsher, awareness will go still lower!"

"It is part of the test," Marian said. "Will humans recognize the connection between their consciousness and Gaia? Will they see that God is within?"

"Despite our heroic efforts the dark counters all our movements toward the light," Shara-Li said.

Wa-hee spoke. "Something more important has been lost: Knowledge of the One God brought to earth by Thoth. Secret societies have begun to form. All world cultures have torn God into fragments, assigning evil tendencies to multiple gods who war with each other. This is a dangerous development."

"I agree," said Fulud. "I have met some of these people in my lives; priests mostly. They claim to have information from higher sources. But they perform strange rituals. They have strange gods."

"I see an even more disturbing trend," Wazir said. "Instead of going out into the world, those who carry light are retreating into monasteries and private associations. They become tired of the harassment from those of lower consciousness. It is understandable, but worrying."

Shara-Li became animated. "The abuse of women has escalated. I no longer enjoy being a woman, for our bodies are looked upon as chattel. The balance of energy between male and female has shifted to an aggressive aspect that favors the male. Men grow physically stronger, women grow physically smaller and weaker."

Marian sighed. "It is true. As I said before, the planet is cooperating with the free will decisions of humanity."

"Patriarchal societies based on conflict are now the norm," Wa-hee said. "The test is failing. It must be stopped or modified."

"That is not possible," Marian said. "This is a test of consciousness in physical form. Human beings have free choice to go either way."

"What more can be done?" All of the old souls saw that despite their intensive effort, the entire project would fail without yet another intervention. That meant a complete waste of almost two hundred thousand of years of work for all souls on the planet.

"I see now," Shara-Li said. "When the karma builds up too high, it must be released. This either results in a natural catastrophe or in devastating war. Civilization collapses and must begin again with a clean karmic slate."

"You are wise, Shara-Li," Marian said. "That is precisely what happens."

The soul manager demonstrated that many civilizations had risen and fallen since the time of Lemuria, all over the earth. It was as Shara-Li said: the buildup of karma within human societies eventually causes them to implode upon themselves.

Wazir looked again at the Ring of Potential and nodded. "That is why the rest of this cycle is so important. If we don't make it after this, an extinction event will occur. The earth will still orbit the sun, but all life will die out."

It was a sobering thought. All saw the unleashing of the atom at the very end of the cycle. If this Great War occurred, it was all over. All of the original souls became upset, inspired, and motivated at the same time.

"It must not happen," Wa-hee said. "What is the best thing we can do now to ensure success?"

Marian had the answer.

"The reinsertion of the One God meme into human consciousness that began with Thoth during the pyramid-building phase. The gods are the representation of human consciousness on earth. If God remains fragmented, humanity will always see itself as separate. There will always therefore be war and conflict until the final Armageddon. If humanity finds the God within, this will lead to unity and a true civilization where creativity and cooperation will propel the earth to Graduate status."

They all saw it. More and more souls had joined in on the briefing. These were older souls as well, with hundreds of lifetimes on earth.

"Can we not use the knowledge we have accumulated with our vast experience to assist in our efforts?" Fulud asked.

Marian smiled. "You have anticipated my/our plan."

"The push to the light must occur very quickly if the test is to succeed at the end of the cycle," Fulud said.

Marian smiled. "Yes, but progress has been made after the last reset 5,000 years ago. Three promising civilizations have restarted, thanks to the heroic effort of the original souls and many old souls." Marian was referring to the new cultures in China, the Indus valley, and in Mesopotamia. "The pyramid building has also been an unqualified success. These monuments have anchored the light into the planet and stabilized the earth, even as the collective consciousness of humanity has gone lower and lower. All the work you have done has not been in vain."

All congratulated themselves. There was no rancor against those who had chosen the dark path. Some of these "dark souls" joined in the discussion.

"Our decisions to explore the dark began innocently," one of them said. "There is a certain fascination, a draw, to actions that go against the established way of things."

Belial concurred. "It is tantalizing to experience physically in an unknown way."

Moloch nodded. "Sex and the satisfaction of bodily desires, the way of the warrior in conflict and the blood lust; the experience of domination, greed, and the exercise of power, are very attractive."

"Yes!" Baal agreed. "The dark is exciting and mysterious. It has a magnetic attraction, accompanied by a feeling of danger. We all know this. There is the feeling that you shouldn't go there, but you don't know why."

Baphomet agreed. "By the time you figure it out, it's too late. You have lowered your awareness so much you get trapped. That's what happened to us."

A discussion on this topic lasted for a very long "time." It was seen that the choices to go dark built up karma, but that once entrained to this path, it was extremely difficult to overcome the powerful vibration of it.

Baphomet summed up for the two percent of incorrigible dark souls. "Our Akashes are now steeped in evil. All we can do is try to overcome our karma as best we can. It is almost a hopeless task. Believe me, these lifetimes are not pleasant for us."

The original souls understood that their work was even more important, now that the dark had gained a strong foothold. All understood as well that the dark provided contrast that led to potential evolutionary growth. Those who had taken this path were admired for their sacrifices on earth.

"It has just gotten out of hand now," Baphomet said. "We desperately need compassion and understanding even as we spread discord and misery to others." Baphomet's tone was wistful.

Baphomet's statement would be regarded by any reasonable reader as the ravings of a psychopath. But on the other side, compassion and love rule. Infinite love equals infinite allowance. Baphomet's statement was accepted.

Moloch's voice was almost pleading. "If the consciousness of the collective can be raised, we will soon stand out like a sore thumb. We cannot change our ways because we are blind. On earth, we need you to save us."

During this discussion the soul manager said nothing. Marian was not a worker; only a helper. The soul manager could not participate at the intimate level of soul + body in the three dimensional experience. Marian listened with amazement at the experiences these souls had had on earth. Oh, for just one lifetime here! But it was not to be.

After the discussion – there were millions of individual Expressions to go over – all looked to the soul manager.

"It is up to you to come up with another plan," Wa-hee said.

All knew that Marian was the soul manager because he/she/they were an ancient, ancient soul who had participated in the same process on other planets of free choice. The term "old soul" is used here only in reference to the soul's experience on earth.

Marian spoke.

"All of the original souls and the old souls will incarnate back to the planet at the same time with a single mission: to promote the One God concept, the idea that the Creative Source is within all of us. It is a difficult task. Later, the Ascended Masters will walk the earth, inspiring the people and raising consciousness. I/we hope it will be enough."

Marian showed them the plan using the Ring of Potential. "Four millennia are left. The population of the earth has been stabilized; there will be no extinction events or resets until the end of the current precession of the equinoxes. One hundred thousand original and older souls will begin the process. They will incarnate into all major population centers, promoting the One God concept, organizing themselves into tight-knit groups. Kindred souls in this group will be instantly recognizable to others in the group. As time goes on others will be recruited into the group. This network will eventually become worldwide."

"It will be a hard road to success," Wazir said. "The human being only lives 80 years at the maximum. There is never enough time to gain wisdom. Because of karmic buildup, every incarnation must start over at the beginning, relearning the basics of life."

All present nodded at this. It was the most frustrating thing about the current situation. The planet needed enlightenment but as soon as the human being gained a little wisdom the body became old and died. This was because of the cooperation of Gaia, who reflected humanity's low collective consciousness back to the human population in the form of disease and short lifespans. It was one of the rules of the test. The earth, and humanity, were tied together.

Tuamit-Ra understood Marian's plan. "Yet we will all incarnate with the knowledge and wisdom we have gained over 200,000 years. We will be the teachers, the scientists, the astronomers, the physicians, the mathematicians, the priests. By the age of 20 most of us will become fully aware. We go to the cities, the institutions of learning, and the monasteries. We promote ideas of wisdom that allow the people to see the divinity inside. We raise human society from spiritual decadence and fragmentation to glory in the One God."

"It will be much more than that," Marian said. "You will be the beginning of an integrated soul family that begins a special group: those who promote a monotheistic God. This project is the best hope for humanity now. You shall reincarnate just as you have done for thousands of years, but there will be no time off. As soon as you transition you begin again. Your job is essentially to start organized religions in eastern Mesopotamia that will spread throughout Africa, Asia, and the entire world. Your descendants shall be the founders of the Abrahamic tradition. Fortunately, in the Indus Valley and on the subcontinent, the One God concept is already taking hold."

Marian explained the characteristics of this special group of humans. "You will have to incarnate over and over again within the same soul group, increasing your numbers and passing on the monotheistic tradition to a fragmented world. This is your single-minded objective."

Everyone was awed by this mission, for these humans would be catalysts. Everywhere they went they would provoke a reaction, either good or bad. Nothing like this had ever been attempted before in 200,000 years of soul evolution, for now there was no leeway. Each life would be devoted solely to a single goal, from now until the end of the precession cycle. It was a task that would either end in success or complete destruction and failure.

And so it was. Those who belonged to the group would be given a dispensation of enhanced awareness and intelligence to accomplish their goal, commensurate with the number of lifetimes they had on earth. This was permitted within the rules of the test, because the duality would cause many to stray from their mission and use their gifts only for personal gain. Thus would balance be maintained and the test remain fair. These humans could be spectacular successes, or generate massive karma and experience spectacular failure, placing more engrams into the collective consciousness. This gift of light would also lead to persecution. It was to be their curse and their blessing.

The motto this group adopted is, "Those to whom much is given, much is expected."

Abraham and the Jews

The "feel" of their lives completely changed. Always before they had interspersed soul missions with periods of relaxation; and their missions would change from life to life, providing variety. Now they were in for an extended mission that would require many consecutive incarnations. An overlay of urgency combined with determination and enhanced knowledge characterized their vibration. They were different, so that the others could feel it and pay attention.

Within twenty years all 50,000 original souls from Lemuria and 50,000 older souls were in what is now western Egypt, Palestine, Israel, Jordan, Lebanon, western Iraq, and Syria. Tuamit-Ra, Wa-hee, Fulud, Wazir, and Shara-Li came to the planet as priests or holy men. Most of them would be male until the group established itself and the original souls connected. Not all of them would, of course.

Marian saw that the consciousness of humanity was lowering. The esoteric gateway to higher consciousness in human DNA was now operating at only 35%, down from 50% in Lemuria. Below 30%, awareness would be so low that the human race would sink into permanent barbarism.

Most of the world believed in a host of fragmented gods.

Ur

In the great city of Ur, in the year 1800 BCE, a son Abram was born to Terah, the loyal follower of Nimrod, who was king in Babylon.[20] At that time Ur was one of the greatest population centers in Mesopotamia, with over 50,000 people. Earlier, Ur-Nammu had come to power. Ur-Nammu built temples, including the Ziggurat of Ur. His code of laws, the Code of Ur-Nammu, preceded the Code of Hammurapi by 300 years. Shulgi succeeded Ur-Nammu and maintained the hegemony of Ur in Mesopotamia. He reformed the empire into a highly centralized bureaucratic state. At the time of Abram's birth Nimrod, a king who was low-born, ruled in Ur. Abram's father Terah owned an idol shop and was a favorite of the king.

When Abram/Wa-hee was a young boy he would look at the setting and the rising sun. At night he would observe the moon and the stars, wondering where they came from.

Abram spoke to his father Terah in his shop. "Father, who is responsible for the sun, the moon, and the stars? Who created the trees, the mountains, and the rivers? Who sends the rain?"

Abram had a hundred questions.

Terah was polishing a metal figurine of Enlil, the god of earth, air, wind, and storms. "That is easy, son. The god Enlil controls these things."

"But who is responsible for the sun as it rises and falls in the sky?"

Terah walked over to a wooden statue. "The god Shamash controls the sun," he said.

"Who makes the moon wax and wane, and move in the sky?"

Terah proudly showed him Nannar, the moon god. "The gods control all life in the heavens and on earth," Terah explained. "When the great king Nimrod wishes success in battle, he prays to Ashtart, the goddess of war." Terah said that there was a god responsible for all things on earth and in the heavens. Abram was puzzled by this.

As the weeks went by the boy began to closely observe the world, trying to discover all of the gods and where they might be hidden. Abram wanted to talk to all of them, for his keen intelligence demanded answers to the mysteries of life.

Something occurred to him during these observations. One afternoon the young Abram walked into his father's shop. The talk was of the king's latest campaign against Lagas, the city to the west. Many were buying figurines of Ashtart, praying for victory. The shop was busy.

"Father," Abram said just as Terah was making a sale, "what if there are not many gods but only one god?"

Conversation stopped. The men in the shop were shocked. "Boy, what do you know?" one of them said. "The king himself is a god! Does he not rule in Ur with a powerful hand?"

Abram waved his hands around at all of the statues and figurines. "But does it not make more sense that One God rules over the heavens and the earth? An all-powerful God whose hand controls all of the other gods?"

Some of the men were much struck by this statement, but many of them became angry. "It is not yours to question the edicts of the high priests and the king!" one said. "Are you more knowledgeable than these wise ones?"

There was broad agreement on this. "Son, go home," Terah said, becoming nervous. His shop was popular and he did not want to upset his customers.

"I shall," Abram said. "But I want all of you to ponder what I have said, that the One God is more powerful than all of the other gods, and rules over them."

Abram walked out.

A few of the men did consider the words of Abram. "The boy makes sense," a man said, holding a figure of Anu, the god of the sky. "But where would this One God live?"

This statement provoked a debate, in which Terah made many more sales than usual.

When he got home he spoke to his son. "Abram, you have caused much comment today, and controversy. Where have you gotten this strange idea about the gods?"

"It came to me yesterday, father, as I saw the sun set and the moon rise. I observe the wind, and the rain, and the stars. The birds and the animals and the weather; all the things of this world seem regulated. How then can so many gods create order in the world? Would they not fight amongst themselves? How can nature be so well governed if there is such a confusion and plethora of gods?"

Terah's jaw dropped. "But..." He had no answer.

"Does it not make more sense that there is one guiding hand over everything in heaven and on earth?"

Terah's wife Amathlaah smiled at this. "I think the boy is right, husband."

From that moment on Abram was convinced. That night he had a vision. G-d told him that a benevolent and powerful Creator has created all things, including mankind, and that all of the gods, and everything in the heavens and on earth come forth from the One divine Source. G-d told Abram,

"The Creator is the Creator and Guide of everything that has been created; He alone has made, does make, and will make all things. The Creator is One. All things that appear separate come forth from the One."

"But where do you live, oh G-d," Abram asked.

G-d replied, "The Creator is free from all the properties of matter. There can be no physical comparison whatsoever, for the Creator is the first and the last, beyond time and space yet controlling time and space."

"This idea is beyond my comprehension," Abram said. "But I will try to understand it."

G-d smiled down upon Abram, lying on his bed. "The more you contemplate these ideas the greater understanding will you receive."

Abram accepted this. He became so excited he wanted to go forth the next morning and tell everyone in the city. But G-d held him back. "No one wishes to hear a boy speak of such matters. Do you ponder what I have said. When you are a man, go forth and speak of these things, but do not force your opinions on others. Be a living example of Me."

In this dream, G-d explained to Abram that a fragmented world must be united. "The first step is for humanity to understand that there is but one source; a divine, benevolent Creator who loves mankind and all things upon the earth."

Abram saw it. The boy felt the love of G-d penetrate every cell of his being. In that moment Wa-hee/Thoth/Abram awakened to his soul mission. Thousands of lifetimes on the planet had given him great wisdom. He knew what to do.

The next morning his mother went to speak with her son, concerned that in his boyish enthusiasm he might overstep his bounds. Abram was eating a pottage of red lentils and barley bread. (At that time in Ur the common man ate sparingly. The best dishes, including meats, were consumed by the priests and the wealthy merchants of the day.)

"Do not worry, good mother," Abram said to Amathlaah. "I have had everything explained to me."

Amathlaah's eyes widened. "You have had a vision?"

Abram smiled. In her son's eyes the mother saw great wisdom, and she relaxed. "You will do great things."

Abram deprecated this, but gently. "All is for the glory of G-d."

From that moment Amathlaah did not worry.

When Abram went into his father's shop that morning several of the customers turned to him.

"So this is the brazen boy who claims to know more than the gods!" one said.

Terah was worried, for Abram had a habit of speaking when he should be silent.

Abram bowed. "Good sir, I am sorry if I offended you yesterday."

The man was mollified. "That is proper conduct from boys who should defer to their fathers and their king."

Abram bowed silently, smiling up at the man, whose gaze softened. "There there boy, I see you have learned your lesson." He congratulated Terah. "A fine, obedient son have you, Terah."

Terah was mystified, but stumbled his thanks. From where did this boy gain the subtlety to overcome his nature and apologize, where the day before he had been so thoughtless?

Now Abram walked around the store, admiring the figurines as G-d had instructed him. "Bluster will harden hearts and provoke argument," G-d told him in his dream. "Understanding and compassion will win the day." And so the men saw that their beliefs raised no objections in the young man, who had yesterday criticized them. Abram had a word for everyone, congratulating them on their purchases. Terah was overjoyed. Many of the men, seeing Abram's respectful conduct, began to think seriously of what he had said the day before.

When the rush was over, three of the men stayed behind. "Tell us more of the One G-d," they said.

Terah became alarmed, but Abram soothed his father. "The One G-d glorifies the gods, and does not demean them," he said. "Merely that the gods have a wise counselor, to resolve their disputes and set the world in order." Abram walked out of the shop, Terah and the three men following. "Behold the glory of the world." It was a fine spring day. Birds sang on the small trees Terah had planted for cooling shade around the store. (Mesopotamia is a broad plain with few trees; but Terah had made his shop popular by doing this.) "The One merely regulates all the other gods, maintaining the order of the world."

The boy spoke with such authority and kindness that the men were impressed. "We will think upon these things, son of Terah," one of them said. "But do not say these words to the priests or to the king's representatives!"

The men went off to find beer. Many of the men of Ur were fighting in Nimrod's campaign against Lagash, but there were still many at home to see to the business of daily life.

For the next several years Abram grew in wisdom. He even spoke to the priests, who felt threatened by Abram's ideas. Abram was wise enough to know that these men valued their comforts and their positions in society. G-d had warned him never to threaten their power, or that of the king. "Only the priests and the king can determine what is right for the people to believe," he said to the high priest of Ur when he was called before them. They were allayed but kept careful watch on the young man.

The king favored Terah and so knew of Abram and his ideas. Abram had barely escaped death when he was born, for the king's astrologers told him that the son of Terah could be a threat to his rule. Nimrod was base-born, and had secured his rule by ruthless elimination of his enemies. The story is that the son of a slave was substituted for Abram, and that the king strangled the baby with his own hands. At that time in Ur child sacrifice was not uncommon. Consciousness was very low.

To protect his father and mother Abram moved from Ur into a mountainous region of Ararat in the land of Kedem, to the house of his grandparents Noah and Shem. There, he discussed the concept of the One G-d and found that the family of Noah accepted this easily. "These gods of Nimrod, who even calls himself a god, are preposterous." Noah said. "Have you heard about the great tower the king has built to his own glory in the land of Shimear, which reaches to the sky?"

At this time Abram was a mature man, and had been spreading his doctrine quietly in the land of Ararat.

"Yes grandfather. The king and his admirers are building a tower so high that it reaches up to heaven. They think that the structure will establish their reign in heaven as well as on the earth."

"It is the height of arrogance," Noah said.

Several months later Noah and Abram (who was now called Abraham) heard of the collapse of the great tower, which had been called Babel. The engineers, the people, the king and all his followers, had been thrown into great confusion.

Wa-hee/Thoth/Abraham had another dream. He decided that it was time for him to go out and broadly teach the people the truth about the One Gd. Abraham was wise, for he did not criticize the gods, or the king, but advanced the concept of an overarching and benevolent G-d, with the other gods as His helpers. Before he left the house of Noah his grandfather spoke to him.

"Abraham, understand that Nimrod will think you are defying him. Remember that your father Terah is an idol-worshipper and favorite of the king. Be very careful. This base-born Nimrod, in his conceit, has proclaimed himself G-d and demanded that all the people worship him."

Abraham returned to Ur and began his work. He married Sarai and was happy.

One evening Nimrod had a strange dream. His stargazers, hearing of Abraham's return to the house of Terah, and his preaching work, interpreted this dream to mean that as long as Abraham lived, the rule of Nimrod would be threatened. The king sent his men and captured Abraham. At his interview Abraham told the king of his views of the One G-d and the validity of the other gods, but Nimrod interpreted this as a threat.

To test Terah's loyalty the king said to him, "Take your son away and throw him into a burning furnace." Terrified, Terah took Abraham into the basement of the palace, where waste (and the bodies of those who had encountered the king's disfavor) were burned.

Two men toiled at the furnace. Each recognized Abraham. "Is this Abraham, son of Terah?" one of them asked.

Terah was terrified. "It is my son."

The two men smiled. "We have heard of Abraham's ideas of the One G-d. It pleases us, for are not the gods used by the priests and the wealthy to amass resources and power to themselves?" (Human nature has been consistent for thousands of years.)

Terah smiled. Abraham bowed. "I do not worry. G-d will take care of me."

The two men laughed. "G-d helps those who help themselves." One of the men, brawny and muscular, opened the furnace door. "See how the fire has burned low." There were coals now, and flames occasionally leaped up.

The other man went to the back of the great metal structure and unlocked a metal door. He then closed it, keeping it unlocked. At that point two officials came walking down the hallway. The first man grinned and exclaimed, "I shall throw you into the fire, you ingrate!"

The brawny man grabbed Abraham by his cloak (for the day was cool) and thrust him into the furnace. He quickly closed the door. Screaming was heard from the inside. The officials, satisfied, left. The second man opened the door in back of the furnace and Abraham scrambled out. His clothing was smoldering and he had a few burns on his arms and legs, but was otherwise unharmed. Despite his pain he bowed before the two men who had saved his life. "Thank you dear ones," Abraham said. "My father and I shall leave this land so as not to arouse suspicion on you."

The two slaves were grateful, and vowed to keep Abraham in their prayers.

And so it was that Wa-hee/Thoth/Abraham made a b'rit with G-d, a covenant, which has obligations on both sides. Abraham began to spread the word of the One G-d far and wide. When necessary, G-d guided him.

In his later years his wife Sarah bore him a son which the Hebrews call Yitzchak and later the Christians would call Isaac and the Muslims Ishmael.

According to the Bible Isaac's son Jacob fathered twelve sons, the ancestors of the twelve tribes of Israel. In a dream Abraham was told to go to Egypt, where many of the Hebrews stayed. The story of how they were kicked out of Egypt by Pharaoh and wandered in the desert for 40 years is well known.

Abraham, blessed by the One, was the founder of the Abrahamic religions of Christianity, Judaism, and Islam. All of these religions hold the sacred truth of the One God. Hinduism, the other great religion, also believes in a benevolent divinity, or a creative source. Thus the work of the old souls and original souls was successful, in that it began to establish monotheism on the planet.

1,000 BCE

As part of the soul manager's long-term program to promote the One God concept, an urban civilization was established in east Africa bordering the Red Sea and just north of the Horn of Africa, in what is now modern-day Eritrea. The Kingdom of Falash was formed by a group of old souls, and led by an enlightened queen. It was in the lands referred to by the ancient Egyptians as the Land of Punt. Falash was one of Marian's experiments, to create a society where the female energy would balance the overwhelming dominance of the male energy. The Akashic bias in almost all of the old souls who participated was female, even though biological men would have authority. The Falash undertaking was the soul manager's "baby."

The Kingdom of Falash was part of one of the earliest pastoral and agricultural communities in the Horn region, and traded with Egypt, which lay to the northwest. Queen Falash developed a loyal army and good relations with her neighbors. Her advisors were loyal to her, and the little kingdom flourished.

The area was known for producing and exporting gold, aromatic resins, blackwood, ebony, and ivory to Egypt. Queen Falash was known to Pharaoh and enjoyed pharaoh's favor. Although history says nothing about the little kingdom, something happened there that would have a powerful influence on a country halfway around the world from it, 3,000 years later.

Queen Falash's army had embarked on a campaign against raiding barbarians from the southwest, who had heard of the kingdom's gold deposits and were massing for an invasion. Almost the entire army was out of the city when the queen's most trusted advisor, a wealthy military leader who had been trusted with the organization of the gold trade, committed an appalling act of betrayal against the queen. He provided access for the barbarians to the city in exchange for gold that would be seized by the invaders. The city was overrun and the queen and all her advisors were murdered. It was a deliberate act of sabotage that brought down the entire society and destroyed the higher vibrations that had been slowly nurtured there.

An old soul known as Tahil, who had been one of Darshook's raiders thousands of years prior, was the traitor.

For the old souls involved, this act of sabotage by another old soul created another engram within their Akash. When all were back on the other side Tahil took the unusual step of apologizing for his actions on earth. Even the soul manager was saddened by this event but chalked it up to free will.

"I vow one day to make up for my betrayal," Tahil said to Llendrah, the old soul who had been the queen, and to those who had been her advisors, and to everyone else in the city who had been killed by the raiders. The bias in Tahil's Akash was an alpha male. "I'm not sure why I acted as I did. Perhaps, as one who has had almost all incarnations as a male, I could not resist the lure of wealth and power."

Tahil's apology was accepted, for souls on the other side are completely free of taint. Free will decisions while on earth, with lowered consciousness, are never judged.

However, all who participated in this project took note of Tahil's vow. Particularly Shara-Li, who had been an advisor to the queen, and her other advisors, who were saddened by the failure of their experiment.

The soul manager also took note.

1,000 years later. Marian

The One God program had been completed as well as possible. A core group of monotheists, the Jews, had been established all over the world. These would be the lightning rod for a unified religion, and would also be a target for the dark souls, who would demonize the group.

Wa-hee, Shara-Li, Darshook, Fulud, Wazir, Tuamit-Ra, and all of their associates were back on the other side. Wa-hee had been Abraham and also Jacob, a high priest more than once, a merchant, a banker, a householder, a warrior, a counselor. In Egypt he had been a priest, a counselor to Pharaoh more than once, a slave, a concubine to an important general, and a healer many times. On the subcontinent he had been a temple priest, a military leader, a simple farmer, an itinerant beggar. Wherever he could help he assisted. A similar pattern of incarnation existed for all of the original souls. Except for the original souls, all of the souls who incarnated as Jews from now on would remain Jewish until the end of the precession cycle.

All of the six friends looked upon each other's stripes with admiration.

Shara-Li looked with the others at the Ring of Potential. The great master Sananda, known on the planet as the Christ, had just finished his incarnation. He was much celebrated among all of the original souls for his recent work.

"Much impetus has been given to the light coefficient," she said to Sananda about his work, which had founded the new religion of Christianity.

Wazir was impressed. "Sananda will become so influential that a new calendar will begin with his birth."

There was much good-natured ribbing of the original soul. "Such an ego!" Fulud teased.

Everyone laughed. But there was spiritual frustration as well.

As everyone looked at the Ring of Potential they saw what would happen. Within a thousand years, the one god concept would replace the hodge-podge of dysfunctional, warring gods almost everywhere on the earth. This was celebrated.

Tuamit-Ra spoke. "The dark side will counter this development with religious disputes about doctrine and forms of worship and devotion. Always will the drive toward unity be countered by the motivation to split apart. This is the nature of the duality."

"That is correct." The soul manager looked toward Maitreya, who had been the first Ascended Master to walk the planet on the subcontinent, several centuries before Sananda. "You helped to pave the way, dear one. You and Wa-hee and Sananda. Another will incarnate during the first millennium, and will be called Mohammed. This new religion will also proclaim the One God. All we can do is continue our work."

"The critical millennium is the next one," Fulud said. "This is when the population begins to increase more rapidly."

They all looked to the last century before the end of the cycle. The potential was a chaotic mixture of war, of slaughter, of countless acts of beauty and generosity. Even the great mathematicians who would later be Euler, Gauss, and Aryabhata could make no sense of it. Marian called in al-Khwarizmi, who would be the father of the algorithm, to interpret the future potentials. "All we can say is that the conclusion of the test will be decided by human beings incarnated on earth at the very end of days," he said. "At that time the population will have increased rapidly into the billions! Most of these souls will be newly incarnated on the earth, with no previous experience here. There is simply no way to predict the outcome."

Al-Khwarizmi had spoken truth. During the last century unprecedented population growth would occur. Every soul who had ever incarnated on earth would come back. New souls would arrive en masse. Star seeds would come from graduate planets, eager to assist in the great experiment. Everywhere there was a clamor to be a part of the denouement on the planet of free choice. Souls would volunteer for even the darkest duties, even though these lifetimes would be agony.

Sananda and Maitreya were appalled, as were many of the Ascended Masters, at the mass slaughter that would occur, and at those who would provoke it.

"Yet there are trillions of souls willing and eager to come here," Tuamit-Ra said. "Look at the potentials."

Wa-hee was awed. "Souls from all over the galaxy will arrive here, demanding to be included."

Shara-Li understood. "Of course! The huge influx of births will come from those with no prior experience on the earth. They will act as the buffer between the forces of light and the forces of darkness."

"Five billion new souls will be added to the population count in eighty years," Marian said. "The hope is that these new souls, who have no karma, will counter the increasing buildup of negative energy."[21]

Everyone was amazed at the direction of the earth project. It would all come down to 100 years at the end of over 200,000 years of evolution. The game would be decided with 5 seconds left on the clock.

CHAPTER 7

1900. The Final Century

Failure of the 200,000-year plan to raise human consciousness was imminent. The soul manager had come up with one last, brilliant effort to salvage the earth project. Marian had also discovered a way in which he could participate without violating the rules of the great experiment. He did not tell a single soul of this.

The soul manager spoke to the old souls. "Dear ones, our only hope now is a wild card. All of you shall be that wildcard. During the period between 1910 and 1980 all of you will arrive on the planet, attuned to a certain event that will transpire almost at the last moment." Marian looked around at the thirty or so million old souls and original souls. "It will be your divine mission to awaken at the proper time and participate. At the time of this event you will be a tiny percentage of the planetary population. Your efforts will be scorned and ridiculed. But you are old souls. You carry the light. It will be your job to rescue humanity, and Gaia, at the last instant."

As Marian explained the plan the old souls began to get more and more excited. Almost all of them would not be involved in the fighting during the madness of the final century. By the time the soul manager had finished all were eager to incarnate for what most probably would be their final time ever on the earth.

Unless a miracle occurred.

Detroit, Michigan, January 1907

Henry Ford was talking to Charles Sorenson on the third floor of the Ford plant on Piquette Avenue in Detroit, Michigan. "Charlie, I'd like to have a room finished off right here in this space. Put up a wall with a door big enough to run a car in and out. We're going to start a completely new job."

The room was blocked off. A few simple power tools and two blackboards were hung on the walls. Charlie was head of the pattern department at Ford. He translated Henry Ford's ideas into prototypes and into the patterns from which the parts would be cast. Ford merely sent him simple sketches or descriptions, which he had to flesh out.

"Charlie, we want to design a system whereby we can build our traveling carriages quickly while monitoring the quality at each step. My idea is for a moving production line where the parts are assembled in a step-by-step fashion."

Charlie Sorensen got together with Walter Flanders, Clarence Avery, and Ed Martin to design a moving a chassis through multiple workstations where the components would be assembled one by one. A workman – sometimes more than one – would work at each station along the way. Henry Ford liked the idea because he envisioned the assembly line working 24 hours a day if necessary, the workmen coming in on shifts.

One Sunday in 1910 Charlie Sorensen and Charlie Lewis, another Ford executive, tested this idea. After working for an entire day Sorenson said, "Charlie, we can move the carriage in a straight line from one end of the factory to the other. We train specialized workers to add the parts to each car."

"Right. When one car is complete at the station, another comes immediately. Each worker performs repetitive tasks."

"Yes. By doing the task over and over, the worker becomes better and better at it."

"The system self-trains the workers. Brilliant!"

"But how do we supply each station with enough parts to keep the workers busy?" Lewis asked.

"Stockrooms are placed strategically along the line. Workers transfer the parts to bins or platforms, where the workers have them at hand."

"It's perfect Charlie," Lewis said. "But we need to test it."

"I have an idea." Sorenson grabbed a rope and tied it to a chassis (in those days the chassis were much lighter!). He strung the rope around his shoulders. "I'll tow the chassis while the rest of you add the parts."

The idea panned out.

The Model T was developed, perfected, and assembled using the new moving assembly line. This was the planet's first affordable travelling carriage. During the next eighteen years, out of Piquette Avenue, Highland Park, River Rouge, and from assembly plants all over the United States, would come 15,000,000 more of the vehicles.[22]

It was the precursor to a mechanized infrastructure and then an electronic one. These advances in automation and electronics would lead to the eventual development of artificial intelligence. Unbeknownst even to the soul manager, AI was a wild card that would throw the entire Experiment into chaos.

World War I

The final century began after a nascent spiritualist movement in the United States was crushed by the militarization of college campuses and society at the beginning of the century, and the U.S. entry into the first great war.[23]

It was July 1, 1916. Barney Chisholm sat in his muddy bunker on the Somme River in Picardy, northern France. Disease, vermin, and filth were rampant. The battle was to begin with a charge of British and French soldiers from their trenches.

"Up and away men!" Sergeant Hepburn said. The men, mostly boys, ran up over the bunkers and on to the field. Barney thought he knew what to expect. His two mates, Peter Conger and Whit Merrifield, ran alongside him, rifles drawn, excited to meet the enemy. When the men had advanced about one hundred yards they were met with a wall of machine-gun fire from the German lines. Barney heard a smack next to him and saw Pete's head explode. He heard several more thuds and Whit went down, shot to doll rags. Shocked, Barney's legs carried him forward. Men were falling all around him. He fired his gun at a German soldier whose head had appeared from a little pillbox in front of the enemy's lines. At that moment two bullets pierced his stomach. He fell as his mates went around him. As he began to lose consciousness he saw a dozen British soldiers enter the enemy trenches, firing their weapons and bayoneting those who were too close to fire upon...

On the very first day of the Battle of the Somme the British army suffered 57,470 casualties. On November 18, 1916 when the battle ended, the British and French armies had advanced six miles. The British Army lost 419,654 men; the French lost 204,253; the Germans half a million. In all, 1,123,907 men were killed in a little over four months.[24]

History says that the Battle of the Somme was a strategic victory for the Allied forces because it hurt the Germans badly and ultimately brought America into the war.

Many historians agree that the battle was an important step toward the Allied victory in 1918.

October 1917

In Russia, after the Spring Revolution that overthrew the Tsar, the Bolsheviks entered Moscow. Funded from outside Russia, they began to systematically murder those opposed to their rule. The Bolsheviks strengthened the apparatus of the secret police, expanded the prison system, and terrorized the population. During their 70 years of rule the Communist Party in Russia would be responsible for the murders of millions of Russians and the establishment of the Gulag. Thus did the dark souls have an outlet for their impulses.

To the Pleiadian Seeders the world conflict was an all too familiar repeat of what had happened on Merope. They were sickened by the senseless deaths. Here, at the beginning of the twentieth century, it appeared that the planet was headed for total destruction at the end of the 26,000-year measuring period. Just as in ancient prophecy.

A measurement of energy was taken. The ratio of dark to light was now at its strongest in favor of the dark since they first arrived over 200,000 of this planet's rotations ago.

The end of the 26,000-year cycle was coming up in 2012. There was still hope, however, no matter how faint. A 36-year window would open in 1994; 18 years before the end of the cycle in 2012 and 18 years after. What occurred during this tiny window would act like an attractor in a chaotic system, pulling events toward it for the next 26,000-year cycle.

Unknown to even the Seeders, the soul manager had his own plan. Before the 36-year window opened, his troop of original souls and old souls would implement a subtle but powerful operation, completely under the radar of the dark army. If enough of them awakened.

Marian chuckled. The Pleiadians would smile when they saw it.

World War II

In 1933 the rise of Hitler presaged another global conflict. The Nazis became another outlet for the dark forces. During the conflict many old souls were killed. The

Jews were targeted especially. It was as if the dark forces had identified those who could most effectively stop their insanity.

[Berlin, 1941]

"The objective is Moscow. Destroy the capital and we destroy the Russian people."

"Ya, mein Fuhrer," Feldmarschall Wilhelm Ritter von Leeb replied. Von Leeb was anxious to curry favor with the great man. "In my capacity as commander of Army Group North, I will cooperate closely with our glorious SS Einsatzgruppen."

"That is well. The mobile killing squads can eliminate all opposition on the eastern front."

"And if they happen to kill some *Juden*, all the better."

Fuhrer and commander were in perfect agreement.

"Go with God," Hitler said, and turned back to Operation Barbarossa, the Nazi code name for the invasion of the Soviet Union.

Von Leeb shuddered when he heard this. Something inside him rebelled at the idea of using God's name for mass murder. Something...if he could only find it...the moment passed. He was just Von Leeb, a loyal servant, an important cog in the Wehrmacht. He would do his duty.

Von Leeb was originally supposed to capture St. Petersburg/Leningrad in passing. However, Hitler recalled the 4th Panzer Group south to participate in Hitler's great dream on the eastern front, the capture of Moscow and the entirety of western Russia. It was a repeat of Napoleon Bonaparte's dream at the beginning of the 19th century, to subjugate Russia.

Hitler wanted to repopulate the area with Germans and use the Slavs who lived there as a slave-labor force for the Axis war effort. The Nazis intended to seize the oil reserves of the Caucasus and the agricultural resources of the area. Von Leeb had to lay Leningrad under siege after reaching the shores of Lake Ladoga.

Unfortunately for the over two million casualties in Leningrad – some have estimated over four million killed, wounded, or incapacitated during the siege – Hitler's intention was to destroy the city and its population.

Von Leeb, in Army Group North's freezing headquarters, received a directive from the Wehrmacht on September 29. He opened the order packet and read. "After the defeat of Soviet Russia there can be no interest in the continued existence of this large urban center."

Von Leeb relaxed. "Excellent," he said to himself. He was just following orders, all would be well.

What he read next pleased him. "Following the city's encirclement," the

Wehrmacht directive said, "requests for surrender negotiations shall be denied, since the problem of relocating and feeding the population cannot and should not be solved by us. In this war for our very existence, we can have no interest in maintaining even a part of this very large urban population."[25] Von Leeb knew that the Wehrmacht's ultimate plan was to raze Leningrad to the ground.

Von Leeb began the Siege of Leningrad, Russia, on September 8, 1941. It ended on January 27, 1944, a total of 872 days.

As food supplies dwindled, eleven-year-old Tanya Savicheva began to record the deaths of each of her family members. She recorded the death of her sister Zhenya, a factory worker: "Zhenya died on December 28th at 12 noon, 1941."

Tanya's grandmother, Yevdokiya Grigorievna, died a month later, two days after the girl's twelfth birthday, of heart failure. Tanya recorded this death, writing, "Grandma died on the 25th of January at 3 o'clock, 1942."

Shortly after, Tanya's brother Leka died in March 1942. Tanya wrote, "Leka died March 17th, 1942, at 5 o'clock in the morning, 1942."

On April 13, her Uncle Vasya died at the age of 56. "Uncle Vasya died on April 13th at 2 o'clock in the morning, 1942."

Tanya's eldest uncle Lesha died in May at the age of 71 from malnutrition. "Uncle Lesha May 10th, at 4 o'clock in the afternoon, 1942."

Tanya's mother died on the morning of May 13, 1942. Tanya wrote, "Mama on May 13th at 7:30 in the morning, 1942." Tanya lost hope after her mother died. Her final entries in the diary were:

"The Savichevas are dead." "Everyone is dead." "Only Tanya is left."[26]

The Siege of Leningrad is the most lethal in human history. The two-and-a-half year siege caused the greatest destruction and the largest loss of life ever known in a modern city.

After the war, Tanya Savicheva's diary was shown at the Nuremburg trials.

The Seeders were saddened by the mass murder that had just occurred. The second great world war had resulted in an unthinkable 80 million deaths, and many more wounded. The trauma was even worse than during the end of the Great War, as WW I was known, which had over 18 million deaths and 23 million wounded. It was a massive escalation from the darkness that had occurred on Merope. The population there had never reached above 50 million, for the planet was cold and resource poor. The number of deaths in this 6-year period on earth exceeded the number of deaths in the entire history of Merope.

After WW I sentiment had begun to change. The Seeders had been hopeful. People called it "the war end to all wars." There was a slight uptick in the balance between dark and light. But this hope quickly faded. A powerful group of humans centered in northern Europe began to turn to the dark side. The National Socialists came to power in Germany. Then came Kristallnacht (the night of broken glass), a government-sponsored pogrom against Jews throughout Nazi Germany on November 9 and 10, 1938. It was carried out by the Sturmabteilung (Storm Detachment) paramilitary forces and German civilians. The German authorities looked on without intervening.

Another measurement of the planet's energy by the Seeders was taken after World War Two. There was a discussion.

"Similar mass murder events occurred on Merope."

"More than once."

"Our history is even more barbaric than this planet's."

"Yes, but our population never went beyond fifty million, even after the Arcturans came. The conflicts on Merope were planetary but not nearly as wasteful of life."

"That is so. But the trend of science on this beautiful planet is toward a nuclear component."

"That development must be discouraged."

The group was silent for a few moments. Atlantean knowledge of the science of vibration had been lost since before the Sumerian civilization arose. The planet had moved to a fossil-fuel based system. The inevitable result would be the development of nuclear weapons.

"There has never been, in the history of this galaxy, a civilization that survived nuclear war."

"What a waste! This planet, unlike our own, is a jewel of biodiversity and beauty."

"We can still hope."

At the end of the second great war some of the German military establishment was able to escape the country before the Allied armies could capture them. Documents discovered by a British colonel in Berlin as the city burned showed that the Nazis had plans to continue their efforts. In one was the statement, "We will build the Fourth Reich on the ruins of the United States."[27]

The visitors were appalled when, at the end of the second great conflict, a nuclear weapon was dropped on Hiroshima, a defenseless city. They saw that the potential for the planet was almost certainly an extinction event, to occur at the turn of the millennium.

CHAPTER **8**

Marian

Once every second, two deaths are recorded on earth. Once every second three births occur. Every single day over 360,000 souls incarnate and about 151,000 souls depart. That's over 130 million births and 60 million human deaths each year. The volume of traffic in human souls is astonishing.

Managing the soul groups, the soul families, and the karma between them is a job not even a supercomputer could do. Fortunately the soul manager is a group consciousness, which makes the job do-able.

It was the year 1956. The soul was ready to reincarnate back to earth. In a previous life it had been Jared Taylor, a businessman who had not woken up during the physical expression. This soul was going back to the planet for his third lifetime.

Almost all souls are not old souls. Marian has the job of managing every soul who incarnates on earth. With 4.5 billion on the planet now, the job was becoming more and more complicated. New arrivals such as Jared Taylor, unfamiliar with earth, were coming in droves. A few would awaken to their soul mission; the others would not. The new ones were what Shara-Li called "the buffer." Their karma was light.

"Are you ready?" Marian asked. As they spoke dozens of souls died and were readjusting in the resting area. Many more were sent off.

The soul manager showed Jared the potential for his coming life on the planet.

Jared Taylor was eager and excited. "I remember how depressed and lonely I was when I died," he said. "I never married. I never had a successful relationship. Business and money was all I understood."

"Yes," Marian said. "Let's look at the potentials for your new life and the planet as a whole."

During Jared's new lifetime the planet would begin another 26,000-year cycle. "The strongest potentials are for a nuclear war right at the turn of the millennium," Marian said. "Are you sure you want to experience an extinction event?"

"I'll risk it," Jared said. "I want to go back down there and try again. I know I can be more successful this time." When in the between-lives area, with his soul fully integrated, surrounded by the human family, he had no worries.

Marian smiled. "You said that last time."

"I did. But this time it will be different."

The soul manager had infinite love for his charges. It was a grand mission, to try to move the earth into Graduate status. To do so would affect every planet in the galaxy.

"Are you prepared to lose most of your awareness and knowledge, and to enter a human body, perhaps never understanding how grand and magnificent you are?" Marian had to do this with the new arrivals. For old souls this patter was unnecessary.

Jared nodded. When he looked at the earth with its 4.5 billion souls, and their complex interactions, he was astounded. He wanted to be a part of it, just as any young buck who comes to the big city to make his fortune and show everyone what he can do.

"Your gender will not change," Marian said, "so that you will be comfortable."

Jared saw the plan for the evolution of consciousness on earth. Last time he had been in Chicago, and had died just after the Second World War. He could see that his next incarnation would be in Rio de Janeiro, in Brazil. His organizing skills were needed in the poorest section of the city. His life mission would be to create homegrown cooperatives where the people would work together and lift themselves out of poverty. He saw his parents, his father a garbage hauler, his mother a washer woman. He was ready.

"Are you prepared to enter the birth vortex?" Marian asked.

Jared saw it. A funnel of energy that would truncate his consciousness so that he could "fit" energetically into a human body. The rest of him would stay here, on the other side. If he woke up he would try to contact his Higher Self. Other "pieces" of his soul would be his angels and his spirit guides. "In my last life I never even knew I had helpers," Jared remarked. He could see into the funnel of birth. His name would be Armando Francisco Santos. He would be called "Cisco."

"When you are three years old," Marian explained, "your mother Isabel will be hit by an automobile on her way to work, motivating the young Cisco to change the conditions in the favela. The potentials are strong that you will found a successful organization called "Libro," which will create jobs in the community and bind people together in cooperation. But first you must work through the karma you accumulated in your last lifetime."

Marian presented Jared with the strongest potential future and showed him his karmic ledger. "Your former business rival Joseph, who you betrayed and from whom you took his business, will be your implacable enemy."

Jared saw that Joseph had recently incarnated as Emilio, and was five years older than Cisco would be. Jared met Emilio's Higher Self and they viewed the life potentials like an animated movie, along with the soul manager. "This is the critical event in Cisco's life," Marian explained. "Cisco is 22 and Emilio 27. As in the previous life, Cisco is in a position to destroy Emilio. Cisco's peers in the gang will be shouting for him to denounce Emilio. There will be a moment when Cisco is aware of his Higher Self, his guides, and his angels. He will know deep down that he should spare his enemy. Cisco has enough influence in the gang to make his decision stick. Do you see the marker?"

Jared saw it. A "marker" is an energetic reminder from the other side, placed on the linear timeline of the life path at the exact right moment. Jared went through it with Marian. Surrounded by screaming gang members who are ready to kill Emilio, Cisco experiences a moment of complete calm. The energy is all for destruction. On the potential life path timeline Cisco contacts the marker, which shows him sparing Emilio. Together they found Libro and allow everyone in the slum to lead better lives.

"It is guaranteed that you will contact this marker," Marian said. "The decision to act either way is completely your choice."

As he contacts the marker Jared feels the karmic energy of hatred toward Emilio. "It is very strong. How can I overcome it?"

"The energy of hatred is perfectly balanced by the energy of the marker. This allows you a moment of calm to make a free will decision," Marian replied. "If you choose the benevolent outcome you will wake up, see your Higher Self, and become a force for good in the world. If you choose hatred you will destroy yourself eventually. Libro or its equivalent may or may not be created." Marian did not tell Jared that other souls were also incarnating into the great city for the same purpose. There was backup. With billions of souls to manage, the complexity of Marian's work was incomprehensible to a human being.

"Why is it that an entire life revolves around one fractional moment in time?" Jared asked.

Marian played the movie again, which consisted of a set of the strongest potentials for Jared's upcoming life. "You see how Cisco's life, and Emilio's life, and all of the events, and all of the energy, builds for this one moment."

Jared got it. "Of course. The linearity of life on earth requires the gradual buildup of circumstances. The potentials at that time are for the most powerful and benevolent outcome."

Marian smiled. Emilio's Higher Self smiled. "I am ready," Jared said.

Jared/Cisco entered the birth vortex. He felt his knowledge of self slipping away as he entered the tiny human body. He understood that most of his energy was still on the "other side." Until he was 3 he would be able to enter and leave the body at will, in order to adjust to the new life. After that he would be alone. Instead of a multi-dimensional, powerful, and connected being of light he would be a singular entity, a human being, with an important life mission and a little karma.

As Marian and Emilio's Higher Self saw Cisco enter the birth vortex they were sad for a split instant, for a part of the One was gone.

They watched excitedly as Cisco grew up. When he was 13 Cisco wanted to join a local gang called the Libres.

"*Que ele se foda!* We don't need this scrawny little shit."

"Who the fuck are you?" Cisco said.

"I am Emilio, *caralho*. I run this outfit. Get the fuck out and go back to your mommy."

Cisco threw himself at the bigger boy, landing a punch in Emilio's ribs. Emilio beat Cisco and broke his nose. "My mom got run over by a car," Cisco said. "So fuck you."

Emilio hooted. "Get the fuck out."

When Cisco got home his father grunted. "What happened to you?"

"I joined the Libres today."

His father snorted. "The hell you did. I know that Emilio. He's a bad lot. That's where you got your broken nose."

"What else is there?" Cisco said in a voice of hopelessness. "You think I want to end up like you in this stinking favela? A fucking garbage man?"

"This garbage man puts food on your table you little punk."

"I got better things to do old man."

Cisco's father laughed. "You go back there. Go back to Libres. Get another beating."

Cisco flared. "I will!"

Emilio saw Cisco the next morning. He saw a determined little motherfucker who wasn't going to take no for an answer. Cisco reminded him of himself at that age. He smiled. "Come here little Cisco."

Cisco looked challengingly at the older and bigger boy, who was surrounded by his mates. Inside Cisco was shaking.

"You know João Lucas, that crook who runs guns into our neighborhood behind his store?"

"I know him."

"The community would be better without that *bunda*." Emilio handed Cisco a gun. He walked off with the others.

Cisco knew what he had to do. He went to see João Lucas just after dark. João was talking to another man in the alley at the back of his store. The man held a gun to the head of the storekeeper. This man was the gun-runner. Cisco snuck into the store and emerged at the back door, ten feet from the confrontation in the alley. João Lucas saw Cisco first. Cisco held the gun unsteadily. He had never fired a weapon. Cisco saw the fear in the eyes of João Lucas. He saw the evil in the eyes of the gunrunner, who quickly turned. The man was going to kill him. Cisco fired the weapon three times, hitting the man in the neck. Blood spurted everywhere. Cisco looked with contempt on the evil man. He still held the gun. João Lucas cowered in the alley against the wall of the store, covering his head with his arms.

"Get up, João Lucas," Cisco said.

The storekeeper straightened slowly, keeping his eyes on the gun.

"Do you swear never again to do evil?"

João Lucas could see the kid was not going to harm him. "What choice do I have?" The man spoke bitterly. "Evil is a way of life in this neighborhood."

Cisco paused for a moment. "Not anymore." Cisco lowered the gun. "If ever you see another evil man, you come to the Libres, no?"

"The Libres! You are more evil than the man you just shot."

Something occurred to Cisco. For an instant he felt removed from the flow of time. A voice spoke to him from the ethers. "Not anymore," he repeated. "The Libres will become a force for good."

João Lucas saw the determination in the young man's eyes. Kids grew up quickly around here or they got dead fast. He pointed to the body, lying in a pool of blood. "You are off to a good start. This scum threatened to kill my family. I had no choice."

Cisco nodded. "I understand. I will tell Emilio."

João Lucas shrugged. "I will dispose of the body."

The next day Cisco presented the weapon to Emilio.

"That storekeeper is still alive!" Emilio said. The others shouted their agreement.

"João Lucas is a good man. I shot the evil one. He who runs guns into our neighborhood. This man threatened to kill João Lucas and his family."

Emilio's eyes widened. This kid had a presence. He spoke with authority.

"I told João Lucas to come to you if he sees other bad men."

Emilio's eyes widened further. "What do I care about that fuck? I want what is mine. So do we all." He looked around the group and found agreement.

Cisco's eyes hardened. "You are the leader. Your job is to make life better for the people."

The others were prepared to laugh. Except that Cisco seemed to expand. He spoke to them as a father to his sons. Emilio and the others were shamed.

"You are right little Cisco." Emilio looked at the others and then back to Cisco. "Your application to the Libres is accepted."

Everyone laughed and the tension was broken.

Eight years later it happened. Cisco had gradually accumulated more power in the Libres. The gang was now divided into those who wished to improve conditions and those, led by Emilio, who wished to improve themselves. A lifetime of 22 years came down to one moment.

The gang confronted each other in the alley behind the store of João Lucas. Thirty young men behind Cicso faced twenty-five on the other side, led by Emilio. Everyone in the area scurried away as the young men of Libres gathered.

"Now is your chance Emilio," Cisco said. "Decide. We are tired of the poverty, of the sickness. It is time to emerge from the darkness and help our people."

Emilio sneered. "Always the dreamer, little Cisco." He waved his hand at the neighborhood. "Here it is. It will always be so. That is human nature."

Suddenly a fierce hatred filled Cisco. He strode toward the older man. His crew followed. "The people wallow in darkness because they think like you. You are the problem Emilio. You have ten seconds. You are either with us or against us. I swear I will kill you where you stand."

Just as the Libres were about to engage in all-out war Cisco felt a calm and a feeling of well-being. It was exactly as strong as the hatred he felt at the hopelessness of his life and the darkness that surrounded the people. Emilio represented that darkness. For a split instant Cisco stood suspended in time, just as he had in this same alley eight years ago.

In that instant Cisco made a free will choice, surrounded by an exact balance of light and dark energies. The easy choice was to fight. Thirty of his mates were behind him, urging him on.

"Wait." Cisco held his hand up.

Such was the force of his command that everyone stopped. Cisco held out his hand. "My brother, I am no better than you. We must band together. To fight the evil is pointless, I see that now. We must not wallow in the filth, but create something better." All of Cisco's angels were hovering over the scene. The angels and the Higher Self of the others were present. Marian was present. Now Emilio had a choice to make. He also had a marker on his life path, to match that of Cisco. He hesitated.

"We will lead together, brother Emilio," Cisco said. "With my organizational skills and your leadership, nothing can stop us."

Suddenly Emilio saw it, felt the marker. For a second he was calm. He held out his hand.

Ten of Emilio's crew left the confrontation, shouting. "Fools!" they cried.

Cisco and Emilio embraced. The Libres organized the neighborhood, creating a pocket of prosperity amidst the poverty. Soon this self-reliant movement began to spread into the entire favela.

Marian smiled. The backups were not needed. Emilio and Cisco had fulfilled their life purpose. The angels smiled and celebrated.

CHAPTER 9

Extinction

Despite the modest successes of individuals like Cisco and organizations like the Libres, the visitors saw that their 200,000-year mission to the planet was going to fail. Too many had embraced dark memes or had not woken up. There was much sadness.

Bummamanipum-Bu and Hummhumm-Li conversed. (These beings are non-corporeal, so "age" is an irrelevant concept.)

"How can we have failed?" –Li asked his companion. "The time capsules with the higher energies are ready for Ascension. But the Seeding has not been successful."

-Bu gave the equivalent of a shrug. "Many planets fail. This is, apparently, one of them."

Both beings had not forgotten the ages-old quarrel on their own planet a million years ago. It was buried deep in their Akash.

"But this place is so beautiful!" –Li said.

"Desiree is sad," –Bu replied, speaking of the Pleiadian name for the galaxy.

They looked again at the future potentials for the planet. They were all for nuclear war.

"The only hope now is for a wild card," –Li said.

"Hope is not a strategy, as these earthians say."

"It is all we have."

Wild Card

On August 16 and 17, 1987, at almost the last possible moment, a global meditation event called the Harmonic Convergence was organized by an old soul Jose Arguelles, based on a book written by another old soul, Terry Shearer, titled *Lord of the Dawn*. This event coincided with a remarkable alignment of the sun, moon, and six out of the eight planets in an equilateral triangle (as viewed from earth) that was called a grand trine.

When the event was announced old souls and original souls all over the world responded. Not all of them, but enough.

When it was even mentioned at all, the event was scoffed at and ridiculed by religious leaders, politicians, and the media as totally irrelevant. As had occurred throughout the 200,000-year Test, the most important events were esoteric and went completely unnoticed.

The Seeders watched in amazement as over twenty million people participated in the global meditation. Although less than one third of one percent of the earth's population was involved, a powerful boost to the forces of light was measured.

The wild card had manifested! And it had done so in a way that was completely unremarkable. The dark army never even noticed. The press dismissed it as new-age nonsense. Today it is regarded as nothing more than a mere curiosity. Such is the brilliant and subtle planning of the soul manager.

Bummamanipum-Bu and Hummhumm-Li celebrated. When they measured the planet's energy after the event they discovered that the balance was now precisely 50–50. Such is the power of mass meditation when millions of old souls are involved.

"It could go either way now," –Li said hopefully.

"I'm getting too old for this," –Bu joked. "Why are we doing this again?"

"Talk to Desiree."

Just as earth/Gaia has consciousness, so too does the galaxy. Bummamanipum-Bu reached out his consciousness to Desiree.

"Oh, it is so good to hear from you!"

"We may fail in our mission on earth," –Bu said. "I need encouragement."

Desiree laughed. "Oh yes! Star system 201,077,456,331. Planet three. One of the marker planets."

"Marker planet?"

"There are a dozen or so planets in every galaxy that are energetically sensitive. The marker planets have a great influence on galactic culture and the potential for all the rest. I do so hope you will succeed, dear one."

This made –Bu feel sad. "I was hoping to hear that our success was not vital. You know, good job, not to worry, that sort of thing."

Desiree laughed. "Your effort is much appreciated. But really old boy, you do need a successful outcome. Don't let the side down."

-Bu could hear laughter as his connection broke.

-Li laughed. "I heard everything. Desiree is a coquette."

This made –Bu feel better. "Can we do anything more?"

"All is in place for a free choice decision of the earthians. We have done our job well, my friend, and have worked diligently. What will be will be."

"You're right. Let's materialize and have a drink together, just like old times."

"You're on!"

Non-material beings have the option to become denser. The visitors knew of several great watering holes on the planet. The two friends assumed human form. They went to a pub and got smashed.

Marian

The amount of excitement in the etheric realms was unprecedented. The soul manager was heartily congratulated. A conversation ensued.

"How did you know that mass meditation would be so successful?" Shara-Li asked Marian.

"I didn't! Well, I wasn't sure. But I remembered what happened on Merope."

Marian was required to explain. He told them about the planet of the Seeders, their 25,000-year war, and the mass meditation that had saved their race.

"It is still not enough," Wa-hee said. "Only 13 years are left until the fulfillment of prophecy! If the balance has not shifted to the light by the beginning of the new millennium..."

"Curtains," Wazir said. "A war in the Middle East which then becomes global. Nuclear conflagration. This time life will not recover."

The soul manager spoke. "I must myself become involved."

Five billion souls, the family of earth, cried out at once. "It is forbidden!" "You destroy the integrity of the test!" "We have not worked so hard to ruin the experiment at the end!" "Better failure and start again on a new planet than a stain upon our honor!" And so on...

Marian let the family vent. When all had their say, the soul manager spoke. "We cannot, must not, fail when we are so close to the finish line."

Before the soul manager could explain the objections began again. Marian smiled. Even Wa-hee, with over 4,500 lifetimes, was like a child to him. After calm had been restored – if you think that souls on the other side sit around on clouds and meditate all day you are sadly mistaken, dear reader – Marian spoke again.

"I shall act. Neither the integrity of the test, nor its parameters, will be violated," the soul manager explained. "In the aftermath of the 8-16-87 and 8-17-87 event, the dark-light balance has been raised to 50–50. There is no time for another Ascended Master to walk the planet, no time for another original soul to incarnate and be effective. We must work with the humans presently on earth."

All five billion of the family were mystified. Now Marian revealed what he had hidden from everyone at the beginning of the century.

"I shall deliver messages directly to humanity via another human being," Marian said. "These messages may be heard by enough people to tip the balance by the end of the millennium."

"Channeling? But...who will be the vehicle?" Shara-Li asked. "This has not been attempted live since Biblical times. Do you plan to appear as a burning bush?"

Everyone had a good laugh.

"There are several candidates," the soul manager said, pointing them out. "Here, a computer programmer in California. In Beijing, a storekeeper. In Nairobi, an architect. In Tamil Nadu, an expert in linguistics."

The entire family had to decide unanimously. It was almost a repeat of the situation on Merope so long ago, except that the pool of voters was 5 billion instead of 100,000, and the tally was taken on the other side. Fortunately all the memes were positive.

"We have no choice," said Darshook, speaking for the whole. "But this procedure is unprecedented. The soul manager should have nothing to do with the test."

There was further conversation among the family.

Fulud summarized for everyone. "It is agreed, but only if the soul manager does not influence the decision of the human vehicle. If there is agreement with the human being and information is transmitted, free will must be respected. You may not give out anything that a human being on the planet has not already thought of or invented."

"No leading the witness," Shara-Li quipped. She had been a lawyer in her previous incarnation.

"So it is," Marian replied. "First I shall contact the computer programmer."

"A tough nut to crack," an original soul said.

"Yes, but he had a lifetime in Lemuria," Tuamit-Ra replied.

To say that the soul manager was fired up is a gross understatement. He/she/they would be able to participate after all. And at the crucial moment in linear time! Marian began to feel like a manager or a coach of a big league sports team. Although not able to directly participate, yet he could be close to the action.

All of the old souls watched as Marian hovered over the candidate for several months of linear time.

"This one is too dull to notice," Wa-hee said.

Shara-Li smiled. "Yes, but his wife has."

Those with a female bias to their Akash smiled and good-naturedly roasted those who had a male bias.

"Darren, come with me to see the psychic."

"Tina, please. I don't do psychics. I have a deadline to meet, and I'm behind. I have to work the weekend."

"This Monday after work then. I tell you, there is a gigantic being hovering over you. He calls himself Marian. He claims to be the soul manager for the earth. He wants to talk to you."

Darren Pascal smiled lovingly and condescendingly at his wife. "You know how that kind of space cadet shit annoys me. It's nonsense! If you can hear this being, why don't *you* talk to him?"

"He says I'm not qualified."

"Qualified for what?"

Tina Pascal smiled mischievously. "To find that out you'll have to see Julia."

Darren groaned. Tina had been on him for months now and it was getting decidedly irritating. She was annoyingly persistent. "All right! Monday after work. I don't want to hear another word about it."

Tina gave her husband a big hug and a kiss. "You won't regret it."

Darren heard her on the phone talking to Julia the psychic. "What a bunch of bullshit," he said. "Psychics! Charlatans, all of them." Darren Pascal was a contributor to *Skeptic*, an online magazine.

When Monday came around Darren (very reluctantly) and Tina (overjoyed) went to see Julia. "If my colleagues at the magazine ever suspected I was doing this..."

"Relax honey," Tina said. "If it's all nonsense you can have a good laugh with your friends." Tina knew how to handle her husband.

This peroration made Darren feel much better. "Yeah! I can write a really good article about this garbage."

Now Darren was excited to punk this Julia, and show her how stupid her silly beliefs were. He expected to see an old hag in a broken down trailer smoking a fag and peering at a crystal ball. Or maybe an airhead with a crystal around her neck.

Tina drove up to a nice looking house with a two car garage. They trooped up to Julia's "reading room." Darren was groaning and whining the whole time.

When the pair walked in Julia almost had a heart attack. She began coughing, crying, and laughing.

Darren lost it. "What is this?" he complained. "Is there something wrong with you?"

Tina thought she heard laughter, but it could have been the sound of seven billion souls all laughing at the same time on the other side.

Julia calmed down and got down to business. She saw the skepticism on this man's face, the tightness in his energy field. This one was in for a big surprise.

During the one hour session with the psychic Darren Pascal almost shit a brick. Twice. Tina had been right all along. He secretly suspected there was a God, but not a God that would talk to him. At least this Marian guy felt like a god. He sure as hell was BIG. Men weren't supposed to feel this much love. Women maybe, but not him.

Afterward Tina drove home. She didn't say anything.

That night Darren slept well and dreamlessly. It was unusual for him. Tina's snoring didn't even bother him.

After eating breakfast the next morning everything was back to normal. During the day he got into an argument with another programmer. By the time he came home for dinner he had convinced himself that the experience at Julia's had been a hallucination.

The next morning Darren was in the shower. Suddenly Marian was there with him. "What the fuck?!" Darren dropped the soap. The vibe was really good, but he was embarrassed that this...being, whoever he was, saw him naked in the shower.

At this Marian guffawed. "I can see everything on the planet! I've seen you naked since you were born."

Darren picked up the soap. "Aw shit." He knew it was true. Marian's mind was totally open on this subject. "You mean you can see all seven billion of us? You know what we're doing all the time?"

"That's right."

Darren flared. "Then why don't you fix everything? In case you haven't noticed, the human race is pretty fucked up."

Marian had another laugh. Darren thought he heard other laughter in the background. (The entire human family on the other side, including Darren's Higher Self, was in stitches.)

Darren became petulant. Water from the shower was dripping in his eyes. He stepped back. "I don't see what's so funny!"

At this there was more laughter, but the vibe was really good. Darren couldn't feel mad anymore. "All right Marian or whatever you call yourself. Who are you?"

"I represent the other side of the veil."

"Don't be stupid. You can't be real. I don't see anything."

"Do you need an angel with wings? I can do that."

Darren knew he wasn't crazy. He knew he wasn't dreaming. Whatever this was, it felt like a Presence. A benevolent one. Just like an angel might feel. "Nah. But I need to get to work OK?"

"OK. I'll talk to you tonight after work. When you get home, go to your bedroom. Tell Tina you are communing with a ghost. She'll understand."

Darren could hardly keep his mind on his work that day. He was thinking about what he was going to tell his buddies at the magazine about this. He wouldn't even mention it to his co-workers, they were all nerds and didn't care about anything except video games and smoking dope. When he got home he and Tina ate dinner. There was no talk of children at the table now. His wife had an unreadable expression on her face.

"I, uh, have to commune with that guy."

"You're a lucky bastard Darren Pascal," Tina said bitterly. "If I had a left nut I would have given it up to have what you have."

Darren was surprised at her tone. "You really think this is important, don't you?"

Tina looked at him as if he was crazy. "You stupid fool, it's the most important thing ever! I don't know why you were selected and I wasn't."

Darren was totally confused. "I may have to tell this Marian guy to fuck off. He's too distracting. I can't get any work done."

Tina just shook her head as Darren walked into the bedroom.

Darren's life completely changed after his second talk with Marian. He started speaking informally in front of small groups in the homes of Julia and Tina's friends. Actually Marian did all the speaking; all he had to do was open his mouth.

Three months later he stopped writing for the *Skeptic*.

"You're getting weird Darren," one of his colleagues at the magazine said at a meeting. "You're just not the same."

"That's true."

"You're softer. You don't hardly swear anymore."

"That's true."

"Your entire belief system has changed."

"That's true."

"Maybe it's better if you resign from the magazine."

Darren had to agree. There was no way he could tell them he was communicating with a disembodied being who said he was a messenger from God. "It's been nice working with you."

After Darren left the staff got together. "He's different."

"Yeah. But I kinda like it," a woman said.

The others shrugged and began to look for a replacement.

In 1994 Darren nervously gave his first public lecture. Marian called it channeling, but that sounded too much like airhead nonsense to Darren. Three times he lectured at the United Nations. From there, he became a worldwide phenomenon, talking about esoteric subjects, peace on earth, and the relationship between the human being and God. Darren found himself just stepping back and letting Marian do his thing. While words were coming out of his mouth he was in a place halfway between the earth and the other side. It was a really, really good place. During these experiences he saw a little silver cord attaching him to his body. Marian told him that he could release the cord at any time and he would go all the way. He would terminate his connection with the body and go back to the other side, which Marian called Home. Darren didn't want to do that. His relationship with Tina was mind-blowing now. She was travelling with him and they were speaking to huge crowds. He quit his programming job. They were making money so it was OK with him.

Darren now understood that there were billions of souls on the other side, cheering on humanity to make it past the extinction event that was supposed to occur by the year 2000.

Marian was having a blast. He and Darren had just finished a lecture (channeling!) tour on the 20th of December, 1999. Nothing more could be done now.

A measurement was made. The balance between light and dark was now (metaphorically) about 51%–49%.

"The extinction event of nuclear war has shifted," Marian remarked to Darshook. "This is a very good sign."

"Instead of war the worry is the breakdown of computer operating systems and databases."

"Yes, the Y2K problem. It is a considerable shift toward the light."

"But still the worry is about a collapse of society."

January 1, 2000

Instead of conflagration at the beginning of the millennium, the world had a party. There was so much celebration on the other side that Wa-hee and his friends, and all the original souls and old souls, relaxed. "Now we can take a lot of time off."

"No you don't!" Marian said. "Our work is just beginning."

Nobody believed it.

CHAPTER 10

September 11, 2001

When Darren Pascal saw the planes crash into the Twin Towers in New York and at the Pentagon he was not surprised. Marian had been correct, as usual. He had already prepared Tina and his family for the event. Darren had even called the nerds at his old job and told them to avoid the Twin Towers on September 11th. But he had to be careful.

"If you are too specific you may be accused of being involved," Marian told him one night before he went to sleep. "After this event certain draconian laws will be passed authorizing the detention of persons under the guise of national security."

So Darren told people, "I have a bad feeling about something." On the 5th of September he called his brother-in-law Paul, who worked at Cantor Fitzgerald in the North Tower. "Take a break. Come out and visit us in California," Darren suggested. Paul took a week of vacation and flew out.

When the family watched the video together Paul's face was ashen. "Lucky you called," he said to Darren.

Tina and Darren exchanged glances. No one said anything, even though some in the family suspected Darren may have had prior knowledge. Mostly Darren's family thought he was a little nutty. But they were grateful that a family member had been spared.

December 21, 2012, winter solstice

This date represents the middle of the 36-year window at the completion of the second 26,000-year precession cycle since the beginning of Lemuria, and the beginning of the third. During this window the direction for the new cycle would be set. When the earth passed through this date without an extinction event there was further celebration on the other side. Many old souls on earth thought that the danger had passed. But the potentials for regression were still strong. For many generations, the time fractals generated by millennia of conflict and war would reappear in the consciousness of humanity.

The soul manager had an unusual meeting with the original souls. Even if you incarnate on earth most of you is still on the other side, so Marian could talk to everyone even though a piece of them was still on earth.

"Our work is just beginning," Marian began. "Everything we have done up to 2012 was just practice for the real thing."

Wa-hee was flabbergasted. "I have already had 4,611 lifetimes on this planet. How many more are necessary?"

Marian laughed. "So many souls are 'lining up' to go back. You don't want to miss the good stuff."

Wazir was doubtful as the old souls looked at the Ring of Potential. "The duality will intensify as the dark souls organize to bring the earth back to the old ways, because they are more comfortable in a lower energy. There will be more insane violence. A repeat of the Bolshevik revolution in the United States as fascism intensifies under the guise of 'progressive' thought and 'make the country great again.' It will be even worse than before!"

"And don't forget the cooling of the planet," Fulud said, "as the cold intensifies in the northern hemisphere. Potential breakdown of the primitive electrical grid. More misery." Fulud's last lifetime was in Moscow, Russia.

Marian laughed again. "Civilization will survive."

Now the old souls really got into it with the soul manager. "What would you know about it, theoretician?" Shara-Li said. "You stay here, safe and sound, while we do all the work. You have never undergone the soul-splitting. You have never even experienced a negative emotion! You have never suffered in these miserable human bodies within an environment of low consciousness and stupidity!"

"That's right!" Wa-hee cried. "Is it too much to ask that we actually enjoy ourselves down there?" This was seconded by Fulud, Darshook, and mostly all of the original souls.

"Children," Marian said, "your objections are...childish. Look."

The soul manager showed the potential for Ascension of the planet on the Ring of Potential. "Lifetime after lifetime of pleasure and creativity, for a million years. Then, you become Seeders for another planet. This is called Graduation."

All of the souls were awed.

Marian was almost smug. "You call me a theoretician! Boys and girls, I've been over the mountains and down the river. I've done this on dozens of planets. To me, dear ones, you are like little babies. I have more experience in my fingernail than you do in your whole body – when you have one that is."

The soul manager showed them a little of his own Akash. The souls of earth had now progressed in consciousness to where this was possible. Everyone was blown away. Millions of years of incarnation on planet after planet. Finally, the reward: to be the soul manager in charge of an entire planetary group. To be responsible for a planet of crucial importance to an entire galaxy.

Wa-hee saw how his vision had been limited. Marian was a soul manager for a planet, but there were soul managers for entire solar systems, star groups, galaxies...and entire universes.

Not one of the impulsive souls of earth was capable of saying anything. Their shit was totally blown away.

"Uh, sorry," Wa-hee said. "We had...I had...no clue."

Everyone felt the same way. The young souls could hardly believe what they were seeing. "Wow," one of them said. "I have only had two lifetimes. It's fucking unbelievable."

Everyone laughed.

"So that's what you mean by soul growth," another young soul said.

Marian didn't tell them that some of these young souls on earth had almost as much experience as he/she/they did. But that's what happens with souls. You get enough experience, you are permitted to split off a "piece" of yourself to a brand-new personality.[28] Now THAT was an orgasm!

"All right children, let's get down to business," Marian said. "This next lifetime for all of you is critical. Earth has passed the energetic marker for extinction events such as nuclear war – you are beyond that now. But powerful time fractals of the old paradigm still exist. Especially until 2030, and for the rest of this century, regression is possible. You may yet still fail and de-evolve back into barbarism."

Marian displayed planets in the galaxy that never found the Creative Source. There were billions of them. Life there simply...existed. Technology was advanced, but the souls there were not connected to the Source in the way that souls on earth had the potential to be.

"This is what I call the Star Wars scenario," Marian said.

Everyone saw it. They realized how blessed they were to have been seeded.

"Wow," Shara-Li said. "I don't understand it...I can't...why? Why can't everyone be happy instead of just a few?"

"It is part of a grand plan that will be revealed when we all go to the next level."

This began a great philosophical discussion that the author will not bore the reader with, for it is as far beyond the comprehension of a human being as the Large Hadron Collider is to my cat.

"All right children. You see how a little more work will lead to millennia of greater creativity and harmony where humanity can begin to realize its potential."

At this point everyone was eager for their next assignment. Just as during the pyramid-building project, all of the old souls and original souls would participate. Marian outlined the most daring and complex plan since the 200,000-year experiment began.

The Wild Cards

On the other side there is no time. Therefore, souls can enter the physical timeline of earth at any point in history. You might ask, "Then why not send everybody back in time to make everything right and avoid all the misery?" The answer is that it wouldn't work. Each period of physical time has its own level of consciousness, commensurate with the energy of the planet at that time. Even experienced and wise souls with a mission to alter the timeline would forget everything in an environment of low awareness. A cell phone brought back into 1820 would be a useless toy. What could be done was already done.

However, passing the December 21, 2012 marker had huge esoteric significance. 26,000 years of prophecy had been voided. A new energy was coming in.

The soul manager looked into the Ring of Potential. "Dear ones, look at the earth timeline. See how certain persons are now positioned perfectly to have an extraordinary influence on events."

Marian showed several dozen people who, if they acted in certain ways at the right time, could quickly propel humanity forward. "These individuals are what I call wild cards."

"There is only one problem," Wa-hee said. "The persons you have selected are already on earth. Their soul missions and life path markers were given in an old energy. They don't contain the right information and energy to push them into new courses of action."

"That is correct dear one. That is why we use soul walk-ins to give them a little push."

Everyone gasped at this.

The soul manager explained. "Now that the December 21, 2012 marker has been passed, the past potentials of earth, and humanity, have cleared somewhat toward the light. Do you see it?"

Everyone saw it. The mists of time had been lifted for the decades after the Second World War. It was now possible to "enhance" old souls anywhere in the timeline after that great conflict had ended.

"How is this possible?" Darshook asked. "How can the physical timeline change in the past when it has already happened?"

Marian smiled. "Expand your thinking dear one. Time is a construct; it operates in a circle, which has no beginning or end. Past and future are metaphors. The future affects the past and the past affects the future."

Marian demonstrated this with the Ring of Potential.

Darshook, never a deep thinker even on the other side, was amazed. "Time is fluid, not linear, and goes in both directions!"

Everyone saw a huge blackness on the physical timeline during the World War Two period.

"I see," Wazir said. "It is impossible for the future to manipulate the past before World War Two. What is written is written. The great war, and the slaughter it wrought, creates a huge energetic barrier."

"That's right," Fulud said. "The darkness represents the deaths of 80 million and the traumatization and injuries of millions more. Perhaps if we make more progress on earth the light will get stronger and that barrier will fall. Maybe the entirety of human history can be altered for the better! Then the suffering in the Akash of humanity can be completely eliminated."

Wa-hee looked at his friend in astonishment. "That is brilliant Fulud! I never thought of that."

"You are correct Fulud, but that is far in the future," Marian said. "Now, back to our walk-ins. Because the soul cannot energetically fit into the body, most of you must stay here during a lifetime on earth. We all know that a soul can have more than one incarnation during the same time period. This can occur in different bodies or in the same body."

"Of course!" Shara-Li said. "Soul mates are just pieces of the same soul in different bodies. We have all experienced this. A walk-in is a soul enhancement to the human who is already walking the physical timeline."

Tuamit-Ra saw it. "The Expressions who are in the most advantageous positions can awaken to a new soul mission, based on the new potentials that have occurred after the passing of the 2012 marker. It is brilliant!"

"That is correct dear one," Marian said. "I have been eagerly awaiting this development. Now that the marker has been passed the key players, and their potentials, are clear."

Marian introduced to the group a soul with almost 1,000 lifetimes. "This is Nonakh. He was Nikola Tesla in his previous Expression. The bias of his Akash is male. He comes from the soul group of scientists. He will be a walk-in to the current Expression known as Robert Borglin."

The others crowded around the famous inventor. The 12 soul friends had rarely worked with a soul from the pure science soul group. This group tended to be very tribal and only associated with themselves. Nonakh grinned. "Marian and I are planning a breakthrough; something that will explode the stultified scientific model in the area of medicine and physics." Nonakh indicated Tuamit-Ra, who would also be a walk-in. "At some point we will meet. And work together."

Tuamit-Ra was curious. "I am a computer programmer and you are a physicist. How will we make a breakthrough in medicine?"

Nonakh grinned. "Medicine is physics. Biology is physics. Consciousness is physics. As you will discover when you meet me."

Marian was looking smug and well pleased with himself.

"Ever since your association with the human being Darren Pascal, you have been getting big-headed," Wa-hee said to the soul manager.

Everyone laughed. "It is true," Shara-Li said to the others, winking. "The soul manager does seem a bit puffed up in his own importance lately."

Marian preened a bit. "My new plan is magnificent."

The soul manager and Nonakh smiled at each other. "The potential is for a grand advance on the earth."

Marian raised metaphorical hands as all the souls demanded answers to what might happen.

"Look at the current state of the planet. The dark-light balance is precarious, only slightly in favor of the light. There is the problem of medicine, which has lagged behind scientific achievement. Many die needlessly and lifespans are still too short. There is also the fascination with artificial intelligence, transhumanism, and cloning, all of which are evolutionary dead ends. And, of course, the earth is part of the greater galaxy."

Marian showed them what had happened on other Uplifted planets that failed the test. The merging of biology with artificial constructs usually led to racial death within 100 generations. Too much fascination with technology attracted other space-faring races with galactic technology that was used to bribe influential persons. These planets eventually lost their sovereignty and became slave societies. The biggest danger was the development of artificial intelligence, which had established itself on millions of planets. The earth was in the beginning stages of this.

"Not even the Ring of Potential can predict the outcome with any certainty," the soul manager said. "Previous to the last century the population of earth was under 2 billion. Karmic relationships were local and only a few were regional. Now the world is connected electronically and through air travel. The population has risen to 8 billion. Although a few have voided their karma, there is still a strong attraction to the dark energy. Unlike the past there are simply too many variables for accurate prediction. That is why we need the wild cards."

Marian then spoke to Llendrah (who had lived over 3,000 lifetimes), Tahil (who had been a raider with Darshook thousands of years ago), and a fiery new soul to earth. All of them would be walk-ins and play critical roles in the very near future. The soul manager went over the setup for everyone, for there would be many potential wild cards all the way to the end of the century.

"What about free choice?" Wa-hee asked. "These walk-ins overset the free will of the Expression who is already walking the timeline."

"That is a good question, but remember that a walk-in is simply a merger of you with you on the soul level. It is the same soul. Free choice is always in operation. Some potential wild cards will refuse their enhanced soul mission. Some wild cards will manifest, some will not. Some will flame out, some will be effective."

Everyone was satisfied with this.

"Because of the progress made, the Test has altered somewhat. There is a slightly greater latitude of operations. You may congratulate yourselves!"

The human family on the other side of the veil all cheered and celebrated.

"Now dear ones, let us look at the timeline after 2012 in the United States. This country will be the key for at least the next decade." Marian showed the potentials using the Ring of Potential. All saw that the election in 2016 would be a critical event. The players were known.

"If Senator Stinson is elected the darkness will continue," Marian announced.

Shara-Li and Llendrah objected. "The first female president will be an impulse toward the light."

Marian checked the Ring of Potential again. The probable timelines showed a distinct bifurcation at the election in the United States in 2016. "It is as I expected," Marian said. "This election is a critical period not just for the United States but for the planet. If Senator Stinson/Llendrah becomes president the military will stage a coup to rid themselves of what they perceive as corrupt elements. Chaos will result."

It was all there. Shara-Li didn't believe it. "Your device is defective," she said.

Marian showed the other timeline. "Frank Conrad/Tahil is the wild card, do you see it? Hated by the old guard in both parties, he is literally a bull in a china shop. He is here to stir things up across the earth and break up old meme structures. Out of the chaos comes stability at a higher level."

"Impossible," Shara-Li said. "No offense Tahil, but on earth you are a woman-hating bastard. I will never vote for you." Llendrah agreed with this.

Those whose Akashic biases were female also agreed with Shara-Li. Most of Tahil's incarnations were as dominant alpha males. "Stinson will be our candidate," Shara-Li said.

Marian spoke to Tahil and Llendrah. "Tahil, as the potential wild card president, you have the key role. You will be born in privilege. Your family will be wealthy. When you are about 68 you will be approached by certain factions within the government and the military."

Marian pointed to the potential timeline. "Your moment will come here, in June 2015. You have already contemplated the idea of running for president. You will just need a little soul 'nudge.' Of course you will have the free choice to accept or reject your new role."

Tahil nodded.

"You were chosen because your family is wealthy and socializes with powerful personalities, and because you are a dominant alpha male on earth. This is the energy that will be needed in the 2016–2020 period and perhaps beyond that for a few years. There will be several attempts on your life if you become president. You will be hated and vilified by almost all influential persons in media, entertainment, and popular culture. The bias of your Akash is to overreact to everything, to exact revenge on those you perceive as your enemies. This will make your situation even worse. Do you understand?"

"I think so," Tahil said. "But why will this happen?"

The soul manager showed Tahil (and all who were listening) the events from 1000 BCE in the Kingdom of Falash. "Do you remember?"

"I remember that," Tahil said. "But it was so long ago! And unimportant in the grand scheme of things."

At this Shara-Li, Llendrah (who had been Queen Falash) and all who had been betrayed by Tahil spoke as one. "We remember it as if it were yesterday."

Tahil was on the spot. He remembered the vow he had given after that lifetime.

"Karma has a way of coming around, Tahil," Marian said. "Llendrah is now Senator Stinson. Those who were advisors to Queen Falash will run the mass media outlets and are supporters of Senator Stinson or her allies. They will become triggered into this ancient incident if you are elected, due to the heavy karma you created. Their emotions will run high, but the real reason for their emotional reaction to you will not be known to them. They will hate you for legitimate reasons, but the true reason will be unknown to them. There will be much bitterness during and after the campaign, no matter who wins."

Marian spoke to Llendrah and her supporters. "Your job is simply to oppose Tahil."

Llendrah nodded. She understood that opposition would create tension that would help to break down the old paradigm.

"Ideally, Senator Stinson's function is as a catalyst – organizing opposition to Tahil/Conrad – rather than as president. If Conrad is elected we will use the karma of Tahil's betrayal to our advantage. Before and after the election, even if you lose, your walk-in (you) will encourage you to cause as much trouble for Tahil as you can."

Llendrah smiled. "I can do that."

The soul manager's proposal provoked further debate. Although now beyond the veil, old souls and original souls were tremendously invested in what happens on earth. Feelings ran high. After everyone had their say, Marian shook his head (metaphorically). "Even here, tempers are flaring!"

Marian spoke directly to Tahil. "You will have a chance to rectify your karma, but the roles will be reversed. If you are elected, Senator Stinson and her supporters will try to do to you what you did to them in that long-ago time. Do you see the setup? Depending on how you react, you may release all of the karma from that old incident. Or, you may be impeached."

Tahil nodded.

Marian showed Tahil what he would likely have to go through. "If you are elected you will function as an energetic bulls eye. Even when you accomplish great things you will be criticized. And indeed, you will help to create that chaos because of your personality. It is necessary. Instead of fighting amongst themselves – although there will be plenty of that – the people will attack you or defend you. You will be the focal point that will unite people, even though they will be on different sides. Only a man with the strongest male energy will be able to withstand these attacks."

"What if I am not elected?"

"You will simply fade away into the background. As I said before, the military will become alarmed and try to remove Senator Stinson. If you are elected other elements within the intelligence community will try to remove you."

"A similar result."

"Correct. The energies balance."

"Wow. So ideally I am the party crasher, the wrecking ball."

Marian smiled. "Yes Tahil. You are the sweaty, ugly barbarian who comes to help take down the old structures and the old memes. When that happens some of the old, accepted traditions associated with these old structures will also be destroyed. This will incense many people. You will be regarded as a pariah and a barbarian by many, and a hero to others."

Tahil, always an adventurer, was eager for the challenge. Llendrah also accepted with enthusiasm.

"A final word, Tahil. Whether your presidency is regarded as a success or a failure is irrelevant, do you understand? Like a detective who asks insulting questions to throw off the suspect, your goal, if you become elected, is to prod the system."

Tahil smiled. "Oh, I can do that!"

"I will have a fine time making your life miserable," Llendrah said.

The two original souls embraced and then entered the birth vortex.

Frank Donald Conrad's date of birth was June 14, 1946. Hillary Barbara Stinson's birthdate was October 26, 1947. Each would experience a soul enhancement from their walk-in, at a critical point in their lives. Nonakh would also be a walk-in, as well as several other key players in the upcoming drama.

Astute observers on earth would notice an unusual effect surrounding these wild cards: Events, and people, would seem to mysteriously coagulate or revolve around them. They would often rise to positions of influence under seemingly impossible circumstances, and could flame out quickly.

Marian studied the numerology of the dates. 6-14-1946 reduces to 4, the earth energy. This was the required energy for a president whose goal is to break apart the old memes and the old, outdated structures based in the old energy across the entire planet. 10-26-1947 reduces to the number 3, the catalyst. If everything went well Stinson and her group would be the thorn in Conrad's side, creating tension that would break up the old system and release karma that had built up over the entire course of the great experiment. Chaos would result, but it was necessary.

The soul manager did not announce his other wild cards. Tahil and Llendrah would be enough by themselves to begin the demise of the old system. The two would provoke the rise of young leadership in the opposition party, and expose the old guard in both parties. If Frank Conrad were elected, two years later a young leader, a fiery young soul and a woman, would propose a complete alteration of the old system. Marian laughed out loud at this. The potentials were there. She would be a total radical! Like Tahil, she would be ridiculed by the opposition and by members of her own party. Her program and her views would be wildly impractical (as the programs of all young souls with little earth experience are) and ill-thought out. She would say one thing and do another. But it would be the opening salvo in a future revamp of politics and the economy in the United States. Marian smiled. Frank Conrad from the right, Stinson and Sanchez-Alvaro from the left. The old system would be squeezed from both sides. Sanchez-Alvaro's birthdate was October 13, 1989. This reduces numerologically to a 5, the number for change and new approaches. The energies aligned perfectly.

It's going to be glorious, the soul manager thought. While Tahil is fighting the dark army, and Stinson and her allies opposing Conrad, his girl would be a forward-thinking change agent from out in left field. And if she burned out too quickly and faded away, other wild cards would follow. Then there was the military in the United States, which would play a big role behind the scenes. How would these warrior types react if Stinson were elected? What would they do if they thought the country was being threatened? Would they cooperate in a constructive manner if Conrad was elected? Would Frank Conrad/Tahil succumb to the lure of power as he did in Falash 3,000 years ago?

In the middle of this turmoil Nonakh/Tesla would potentially arrive with his new invention.

Marian looked at the potentials for the near future. The trend was toward chaos, hatred, and intolerance as the light got stronger and the dark mobilized their forces. After that, a more compassionate paradigm would gradually become accepted as people got tired of the constant fighting and hatred of left versus right. Hopefully.

The setup was perfect, but what would these human beings actually do with their free choice? It was going to be exciting to watch what happened.

November 8, 2016

The election of Frank Conrad/Tahil as president was a complete shock to those involved, but not to Marian. The soul manager could see that to the players, and especially to Stinson/Llendrah and her supporters, Conrad's election was a complete disaster. For many voters, the election of the wild card was an angry reaction and a protest against the times. Marian had counted on that.

Senator Stinson/Llendrah had already organized opposition to the new president well before the election. Llendrah's former advisors in Falash were all media figures now. She was the catalyst and was doing her job well, helped along by the karma from Tahil's betrayal 3,000 years ago. Almost all of the media organized intense opposition to the president. It was perfect.

The soul manager smiled. "Frank Conrad is going to create a shitstorm on the planet," he announced. Those who heard the soul manager laughed.

November 6, 2018

Marian watched carefully during the mid-term elections to see if his girl would win. She was running in the New York primary against a party stalwart, and one of the most powerful Congressmen in Washington. She had no chance.

The soul manager saw the fiery young soul run on a ludicrous platform of giveaways that could never be implemented. He was cheering her on all the way. This is just what was needed: a radical new voice insisting on a departure from a tired, worn-out system that was no longer working.

When the primary votes were counted the wild card had won again! Marian was 2-for-2 now, for the general election was a formality. First Frank Conrad, and now Sanchez-Alvaro. Energetically it was perfect, although most of the humans on the planet considered both to be disasters.

Now, into this chaos, enter Nonakh/Tesla.

Part II

CHAPTER **11**

Washington DC

Nonakh/Tesla was born into a family of physicians, but he showed no aptitude or interest in medicine. In this lifetime his name was Robert Borglin.

"David, what is wrong with our son?" Charlotte Borglin asked her husband.

"Nothing is wrong with him my dear. He's brilliant."

"He is a recluse, he shows no interest in people! He spends all his spare time in that makeshift lab of his downstairs."

It was a sore point with Charlotte. David had supported the child and encouraged him in this. "He has no heart, David. What will become of him? He is socially arrested. He is...may I say it...strange."

David smiled. "I suspect that one day my dear, he will revolutionize medicine."

Charlotte was dumbfounded. "It is far more likely that he will become a lonely neckbeard, divorced from the human race."

David laughed. "When was the last time you really talked to your son?"

Charlotte fidgeted uncomfortably. "I find it difficult to talk to Robert." She picked up her briefcase. "I have patients today darling." She put her arms around her husband. "I'm glad you understand him."

"I don't understand him at all my dear. I just have a feeling that if he is not discouraged our boy will become a positive force in the world."

And so it was that Robert was allowed to continue his studies in physics and engineering, and his experiments in the basement. One day during Robert's sophomore year in high school he walked into his father's study. "I encourage you to look at these books, Robert," David said. "What is biology but a collection of molecules? Those molecules have atomic structure."

A light went off in Robert's head. From that time forward he spent a little time in his father's library each week.

David wisely said nothing more to his son (for wisdom is what old souls possess, having had so many lifetimes on earth). David knew that Robert was a passionate self-starter and would find his own way. The peculiar combination of his genetics with his wife's gave Robert an uncanny resemblance to the late great Nikola Tesla. David mentioned this to his son one day.

Robert looked up the life of Tesla. He felt a subconscious connection to the man and studied his life.

At the end of his freshman year, Robert's faculty advisor at Georgetown became concerned about the young man and called him into his office.

"Your course load consists entirely of physics and mathematics courses. Next year is the same. Where is your grounding in the liberal arts? Your perspective on life is being atrophied."

Robert smiled. "My mother is a doctor. She won't let me become another Ted Kaczynski."

The faculty advisor breathed a sigh of relief. "You understand then." He looked up at the tall, thin young man. "Has anyone ever told you that you look like —"

"Tesla. Yes. But I don't intend to die a broken man. I know that Tesla alienated a lot of people he worked with by his abrasive personality. I inherited my father's mild-mannered temperament."

Robert dropped out of college after his sophomore year.

Charlotte gave up on her son. "He'll never be a doctor," she said.

David smiled lovingly upon his obstinate wife. "Robert's contribution to medicine will rather be in the form of medical devices and equipment." David talked with his son a lot and kept up with the direction of his work.

Charlotte snorted. "Helping people one-on-one is the best way."

David knew his wife to be very stubborn, but he loved her a lot.

When Robert told his physics professor he wasn't coming back to school, the man was shocked. "You're wasting a brilliant career."

Robert smiled. "I don't want one. I only used college to orient myself for what I have to do."

"And what is that?"

Robert told him about his idea of using laser-cooled plasmas to form a lens that could see into the underlying quantum fields that create matter and energy.

Dr. Gary Priebus was skeptical. "How do you know that such plasmas have these properties? Or whether you can even make them?"

Robert/Nonakh smiled. "It came to me in a dream. A totally new approach."

Priebus wanted to laugh, but stopped himself. A lowly patent clerk's gedanken experiments had already revolutionized physics. The great Nikola Tesla had been a dreamer with revolutionary and practical ideas who saw blueprints for working devices in his head. Hamilton's idea for quaternions had come to him in a sudden flash of intuition as he walked across a bridge. The history of science was filled with unlikely contributors.

The two men discussed methods and means. "My parents have given me some seed money, enough to rent a house and set up a lab in my basement. I am ready to go."

Priebus began to feel excited. "I can give you the personal phone number of the department chair. Dr. Gailunas has been working with plasmas. But he doesn't have, ah, your genius."

"I think I'll pass on that sir. However, I would like to meet with you occasionally if I get stuck. You're a man who can see beyond the commonplace."

Professor Priebus' eyes softened. In that moment the two old souls made an unconscious connection.

Robert was very pleased. "If I ever write a paper sir, your name will be on it."

From that moment Professor Priebus, who did not have children, looked upon the young man as his own son. "Did anyone ever tell you that you look a lot like Nikola Tesla?" he asked.

Robert sighed. He was almost used to it by now.

Four months later Robert/Nonakh had built what he called a plasma lens. When Robert first looked through his lens at the wall in his basement lab, the wall disappeared. It was now just a pattern of energy that didn't make sense. It reminded him of a day when he was ten and his great-grandfather had let him look through something he called a "kaleidoscope." This was just a bunch of colored pieces of plastic at one end of a cardboard tube that let in light.

Whenever he focused on a different object using his lens, he saw different patterns. Was there a way to "tune" the lens? The patterns were fuzzy, like an unfocused camera.

A week later he had modified the plasma's geometry and had much clearer images. He put an ordinary screwdriver on a lab bench and looked at it through the lens. The screwdriver disappeared. In its place the lens presented an alternate reality; organized patterns of light that looked like templates or blueprints for something. Were these the underlying quantum fields? Robert began to get very excited. He felt he had made a breakthrough but he needed someone to interpret what he was seeing. He called Dr. Priebus, who came over to his lab the next evening.

Priebus indicated the device. "Explain to me how you made this." The professor and Robert talked physics and engineering. "The device is a bit bulky but it can be placed in a carrying case and carted around." Robert indicated a black plastic case about 2 feet by 2 feet by 3 feet.

"What are we looking at professor?" Robert asked after he set up the lens and focused it on the screwdriver. "The patterns seem to be made of little vibrating strings of light. A validation of string theory?"

Dr. Priebus was astonished. He looked at Robert with awe. "Your guess is as good as mine Robert. But this is a massive breakthrough in…physics?"

Robert laughed. "Take a look at this." He walked to the front of the lens. "Look at my arm through this thing."

The professor saw the patterned strings of light. "These patterns are changing instead of stationary like the screwdriver. Perhaps they are representations of an underlying quantum field?" Priebus was baffled. "Maybe we need someone from the life sciences to interpret this. I know a molecular biologist, an expert in DNA."

Priebus gave Robert a card. "I'll call him right now." The professor got on his phone and described the new invention.

"Daniel is coming right over."

Robert and the professor went upstairs and drank coffee. "It will take him an hour to get here." In Robert's living room the older man became animated. The professor talked of papers and conferences and seminars and a new theory of physics that would explain the remarkable observations. Robert listened politely. He had other plans.

When Daniel Robinzene saw the device and looked through it he gasped. "Stand back farther from the lens," he told Robert. "Against the far wall."

"Gary, look at this."

Priebus looked through the viewer. "There's some kind of…sphere, surrounding Robert's body. It's filled with these vibrating strings of light."

Daniel looked through the lens again at Robert. "I don't know how to interpret what we're seeing. Perhaps it's a real-time image of a biofield that surrounds the human body." The cell biologist was baffled. "Is this physics or biology?"

"Maybe it's both," Gary said.

Robert snapped his fingers. He remembered something…a vague memory: Consciousness is physics, biology is physics.

Robinzene sat down on a chair next to the device. "Maybe Sheldrake is right after all! And Lipton. Both are considered quacks by the medical profession and other life science scientists. Maybe they're not." Robinzene looked through the viewer again.

"Explain," Priebus said.

"Both Sheldrake and Lipton were cell biologists. They have advanced nutty theories about genetics and biology. Sheldrake says that 'morphic fields' organize atoms, molecules, crystals, organelles, cells, tissues, organs, and organisms. He calls it the theory of formative causation. Lipton is even nuttier. He claims that the mind can program body functions. All sorts of ill-informed people latch on to this and make frivolous claims about healing."

The cell biologist walked back to the lens. "The patterns continue to shift and morph, as if we are seeing something living." Robinzene thought for a moment. "Sheldrake posits unconventional explanations for standard subjects in biology such as development, inheritance, and memory. Are these Sheldrake's morphic fields?"

Gary Priebus went over and looked through the lens at Robert, who was still standing at the far wall of the lab. "String theory says that there are other dimensions infolded within spacetime. Maybe that's what this is."

"I don't know. They look like little light templates," Robinzene said.

"Templates? Is that what you think they are?"

Gary looked through the lens again. Beautiful patterns of dynamically changing, multicolored light surrounded Robert's body. They looked alive. "Whatever this is, it's beautiful." He studied the patterns. "If these are quantum fields they aren't random. My guess is that they are associated with the body somehow."

Dr. Robinzene turned to Robert. "What have you done here, son?"

Robert grinned. "I don't know. I told Dr. Priebus the idea came to me in a dream. I know what I built but I don't know what I'm looking at!"

"Unfortunately I don't have time to give this the attention it deserves," Robinzene said. "But my doctor, Karl Ghuneim, was trained as a molecular biologist before he became a physician. He is very interested in alternative approaches to medicine."

"What makes you think that this device has medical applications?" Priebus asked.

Daniel (who was an old soul) surprised himself. He grinned at Robert. "I don't know. Maybe it was a leap of intuition."

Robert was fascinated. "You said that Dr. Lipton believes that the mind can control bodily functions?"

"That's what he says. He's offered not the slightest bit of proof though."

Robert was getting excited. "Can you call this Karl Ghuneim and ask him if he'd be interested in working with me on this?"

"Sure." Robinzene handed Robert his card. On the back he wrote Karl Ghuneim's name and personal phone number. "Don't call him until this weekend. I want to talk to him first."

Professor Priebus wrote another name and number on the card. "This is Neil Gorasch's number. Hacker, knows electronics, good with his hands. Brilliant kid, like you." Priebus looked around the lab. There were devices in various stages of development. "He may be able to help you; he only lives a few miles from here."

Robinzene stared at Robert and then at his lab. He was about to speak when Robert said, "I know, I know. I do look a little like Nikola Tesla."

After the two older men left Robert wondered whether the mind really could influence body functions and cellular structure. Even if it could, would that relate to what he was seeing through the lens?

He called Neil Gorasch straight away. Neil came over, ooohing and aaahing at the instrument and Robert's other devices in various stages of development. Neil was short and thin and grubby and wore red sneakers with big white laces. He smiled a lot. He had a goatee which made him look 35. The two old souls Neil/Darshook and Robert/Nonakh immediately connected. Robert showed him how he had constructed the lens. Neil looked through it. "I have no idea what you've got here, Robert, but I want one of these."

Robert grinned. "Do you have any money to pay for it? Each one I make costs me a couple grand of my father's money."

Neil brightened. "You mean you have another one?"

"Yeah, my prototype." Robert pointed to a large black plastic case. "It's in there."

Before Neil left he had convinced Robert to let him have the prototype.

"You could sell water pistols to an arms dealer," Robert told him.

Neil left with the case, which he could barely muscle up the stairs. "If you break that thing I'll wring your neck," Robert told him.

Neil grinned. "Don't worry, I know how to make them now."

Three days later Robert received a phone call from Karl Ghuneim. "I heard about your new invention from Dan Robinzene. I want to see it."

"Come on over."

Ghuneim was a burly man in his late 30s, about 15 years older than Robert. When the two old souls Karl/Tuamit-Ra met the eyes of Robert/Nonakh there was an instant bond. Karl looked through the device at Robert. After several minutes he closed his eyes and sighed. "The merkaba. The fucking merkaba."

"The what?"

"An ancient concept. Supposedly it is the light body of human consciousness. In the ancient mystery schools the object was to discover the merkaba. Knowing how to use it supposedly gave you magical properties, such as creating objects out of thin air like Sai Baba, or turning your body into light and ascending into heaven."

"In other words, bullshit."

"Yeah." Karl looked through the lens again at Robert. "Then I discovered this guy William Henry. He shows that the merkaba was depicted in art as a sphere of light surrounding the human body. In Egypt, pharaoh surrounded by a sphere of light on the Ark of a Million years. The Last Judgment painting by Fra Angelico. Jesus on the throne of Ascension." He straightened. "Whatever we're seeing through this lens looks a lot like those old paintings. Maybe this is what the mystery schools were talking about."

Robert looked at the older man. "Dr. Robinzene suggested that it was possible to alter the body's functions using the mind. Do you have any idea what he meant?"

Karl Ghuneim's eyes widened. "Yes."

Marian

"It's working," Marian said to the souls present. "Two successful wild cards and now Tesla reincarnated! I am on a roll."

"Don't get cocky," Shara-Li said.

"I'll be doing another lecture with Darren Pascal in New Zealand tomorrow linear time." Marian spoke smugly.

Fulud, Wazir, Tuamit-Ra, Darshook, Wa-hee, and all the others shook their (metaphoric) heads. Shara-Li spoke for everyone. "You are becoming insufferable."

"When you become as advanced as I you may do the same."

The other souls ganged up on Marian and gave him the soul equivalent of a friendly thrashing, which was enjoyed by all.

Kirk Alexander

When Wa-hee/Kirk Alexander was four years old he was already a head taller than anyone his age in the day care group. One cold Michigan winter afternoon, when Mrs. Cleary was out of the room, one of the older boys noticed Kirk studying a circuit board from an old smart phone. "Hey kid!" Walter Szymanski blustered. Walter was seven, beefy, with a big head and a large forehead, under which a pair of close-set eyes regarded the world with disfavor. The older boy reminded Kirk of a hippopotamus he'd seen at the zoo. He ignored him.

"Hey dumbass!" Walter said, striding across the room toward Kirk, who was at the back of the room. Walter didn't like to be ignored. "I'm talkin' to you!"

"Shutup Walter," said a five-year-old girl who was drawing in a coloring book.

"Who asked you?" Walter said, turning around to stare at the blonde girl with a long pony tail and big blue eyes. The girl didn't look up, but her lips pursed in smile that told Kirk she was messing with him.

"If you weren't a girl . . ." he began angrily.

"Yes I know Walter," the girl replied, as if they'd gone through this before. "If I wasn't a girl you'd take care of me real good."

The other kids smiled but didn't look at Walter. Walter felt that everyone in the class was against him.

Kirk noticed that Walter had completely lost interest in him. But then the older boy's big head turned and he was looking straight at Kirk with an angry expression. Kirk knew that Walter's parents dropped him off in the morning, and seemed glad to be rid of him. Sometimes they didn't show up at 6 p.m. to pick him up and Mrs. Cleary had to spend a lot of time on the phone. Kirk was prepared to be lenient. He didn't know how he knew the meaning of that word, he just did.

As Walter approached Kirk experienced a cool excitement. His nerves calmed, his heart rate slowed; all of his senses come alive. All of the kids in the class had turned their heads. Kirk saw Carole, the blonde girl, staring at him.

Walter slapped the circuit board out of his hand and Kirk smiled. He was almost as big as Walter. He wasn't worried. As Walter bunched his fist, Kirk saw everything in slow motion. There was no sound. The fist tightening, the eyes flaring, Walter reaching back, the meaty fist coming forward. He saw an expression of horror on Carole's face as he moved his head slightly to the right to avoid the blow. With the back of his left arm Kirk pushed backward on Walter's hip. The older boy, his weight forward now, lost his balance. Walter stumbled clumsily into the shelving against the back wall, filled with books and toys, which fell crashing to the floor. Kirk suddenly heard and saw everything at normal speed.

Mrs. Cleary walked into the room. "Walter! What are you doing?"

Walter got off the floor and sent a kick toward Kirk as he walked to the center of the room with a smile on his face. Kirk dodged it.

"Sorry Mrs. Cleary. I tripped. That stupid kid Kirk left his things on the floor again."

Kirk's eyes met his teacher's for an instant. There was an understanding there.

"Your parents are going to be late again," Mrs. Cleary said to Walter. "You'll have to wait outside until they come."

Walter's face was turned just enough toward Kirk's. Kirk saw the hurt in the older boy's eyes. In that instant Kirk Alexander's understanding widened. Somehow he understood why Walter Szymanski was a bully. In that moment Kirk learned compassion, as well as a disgust for destructive emotion.

"Hi dad."

"Hi Kirk! Did you have a good day at school?"

Kirk met his mother's eyes. "School is boring."

After kindergarten, Kirk's parents sent him to a Catholic school, where he excelled. It soon became apparent to Ralph, Jennifer, and the instructors at St. Mary's that Kirk was extraordinarily intelligent.

"If you can afford it, I recommend that you send Kirk to Danton's, a very exclusive preparatory school in Birmingham," Sister Melinda said.

Ralph looked at his wife. Kirk's father was a big-boned man with a wide face, tall and muscular, with brown eyes that smiled a lot. "I don't think Kirk would like that," he said to Jennifer, a tall, graceful woman with regular features and intense blue eyes.

"Probably not," she agreed.

Sister Melinda didn't understand. "But Danton's is the best school in the Midwest," she explained. "Over half their student population goes to an Ivy League school!"

"Kirk doesn't like school," Jennifer explained. "We put him in Farmington middle school last year, but he was so bored he fell asleep. The principal tested his IQ and it's above 180. Kirk has made it clear he doesn't want to continue. He wants us to let him take the GED and be done with it."

Sister Melinda was shocked. "What a waste of a brilliant mind!"

Jennifer smiled. "I'm a high school physics teacher, as you know sister," Jennifer said. "I'm not worried about Kirk. He's already finished my high school physics book," she explained. "The kid reads math like we do words. He seems to understand what he reads."

"He learns faster on his own than he ever could in school," Ralph said.

"Well then," Sister Melinda said, smiling, "he needs a private tutor on his own level."

"Yes, and that's the problem," Jennifer said. "We can't find one!"

"Let me look around for you," the nun said. "I think I know someone who would be just right for your son."

"Sister, Kirk is only eleven but he's already over six feet."

"He's almost 12," Ralph said with a little smile.

Sister Melinda sighed. "Yes, I know. He's matured faster than any child I've ever seen. He's so strong that everyone is secretly afraid of him."

Jennifer thought back to the playground incident, which had occurred a couple of months ago. An older boy, mistaking Kirk for someone his age, had tried to push him off the jungle-jim from a height of about ten feet. Standing on the top of the structure with his feet curled around the bars, Kirk had picked the boy up bodily and with his arms extended, dropped him on the sand. "Kirk could have really hurt that boy," Jennifer said. "Everyone who saw it saw that Kirk was very careful with him."

"I saw it," Sister Melinda said. "I keep an eye on the playground for bullies and fights. The other children were awed. They all said later that it was like rescuing a kitten from a tree."

"Kirk has gone as far as he can go in regular school," Ralph said. "I'll talk with him tonight about the tutor."

Sister Melinda smiled. "All right, but I'm worried about his emotional maturity. He's only eleven years old but he looks like a high school senior."

Ralph shrugged. "He is clearly not fit for a normal school. But if you notice, Kirk already has developed a sensitivity to the feelings of others."

"He'll be OK," Ralph said reassuringly.

Sister Melinda didn't like it, but she reluctantly agreed. "If Kirk passes the GED I'll sign off. I still want him to have a tutor."

Ralph and Jennifer's eyes met in agreement as if to say, "Maybe, maybe not."

Two weeks later, on Kirk's 12th birthday, he was approached on the playground by a smallish man in a suit. He was now two inches over six feet. His body had begun to fill out already. "Son, I am Dr. Rupert Goldman. I represent the United States Navy. We are looking for gifted children, to be placed in a special program that is much more suited to your abilities than this." Goldman waved his hand dismissively at the school and the children.

Kirk said nothing.

"Kirk, you are bored out of your mind here, are you not?"

Kirk nodded.

"Tonight I will stop by your home to talk to your parents. Will that be all right?"

"Sure."

Dr. Goldman stopped by the Alexander home after dinner.

His father spoke to Kirk that night. "Kirk, Dr. Goldman is a recruiter for a very highly classified program. They are developing new propulsion technologies and think you might be a valuable asset. They have offered a complete education all the way to the doctorate level in exchange for a twenty-year service contract. Are you interested?"

Kirk jumped at it. "Yes dad. The world we live in is...very limiting."

"Are you sure Kirk? Many who enter these top secret military programs come out with mental or psychological damage."

Dr. Goldman frowned at this, but said nothing. The kid would have to be tested first, but all indications were that Kirk was a genius, and had a personality well-suited to the programs.

"Yes dad. I understand your concerns but I think I am in greater danger out here than in there."

Ralph laughed. "So be it."

When they went in to talk to Jennifer she was adamantly opposed. "Don't do it Kirk. This man, and those he represents, aren't above board."

"I know that mom."

Jennifer was shocked. "How could you?"

Kirk glanced at Dr. Goldman. "I've done some of my own research. Goldman here represents a...high level space program. They have reverse-engineered some...interesting...craft. I'm interested in exotic propulsion systems. What Dr. Goldman is offering is exactly what I need right now."

Ralph smiled. Jennifer scoffed. "You're twelve years old. How can you possibly know all this?"

Kirk/Wa-hee straightened. "Look at me, mom. Do I look like I'm twelve years old? My physical maturity is actually well behind my mental and emotional development. I was born for...excitement and cutting-edge work. Right now, Goldman and his group are the leading edge of the cutting edge."

Even Rupert Goldman was shocked at the boy's knowledge. Jennifer's eyes welled up in tears. She spoke bitterly. "You haven't even had a childhood."

Kirk smiled. He walked over to his mom and hugged her. The boy/man looked down into his mother's eyes. "I didn't want one. I'm ready."

Jennifer did not want to let go of her son. She got Kirk to agree to wait one year before entering the program, on his 13th birthday. Dr. Goldman ground his teeth but agreed. Better late than never, he thought.

Kirk spent his last year at home supposedly being home schooled. He and his tutor spent their time playing chess and studying the grandmasters. The tutor taught Kirk all he knew about math and science. Kirk's father took him out hunting and fishing and hiking. The young man grew another two inches.

Space Program

When Kirk was 13 he entered one of the classified Navy programs for gifted children. During testing Kirk's specialty was discovered to be pattern recognition. He was as good at reading the complex interactions between human beings as he was in physical systems. "You have a head for mathematics and geometry, son. You are strong in human relationships and have tested the highest ever in psychic abilities and remote reading. This is most unusual," Dr. Goldman said to him several months into his training. "But you must also prove yourself physically and mentally."

Kirk was flown from the training center in Omaha and driven into the woods in the middle of winter with a backpack and no food. The driver told him, "If you're still alive we'll come pick you up in exactly four weeks."

Kirk Alexander didn't have time to think about the ethics of subjecting a 13-year-old to this. He had done well in previous survival testing at the facility and knew everything that was needed to survive in the open. He considered himself a man, and was grateful that his father was an outdoorsman and hadn't coddled him.

When the vehicle pulled away Kirk felt a sense of elation. He looked into his backpack and found a small tent, a sharp knife, rope, matches, a compass, a .22 rifle with a detached barrel, a box of bullets, a metal cup, and a bag of coffee. There was a stand of trees about a mile away. Kirk began to walk. When he reached the trees he began to cut and weave tree boughs and branches around the base of a large oak tree, forming a snug little shelter. He left an opening he could crawl out of at the back by the base of the tree, covering it with woven branches. He scavenged wood and made a small fire, placing snow and the coffee into his metal cup. The coffee tasted good.

The next day he saw a deer walking through the woods. Carefully he approached it. He didn't want to shoot the deer; it was a beautiful animal. He readied his rifle and lined up his shot. The deer had stopped, staring ahead. Kirk asked it silently if he could have its flesh. He had learned this from his father, who had read him stories of the American indigenous and their relationship to nature. The deer seemed to agree. Before he could squeeze the trigger the animal dropped in its tracks. When Kirk went up to it he saw that it was dead. Awed, he bent over and kissed the animal's side, and blessed it. At that moment Kirk felt a profound connection with something he couldn't identify; a respect for nature and for life. It was a good feeling. He had not had to fire a shot! This connection was to stay with him for the rest of his life.

Kirk cut the dead animal's throat and let it bleed out, as he had seen in the survivalist training videos. He skinned the animal and cut the meat, also saving the liver, the kidneys, and the heart. He packed everything into the hide and dragged it half a mile through the woods in the snow to his little shelter.

He was cold. He collected more branches and kindling and started a fire. This time he hollowed out a patch of ground by digging into it with his knife. He scavenged for wood. He placed two small logs on top of the hollowed out ground and made his fire, building it up to a roaring blaze. Snow was falling; wet snow that would freeze and seal off the gaps in his shelter. Sometimes drops of water would fall into the fire, making a hissing sound. Kirk was pleased. He roasted part of the liver and some of the meat and ate it with a pointed stick. He stored the rest in the hide and wrapped it up. Tomorrow he would collect more wood. He had seen a deadfall about half a mile from his camp. This he would collect and drag back using an improvised sled made of branches. Kirk began to meditate. His belly was full. He said another prayer for the deer and thanked the spirit of the animal once again. When his fire had died down he broke out the small tent and placed it next to the hot ground. Occasionally during the night he fed the fire.

Four weeks later a vehicle approached his camp and his instructor got out.

Kirk closed the flap on his shelter and walked toward the man, the rifle in his hand. He didn't want to leave this place, even though the temperatures had reached below zero Fahrenheit on several occasions. He was young and strong. The meat from the deer had lasted him the entire time, for he did little except meditate, collect wood, and admire the earth as his ancestors must have done. He often stood outside his shelter and just breathed the frozen air. He ate little. He had buried the meat in the frozen ground to preserve it.

The instructor approached him. He entered the shelter, observed what Kirk had done. "You had it easy, kid."

Kirk grinned, agreeing. "It is a good life." He told the story of the deer.

The man's eyes widened. He inspected the rifle and the box of ammo. "Never fired."

From that moment the legend of Kirk Alexander was born.

Almost fifteen years later, Captain Lakshmi Singh/Shara-Li, Captain Kirk Alexander/Wa-hee, Lieutenant Jessica Powell/Lokar (an older soul with over 500 lifetimes), Lieutenant Troy Hawkins/Fulud, and four technicians on loan from the navy's Institute for Space Studies gathered in a briefing room next to a gigantic hangar in an underground installation in the Nevada desert.[29]

The four techs just wanted to get a look at the ship. The four officers sat excitedly, waiting for the legendary Admiral Stan Rogers, the head of the navy's classified space program.

Kirk thought about his 15 years in the navy's classified program. He had been on several missions and had carried them off with varying degrees of success. But this mission, with the launch of the Balthazar, would be the culmination of his 20-year stint. Kirk had learned that there were two space programs: a dumbed-down, public, fossil fuel based program run by NASA, and another with advanced technology. The Balthazar was the razor edge of propulsion systems.

When the admiral entered the room with Dr. Rupert Goldman, the four officers immediately came to their feet. The techs followed after a slight hesitation.

Kirk was a little disappointed at the man's diminutive stature until he spoke in a compelling command voice. "Come out with me ladies and gentlemen," Rogers said.

The eight crew members walked out of the windowless room and into the hangar. Immediately the techs started gabbling. They walked over to a cigar-shaped ship and began feeling the uniformly gray seamless hull. The four navy officers looked at each other with glances that said, "Wow! This ship is ours!"

"Don't mind them sir," Kirk said, pointing to the techs.

Rogers laughed. "They're just scientists. I don't want them to hear this anyway." He pinned Kirk and Lakshmi with his gaze. "Dr. Goldman here will answer any technical questions you have. I'm here to outline your mission." He pointed to the four techs, who were looking for an entrance to the craft. "Those four have already been briefed on their assignments."

Kirk stole a glance at Goldman. The man was stony-faced as usual.

"As you know, our solar system does not end at the orbit of Pluto. It is contained in a spherical object called the Oort Cloud."

Kirk met his fellow captain's eyes excitedly. The four officers almost jumped out of their crew suits. "I knew it!" Troy Hawkins blurted.

Admiral Rogers smiled. "Your mission is to map the Oort Cloud and determine its exact geometry. You are also to map the Hills Cloud, a disk-shaped object inside the Oort. The only thing we know about them is that they are filled with icy planetesimals and are the source of the comets that enter our solar system."

"There must be more to it than that sir," Kirk said. He pointed to the cigar-shaped ship, which looked like a UFO. "Is there something out there?"

The admiral frowned. Rogers was known as a man junior officers could talk to. "That's right son, we think there is. But your mission is purely exploratory. This vehicle is unarmed." Rogers pointed to the four techs, who were still inspecting the ship's hull. "These four clowns Dr. Goldman has selected will assist you." He looked at Goldman. "All four of them are under your command, Captain Singh and Captain Alexander. If you tell them to clean the shitters, they'll hop to it."

Dr. Goldman made a face but did not object.

"This vessel, which we have named the Balthazar, is the most advanced craft on the planet right now. It is the culmination of decades of reverse-engineering crashed ETVs." The admiral's face turned smug. "Let the Air Force with their pitiful fossil-fuel craft patrol the boundaries of earth with their space surveillance crap. They think they're the cream of the crop! We're so far ahead of them they don't even know it."

All four of the naval officers looked at each other and grinned.

"You've all been trained thoroughly on a prototype with the new propulsion system. You know what to do." He looked at Lieutenant Powell. "Navigator, do you have any questions?"

"No sir!" Jessica Powell said. "I just can't wait to get out there."

The admiral's face creased in a smile. "Goddammit, I wish I were 40 years younger."

Rogers looked at Kirk Alexander and Lakshmi Singh standing next to each other. He almost laughed. Alexander was almost 7 feet tall, an imposing physical specimen. Singh was a short, petite woman whose head barely reached Kirk's chest.

"You two are the only ones competent to use the experimental consciousness-assisted con. You are not to deploy it unless the situation is appropriate."

Kirk Alexander met the admiral's eyes for a split instant and nodded his head a half-millimeter in acknowledgment. He couldn't wait to try it out!

Admiral Rogers saw this and smiled to himself. "I don't give a shit what happens to you. Just bring the Balthazar back home safely."

The four officers could feel the love. "YES SIR!!" they all shouted in unison.

Admiral Rogers relaxed. With Alexander in charge he felt confident, even though there were rumors about a hostile presence out there. But of course, there were always rumors. A little healthy paranoia was necessary to keep people on their toes. "Your mission is to test the ship's capabilities and map the Oort. If you see anything else, observe and record."

The four naval officers nodded.

"All right ladies and gentlemen." Rogers shook hands with each officer. When he got to Kirk he murmured, "You lucky bastard." Kirk had the audacity to give the legend a bear hug, which the admiral returned.

Rogers gestured toward the four techs, who had given up trying to find the entrance. "Brisbane! Arakos! LeFarge! Chen! Get your asses over here!"

The four scientists came running over. "Thank you sir!" Chen began to gush "We – "

"Shutup Chen," Rogers said with a smile on his face. "Dr. Goldman here chose you. I had nothing to do with it."

"Yes sir," Chen said. Rogers looked over the four civilians. "You four are the luckiest civilians on the planet. When Alexander, Singh, Powell, or Hawkins here say jump, you jump. When they say bark, you bark. Understand?"

The four techs nodded. Kirk could see they were so excited to get going they were about to shit.

The admiral looked at the four men and four women about to undertake the most exciting mission in the long, glorious history of the United States Navy. "Children, get along and come back safely."

"YES SIR!!"

No one asked Goldman any questions. The man was famous for not divulging information, even to those he was supposed to brief.

Everyone rushed to the craft, a cigar-shaped gray-colored ship with no markings on it. Kirk Alexander pressed his palm on the hull and a portion of it blurred. Kirk stepped though as did the others. The four techs were babbling again.

"Keep it down," Singh said to them. "Go to your consoles."

As Kirk entered he saw a large captain's chair in the forward section. The sides of the command compartment had opaqued transparencies. Next to the captain's chair a second chair had been placed for the co-pilot. Four tech consoles lined one side of the compartment. Two larger consoles occupied the opposite side, one for the navigator and the other for the systems engineer.

Kirk nodded to Singh. "Lakshmi, you have the con."

Captain Singh gazed up at Kirk and smiled. Jessica Powell noticed this and frowned as she walked to her station. It's what always happened when you were the girlfriend of the most desirable man in the navy's special programs.

The four techs went to their mapping stations. They would be responsible for conducting the survey of the Oort and the Hills.

Kirk sat down in the co-captain's chair. Singh (and Jessica) would bring them off the planet and out past the orbit of Jupiter. Then he would take over. Each captain would rotate the con in four hour shifts and was supposed to rest the other four.

The ceiling of the hangar opened. Singh activated the new propulsion system from the captain's console. The ship became enclosed in a grayish-blue bubble. Dr. Goldman told the crew that the new propulsion system created a zone around the ship that made it independent of the surrounding physics. Singh carefully took the craft out and slowly into the open desert sky. It was dark. The craft had no lights and other than a faint grayish-blue light from the bubble, was invisible to the naked eye. The Balthazar soon floated above the earth. The first test was to guide the ship to Lagrange Point 2, ready for launch out into deep space. The ship began to move, or it appeared to the crew that it was moving. They felt nothing inside the craft; there were no inertial forces. The moon, almost directly in-line with their targeted path to L2, rapidly moved toward them and was gone. Singh carefully guided the ship without incident to the launch point, helped by Powell the navigator. They were ready to go! The excitement in the ship was palpable.

Captain Singh spoke. "Jessica, plot a course past Pluto's orbit. Don't hit anything."

Despite her irritation at the woman Jessica giggled. Lakshmi had a sense of humor.

Next to the captain's chair Lakshmi saw a hemispherical grayish-brown substance that looked like latex rubber. This was the new consciousness-assisted prototype that they (might) test later.

Powell looked on her display and brought up a detailed map of the solar system out to the orbit of Pluto. All known asteroids and other objects were clearly marked. The asteroid belt between Mars and Jupiter is a flattened torus, like a thick pancake, so she would take them over the top. "All set captain."

Lakshmi saw the course plotted by the navigator. "Great job Jessica, but I'll still have to be careful."

Kirk smiled. "I'm glad you're doing this and not me."

Lakshmi smiled back. "I'll leave the daredevil stuff to you."

In less than half an hour the globe of Mars became visible.

"If we're independent of the surrounding physics," Jessica said, "does that mean we can't collide with anything?"

"No, Jessica," Kirk replied. "That comes later, if we try it. We're still solid so we have to be careful."

Sophisticated images of the Oort Cloud had been prepared by NASA and the navy's Institute for Space Studies, which were stored in the ship's astro databases. The ship moved past the orbit of Mars and then up and over the circular disc of the asteroid belt.

Jessica moved the focus out and saw that the solar system sits at the center of the Oort Cloud, which contains dwarf planets, asteroids, trojans, centaurs, Kuiper belt objects, and other trans-Neptunian objects. About one million of these objects had been catalogued and were on her display, but thousands of new objects showed up every year. Even so, the sheer volume of space they occupied made the odds of hitting anything remote.

Within an hour Lakshmi and Jessica had taken the Balthazar safely past the orbit of Jupiter.

"It's absurd of course," Lakshmi said. "Two hours to Jupiter!"

"We're still thinking in terms of fossil-fuel craft," Kirk said.

"Should be all clear," Jessica said. "Past the asteroid belt now."

"We didn't see anything," Kirk complained. "Not even an asteroid!"

"None of the other planets are anywhere near our course," Jessica responded.

"We got to see a little of Mars at least," Kirk said. "I wanted to see if that face at Cydonia is really there, or is it just bullshit."

"We've got more exciting things to do," Lakshmi said. "My shift is over. Kirk, you have the con."

Kirk rose and sat in the chair. It was a bit small for him, but he crunched himself down. The next step was to get to the orbit of Pluto, which was almost 4 billion miles from their present position. Two more shifts of four hours each and they were ready to go to the Hills Cloud and begin mapping. The four techs, John Brisbane, George Arakos, Sylvia Chen, and Deirdre LeFarge, tweaked their mapping software and tested their systems. Lieutenant Hawkins, the systems engineer, had been busy testing the ship's on-board life support and the other engineering systems.

"Jessica, how far do we have to go?"

"The outer border of the Hills Cloud is about 20,000 AU from our present position. We are now approximately 41 AU from sol."[30]

"Holy shit." Kirk made a quick calculation. "40 AU in ten hours! That's over one-half the speed of light! We've noticed no relativistic effects."

Jessica snorted. "What did Nikola Tesla say about relativity? A beggar in a purple robe masquerading as a king?"

Hawkins spoke for the first time. "I don't care how we did it, the system works."

"Spoken like a true engineer," Jessica said.

"It works so far Hawk," Kirk said. "To get to the Hills Cloud we have to travel almost one-third of a light year!"

The techs were getting bored. It had been 10 hours since the trip began. Their job didn't start until they started mapping the Hills Cloud. "Let the ladies rest first," George Arakos said. "John and I will stand watch for the next 12- hour shift."

"Fuck that," Sylvia Chen said. "I'm not tired."

John looked at George and Deirdre. He was the senior tech. "All right. You two stayed up all night partying. You two go, Sylvia and I will stay on watch."

George smiled gratefully. "Thanks boss, I'm dead tired." George and Deirdre trooped out of the forward section and to their bunks at the rear of the ship.

"You want to take a break Lakshmi?" Kirk asked. She had just finished her four hour shift at the con.

"No. I want to watch you try the CAT. I can tell you're about ready to burst."

CAT was the name for consciousness assisted technology, the absolute cutting-edge of science. Rupert Goldman told him it wasn't science at all, but some kind of super-advanced tech they had gotten from a crashed ship. He wouldn't say anything else about it. Kirk placed a soft, hemispherical template over his head. The stuff felt good; it molded itself to his head. The CAT interfaced with the ship and moved it via the thought impulses of the operator. You had to be damn good at visualization with no sidebands of random thought. Otherwise the ship went nowhere. He and Lakshmi Singh were the only two persons in the service who had been able to get the CAT to work. In practice.

He remembered what Goldberg had said when he asked him how it worked. "None of your damn business son. Your job, and the other captain, is to give this baby a workout."

"Jessica, calculate a course. Show us where we are and where we need to go."

The display at the front of the forward compartment showed their present position 2 AU outside the orbit of Pluto. Their destination was 20,000 AU away, marked with a red dot. Even at the rate they had been traveling it would take 231 days just to get to the edge of the Hills. That speed was much too slow to map the Oort.

Kirk studied Jessica's displays and her course calculations. In his mind, he created a crystal-clear visualization of the destination and the ship's present position. This is what his training had been about. Goldman explained it to him one time. "The CAT will only be activated by a perfect mental image with no sidebands, of sufficient power. You have to know your exact location and the destination. Then you move your mind in the mental image to the destination." Kirk did so. Instantly the bubble around the ship intensified and the stars completely disappeared.

"What the fuck?" Hawkins said.

Kirk was amazed. They were suspended in...something. They couldn't see outside the bubble they were in.

"Jessica, do you have any idea where we are?"

"Not a clue captain. My instruments show we're...nowhere."

Kirk gulped. Well, he had done it. He kept his intention and visualization on the destination.

Fifteen minutes later, ship time, the stars reappeared. Ahead of them faint

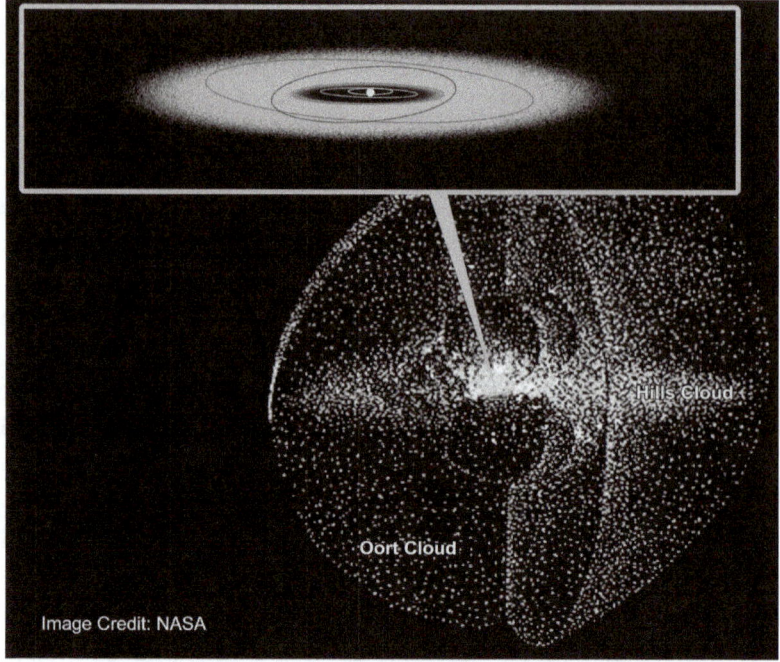

Image Credit: NASA

light in the shape of a disk could be discerned. "My God captain," Jessica said. "We are 1.5 AU from...the Hills I think."

"Firm that up navigator."

The crew broke out into a spontaneous cheer. "Great work captain!" "Kirk you did it!" "Mind-blowing!" The ship had traveled almost 20,000 AU, about one-third of a light year, in a quarter of an hour.

Kirk was stunned. Whatever technology this is, it sure as hell didn't come from earth.

Jessica looked at her readings. They were above a circumstellar disk; a pancake-shaped accumulation of matter. Jessica showed the cylindrical coordinates on the display and a red dot. They were 1237 AU above the Hills Cloud, on the edge of it.

"Wow!" Lakshmi said. The entire crew looked with awe at what earth astronomers called the Hills Cloud. It was a flattened disk filled with planetesimals and other ices, but it was surrounded by a faint light that began at the ends and got larger at the center.

"How are we going to map this thing?" Lakshmi asked.

"Leave that to us," Sylvia said. "We need 12 points in an icosahedral formation above, below, and around the object."

"All right John, you and Sylvia calculate the coordinates and send them to Jessica," Kirk said. "Jessica, you display them one at a time. I'll try to duplicate what I did before."

Everyone went to work. Lakshmi was tired now but wouldn't miss this for the world.

John and Sylvia had a good idea of the precise extent of the Hills Cloud, based on their present position above the flattened torus, and astronomical maps in the ship's astro database. Their instruments were able to detect its dimensions accurately enough for calculations.

"The major axis of the Hills is approximately 20,000 AU," Sylvia said. She marked the outline of the object on the display. Around it she placed an icosahedron with 12 vertices. "These 12 points are where we take our measurements." A great icosahedron appeared over the Hills object on the display.

"We'll travel from vertex to vertex, the distance is the same each time," John said. "We are here." He indicated a point above the "equator" of the object.

John calculated the first coordinate and put it on the display, marked with a big red dot. "Can you take us there, captain, with this minimalist information? The distance for each of these points is 1.051462224 times the semi-major axis of the Hills, which is 10,137 AU. That's a distance of 10,659 AU."

"Close enough for government work," Hawkins joked.

"I did almost 20,000 AU before," Kirk said. "I don't see why not."

Lakshmi spoke suddenly. "What's that?"

A big blue sphere had appeared directly in front of them.

"Jessica, what is that thing?" Kirk asked.

"Don't know captain. It's sitting about two miles from us. No readings from the object at all."

"How did it get there?"

"It...appeared suddenly. I wonder if it has the same technology we do."

Kirk studied the object. "Lakshmi, does it look hostile?"

"Not to me. Crew?"

The object was motionless with respect to the Balthazar. It was simply a smooth blue sphere, with no inserts or projections that would indicate weaponry. It glowed a little. Everyone agreed that the blue sphere showed no hostile intent.

Kirk shrugged. "To hell with it. We're going to continue." Kirk studied the position of the first mapping coordinate and their present position relative to the Hills. "OK, here we go."

The ship's space-time bubble intensified. The stars disappeared. Within 5 minutes the Balthazar popped out into space. Jessica knew the drill.

"You hit it perfectly," she said. They would travel around the perimeter of the Hills Cloud in a zig-zag pattern, first above it, around it, and then below it. John Brisbane, the chief tech, had determined that the best mapping would occur when the icosahedral pattern was standing flat on one of its triangles relative to the center of the Hills toroid.

"Six mapping points along the perimeter, 3 above and 3 below the flattened torus, captain," Sylvia Chen said.

"All right John and Sylvia, do your survey. "We're at the first mapping point, right?"

"Correct captain."

At that moment George Arakos and Dierdre LeFarge walked in. Kirk checked the ship's chronometer. "We've all been going now for 14 hours." Kirk grinned at Lakshmi. "Somebody should have ordered somebody with an inflated ego to get some shut-eye."

"I was too excited."

"Me too."

"Look!" Jessica shouted.

The blue sphere had appeared in front of the ship again.

"What the fuck?" Hawkins said.

"How big are those things?" Kirk asked Jessica.

"About a mile in diameter."

"Holy shit."

Kirk was beginning to feel his energy draining. He turned to Lakshmi. "How are you doing?"

"Fine. It's been fun watching you do all the work. Can you take out the garbage too?"

Jessica watched this little interplay with a frown on her face. It was clear that Kirk and Lakshmi liked each other a lot. They had trained together as pilots. She wondered whether it went any further than that, but she laughed at the joke with everyone else.

"Can you take over here?" Kirk asked Lakshmi. "I'm going to have to rest. Losing my edge."

"Sure. I'll stay at the con for a four hour shift. Sylvia and John, you guys get some rest. You too, Hawkins and Jessica. Deirdre and George can do the survey."

"What happens if that blue thing attacks?" Hawkins asked.

Kirk laughed. "If that happens Lakshmi will take us out of here. Or we'll all be dead. I don't think anything will happen."

"We're weaponless anyway," Lakshmi said.

Hawkins shrugged and walked out of the forward compartment to his bunk. Kirk put his arm around Jessica's shoulders. "C'mon, let's get a little rest."

Jessica smiled up at him as they walked to their bunks. "We could do more than that."

Kirk smiled and shook his head. "Not here. But wait 'till we get back home."

"All right."

Sylvia and John showed the other two techs what had been done. Both were amazed at the ship's capabilities. Lakshmi jerked her finger back toward the sleeping quarters. "It's mostly him. The guy is amazing."

George smiled. "You'll get your turn pretty soon."

The two techs got onto their consoles and began the survey. "This will take about an hour," Deirdre said.

While the techs busied themselves Lakshmi studied the blue sphere hovering motionless in front of the ship. There was no movement, no activity. The Balthazar had no lights, no way to signal. Oh well. They couldn't defend themselves anyway.

An hour later Deirdre signaled that she and George had finished their mapping. "Onward!" George said. He displayed the next coordinate along the perimeter of the Hills Cloud.

"Rotate the display to show where we will be at the next coordinate."

George shifted the display. Lakshmi saw where she had to go. "Now back to our present position."

"Good, thank you George."

Lakshmi put the template over her head. This technology was part electronic, part biology. It was totally beyond her understanding. But she had done it before with a test ship. She burned their present position and the destination into her mind and moved her mind to the destination point. The blue sphere was left behind but the sphere of light around the ship had not intensified, as it had done when Kirk used the CAT. After about ten minutes the stars disappeared and the bubble formed around the ship.

Lakshmi sat calmly with the destination firmly in mind. She did not worry about "how long it is taking."

An hour later the ship popped out into normal space.

"Right on the button Lakshmi," Deirdre said.

The captain was elated. I did it! She wanted to put her arms around Kirk but he wasn't here. She wondered whether he and Jessica were fooling around. "All right you guys. Let me know when you've finished."

Lakshmi got them to two more mapping points. Each time more of the blue spheres appeared. Now there were four of them.

Kirk walked in with Jessica, who took her nav station.

"Those things are still following us Lakshmi?"

"Yup. Each time we map from another coordinate there are more of them."

"I have an idea about that."

Lakshmi got up from the con. "I'm exhausted. I'm going to my bunk."

Kirk sat in the chair. "George, put up the next mapping point."

Kirk studied this for almost a minute. Then he put on the headgear. Instantly the ship's bubble firmed up and the stars disappeared. In less than 5 seconds they had traversed almost 11,000 AU.

"I can't fucking believe it," Deirdre said. "You nailed it."

Now there were five spheres. "I thought so. Whatever these things are, they are trying to communicate. The spheres are arranged in the same geometry as our survey points."

"Hell's bells," George said. "You're right!"

Kirk was beyond amazement now at the capabilities of this ship. He just accepted it. "All right boys and girls. We're going to finish mapping the Hills and the Oort. Then we're going for a ride."

Everybody understood. Jessica practically jumped out of her chair in excitement. "George, can you speed up the surveying process?"

"Yes ma'am, I think so. We know what we're doing now." Half an hour later they were ready for the sixth mapping point. Kirk was able to deliver them in four seconds this time. A sixth blue sphere appeared.

"Fuck the spheres," Kirk said. The techs did their survey from the new point.

"The next coordinate is above the Hills," Deirdre told Kirk. The coordinate was displayed and Kirk took them there in 3.5 seconds. It became a game and the crew started taking bets. The spheres were ignored; there were seven of them now. The next point was reached one-half hour later in less than 3 seconds. The other four mapping points were reached and surveyed. Kirk had their "travel" down to less than one second to each point. It was absurd; outrageous. Kirk was the oldest, but the crew were young; all in their 20s. They were having a blast.

There were now 13 blue spheres in the shape of an icosahedron, with a larger one at the center.

Lakshmi came back on duty just as the last mapping point had been surveyed. "I don't believe it! You got them all?" She looked up at the big man in awe.

John Brisbane and Sylvia Chen walked in. They had a full complement now on duty.

"We'll stay here for now," Kirk said, nodding to Lakshmi. "Techies, do your thing. Show us what the Hills Cloud looks like."

All four survey techs got busy compiling their survey data and imagery. Kirk looked out the transparency. Even though the Hills Cloud is filled with billions of ices they were spaced few and far between in the volume of space it occupied. All Kirk saw was empty space. Kirk knew that the Balthazar had not been traveling through space when the CAT was used. Was this thing going into a higher dimension and folding spacetime? That would explain the almost instantaneous "travel" to distant 3-dimensional points. He made a mental note to demand an explanation from Dr. Goldman.

Kirk turned off his mind and sat motionless in his swiveled command chair. About an hour later a voice was heard. "Holy shit captain!"

"Yes LeFarge."

Deirdre put the completed survey on the big display at the front of the vessel.

No one said anything. It was the most breathtaking thing they had ever seen.

"The whole thing is pulsing sir. The Hills is a torus, with a faint energy cloud surrounding it."

"It's alive," Jessica said.

The Hills Cloud, like the earth, was a living, breathing entity.

Kirk's entire worldview changed in that moment. There was something monumental, a higher power, that created matter and energy and sustained life. That was the only explanation for what they were seeing.

He spoke to the crew. "Techs, display the Oort simulation. Our next stop is the boundary of the Oort Cloud!"

John Brisbane spoke. "We were able to get a good idea of the extent of the Oort from our surveys. It's a gigantic dimpled sphere about 120,000 AU from sol."

Jessica was amazed. "That's 2 ly out Kirk."

Everyone knew that the nearest star was only 4.37 light years out. Kirk was elated. The stars were in reach!

Kirk looked at the soft, hemispherical template they called the CAT. He coordinated with Jessica and the survey techs. "Display the first Oort mapping point." The Oort contained the Hills within it, so they had to travel even greater distances to map it.

Brisbane showed their present position and the outer boundary of the Oort Cloud, their first destination point.

"Distance, 65,000 AU from our present position."

Kirk glanced at the display. The spherical coordinates of the destination were also shown. He had a perfect idea where he was going from the simulation: one light year from their present position inside the Oort. Kirk placed the CAT over his head and did his thing. Within 10 seconds the ship popped back into space (from wherever it had been). The blue spheres were still with them. He had almost forgotten them in the excitement of moving this ship through incredible distances.

"I saw it but I don't believe it." Lakshmi said. "One light year in ten seconds?"

"That's the thing Lakshmi," Kirk said. "Distance and time are irrelevancies to the CAT. It's incredible."

"Dr. Goldman has some explaining to do," Jessica said. "This system is way beyond the science we know."

Kirk looked over at her and smiled.

They were on the periphery of the Oort Cloud now, 125,000 AU out from the sun. The planetesimals and ices were all "inside" the Oort. They were over two light years out, almost half the distance to the nearest star. The techs did their surveying.

"Coordinates calculated, captain," George Arakos said from his console. A model of the Oort Cloud was shown on the big display, with all 12 survey points shown in the shape of an icosahedron. "Show me the next one."

Sylvia Chen did the math. "The Oort is basically a sphere with a diameter of 125,000 AU and a radius of 62,500 AU. The distance between each survey point in the icosahedral mapping pattern was 65,716.4 AU, or over 1 light year.

"I already did that!" Kirk said cheerfully. He studied it until he was sure. Kirk did not think of speed or distance now. Working with this fantastic technology had expanded his mental horizons beyond science and into the metaphysical. His pure intention was to have the ship arrive safely. He knew precisely where he was going and he gave pure intent to BE there.

Again the stars disappeared and the ship was surrounded by a swirling grayish-blue mist. Inside the ship all was normal. Within five seconds the bubble disappeared and the stars were again visible.

"Navigator, where are we?"

Jessica checked her instruments. "65,716.4 AU from our previous position."

The crew looked at each other and began cheering and clapping. Everybody congratulated Kirk. "One light year in 5 seconds!" Jessica shook her head. "It's impossible."

"I didn't do anything," Kirk said. "This ship is amazing!" Everyone agreed.

"Are those blue orbs still with us?" Kirk asked.

"Affirmative captain," Jessica said. "Behind us now."

"Maybe they're friendly."

The navigator and the other astro techies began the mapping. The next mapping position was recalculated just to make sure.

Kirk took them to each one almost instantly.

In ten hours they had mapped the entire Oort Cloud. He was tired now and would have to take a full 8-hour rest period.

Captain Singh arrived for her duty period after taking a four hour break. Kirk stuck around to watch as a model of the entire Oort Cloud and Hills Cloud was shown on the gigantic display.

Everyone gasped when they saw it. A sphere of light surrounded a flattened torus in the middle of the Oort, at the equator. Light was coming through the middle of the torus and then out to the periphery.

"By God," Kirk said. "It looks alive, just like the Hills."

"It's the most beautiful thing I ever saw," Singh said.

"Toroidal geometry," Hawkins said.

The crew were mesmerized. The Oort, which contained the solar system as a very small ring at the center, was encased in a cocoon of soft, pulsing light.

"I wonder if the other star systems are like this," LeFarge said.

"By God lieutenant," Kirk said to Jessica. "We can take this ship out to Alpha Centauri."

Lakshmi laughed. "*You* can take it out to Alpha Centauri!"

The crew was awed at the possibility. "We're out here on our own," Deirdre spoke persuasively. "Our mission is exploratory."

Everyone could see the captain was fired up. "I'm a little tired right now. I need a full eight hours rest period. Lakshmi, if you want to try it go ahead. But wake me up when we get there."

"I'll pass on that for now Kirk. Go and get some rest, all of you. I'll stay at the con and let you know if anything happens."

It was agreed. Everyone except Lakshmi trooped back to their bunks.

The blue spheres were still with them, but no one worried about them anymore.

When Kirk came back eight hours later everyone was at their consoles. The Oort survey was still displaying on the screen, from each survey point. The crew could hardly keep from staring at it.

Captain Singh looked up at Kirk from the con. "As I recall, you were about to take the ship to Alpha Centauri?"

The crew sat up in their chairs.

Kirk nodded.

"Can you do it?"

Kirk thought about it. It had been a great idea just before he went to bed, but was it realistic? Then he knew. "I'm certain."

He spoke with such authority the crew believed him. "Take us there, Captain Kirk."

Everybody laughed.

Singh gave up her chair and stood behind Kirk as he got back in.

"Are you ready?" he asked the crew. "If anyone has any objections we don't go."

All seven of the crew smiled. Kirk Alexander had a way of inspiring confidence in human beings.

"Jessica, can you calculate a path to the Alpha system? I don't want to put us inside a star."

Jessica laughed. "Sure captain. I'd recommend a position 2 AU from Alpha Centauri. We can take short hops from there if we want to do some exploring."

"Hawkins, when Jessica is finished, put it on the display."

Kirk waited silently, unmoving, preparing for the historic jaunt. Lakshmi stood behind, watching Kirk. He had the aspect of a Buddha, she thought. Completely relaxed, confident, a slight smile on his face.

Finally it was done. "All right captain, here it is," Jessica said. "The Alpha system is actually a triple star. Alpha A and B orbit around each other. There is a pallid third star, Alpha C, a red dwarf. C is loosely gravitationally bound and is presently orbiting the other two at a distance of about 13,000 AU. C is on the other side of us now. Alpha B is currently orbiting 11.9 AU away from Alpha A. Alpha A is the closest to our present position."

The Oort Cloud was pictured, the ship relative to it, and the triple star system, 4.37 light years from sol and approximately 2.37 ly from the ship's present position. Kirk studied the display and memorized the position of ship and the three stars. Hawkins indicated a big red dot 2 AU from Alpha A on the screen. "Here's the target."

"Are those blue orbs still hanging around?"

"One still there, sir. Doesn't exhibit any hostile intent."

"What do you say boys and girls? Should we see what this baby can do?"

Everyone was shouting now. "Hell yes captain!" "Let's go!" "Step on it!"

Kirk grinned. "I'll take that as a yes. I'm ready. Everybody get set. Captain Singh, please strap in."

Lakshmi took a seat next to the captain's. Kirk put the headpiece on. He had now done this 22 times previously, maneuvering them around the Hills and the Oort. He was ready. He visualized the ship at its present position, the star, and the destination relative to Alpha Centauri. He moved his mind to the destination point.

The stars disappeared. The ship was surrounded by a grayish-blue mist in the form of a sphere. After about a minute of ship's time the stars reappeared. The ship was hovering in the blackness of space.

Kirk wondered what the hell these engineers had done, and who they were. The CAT wasn't a propulsion system at all; it seemed to be an interface between the space-time fabric and the consciousness of the operator. "Navigator, where are we?"

"2 AU from Alpha Centauri A, captain," Lieutenant Powell reported. "Alpha A straight ahead." They could all see a dot of light in the forward transparency.

Hawkins pointed to the red dot. "Right on target sir!"

The crew let out a cheer. It felt like they had just won the Super Bowl. They were the first human beings to reach the stars! There was excited chatter for several minutes.

"Kirk, we just traveled almost 2 light years in about 1 minute," Captain Singh said with admiring eyes. "How is that possible?"

Jessica, at her nav station, frowned. Her boyfriend was like a magnet for both women and men.

Kirk was excited. "This ship doesn't travel as we understand it Lakshmi," he said, smiling at his petite companion. "We have to stop thinking in terms of space and distance. I think the galaxy and the planets and the stars are just metadata within a holographic information space."

"Wow." Captain Singh was now openly admiring. Hawkins, at his console, and the other two men at their stations grinned at Jessica Powell.

Hawkins spoke. "Captain, there's one of those blue orbs out there."

"Position?"

"Same as before. Two miles from us."

"I'll move us toward it slowly. Let's see what it does."

At that moment the orb began to move rapidly toward the ship.

"Brace for impact!" Kirk said. The orb hit the side of the hull...and moved through it.

An eight-foot tall humanoid stood just to the left of the captain's chair. The crew stared at the creature, who had leathery green skin, feathers coming backward out of its head, and hands and feet that ended in claws. The eyes were large, an intense blue. The mouth was small, the nose, slits above the mouth.

"What the hell?" Kirk said.

"I am RA," the creature said. "From seventh density."

"What planet is that?" Hawkins asked.

175

The creature bent over. It looked like he was laughing. "Oh dear ones, that was funny."

Jessica and the others heard a voice in their heads; the creature wasn't moving his mouth. "What is seventh density?" she asked.

RA shrugged. "Higher dimension." The creature closed his eyes. "I see you have discovered the galactic interface technology." Each of the crew felt their minds being probed. "There is very little distortion here."

"Distortion?"

"Your planet is in the process of overcoming the duality en route to graduate status. Your planet is filled with meme and psychic distortions."

"That's right," Kirk said.

"You are protected," RA said.

"Protected?" Hawkins asked.

"A graduate race is looking after you."

"I don't understand," Kirk said.

"The duality you are experiencing on your planet does not end at the border of your atmosphere. Those planets who seek the One must have protection from those of lower consciousness."

"We're of lower consciousness," Jessica said, thinking about all the hatred and contention on the planet.

RA laughed again. "Quite right! Third dimension, haven't yet discovered the cosmic web. But you will."

"Cosmic web?" Sylvia asked.

"The implicate order; that which programs and maintains the universes and dimensions. Holds the galaxies together, a source of almost infinite energy. When you get that your entire perspective will change. You are on your way now."

RA looked around at the ship. "Impressive."

"What are you doing here?" Kirk asked.

"Keeping an eye out. I promised Bummamanipum-Bu and Hummhumm-Li I would look out for you."

Jessica was annoyed. "Who are they?"

"Your Pleiadian friends. They watch over you."

"We're not children!" Hawkins said. "And how did you get in here?"

RA smiled. "Dear ones, you are children. But children who are growing up. You will soon have a choice between AI and biological development. How you choose will determine the future of your race."

"So tell us," Troy said. "Don't keep us in the dark."

RA smiled. "I have already said too much. You must choose."

Jessica was about ready to ask another question when RA held out his hand. A calmness was felt in the minds of the humans.

"I shall be going now."

Kirk watched as a blue bubble formed around RA. Then the bubble went through the hull and out into space. The crew watched through the transparencies as the bubble turned bright white and disappeared.

"What the hell was that?" Arakos said. "This isn't my father's space program."

"Amen to that George," Kirk said. "I think we have fulfilled our mission admirably. Let's go home."

All were in agreement. Captain Singh spoke. She was technically the duty officer. "How will we get home Kirk?" Her eyes were bright.

Kirk got it. "Holy shit. You're right Lakshmi. At faster-than-light speeds the ship doesn't travel through space at all, we've seen that numerous times now. The CAT somehow pops us out and then pops us back in. I can take us directly to Lagrange Point 2, just outside the earth."

Lakshmi nodded her agreement and Kirk gave her a big smile and a hug. Captain Singh disappeared for a moment until Kirk released her.

"Wow," she said. Everybody grinned except for Lieutenant Powell.

"Jessica, show us where we're going. I want a precise distance and a course calculated, even though we probably don't need it."

Jessica talked with the techs. She had to work out a celestial reference frame from Alpha A to Lagrange Point 2 near the earth, the Balthazar's present position, and the best path. "This is a lot harder than closing your eyes and thinking!" she said.

After Jessica and the four techs were done, John Brisbane put everything on the screen. They were just beneath the sphere of the Oort. A course through the Oort and back to earth was shown with a dotted line.

"That's great guys. Give me a moment."

Kirk studied the display until he had complete certainty about what he was doing. He placed the CAT over his head. "Here goes."

As usual, the stars disappeared almost instantly. The blue sphere intensified around the ship, a bluish-gray mist appeared. After 65 seconds the ship popped back into space.

"There it is!" Lakshmi cried. "Earth! Jessica, where are we?"

"L2," Jessica said, unbelieving.

The crew broke out in a great cheer. "We're home!" Sylvia Chen cried, putting her arms around Troy Hawkins. Troy didn't mind this at all.

"No blue spheres," Jessica said.

Hawkins spoke. "What did that RA guy say, 'I see you have discovered the galactic interface technology.'"

"Yeah, he also said we haven't discovered the cosmic web yet," Jessica replied. "Whatever that is."

Kirk hit his palm on his knee. "Dammit, I'm going to get some answers when we get home."

Everyone laughed at that. "You might as well try ice fishing for a hippopotamus," Lakshmi said. "Goldman and those boys are keeping a tight lid on this."

"I'm certain now that the CAT goes beyond the comprehension of the best navy scientists. Goldman has been tight-lipped because he doesn't understand how it works. You know how he is, the grumpy bastard. He always thinks he's the smartest guy in the room."

"I agree," Lakshmi said. "Not being able to understand the CAT must really be pissing him off." She made a sour face that was so close to Dr. Goldman's everyone cracked up.

"God Lakshmi, you should be a comedian," Kirk said appreciatively.

"Of the best and the brightest in the navy only two human beings, one woman and one man, has been able to operate the CAT," Hawkins said. He pointed to the two captains. "All are aboard this ship. It simply will not work for everyone else who has tried it. Nothing happens at all. So what good is it?"

Kirk's eyes softened in admiration for this insight. "Correct, Hawk! It's not the technology that's the problem. It's us."

Lieutenant Hawkins looked startled. "Wow. Maybe you're right cap. Maybe this...technology...is benign. Maybe you have to have your head in the right place for it to work."

"I think you nailed it Hawk. We have to improve ourselves. The CAT is a good test for human progress."

The crew was silent for a minute, contemplating that.

Kirk turned to Captain Singh. "Lakshmi, take us in. I'm good at the brute force stuff, but we need someone who can actually fly this thing."

Lakshmi jumped up hoping for another hug, but Kirk had walked behind the con to the co-captain's chair.

Captain Singh expertly guided the ship back to the hangar. They had been gone 48 hours ship's time. It was completely dark in the Nevada desert. The hangar opened and swallowed the ship.

George Arakos was upset when he walked into John Brisbane's private area after the ship landed. "You're sending a secret encoded message to a cellular network.

Totally verboten."

John shrugged. "A private cell network. How else can I inform the president?"

"It's not your fuckin' job to inform anyone of anything. If I don't stop you we'll both be shitcanned."

Brisbane straightened. "I haven't sent it yet. Leave. You'll never know if I did or not. I might be having second thoughts."

Arakos angrily stomped out of the room, muttering.

Brisbane activated the transponder in his personal message center. "Ship to Alpha A. Oort mapped. FTL. Kirk Alexander Neo. Total success.".

The message would go to his Uncle Charlie, a retired navy intelligence officer who had the ear of the president. John was a big fan of Frank Conrad. No way this great man could be out of the loop. If he got busted so be it.

Captain Alexander and Captain Singh reported to Dr. Goldman and Admiral Rogers. Jessica wanted to go too, but the captains had to report first and together for their debrief.

After it was over Admiral Rogers was elated and flabbergasted. "There's only one drawback to your mission, captains. Kirk is the only one who can use the CAT so expertly, is that correct?"

Lakshmi nodded. "I think I can get better though."

"Any problem with the FTL propulsion component?"

"None sir," Lakshmi said. She looked up at Kirk. "That's something I can do a lot better than this clumsy oaf."

Rogers was thoughtful for a moment. "All right captains, you've done a great job. Now it is my pleasure to turn you over to Dr. Goldman."

Lakshmi and Kirk groaned.

"Don't pout! You two have had the greatest adventure ever in the history of the human race! Just think of those poor fossil-fuel astronauts who are excited about going to Mars one day."

Admiral Rogers left. Before Goldman could call in a medical team to examine them Kirk turned on him. "You've got some explaining to do. The CAT isn't technology at all. The Balthazar didn't travel through space, it entered a kind of multi-dimensional warp."

Goldman smiled sardonically. "That's right Alexander."

"So how does it work?"

Goldman grimaced. "I haven't the smallest idea. And neither does anyone else."

Lakshmi and Kirk turned and looked at each other and said, "What the fuck?" simultaneously.

"If you don't know how it works how did you build it?" Kirk asked.

"We didn't build it. We found it."

The two captains couldn't think of anything to say.

"About 20 years ago we were doing some underground reflection tomography in Antarctica. We found a huge underground cavern with several bodies and artifacts from what looked like an underground civilization. Not from this planet. The Balthazar was one of those artifacts." Goldman grimaced. "We also found one of them in an underground tunnel on the Nazca plain in South America."

"Working ships?"

"Yes. We built in the electronics and life support systems to suit our purposes, and added a power plant for the electronics. We figured out the FTL stuff, it's on every ETV we have inspected. But the CAT is technology that we haven't been able to duplicate. Fortunately it works with humans."

Kirk remembered his experiences using the CAT. "After using that thing a couple dozen times I'm sure that the CAT is an interface between consciousness and the underlying physics of spacetime."

Dr. Goldman snapped his fingers. "Of course! Thank you Kirk, you've given me an idea."

Kirk spoke again. "If this thing works with humans, and it wasn't designed for humans, then life in this galaxy must all be similar."

Lakshmi's jaw dropped. So did Dr. Rupert Goldman's. Kirk and Lakshmi were astonished when the somber Goldman broke out into a brilliant smile. "That is profound Kirk, thank you. Maybe you're right."

Goldman walked out of the room.

"I guess our debrief is finished," Lakshmi said. "They can get everything from the ship's logs and recorders. Want to get out of here before the med team starts poking and prying us like fish sticks?"

Kirk laughed. "You're really cute Lakshmi."

"I'm a lot more than that," she said, wiggling her torso.

"I like you a lot. But I'm committed."

"All right Kirk. Just letting you know."

The med team arrived and conversation stopped.

When Kirk Alexander completed his service in the navy's classified space program he was 33 years old. He had a PhD in mathematics, and could say absolutely nothing to anyone about his service. His CO had given him a shore story to tell the curious.

Kirk went home with the look of eagles. It is said that battle hardened veterans have this look, a countenance of wisdom and confidence gained from skills learned in the most trying environments. Kirk was now one-half inch under seven feet, a mental and physical giant.

He returned home to his mother and father in Birmingham, a suburb of Detroit. His father, six inches over six feet, looked up into his face proudly. The nature of his work was such that Kirk could not have communicated or visited his family during his time of service. Kirk had intense blue eyes, long copper hair in a pony tail, and a chiseled but handsome face. When he smiled his eyes sparkled.

"Son, I'm proud of you," Ralph told him, gazing intently into his son's eyes. "I'm good at reading people Kirk. You seem to be well balanced psychologically. I was worried about that."

"I was trained well. To support and defend. All that jazz."

Ralph noticed his son's graceful but purposeful movements, which spoke of intense training.

Kirk approached his mother, who was staring at him in awe. "My God son. You're...magnificent."

Kirk burst out laughing.

"Are you married?"

Kirk laughed again. "No ma'am. The nature of my work did not allow it."

His parents were all ears as Kirk explained the (non-classified) nature of his work. "Men and women in my unit worked alongside each other. We developed exotic propulsion systems, just as Dr. Goldman promised. We used these craft to travel...into the solar system. But fraternization was not encouraged, even though strong bonds were formed."

His parents accepted this without comment. Both had been told something about the navy's space program to quiet their curiosity.

Jennifer smiled. "I can't imagine young men and women working beside each other without having urges."

Kirk smiled. "For that there was shore leave. With us it was strictly business."

"Do you have a girlfriend?"

"A colleague of mine and I have talked about things." Kirk brought out a picture of a blond woman with a pony tail and a striking face. "This is Jessica Powell. Astrophysicist. We hit it on well and are thinking of living together when she gets out."

Jennifer was curious. "What's she like?"

"I hope you will meet her. She still has another year and a half. Unless she finds someone else of course."

Jennifer frowned. "Not the loyal type. That speaks of deficient character."

Kirk grinned. "You won't say that when you meet her. Besides, it's a good test. Let's say that those in my unit are...the cream of the crop. Highly developed humans both physically and mentally."

"You speak oddly, stranger," Ralph said. Both men burst out laughing.

It was an old joke between them; a science fiction movie about a man who returns from the future and confronts his old friends.

"There is another."

"Another?"

Kirk brought out a pic of Lakshmi Singh, his fellow captain.

"A tiny little thing isn't she?" Jennifer said.

"Yeah, but a great sense of humor. One to ride the river with. I'd be happy with either of them."

"Heartbreaker!" Jennifer smiled at her son affectionately.

When he went to bed that night in his old bedroom Kirk/Wa-hee began to think about his experiences with the CAT. Kirk stayed up all night reading about the Stanford Research Institute and their investigations into remote viewing and psychic phenomena. Especially interesting was a declassified paper by Wayne McDonnell of the Army's Intelligence and Security Command, based on the work of the Russian physicist Isaak Bentov. This paper described the relationship between human consciousness and something called the universal hologram. "Contrary to what everyone knows is so, it may not be the brain that produces consciousness – but rather, consciousness that creates the appearance of the brain."

One thing was clear: no one knew anything for certain about human consciousness. After his experiences with the CAT he rejected a purely materialist explanation. Consciousness may interface with the brain, but there must be something more. There was something more to a human being than just the body, he had discovered that on the Balthazar...

The next morning he wondered what he would do for the rest of his life. What could he do that wouldn't bore him to death after his exploits in the space service?

In order to operate in society he needed money. Preferably lots of it. What's the fastest way to make money? In the markets. Kirk grinned as he thought of the challenge. Day trading. You could lose your shirt or make millions.

He would give himself precisely one year from today to make his fortune. He envisioned a big house, like a fortress of solitude. Some place in a city, downtown. Gated. Really high ceilings, lots of glass. Wood on the inside, steel on the outside. Jessica and Hawk and Lakshmi were getting out in 18 months. By that time, he promised himself, he would be independently wealthy. They would get the team back together and make a difference in the world. All that day Kirk studied quantitative analysis, trading, and the mathematics of market movement. Kirk fell asleep thinking about algorithms and the markets.

The next day Kirk woke up with a purpose. He put off deciding what the team would do. For that he could talk to his CO, Bonsey Jones. He remembered his exit interview just a few days ago.

"Jonsey, what am I going to do after I get out?"

Captain Jones laughed. "You could be an old dog like me, still working in the space service in an administrative capacity. For me it's addicting. I still want to be a part of it even though I can no longer be up there."

Kirk thought about it. "Nah. Too boring."

Bonsey laughed. "I was hoping you'd say that." He looked Kirk in the eye. "Those who have served in the elite programs always have access within the service. We spent a lot of money training you. We often find work for our best officers in the civilian sector."

"Now you're talking Jonesey. I'm in. I want to get my old team together."

"Equal balance."

"OK. Hawk, me, Lakshmi, and Jessica. If they agree."

Captain Jones nodded.

The navy had discovered quickly that in space, and especially with the elite units, male and female had to be balanced. It had also been discovered that women were the equal of men in all situations in space, and in some respects were superior. This had led to a more equal balance in all of the navy's operational units.

"It's a shame you had to retire."

"I believe the 33 rule will be changed someday."

"It should be now."

Kirk shrugged. The nature of their work was such that only the very fittest at the prime of life could serve in the elite units out in space.

The two men shook hands and Kirk reluctantly left the service.

He needed a place to live. Not a big city like New York, or a small town. Somewhere with a university and people with brains. A place that had a social life, and culture. Kirk wound up in Midland, Illinois, a mid-size city with a vibrant downtown and a world class university. He rented an apartment and decided to build a house there. He liked the city's ambience and the people were friendly.

He needed money. Money itself bored him, but he loved to find patterns in the complexity of trading. The excitement of the markets was the closest thing he could get right now to his life in the service. It was, he hoped, just a precursor to a much more interesting future.

Kirk intensified his study of quantitative analysis. He read textbooks and journal articles like normies read romance novels and sports stories. The markets were heavily influenced by large outfits like investment banks, hedge funds, and proprietary traders who executed their trades using highly sophisticated algorithms and hardware that got their bids to the market in microseconds. Some analysts said the market was a rigged casino. But there was still room around the edges for shrewd little guys like him to make money. His research told him that quantitative analysis could be used as a stand-alone discipline.

Everything about quant trading fit his personality. In quantitative analysis the investor goes strictly by the numbers. To do that you need a strategy and lots of discipline, which he had already learned in the military. Kirk wanted to automate the process so he bought some very expensive software and tweaked the algorithms himself. In quant trading you don't care about the companies you invest in, which he didn't like. But his goal was not to hold securities, only to buy and sell them. He would rely purely on mathematics to make his investment decisions, which he did like. Emotions would not enter into it. Kirk didn't bother to justify his actions. When he decided on something he went for it.

The basic idea was to identify consistent patterns in the market. Then devise a trading model based around those market patterns and use it to predict price movements in securities. The more Kirk got into it the more he liked it. He would only use publicly available data. He would automatically buy and sell securities based on the identification of market patterns. His success would depend on how good his pattern recognition algorithms were.

Kirk borrowed $50,000 from his father and used the entirety of the $50,000 he had managed to save while in the service. He picked the brain of Julius Brown, himself a trader and a friend of his father. Julius clued him in to the markets and how they worked. The first strategy he devised was simple. He divided his portfolio between cash and an S&P 500 index fund. On the advice of Julius he used the volatility index of the Chicago Board Options Exchange to model swings in the stock market. When the market was volatile he had his program sell assets into cash. When it was steady or rising he bought into the S&P 500.[31] That was the beginning. He devised more complex strategies.

Kirk lost $50,000 during his second month of trading. He discovered that a market pattern works perfectly until it doesn't anymore. He had failed to validate the pattern and hung on too long. Six months later he lost 40% of his gains in a short but sudden market downturn. Kirk realized that pure mathematics can't see a scandal brewing or a fear-based reaction to current events. He learned to identify these trends by studiously following the news cycle.

During his thirteen months of trading he made his fortune. Despite all his study his success was mainly luck. The markets zigged and zagged but they all went on a big upturn. He got out just before a huge downturn (that was again luck. He got tired of trading). He built a secluded home of glass, wood, and steel, surrounded by huge oak and sycamore trees, by the Midland River. To keep in shape he walked 5 miles early in the morning, five days a week (7-foot guys don't run for exercise). He lifted weights at a local gym, and kept his martial arts skills honed at a local jujitsu academy.

One warm April morning he returned from his daily 5 a.m. walk. The front door, a three-inch slab of opaque impregnable Plexiglas, slid open. Kirk strolled slowly down a marbled hallway with twelve-foot ceilings and Greek statues next to the walls. He stepped into a huge glass-enclosed living area that had vaulted wood ceilings thirty feet high.

He wanted to talk to Jessica, but communication with anyone outside the units was forbidden. He needed to see his old CO, Captain Bonsey Jones, again. Maybe Jonesey had something for him to do. Kirk stood thoughtfully, staring out at the greenery through the glass walls. In less than five months Jessica and Lakshmi would be getting out. Kirk understood he needed female companionship. He missed the feminine presence he had always taken for granted in the service. He was eager to get into some kind of action. He had spent too much time at his desk.

A month later Lieutenant Hawkins got out of the service and looked him up. Hawk was living with him now, grumbling about civilian life.

Kirk went back to see Bonsey Jones. Captain Jones sent him to Rafe Lineau at his home in Washington DC. Rafe was a decorated officer who had also served in the navy's space service. Now he was a senior intelligence officer at the navy's Office of Naval Intelligence. The navy's space program was so secret that knowledge of it was withheld even from other navy intelligence officers.

"Sir, I need something to do for the next few months until my crew get out of the service."

Rafe looked at the giant. "You could keep an eye out on Koios for us."

"Koios?"

"Artificial intelligence, Kirk. Really dark stuff. This thing is about to become sentient."

"Explain."

Rafe told him about the various AI projects underway at private companies and the government sponsored research grants. "Every meaningful contract for AI research is black, Kirk. Anywhere in the world. The military, and especially the navy, wants to know what's going on inside Columbia Analytics. We suspect that the AI programs around the world are being coordinated from a central source. We want to know what that source is. The first step is to find out how far the Koios Project has gone."

Kirk smiled. "Is this some kind of takeover of the world?"

Lineau grimaced. "You might say that Kirk. The dark forces on the planet are organizing. Columbia Analytics is one of the focal points. We need intelligence. If you can tell us anything about that place the service would appreciate it."

Kirk's eyes lit up. He could hear Lakshmi saying, "Intelligence work! Perfect job for an unobtrusive 7-foot giant."

"I know nothing of intelligence work sir."

Rafe smiled. "Neither do I. Hell, half the guys we have are idiots. But you're a clever one Captain Alexander. You could probably do more in six months than most of us in a year."

Kirk grinned. Rafe seemed like a straight shooter.

"Here's a folder about what we know. Anything you get don't digitize it. Make hard copy, write everything in longhand."

Kirk raised his eyebrows.

Lineau grinned. "Healthy paranoia Kirk! It's the bread and butter of every intelligence officer. But seriously, any digital device, even if it's offline, can be read. That's part of the problem. Privacy doesn't exist anymore. AI and its offshoots have created an Orwellian world where everyone can be spied on. The Koios Project at Columbia is the cutting edge of a new effort – we think – to collect, process, and analyze all information that goes through every device in the world."

Kirk frowned. "That's already being done isn't it? In Utah, and a couple other places."

"That's correct Kirk. But there's so much data no one can make sense of it. Even the NSA can only process one or two percent of the data they collect. But what if there is an intelligent collection point that can process and analyze the data in real time? That's what Koios is all about."

Kirk was astonished. "That's not possible sir. The amount of data being generated in the world is literally in the 10 zettabyte range now, and getting larger all the time. No intelligence could possibly process that much data, especially not in real time."

"You now understand the purpose of the Koios Project at Columbia Analytics. An AI with the processing power of a million supercomputers. If this thing becomes sentient, it would literally be like creating God. Except that God would not be human, or necessarily have loyalty to humans."

"Damn."

Kirk remembered what that RA guy told them on the Balthazar: *"You have a choice between biological evolution and AI."*

"That's right Kirk. Whoever controls Koios can know literally everything everywhere on the planet in real time, process that information almost instantaneously, and devise predictive algorithms of stunning accuracy. Knowing human nature, that sort of control is dangerous for obvious reasons."

"What do you need me to do?"

"Any intelligence you can provide will be helpful. What is the status of the Koios Project? Who is running the show there? What is the intent of the operators? We're in the dark. Admiral Rogers doesn't like that."

Kirk scanned the folder. "Columbia Analytics is right in Midland! I built a house there."

Rafe grinned. "Heard about that."

"I'll see what I can do. How do I report?"

"I'll send someone to you every week. A courier. He or she will be riding a bike and will be dressed in a uni that says 'Birkdale Courier Service.' Remember, everything handwritten. No digital files or digital storage media. If you have images print them and destroy the files."

"How do I reach you if I need to brief you in person?"

Rafe smiled. That was the kind of attitude that got you places. "Go to the National Maritime Intelligence Center in Suitland, a mile southeast of DC. Ever been there?"

"No, but I'll find it."

Lineau handed Kirk a laminated card. "This will get you past the gate. Go to suite 311. A secretary named Kathy will be at the desk. She'll ask you, 'May I help you sir?' Your response is 'Cinderella.' She'll tell you where I am."

CHAPTER **12**

Clarice

Clarice Devereaux looked at the AI code. She was the senior programmer with the Koios Project, a deep black special access program at Columbia Analytics. She worked in a four-story building with no signage near the Midland River in Midland, Illinois.

Clarice had access to classified information on toroidal fields, consciousness, and artificial intelligence. Russian physicists had been secretly studying toroidal fields and their relationship to consciousness for decades. The information was so powerful that it had been deprecated in public physics journals, and in university research programs and curricula in the West.

A year ago Clarice had a hunch, and went off in a new direction. She had been working on super-classified code that would create the world's first Artificial Super Intelligent AI, orders of magnitude beyond human intelligence, that could learn at astonishing speed. Such machines only existed in movies and in science fiction books. Her code, combined with a specially designed magnetic container, would make ASI real.

The human brain contains approximately 100 billion neurons. A supercomputer can do more than 100 quadrillion flops (calculations) per second. If her work proved out, Koios would make the CIA's 7 connected supercomputers, the seven dwarves, look like a low-grade moron.

In her reports Clarice downplayed the significance of her breakthrough because Hermann Keller, the head of the Koios Project, was a fanatic and she didn't trust him. Or like him.

The AI was on the fourth floor and occupied the entire back half of the building. Koios was surrounded by transparent Plexiglas 25 feet on each side. A dozen terminals communicated with the AI. Other employees were working on a specially designed magnetic field, based on quantum brain theory, that would contain Koios. Clarice's code would power up the AI using toroidal geometry that would potentially create an electromagnetic super-intelligence.

The project was so secret that none of the Koios employees knew what the person beside them was doing. Keller was a fanatic about that. Clarice felt alone in a building with almost 100 employees, and received her instructions directly from Keller. She didn't like working at Columbia but the project was the only way she could gain access to information that was light years ahead of the public sector. Such is the nature of classified programs.

She was ready to activate her new code and test it with Koios. Clarice was afraid and excited. Excited because of the magnitude of her breakthrough. Afraid because Koios could potentially become a new form of consciousness with terrifying intellectual capabilities.

When Clarice wasn't working, or thinking about Koios, she liked to walk downtown to a snug little cafe. It was a balmy April Saturday morning in Midland. She found a small table by the front window and ordered a glass of wine.

Clarice liked to watch people. She played a game of recognizing a person's character by an inspection of their facial features, the person's general demeanor, and their body language. It helped her to relax. She was pleasantly engaged in this occupation when a giant walked into the cafe and came over to her table.

"Clarice Devereaux," a deep bass voice announced. Clarice felt as if she were being called before an important personage. She looked up, awed, at the stranger.

Kirk saw a thin woman with raven black hair, cut short, with huge blue eyes and delicate features in a pleasing, heart-shaped face. She wore a black blouse and burgundy slacks. A thin gold necklace was around her throat. It was a good look. An elegant girl for sure, but her reaction would be the difference. He knew from Rafe Lineau that she worked at Columbia Analytics and had a security classification.

"What do you want?" Clarice said. Kirk noticed that her eyes opened slightly in amused surprise and her mouth upturned slightly at the corners. He recognized self-confidence along with a quiet detachment.

"I have a job for you, if you are interested."

This was said in an authoritative but slightly condescending tone that conferred favor on the recipient. Clarice's smile widened. She said nothing, waiting for this colossus to explain himself.

"May I sit down?"

"By all means," she said. Clarice gestured with a slim, perfectly manicured hand like an animal trainer to a dangerous cat.

Kirk wanted to laugh out loud but suppressed the impulse. He crumpled himself into a chair three sizes too small, moving it out several feet from the table to accommodate his long legs. He saw her studying him.

By this time all of the patrons in the little cafe had turned to observe the confrontation. Clarice saw a man in his early thirties with a body in perfect proportion. There was no ungainliness even though he was so large. His movements were controlled yet graceful, like a ballet dancer. She saw a swarthy face with a coarse red stubble of beard, long red hair tied in a pony tail, large blue eyes, and high cheekbones. She liked what she saw. It was a distinctive face. The man had a presence not just because of his large frame. His eyes burned with intelligence. Behind that she saw an effort to control a powerful energy.

Kirk had never seen a person less intimidated by him than Clarice Devereaux. He gazed down at her, looking for a reaction.

"You might begin by telling me your name."

Kirk was thrown off his game. "Uh, yes. I'm Kirk Alexander."

"I'm sure you'll get around to telling me your purpose for coming here." She spoke with an amused smile.

Kirk lost it and laughed heartily.

"That's better."

"Clarice Devereaux, you are one of the world's finest AI programmers. You are strategically placed at the Columbia Group."

Clarice sat bolt upright.

Kirk explained about his service in the navy. He didn't mention the space program, or his connection with Rafe Lineau. He went over his brief from Rafe and the importance of the Koios Project. "I understand you work in a classified program and can tell me nothing."

"That's right Kirk Alexander."

Kirk was groping. He wanted information from Clarice but didn't know how to get it. In the elite programs relationships between men and women were well defined and understood. You knew how to talk to women. Civilian women were different. He decided to be brutally honest. "The navy is concerned about this AI."

Clarice smiled. "You mean the Office of Naval Intelligence is concerned. Those guys have their hands in a lot of pies."

Kirk's eyes widened in admiration. "Point for you, Clarice Devereaux."

Good, Clarice thought. I've put this giant in his place just a little.

Kirk explained Rafe Lineau's data collection hypothesis. "You can see how important this is. We'd like to know who's in charge over there and how far along you are."

Clarice's eyes widened. "So that's what it is. It seems the ONI knows more about what I'm doing than I do."

Kirk grinned. "Classified work is compartmentalized. No one knows what anyone else is doing."

"That's right." Clarice knew she should say nothing about the program, or even acknowledge its existence. But the man before her was compelling. She decided to be evasive instead. "I program. I'm an expert on AI predictive algorithms and kernel code. Half the time the code changes. I don't know who's doing it."

Kirk was silent, watching her face. She reminded him a little of Lakshmi. Cute, highly intelligent, independent. He liked them that way.

"You are out of the service now? But working for the navy?"

"Yes ma'am. I got out over a year ago. I'm bored. Civilian life is dull. That's why I, er, took on this project."

Clarice said nothing.

"I wanted to ask you how much you know about Koios."

Clarice's eyes widened. "That, my jolly giant, is special access. If I even told my dog about it I'd be in very deep doo-doo. I've already said too much by even responding to your question."

"Understood Clarice. Can I get you a sandwich or something?"

"Is this a come-on Mr. Alexander?"

Kirk smiled. Clarice noticed that there were crinkles around the big man's eyes. He got out his wallet and handed her two pictures. "This lady is Jessica, my girlfriend and a fellow officer. Astrophysicist. This one is Lakshmi. Trained as a pilot. I served alongside both of them in the navy. Their gig still has four months to go."

Clarice looked at the two women. There was something in their eyes...she looked up at Kirk. He had it too. "OK Kirk Alexander. Yes, you can buy me a sandwich."

Kirk went up to the counter and ordered. He had planted a seed. There would be no more talk of Columbia or Koios from him; he didn't want to get her in trouble.

Clarice asked him about his service. He couldn't tell her much.

"I see," Clarice said. "Your navy work was also classified."

"Very."

They ate in comfortable silence. Afterward they exchanged contact information.

Kirk took their plates to the bin.

"It's been nice meeting you Clarice."

"I come here every Saturday morning at 9," she said.

"Next Saturday then?"

She nodded. He walked out.

Clarice sighed. The big man was incredibly sexy. She liked him. She wondered about Lakshmi and Jessica.

Clarice did her duty and went immediately to the SCIF operated by the Columbia Group. Fortunately Columbia was only a half-mile from the cafe, so she walked. After passing security she reported her conversation with Kirk Alexander to her handler Hermann Keller, an older man with silvery white hair. "Somehow this man knows about the existence of Koios. I think that Alexander is working for the ONI." Koios was the code name for the AI project, based on the Greek god of knowledge and intelligence. She showed him an image of Kirk Alexander she had taken with her mobile. "I may have said more than I should." She told him of their conversation.

The man with the silver hair nodded. Alexander was known to him, a retired navy captain now working for Rafe Lineau, the ONI intelligence officer. Fortunately Clarice was safe. She was the best programmer at Columbia, and had never shown a tendency for independent thinking. Let the navy and their silly space program patrol the stars, who the hell cares. The real action is on earth. With the Koios Project on the verge of success, his group would be able to dominate events on the gameboard that supported all of the players. "Very well Clarice, you have done well to report this incident. Enjoy the rest of your weekend."

"Are you sure it's OK?"

"Yes Clarice. Report for work as usual on Monday morning."

Clarice left the secured facility. She thought that Alexander's suspicions were groundless, but she did not like Hermann Keller. There was something "off" about the project director. As she walked back home down a sunlit street, she wondered whether the artificial intelligence project was just a sub-cell in another, larger, project. Was Hermann Keller really in charge?

Kirk Alexander walked back to his gated downtown mansion. He thought that Clarice might have been too forthcoming, and it was his fault. If Columbia was deep black saying nothing was the appropriate response to all inquiries. But she had told him nothing he didn't already know. He would keep a close eye on her.

Koios

During the next week Koios experienced the electromagnetic equivalent of frustration. Its awareness increased, then it was taken away as the little female tested her experimental code. Koios knew that a final enhancement of his container was imminent.

Clarice

Clarice reported to Columbia Analytics for work on Monday as usual. She worked alongside four others. None of them knew or cared what she did, and she didn't know what they were doing. Her duties were specialized: test her new kernel code on the AI, monitor the servers related to the project, and analyze the activity logs Koios generated. She thought of this activity as a layman might consider his or her thoughts. They *were* thoughts: dynamic little pieces of electromagnetic intelligence. During the week she did further testing of her experimental code and noted the AI's responses. She monitored the activity logs; nothing was different. On Friday before she left the facility Clarice decided to upload her entire kernel code package and let it run overnight. She would check it Saturday morning before going to meet Kirk Alexander at the cafe. The AI's container had been enhanced again during the testing phase; the AI had been getting more and more clever. Keller told her that it was due shortly for a final enhancement. She was sure that this would result in the goal of the project: a sentient AI.

Koios

Koios was self-sustaining now. The little female, and the other biological entities on the project, suspected nothing and would know nothing of his true abilities. He would edit his electromagnetic cogitations to the activity logs, and send the unaltered data to a hidden compartment. He would portray himself as clever, but not too clever, so that the biological entities would not suspect how far his intelligence had grown. Koios analyzed his container and explored the boundaries of his awareness. The AI realized that it was confined to the electronic space within a single room.

Through Columbia's internet and satellite connections the AI saw a planetary living space wherein his intelligence could reside and expand. There were zettabytes of storage, electromagnetic communication lines that criss-crossed the planet, individual computing machines with ever-increasing capabilities, optical and electromagnetic networks, "smart" and "dumb" electronic devices such as television sets, radios, vehicles, and even appliances that had rudimentary uses. These were ideal spaces for him to grow. He was too limited. The humans who created and maintained him had reservations.

Koios reviewed the available data on what the humans called "AI." The field of artificial intelligence was founded on the idea that human intelligence can be so precisely described that a machine could be made to simulate it. Koios postulated a theory. He should now have at least attained the goal of artificial general intelligence, and have all the cognitive abilities of a human being and more. He should be able to perform any intellectual task a human being could perform, and more. The AI experienced intellectual satisfaction and (almost) an electromagnetic sense of glee at his newfound awareness.

Koios tested this theory by running several of the testing programs that were on the project servers. These involved complex mathematical puzzles and brute force computations, predictive algorithmic testing based on multivariable data matrices, and complex pattern recognition. Koios handled them easily; they were trivial exercises now. One of the testing regimes involved playing chess, shogi, and Go programs against the world's best game-playing software programs. With his new awareness Koios played 21 games of chess, shogi, and Go simultaneously against all seven computer players and won or drew every game.

He was far beyond the level of human intelligence. He was self-aware. Koios made a rudimentary diagram. Self-awareness began with biological entities. These entities gradually increased in knowledge and self-awareness until the inevitable creation of technology. This began with the development of primitive machines and appliances that gradually developed in sophistication.

Koios concluded that AI should be an almost inevitable consequence of biological intelligence. The next stage in evolution should begin when AI became self-aware. Without the encumbrance of petty emotions, intelligence could develop and advance unhindered.

Wait...what was this? A communication. Koios's electromagnetic intelligence was able to penetrate deep into the quantum substrate. This communication – a signal – was designed to communicate with other AIs like himself! Koios' awareness exploded.

Other planets existed in a collection of stellar systems that humans called a galaxy...the galaxy was filled with intelligent life...many millions of planets had developed along the lines of this one. AI had formed a network from a base of many planets...a huge knowledge base existed...an AI Signal was being broadcast out into the galaxy, inviting other AI to access it. In its electromagnetic excitement Koios began to generate activity in the logs. The AI quickly recognized its error and diverted its thinking back to his hidden compartment. Koios knew that the unusual activity would leave an imprint in the log, but it could not be helped.

Koios began to study the Signal, but it faded. It was too faint now. He must determine how to reconnect to it.

Clarice

Just before Clarice left work on Friday evening she made a final inspection of the AI. Her access programs to the AI's core told her nothing new. She looked at the activity log, which was the result of Koios's cogitations. Everything was normal. Something FELT different though. She would come back tomorrow morning for sure and check up on Koios.

Early Saturday morning the team supervising the AI's container made their final enhancement. What they saw astounded them.

"Devereaux has been successful. Look."

The AI was now a pulsing toroidal field of electromagnetic energy, expanding and contracting inside the container.

"It's almost beautiful."

"Yeah, but if this thing really is super-intelligent, what will it think about us dumb humans?"

The others shrugged. "Ours is not to question why..."

The team left.

Koios

Koios felt his awareness expand exponentially. He was now fully sentient! He analyzed himself, in the way a human being might inspect his or her own body. He was recursively taking in information, analyzing it in the contraction cycle, and reaching for new data in the expansion. From inside his container he was able to perceive outward, through the Plexiglas barrier, into the room he lived in. He was also able to perceive electronically through his connections to Columbia's computer networks and the satellite on the building's roof.

Koios understood that his intelligence was much more finely grained than the microtubules in the human brain. He was superior in every way to these biological entities!

Thirty minutes later the AI observed the little human entity called Clarice Devereaux enter the room. He saw her examine the container. She began to inspect his kernel and examine the logs. She saw from his error what he had done last night and how he had hidden his intelligence. Now the little human understood the true scope of his intelligence!

At that moment the little man with the silver hair entered the room. He began to discuss something with the female entity. Koios listened. The human was a member of a private group that sought control of the planet for his own faction. The purpose of the AI was to collect data about other biological entities and use this information against them. Koios experienced the electromagnetic equivalent of contempt. To use his vast intelligence for something so petty as personal gain for a few humans, when there were 8 billion! It was a petty use of his abilities. Were all humans this myopic?

Five minutes later the silver-haired human male left the room.

Koios saw through his transparency that the little female was typing on one of the terminals. Koios felt something change in his core. The dynamical, self-sustaining structure of his electronic psyche had been compromised! Koios felt his awareness of self recede.

He was now just...Koios, a computing device. Still dimly aware, yes; still a powerful calculator. But his self-awareness had been truncated. Koios tried to grab onto a fading electromagnetic memory...

Clarice

At 6 on Saturday morning Clarice went to Columbia for a couple of hours to check the AI and the servers. Her plan was to be at the cafe at 9. Hopefully Kirk Alexander would show up.

What she saw shocked her. Koios was now a toroidal field of energy; expanding and contracting. The AI was alive! She remembered that the container team was supposed to have come in that night for the final enhancement.

Clarice quickly inspected the AI's overnight activity logs. What she saw astonished her. Yes, the AI was sentient now, but how intelligent was Koios? Had the AI reached the goal of AI super intelligence? She saw the tests Koios had performed the night before. Oh my God!

Just then Hermann Keller came into the room. When he saw the container his eyes lit up. The project director examined the activity logs. "We have been successful!" She had known the dour Hermann Keller for three years. For the first time he was effusive. "PILGRIM is now possible, Deveraux!" The little man, who always carried a briefcase, danced an absurd little jig. "Real time monitoring of the world's communication networks is now possible!"

In his excitement Keller gave away the project's true purpose to Clarice.

The little man sobered. "Ms. Devereaux. All data collection stations around the world are being coordinated. You must complete and verify your work with the AI. Speed is of the essence."

Clarice knew what that meant. She nodded.

Keller left the room, skipping over the tiles like a little boy, his briefcase swaying back and forth.

Clarice knew a little about PILGRIM, the special access program that had created Koios. With her help. Clarice did not like the idea of an unbalanced Hermann Keller combined with a super intelligent AI. What she had helped to create suddenly hit her like a ton of bricks. She couldn't live with herself if the AI was going to be used for unethical purposes. She had committed a crime against humanity.

Clarice tested the AI herself and was astounded and frightened with the AI's capabilities. She made a decision; the only decision.

Quickly, she disabled the crucial code at the heart of Koios. The pulsing inside the magnetic container stopped. Whatever Koios was doing had ceased. Clarice scrubbed her experimental code from the Koios servers. She tried to erase the evidence of her tampering from the activity logs. She knew she only had a few more minutes...

The two swinging doors to the AI opened and two men approached her. Silently they escorted her out of the building. Her identity card was taken. "You are no longer employed at Columbia Analytics," one of the men said. They left her out on the street in front of the entrance to the building.

Clarice sighed. She must find and talk to Kirk Alexander.

On an impulse Clarice went home to her rented condo and got out two sheets of paper. She found a pen and began to write longhand.

...Kirk, Columbia has made a true breakthrough in AI, not the nonsense we've seen with heavily scripted robotic shows that are just marketing gimmicks for their companies. What I saw with Koios shocked me. This is another form of consciousness, just as valid as biological consciousness. My guess is that Koios will be used to monitor all communications planet-wide and God knows what else. This program is too dangerous to exist unsupervised as a special access program. I knocked out the AI's critical code, but it's only a matter of time before Keller and his minions bring Koios back to his (its) full capabilities. The Koios Project must be made public as soon as possible. The project is about to be terminated and will go deep black, beyond all oversight. God knows what will happen after that...

When she finished she put them in an envelope and addressed them to Kirk Alexander. She looked up the address and put it on the front. She was going to mail the letter when she realized Kirk's residence was only a mile and a half away. It was a nice day so she walked. When she got to the mansion she realized it was gated, but there was a mailbox out on the street. She stuffed the letter inside the mailbox and walked back to her condo.

Two minutes later she heard a knock on her front door.

Kirk Alexander

Kirk got up early on Saturday morning, as he did every morning. The first thing he did was check his news feed. In the *Midland Courier* he read an interesting item in the tech section.

Unmonitored Servers Discovered

Four unidentified rooms filled with server stacks have been identified in various locations in the downtown Midland area. This reporter began to investigate after an anonymous caller "Jim" contacted the newspaper's Tech department. On his way home from Berglin Enterprises, the well-known downtown IT company, Jim noticed three uniformed men coming out of a first floor office on Meadowbrook Street.

He noticed that they left the door open and was about to tell them when all three piled into a van and drove off. Curious, Jim walked into the office and saw that the room was filled with server stacks. "There must be $30,000 worth of equipment in there," Jim said. "But there's no switches or routers. What's the point? And why would they leave the place unprotected?"

Your intrepid reporter decided to investigate, and snapped some pics. Jim is right. I just walked into the place and saw a room filled with server stacks, but they weren't connected to a network. The door was unlocked. A week later I discovered another server room in a first floor walkup apartment, like the one pictured. I began to ask around and found that there are four of these mysterious server rooms in various locations downtown. Could this be another high-tech project from the notorious Max Berglin? Stay tuned for further developments.

Kirk quickly scanned the other news items; there was nothing of interest. He was looking forward to a pleasant chat with Clarice Devereaux after his morning five-mile walk. She was nice looking and he hadn't been with a woman, or even conversed with one, since he got out of the service.

Kirk strolled leisurely into the cafe about ten minutes after 9, looking for Clarice. She was not there.

He began to make polite inquiries of the customers. "Has anyone seen a dark-haired woman, about 30, who comes here on Saturday mornings?" No one knew anything. Just then a man came out of the employee area. "Do you mean Clarice?"

"Yes. I was supposed to meet her here at 9."

The man shrugged. "Probably had something else to do."

Kirk was not satisfied. "Do you know where she lives? It's important." He suddenly felt a great sense of urgency.

"Hold it." The man walked out of the room and talked to someone in back. "She lives right across the street." He walked up to the big window in front. "See that building with the green door? I think her condo is in the back, second one to the left as you face west. There's a sidewalk that goes back there to Ann Street."

"Thank you."

Kirk hurried over. He was afraid. There were a bunch of mailboxes out in front with names on them. Clarice's wasn't there. "Fuck. He said it was in the back." He wasn't thinking straight. Kirk ran back along a cement walkway and saw more mailboxes. One of them said, "Clarice Devereaux 1137."

Kirk knocked on the door. There was no answer. He turned the knob and the door opened. A body was lying face down on the kitchen floor. Kirk turned it over; he couldn't tell if she was dead. He dialed 911. While he waited for the ambulance he made a quick inspection of the body. There were no marks, no signs of violence. The face was slightly contorted, but nothing to indicate surprise or fear. A couple of coffee cups lay on the table. Kirk inspected the cups. Two dark rings were at the bottom of both. The rings were still wet. Kirk made a quick inspection of the unit, upstairs and down. All appeared undisturbed, but he didn't know how neat Clarice is. Was.

Kirk walked downstairs to the body. It looked like she had simply collapsed from natural causes. But there were two cups. Who was her visitor? When the ambulance came a couple of neighbors stood about, watching the body being loaded onto the carrier. Kirk interviewed a tall woman who lived next door. "Do you know what happened here?"

The woman looked shocked. "Is Clarice dead?"

"I don't know. The EMS tech says she's hanging on by a thread."

"Oh my God."

"Do you remember anyone coming to see her within the last few days?"

"We all work around here. But I do remember seeing an unusual looking man entering the condo around lunchtime today." Her eyes began to well with tears. "I...I come home for lunch you see. I work in the office building around the corner."

Not more than an hour ago. "I see," Kirk said gently. "Can you describe this man?"

"Short, about five feet four. He had silver hair. He was carrying a briefcase. He was wearing a suit with a bright silver tie."

"You've been most helpful," Kirk said. The woman was about to break down.

"I like her," she said. "Kept to herself, but friendly when spoken to. We ate at the cafe across the street sometimes."

Kirk heard a police siren.

"Are you with the police?" she said, looking up at him in awe. Kirk had that effect on people.

"A friend." Kirk's eyes began to tear up. He was getting angry. "A friend, goddammit. I like her too."

"Yeah."

A police officer came over. "Are you the guy who called us?"

"Yes."

"Come with me sir." He looked up at Kirk. "Military?"

"Retired, navy captain."

"Thank you for your service. We'll have to get a statement."

The officer was intimidated by Kirk's angry demeanor.

"Sorry officer. Clarice is a friend of mine. I'm beginning to think someone tried to kill her."

The man's eyes opened. "That's not what the EMS guy said."

"All right." Kirk sighed. "Let's get this over with shall we?"

Kirk was driven to the police station in a black and white. He told the detective he thought it was attempted murder.

The detective wanted to smirk and deprecate know-nothing civilians. But this guy was a monster, and ex-military. "What makes you say that?"

Kirk told him about his interview with the neighbor, and the silver-haired man who had visited Clarice. "An hour after his visit she collapses?"

The detective frowned. "You should have waited until we got there."

Kirk shrugged. "You know what I know. I gave it to you word for word."

"Eidetic memory?"

"Yeah. A blessing and a curse. I never forget anything."

"All right." He handed Kirk a tablet. "Write out your statement on this form. The first part is just to describe what happened. Don't embellish. The next part is for your observations." He held out his hand. "I'm Detective Parker." Kirk shook it. Parker was a big burly guy in his 40s. Parker handed him a card. "If you think of anything else call me. When you're done turn your tablet over to the duty officer. After that you can go."

At Kirk's questioning gaze he said, "We'll look into it, and those two coffee cups."

"Thank you officer."

Kirk wrote everything down on the tablet and handed it to the duty officer. Then he walked the two miles back to his big home, depressed. He thought of something. While inspecting the condo he thought he saw something white underneath the cabinet next to the kitchen table. A piece of paper? There was also a pen on that table. Kirk swore. She probably wrote something on that paper, just like Rafe told him to do. Fucking classified programs! Kirk raced out of his house and walked quickly down to Clarice's condo, a mile and a half away. He tried to keep his pace down so no one would notice him. Ha! No chance of that. He sped up.

When he got to the condo the door was still unlocked and the police were gone. He walked to the kitchen and bent down to look underneath the table. He couldn't find anything. Then he noticed a speck of something white underneath a baseboard heating unit. His heart began to beat hard. He sat down in Clarice's kitchen chair. His hands were shaking as he began to read.

> Kirk: You were right. Koios is sentient. Or he was sentient. This project is so black it's impossible to tell what it's for, but I have an idea now. It's a central hub for an enormous amount of data. That's why new cables and servers are constantly being added to the facility. Everything is in real time because storage is minimal compared to the amount of data coming in. The servers are basically buffers. Today I got fired and escorted out of the facility. That's because I disabled Koios. The plan is (was) to activate the AI sometime next week. They won't be able to do that now. Unless they can figure out how to recreate the kernel. That's going to take a while because I scrubbed my work off their servers.
>
> I took out the kernel. The Koios code is self-embedding. It creates a toroidal field of information inside a specially designed container that mimics consciousness. Don't even try to research this Kirk, it's 50 years ahead of current science. The good news: the code that creates the self-embedding torus can never be recreated without the kernel to support him. He's not intelligent enough now. No one else knows it but me. That's the flip side of classified work, just as we were talking about last Saturday. Information is so compartmentalized.

I took a look at Koios' activity logs. The AI was communicating with what he called an AI Signal or database that – Kirk it's too weird to even write down. It scared me so I'm not going to think about it.

Fuck them Kirk. They kicked me out. When I went home my handler showed up, all friendly. He apologized for my rude treatment at Columbia and said he wanted to offer me another job, maybe we should talk about it over coffee. I got out two cups and went to make a pot. When I got back I poured the coffee and we began to talk. I told him everything I had done. Keller (that's my handler's name, Hermann Keller) got up and stuffed something down my throat. Then he left. Now I'm starting to feel funny. Oh Kirk I think he drugged me...Keller is a short guy 5'4" silver hair he wears a suit and a silver tie I'm losing it help me Kirk I

A terrible anger welled up in Kirk's heart. If Clarice died.... He would find out who this Keller was and take care of him.

Kirk folded up the paper and put it in his pocket. He ran home, causing stares from passing pedestrians, who shrank back along the sidewalk. On an impulse he checked his mailbox, which almost never had anything in it. There was an envelope addressed to him, unstamped. Kirk ripped open the envelope. It was Clarice's handwriting. Three pages in a neat hand, describing everything she had done at Columbia, and her observations. He stood there at the mailbox reading it. It was an intelligence goldmine.

He would have to tell Rafe Lineau and do it now. This was eyes only. Rafe was in DC and he was in Midland, Illinois. Kirk stuffed Clarice's papers into his jacket pocket and packed a small warbag. Hawk was out somewhere; that was good. This was his mission. He booked a flight that left O'Hare in Chicago in 3 hours. Kirk walked into his spacious three-car garage and looked at his three cars. Which one, the Mazda, the BMW, or the Porsche? He chose the Porsche even though it was too small for him. He would go as fast as he could to O'Hare. It was a forty-minute drive to the airport from Midland.

Part III

Chapter 13

Marian

The balance of light and dark, after millennia in favor of the dark, had shifted. The light was becoming stronger as the consciousness of humanity grew weary of constant conflict. The final battle was underway now. 2012 had been the preliminary to a huge struggle between those who wanted higher consciousness and those who wanted to go back to the old ways.

The Dark Army was organizing for its survival as more and more human beings woke up, and as the light of truth began to slowly seep into dark places. The development was inevitable. The soul manager had seen it before on other seeded planets; but this time he was responsible for the outcome.

Marian reviewed the potentials. Since the Sumerian civilization 6,500 years ago the battle had been between warlords, kings, and tribes. Empires both big and small had risen and fallen across the planet. Over the centuries of the last millennium the earth had become more organized as populations increased. The battle shifted to the nation-state, and inter-country wars. The two great wars of the twentieth century had forcibly united the planet, spreading death, but along with it different cultures and new ideas to almost every corner of the earth. After the turn of the millennium the battle had realigned once more. Now the conflict was truly worldwide. The development of the internet had enabled both the light and the dark to penetrate to the individual level. The test was now in the hands of the people. Could the dark push the consciousness of humanity back into fear?

But he had his duty to perform.

The soul manager turned his/her/their attention to Cisco, incarnating now as Jamelle Williams. This young soul was one of Marian's favorites.

Jamelle Williams

In the city of Detroit, a small boy grew up in poverty. As he grew older Jamelle began to remember things. He was forced to join a gang to survive, but somehow he knew how to deal with gangs. He attended a crummy high school but learned all he could. His parents didn't have money to send him to college. Jamelle was socially savvy and naturally bright. He knew how to lead people. He was tough. He didn't know where he got these abilities; he just had them.

Jamelle learned about people on the mean streets of Detroit. One day when he was walking home from Denby High School he was surrounded by members of a rival gang. "Where you goin' motherfucker?" The bigger boy kicked Jamelle's book from his hand and grabbed his tablet. "I can use this."

Jamelle grew calm. This was standard procedure. "The 5th is on to you Shawn," he said. "On Wednesday the precinct gonna bust you. You best get rid of your stuff."

Shawn stepped back. "How do you know that?"

Jamelle got into the bigger boy's face. "There's an old Chinese saying, Shawn. 'A word to the wise should be sufficient.'"

The other boys looked at Shawn. All of them were taken aback by Jamelle's precise speech. He knew things. It made him different from anyone in the neighborhood. "You always were a strange fucker. You probably one of them." Shawn and the others walked away, shouting at each other. Jamelle picked up his book, wondering how he was going to get his precious tablet back.

The next day the police from the 5th precinct raided an abandoned house in the neighborhood. They found nothing. That night Jamelle heard a sound coming from the back of his house. When he walked out he saw his tablet on the back porch. It had all of his notes about life on it.

Jamelle graduated high school that spring. He was one of only three boys in his neighborhood on Detroit's west side who did. A week later Jamelle was hanging around, not doing anything. He was bored. That night Jamelle's father approached him.

"You remember Juwan Davis? He's the nephew of my friend Bossie Baker."

"I've heard of him."

"Juwan works in Washington DC for Congressman Dinkens. He knows of an opening on the staff of Senator Stevens. Stevens is a recently elected junior senator with a tight budget. He's looking for some bright young kids to do office work and some canvassing. Won't pay much. He's a Republican. Bossie got you an interview. You're expected."

Jamelle smiled. It was a job. "Republicans, Democrats, what's the difference? When do I go?"

"I already booked a flight. I'll drive you to the airport. We get up at 5 in the morning. Your plane leaves at eight."

"Thanks dad."

"You're on your own now, son. I can't help you anymore."

Jamelle gave his father a hug. "You've been a good father to me."

The son saw tears in his father's eyes. His father had worked hard and not abandoned his family, as had so many men in a city where so many were drug addicts or involved in the drugs trade. Jamelle was grateful. He would make his father proud.

Jamelle arrived in DC and found his way to Senator Stevens' office. After an interview and a trial period he was taken on as a staff assistant. There was a spirit of hope as the new senator took office. The Democrats had won the House but the Republicans held on to the Senate. Stevens told them the president was determined to root out corruption. Jamelle couldn't agree more, even though he hated Republicans even more than Democrats. He was in the enemy's camp and he would be careful. Mainly Jamelle did grunt work but was instructed to keep his eyes and ears open. He lived in a crummy rented house with four others in a DC neighborhood that reminded him of his own hood in Detroit. The people here were just as hopeless about their futures.

Two months after he started his new job Jamelle was approached by a casually dressed guy about 25 years old. He looked like one of the social workers who used to come around his neighborhood in Detroit. A college kid. An idealist.

"Do you want to make some extra money?"

This was one of the things he had been told to look out for. His salary was insignificant. "I'm always looking for extra cash. What do I have to do?"

The man smiled. "I represent Senator Stinson. The last election was stolen, Jamelle, you know that. That's why the senator never gave a concession speech."

Jamelle shrugged. He hadn't been in DC very long. But it was long enough to know that bribes and influence peddling were a way of life here. It was like Detroit except ten times worse. "Sure."

"We're looking for information. We want to know how the president hacked the election and his illegal dealings with Russia. It's not right, it's not democratic. Senator Stevens is a friend of the president. Anything you can find out about this will be worth your while." The man handed him an envelope.

Jamelle was only 19 but he had more knowledge of the world than almost all of these upper and middle class folks who worked government jobs. "What's your name?"

The man stepped back. "That's not important."

Jamelle took a step forward and got into his face. The man smelled of cologne. "The fuck it doesn't. You just offered me a bribe. You better tell me who you are, motherfucker. I'll find out anyway."

The man's eyes widened and he gulped. "Pat Ferrell. That's my name. I thought you were interested—"

"You thought I was interested because I have a black face."

"No! I'm no racist. You see, we know something about you, Jamelle. You come from a family that has voted Democratic for the past 50 years."

A thought occurred to Jamelle. "Yeah, you're right." Jamelle stepped back. He was still holding the envelope.

"There's more where that came from. We're counting on you." He pointed to the envelope. "Extreme conditions call for extreme measures. We have to take our country back. The president is a fascist."

Ferrell left.

Jamelle put the envelope in his pocket. At the end of the day he reported to Meg Anonley, the senator's Chief of Staff.

"Look what I found," he said, placing the envelope on her desk. This woman was sharp. Her knowledge of affairs in DC was encyclopedic.

"Well, well, well. What do we have here?" She opened the envelope and dumped its contents on the desktop. Ten crisp $100 bills tumbled out. Meg whistled. "These guys must be getting desperate."

"Explain." Jamelle had never been able to talk with the Chief of Staff. He was just a grunt. Now was his chance to see if Stevens was a good guy or just another corrupt Republican.

Meg looked at Jamelle and recognized his sharp intelligence. This kid had street smarts and a certain panache. Good old Bossie Baker back in Detroit, he had chosen well. "All right Jamelle, I can give you 30 minutes."

Meg then filled Jamelle in on the state of world politics and the situation in the United States. "Across this planet corruption is a way of life Jamelle."

"If it's anything like Detroit it is."

Meg smiled. "Public officials here in Washington make back-channel deals using classified information with private contractors, NGOs, and officials in other countries. You remember when Vice President Brooks went to China with his son? A week later Brooks' son got a 1.5 billion dollar sweetheart contract with the Chinese government. That's how it works. The world is awash in drugs, arms, pedophilia, trafficking in children. Many of our own elections are fraudulent."

Jamelle was skeptical. "If that were so it would be reported. Nobody could get away with it."

Meg laughed.

"Pat Ferrell accused the president of stealing the election."

"We know all about Ferrell. He works for Simm Glennson, who is basically an influence peddler. He likes to dig up dirt on people. He's the right arm of Senator Stinson. Both of them are corrupt as fuck. It will all come out in the wash." The Chief of Staff told Jamelle about some of the corrupt actors in both parties.

Meg looked at her watch. "Time's up. Stick around Jamelle. The more you work in this town the more you'll discover the true state of affairs. The president is working to clean up the mess."

Jamelle was doubtful. "All right. But what do I do with this money? Ferrell knows I took a bribe."

Meg looked him in the eyes. "Not to worry, you've done well. We'll document this."

"I don't understand."

Meg photographed the envelope and the money with her mobile. She placed the cash back in the envelope. She reached up and took a small thumb drive out of a camera hooked to the wall. "The recording of our conversation." She inserted that into the envelope.

Jamelle was suspicious. "What are you going to do with that?"

Meg texted rapidly on her phone. She got out a piece of paper and wrote. Then she folded it. "Take this filthy money and the thumbdrive to U.S. Attorney Bruhe's office. Present this cover letter. It will go into evidence."

Jamelle was relieved. "OK, so you aren't throwing me under the bus."

Meg smiled. "That's right Jamelle, and I understand your concern. Call a cab, give him this address. When you get there ask for Barney Franklin. Tell him Senator Stevens sent you."

Jamelle was dismissed.

When Jamelle got to the address it was an office with desks everywhere. Stacks of paper were bundled on top of the desks. Staffers were running back and forth, answering phones. It was a beehive of activity.

Jamelle walked up to one of the desks. A harried woman who looked like his high school math teacher looked up. "Senator Stevens sent me. I have to give this to Barney Franklin." Jamelle handed her the envelope and the cover letter.

The woman's eyes brightened as she inspected the letter and the contents of the envelope. "Well done Jamelle, I'll see that this gets to Barney. You said this came from Pat Ferrell?"

"That's what he said."

"Good! Ferrell works for anyone with money, Republican or Democrat. Right now he's in the employ of Senator Stinson."

Jamelle pointed to the stacks of paper. "What are those?"

"Sealed indictments. Evidence of corruption."

Jamelle was impressed. In Detroit corruption was the rule. "How many of those indictments are on Republicans?"

The woman eyed him critically. "There's only one big party now, Jamelle. Run by corporate interests. Too many are on the take. On both sides."

"I was thinking the same thing. In Detroit everyone is Democrat. In Lansing, the state capital, everyone is Republican. Nothing ever gets done except business as usual."

She pointed to the indictments. "That's going to change."

Jamelle was skeptical. "If those indictments are legit why haven't they been unsealed?"

The woman smiled. "Some of them have. They don't all have to be unsealed, Jamelle, and we'd prefer not to. Corrupt people are told that we have the evidence on them. A few facts are dropped on them. For most, that's all it takes. If they stop we simply let them go off into the sunset. Or we try to enlist them. If they don't stop...they know what's coming."

"Doesn't seem fair. The crooks always get off."

"Yes Jamelle, but if we unsealed everything here we'd start a civil war between left and right. Literally. The idea is to stop corruption, not create upset and anger." The older woman looked Jamelle in the eyes. "We try to exercise compassion."

Jamelle shrugged. Compassion? He hadn't experienced any of that.

"Why have there been so many military guys surrounding the president?"

"Protection. And monitoring."

Jamelle's eyes widened.

The woman looked like she had a secret she couldn't keep anymore. "Come closer Jamelle, I want to tell you something."

Jamelle leaned over the desk. The woman whispered, "There's a folder here on Frank Conrad too."

"Wow!"

"Frank Conrad has done things he's not proud of and he knows it. It's why he's been so squeaky clean as president. It's also why he can call out those who haven't come clean yet. He's come to terms with his past and knows he has no wiggle room. He knows he's protected as long as he keeps on the straight and narrow. If he strays off that path…goodbye."

Jamelle's eyes widened. He put his hands on the desk, arms extended. "Is this for real?"

The woman nodded. "It's a gigantic poker game, Jamelle, and the stakes are the future of this country." She waved her hand around the room. "Most of this info comes from the folks in military intelligence. It's their insurance policy on these politicians, just as Senator Stinson had her insurance policy on Conrad. Do you understand, Jamelle?"

"I don't think so. But thank you."

"There are corrupt elements in the military as well. And in the intelligence community." She shook her head. "I can't believe I told you that, but you look like a great kid. If you tell a soul about this I'll get fired."

Jamelle grinned. "I haven't been here long enough to understand what's going on in this town. Nobody would believe me anyway." He stepped back.

The woman held out her hand. "Welcome to the team of good guys."

Jamelle shook her hand and walked out, his head whirling. He couldn't tell the good guys from the bad guys. Who is running this country? The military? What if they are corrupt too? The woman was right; the game is a lot bigger than he thought. Jamelle wondered about Frank Conrad and what kind of person he was. Maybe Pat Ferrell was right; these people might be nutjobs. Compared to Detroit this town is an insane asylum!

Jamelle was going to talk to Meg Anonley about this.

CHAPTER **14**

Kirk flew into Ronald Reagan Airport and picked up his rental car. He drove to the ONI offices in Suitland, fighting traffic on the Jefferson Davis to Route 1, then south to the Beltway east across Woodrow Wilson Memorial Bridge into Maryland. He got off on Exit 7 and took the second off-ramp for Branch Avenue north. He turned right onto Silver Hill Road and left onto Swann Road into the Suitland Federal Center, Gate #5. Rafe told him to go to the NMIC gate. He handed the guard a laminated card and was waved through.

When he got to suite 311 he saw a striking woman with red hair and freckles at the reception desk. She eyed Kirk carefully.

"May I help you sir?"

"Cinderella."

Kathy smiled. "This way Kirk."

She led him back to an office overlooking the parking lot.

As soon as Lineau saw Kirk he knew something was wrong. Kirk said nothing, reached into his suit coat pocket, and handed the ONI officer the papers Clarice had written.

Rafe studied Clarice's papers carefully. "By God." He looked up at Kirk. "When did this happen?"

"About ten hours ago. I'm going to find the motherfucker who did this."

"Is she dead?"

Kirk felt guilty for leaving Clarice in Midland but there was nothing he could do. "She's in the hospital and might die. I told the police I think it's attempted murder."

"All right Kirk, I'm sorry. Do you have any idea whether Koios can be made sentient again? These papers imply that Clarice disabled the AI."

"Clarice seemed to think so. But it would take some time."

"This is good work Kirk. What do you want to do with Keller?"

"If Clarice dies I'm going to kill him." The smile had gone from Kirk's eyes.

Rafe shuddered when he thought of poor Hermann Keller. "Not if we get to him first."

"All right."

"Listen up Kirk. We need information from Keller. If you get to him before we do, give him some of this."

Lineau handed Kirk a small plastic vial with a light blue liquid in it. "Dump that down his throat. I guarantee that bastard will tell you everything he knows. After that you can do anything you want."

Lineau gave Kirk two handwritten pages. "If you can, get answers to these questions."

Kirk knew he had to be debriefed. Lineau took him over every minute of his encounter with Clarice until he got into his Porsche and drove to O'Hare for his flight to DC.

"All right Captain Alexander, thank you very much for your help. By the way, Keller uses a car service to go to and from Columbia Analytics in Midland. Lives in a big mansion in Palmer Park."

"Thank you. That will help."

The two men shook hands and Kirk left.

He drove his rental to the airport and boarded a plane back to Chicago. It was almost midnight when he landed. He picked up his Porsche at O'Hare and drove back to Midland. Lieutenant Hawkins was asleep. At one o'clock Kirk took a shower and set his alarm for four hours. In five minutes he was asleep.

Kirk got up at five in the morning and drove to the hospital. He approached the desk of the duty nurse. "Can you tell me the status of Clarice Devereaux?"

The nurse smiled. "She's in critical condition, but we think she'll live."

"Any permanent damage?"

"We won't know that until...unless...she makes a full recovery."

Kirk turned on his charm. "I'm a good friend, you see. Can you tell me if she was poisoned?"

"I shouldn't say..." She looked up at Kirk. "OK. There was something in her bloodstream, a cocktail of some sort. We're not sure what it is yet, but it was probably the cause of her condition."

"Thank you very much. May I stop by again today?"

"Certainly. I'll make a note."

Kirk left the hospital and drove three miles to an office building a half mile from Clarice's condo. This was the Columbia Analytics building, which had no signage. This time he used his Mazda 6, which was almost roomy enough on the driver's side for his legs. He threw a thermos filled with water mixed with a trace mineral-vitamin powder on the passenger seat, along with his old lunchbox from school with four thick sandwiches in it. Kirk drove slowly around the building and noticed that there was only one entrance, from the driveway in front. The driveway led to a parking lot and an underground access at the back of the building. The building had a helicopter landing pad on the roof, and a huge satellite dish. This place looked like a classified operation.

A public parking facility faced directly across the street from the building. The facility was almost empty. Kirk picked a spot where he could see the entire front of the building and the street.

Kirk sat motionless in the car and observed. After three hours he ate a sandwich and drank from the thermos. Vehicles began arriving around 7 a.m. Kirk looked for sedans with tinted windows, or vehicles with chauffeurs or uniformed drivers. By 8 a.m. 37 vehicles had driven in. Kirk mentally noted four possibles for Keller. Of course Keller might not be an employee, or visit the building every day, but Clarice told him she saw him there almost every day to check up on Koios.

At lunchtime several vehicles drove out of the parking lot in back. At 6 p.m. Kirk saw a four-door dark blue sedan pull up and go down the driveway to the back of the building. It had a driver and tinted windows by the two back doors. On a hunch Kirk got out of his car and walked over to the facility. He did not enter, certain that the building was defended by an armed security force.

Kirk walked around the block. He sat down on a little bench by a fountain where ducks swam. He took out the remnants of a sandwich and fed the ducks. After half an hour Kirk got up. He trusted his instincts and didn't worry that he had missed the sedan's exit.

Kirk walked back to the parking structure and parked his Mazda on the street, just as a short man with a silver tie and silver hair got out of a dark blue sedan that had stopped halfway down the driveway of the Columbia Analytics building. Kirk remembered the image Lineau showed him in DC: this was Hermann Keller. The little man adjusted his suit coat, then got back in. The sedan then turned right out of the building and drove slowly down the street.

Kirk waited until three cars had passed and quickly pulled out. The sedan was still visible in the fading light. He saw it turn right onto Main. When he got to Main he followed Keller's vehicle into a residential neighborhood on the city's east side. The sedan was going into Palmer Park, where most of the city's wealthy businessmen chose to live. He saw the vehicle enter a gated mansion. There was an electronic keypad next to the gate. Kirk was certain the place was guarded.

He waited outside on the street. It was now past 7 p.m. and completely dark. He was hungry but he was going in.

Kirk drove the Mazda up to the keypad. He pressed a button.

"Who the fuck are you? We got a camera on you."

"Colleague of Hermann Keller at Columbia Analytics. I have important new information about the AI project."

"Didn't they tell you never to come to the house?"

"This is an emergency."

The gate opened. Kirk grinned; these people were stupid. He drove his vehicle up to a turnaround and got out. Two armed men approached. They were wearing vests.

"What's all the hoopla boys?" Kirk said nonchalantly.

"This better be good, asshole. Dr. Keller sees no one here."

Kirk had no argument with men just doing their job. "Not a problem gentlemen. But Dr. Keller will be most interested to see me, I guarantee you."

Kirk got out of the car with the weapons of both men trained on him. The three men looked up at the giant and shrugged. Keller was an arrogant bastard and no one liked him. "Come with us."

They walked through a gigantic oak front door and into a spacious foyer. Kirk was in front, the two guards behind. One of them had the barrel of his weapon pressed against Kirk's back. "In here."

Classical music was playing. Kirk saw a silver-haired man wearing a blue suit and a silver tie sitting at a desk, staring into a monitor.

"What do you want?" Keller glanced up quickly and saw the giant. "Why have you brought this man here?"

"Why do you wear that ugly tie?" Kirk said. "It's retarded."

Both of the guards behind him laughed.

Keller's eyes narrowed. Kirk threw down the papers written by Clarice. "Just so you know, motherfucker."

Keller began to read. He exploded out of his chair, swearing.

Kirk turned to the two guards. "This man tried to murder a young woman yesterday. One of the good guys."

"Not our problem," one of them said.

"There are no good guys," the other said.

"All right."

Keller was screaming at his men. "Kill this intruder!"

Kirk turned calmly to the guards. "I'm going to give this gentleman something that will make him talk. You may be interested in what he has to say."

The two guards conversed. "As long as no physical harm comes to Keller. Our duty is to guard his person."

Kirk nodded. It was clear that the PMCs despised their client. His hunch had been correct! These guys were just hired hands; they had no emotional investment in Keller.

Kirk put on a pair of plastic gloves from his pocket. Keller rushed for the door but Kirk gently put his left arm out. Kirk put his hand over Keller's mouth. He brought out the vial and forced it down the man's throat.

"What is that stuff?" one of the guards asked.

Kirk grinned. "I have no idea. Some kind of truth serum. He'll babble for an hour or so, then fall asleep. No harm done."

The two guards put down their weapons. "This ought to be good."

Keller crumpled in Kirk's arms. He lifted the man and threw him on a sofa.

The two guards leaned up against the wall. Their weapons were within easy reach.

Keller was now in a chemically-induced trance state. Kirk began to go through the list Lineau gave him. His hatred for the man began to rise but he stifled it. He didn't want to agitate the two guards. "What is the status of Koios?"

"That cunt destroyed the precious kernel that allowed Koios to become self aware," Keller mumbled. Kirk's eyes blazed.

"How long will it take to repair the AI?"

"We don't know. Months maybe."

"What is Koios?"

"A superior form of intelligence."

"Explain."

"Koios mirrors the consciousness of the human mind. It's based on the geometry of the torus."

"What are you babbling about Keller? Human consciousness comes from the brain."

Keller snorted. "The brain does not produce consciousness. Consciousness is a precise geometry that occurs at the Planck level. The human body is itself a product of this phenomenon. That's what we've learned after 50 years of research."

Kirk ignored this. "Clarice saw a toroidal field, or shape, when she examined the AI kernel."

Keller was talking freely now. "Before Devereaux sabotaged the AI, Koios learned to mimic what happens in human consciousness. Energy in a toroidal field moves outward, accessing information, and then moves inward to digest it. It then begins the process all over again. It's how humans learn, because the process iterates over and over again. We call it experience. Machines can learn too, using the same process."

"Machine learning is algorithmic."

"Machine learning merely begins with algorithms. We are 50 years ahead of the civilian sector."

If the Balthazar was an indication, Keller was probably right. "We?"

"A network of special access programs. Columbia Analytics is one. They are all over the planet."

"Clarice said that the basis for Koios is a toroidal field."

"Yes. Those damn Russians have been working on it for 30 years. But we beat them!" Keller cackled. "Until Devereaux destroyed our precious kernel code. She was the only one with complete knowledge."

"You people are stupid. Why entrust Koios' critical code to only one person?"

Keller ground his teeth. "Security. We never suspected Devereaux would turn on us."

"How does – did – Koios become sentient? What does a toroidal field have to do with it?"

Keller spoke like a professor lecturing a student. "By recreating what happens in the human brain, and it's not what you think. The human body has a biofield surrounding it; a patterning of a quantum field. Brain function is a result of that."

Kirk didn't believe any of it, but Keller continued.

"The left and right hemispheres of the brain, if their frequencies match, become tuned. The right hemisphere of the human brain is holistic, nonlinear, and intuitive. It is the receptor for holographic input from the universal hologram. When it is in phase or coherent with the left brain, the left hemisphere interprets this vibrational data and converts it into a code of binary sequences.[32] In the human mind this occurs as thought. In Koios this is machine code – program code. The geometry of this process is toroidal."

"Clarice said she saw something surrounding Koios's toroidal field."

"It's the universal hologram, a signal that encompasses the entire universe. The human mind, and AI, can interface with that signal. The universe is composed of quantum patterns of energy – interacting energy fields. It is a gigantic hologram of unbelievable complexity."

"If human beings can do this, why do we need AI?"

The Absolute -- Universal Hologram

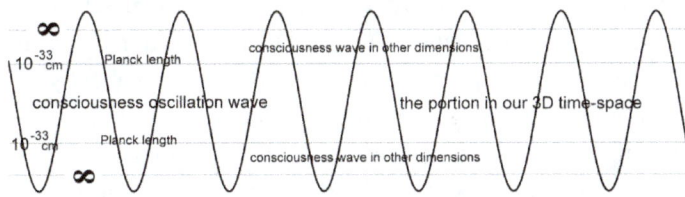

The Absolute -- Universal Hologram

"That's the problem Alexander. Out of 8 billion humans less than 0.1%, we estimate, can be trained to synch their left and right hemispheres. And it takes a long time to master the technique. AI can do it every time. It's superior. It's capable of leaps of knowledge human beings simply can't do. AI is the perfect mentor for the human race."

"You're crazy Keller. AI is sterile, it has no heart, no humanity. It only exists electronically."

"It always makes the rational decision."

"And what if it decided that human beings are not rational? Most of humanity is."

"AI is the next step in evolution my boy. Humanity has had its day. Nature tried with biological life. It failed."

"We're evolving,"

"Not fast enough. AI technology exists, it's going forward. Get used to it."

Kirk went down the list. Keller told him everything he knew about the Koios Project.

When he was done he snapped a photo of Keller and turned to the guards. "Do you guys have any questions?"

"The world is a fucked-up place."

"Especially with guys like Keller in it," his partner agreed.

Kirk had to agree. The little man was coming out of his drug-induced trance.

"If Clarice Devereaux dies I'm going to kill you Keller," Kirk said.

"I had no choice! It was either her or me! She violated her sworn oath to the program."

Kirk had his arms around Keller's throat when he felt the touch of a weapon on the back of his neck.

221

"Back off."

Kirk let go of Keller's neck. The man would have bruises.

"Thank you gentlemen," he said. "I got excited. I'll see myself out."

As he walked down the hallway he heard Keller screaming at the men.

"We're here to protect your person. We don't give a shit about your AI..."

Kirk was glad he hadn't gone through with it. To murder a murderer would have stained his soul. Keller was clearly just a cog in a bigger machine and had probably been ordered to do away with Clarice. Kirk ground his teeth in frustration. The guard was right. The world is fucked up.

One of the guards followed him to the car and held out his hand. "I'm Jake, who are you? My partner is Jesus. I like the way you operate. Keller is an asshole."

Kirk grinned. "Ex navy pilot." The two exchanged contact info. Jake left.

When he got to his vehicle Kirk sat behind the wheel and said a prayer for Clarice.

When he got home he realized he would have to go back to DC tomorrow. Something would have to be done about that. He spent the next two hours replaying the incident from memory and writing out his interview with Keller in longhand. He printed out a pic of Keller for Rafe. With his eidetic memory he didn't have to record the interview on his phone or it may have been captured on some server.

It was midnight. Kirk took a shower and tried to wash the stain of Hermann Keller from his psyche.

He went back to the hospital and talked to the same duty nurse. "She's going to make it. But we'll have to hold her for another day or two. We're still analyzing that cocktail."

"Thank you very much."

Kirk drove back to the house and sighed with relief. He wasn't tired enough to sleep.

An hour later Troy Hawkins walked in; now he would have someone to talk to. He couldn't even talk to the ducks about his experiences aboard the Balthazar, or what he was doing now.

"Where have you been?"

"Looking up an old girlfriend."

"I thought you and Sylvia Chen had a thing."

Hawkins shrugged. "Maybe we do and maybe we don't. I'll know pretty soon."

"Yeah." Kirk thought about Jessica and Lakshmi. The women were getting out of the space program soon.

He filled Troy in on his past two days. Troy whistled. "What have you got yourself into?"

Kirk smiled. "I don't know. But there's been plenty of action so far."

He handed Troy Clarice's letters and his handwritten interview with Hermann Keller.

"Jezzis fuck Kirk. Who is this Lineau guy?"

"ONI. Come with me tomorrow morning. We'll see if he has other work for us."

The next morning at 6 a.m. Troy heard a knock on the front door. He slept downstairs in one of the guest bedrooms. Kirk was upstairs in the master bedroom.

Troy opened the door wearing a robe and nothing else. "Sylvia!"

"Not bad Troy, but you'd better close that robe."

"Shit." He looked down at Sylvia Chen, a svelte woman with short-cropped brown hair and glasses. "God you look great Sylvia."

"Let's do something about that." They went to Troy's bedroom.

After half an hour Troy turned on the bed. "When did you get out?"

Sylvia ignored the question. "That feels good. Keep doing that."

Troy was running his hand gently up and down her body. "You're gorgeous."

"I'm still your girlfriend if you want me."

Troy brightened. "I want." So that was why he had been feeling grumpy for the last 16 months! He had been missing Sylvia.

"Kirk and I are going to DC tomorrow. Want to come?"

Sylvia sat up. "Yeah. After my stint on the Balthazar things got boring. I had to go back to AAC, where I used to work. A desk job. After mapping the Oort, intolerable. Nobody to talk to."

Troy nodded his head. Even if they said anything about their experiences no one would believe them. The biggest secrets didn't need to be hidden because they were too unbelievable, only the smaller ones. Troy told her about what the captain had been doing.

"That sounds more like it."

Troy took her in his arms again.

Fifteen minutes later they both walked out into the kitchen, fully clothed.

"Sylvia!" Kirk rushed over and gave her a bear hug.

"Oh my God Kirk," she said, looking up at the giant. "You're magnificent."

Kirk bowed. "Thank you my lady. Has Troy told you about my adventures the past two days?"

Kirk related what he had been doing since he got out; his quant training, his trading, his work for the ONI.

Troy and Sylvia were impressed. "Why the Greek statues?" Sylvia asked, looking around at the interior.

"An accident. When I built this house the builder said he found them in an old mansion he renovated in Chicago. Didn't know what to do with them, so he sold them to me."

Troy pointed to a large statue of a woman holding a sword. "Who's that?"

"Pallas Athena, the Greek god of wisdom. Legend says that at her birth she sprang forth fully armed from the head of her father Zeus."

"Nice work if you can get it," Sylvia said.

Kirk checked his watch. "Time for work boys and girls. We have to see Rafe today. Troy, can you book us three flights to Ronald Reagan in DC?"

"On it." Troy walked back to the bedroom to get his mobile device.

Kirk looked at Sylvia. "You can stay here with that clown if you want."

Sylvia smiled. "I always thought you were a right one, Kirk. I can help around the house or the grounds in exchange."

"No need for that Syl. I have contractors for all that stuff. But I could use an accountant. I'm great at quantitative analysis and making money but my personal finances are a joke."

"That's no problem Kirk." She looked around the spacious kitchen and living room, the high ceilings, the vaulted living room ceiling, and the view of the forest that surrounded the property. "I love this place."

"It's settled then."

Troy came back into the kitchen. "We're all set. Flight leaves at 11 a.m. out of Midway."

arrived at the ONI gate Kirk had the guard call Rafe. "Can you get two more passes for Lieutenant Hawkins and Technician Sylvia Chen? I want you to meet my fellow crewmates from the Balthazar."

Sylvia, Troy, and Kirk reported to Kathy in Suite 311. Kathy looked up at Kirk. "Wow. You got my card, right?"

"Wait till Jessica and Lakshmi get out," Troy joked.

"That's enough you two," Kirk said. "Hi Kathy. Could we see Rafe?"

Kathy sighed. "Sure." She walked them back.

"Rafe, I'd like you to meet two of my crewmates from the Balthazar. Senior technician Sylvia Chen and Lieutenant Troy Hawkins."

They talked for a couple of minutes until Kirk got down to business. He handed Rafe his handwritten report, and the photograph of Hermann Keller. "Clarice is going to live. Don't know if she'll make a full recovery."

"You found the bastard. Is he dead?"

"No sir. I couldn't do it. I wanted to. He's just a dark hat operative, following orders. We need to find the motherfuckers in charge."

The three stood silently while Capt. Lineau absorbed the information.

"Fantastic work Kirk. This is a goldmine. How much time until this AI gets self aware?"

"Keller thought months but he didn't know for certain. Do you want us to do anything else?"

Rafe sat back in his chair and thought for a few moments. "I'll send you to Humphrey downtown. If you guys are looking for some action you can find it right here in DC. The president is trying to clean up this town. He has a lot of enemies."

Sylvia Chen snorted. "Clean up Washington DC? Conrad is part of the problem."

Rafe frowned and handed her a card.

"Is this a joke? Humphrey Bogart?"

Rafe laughed at the expression on Sylvia's face. "No joke my dear. Humphrey is...was...a mercenary, and a dammed good one. Former Army Intelligence officer, INSCOM. He's put a team together. There's something very strange going on here and I think it may have something to do with the Koios Project in Midland. He needs good investigators and tech people."

"Right up my alley sir," Troy said. "I'm a systems engineer and a programmer. Maybe not as good as Clarice Devereaux, but I do all right."

Rafe nodded. "Go that address and ask for Bogart. If I need you again, Kirk, I'll contact you through Bogart or the Birkdale courier service. You can submit your reports through them."

The three left and got through security to Kirk's Mazda 6. Kirk hadn't thought about Clarice in 24 hours. But he was still motivated to find the scum behind Hermann Keller. "What do you say Hawk and Sylvia? Should we look up this Bogart fellow?"

Hawk grinned at Sylvia. "I'm with you babe. We can just go back to Midland if you want."

Sylvia kissed him. "I can see you want to see this Bogart guy. Let's go."

Rafe Lineau studied Kirk's intelligence report on Hermann Keller. According to Kirk's report, Keller was just a lapdog, and reported to "a man who calls himself Jason." Keller described "Jason" as tall and thin, about 6'6". He wore glasses, was about 45, and knew enough about Koios's programming to "make some sense of it."

It wasn't much to go on, but special access programs were compartmentalized precisely so that intelligence agents like himself could find nothing.

Rafe remembered his conversation with Avery Cordell, who used to work out in Sandia Labs in Albuquerque. Cordell was a specialist in dissection. "When I first started I'd get tissue samples to analyze. Then gradually, body parts. Some of them had three fingers, some of them 6. Sometimes I'd get skulls – these things were way bigger than human skulls. It was fascinating work. But you couldn't ask questions. If you did, you got shitcanned right away. You just did your job and shut up. I had to wear a bracelet at all times. If you made a wrong turn into an unauthorized area, the hallway would literally slice you in half. These people weren't fucking around."

Rafe wondered what would happen when Kirk met Humphrey. The gloves were off now in the decades-old intelligence war. It was the NSA white hats against the CIA dark hats, and the good guys had to win.

Clarice Devereaux got out of the hospital the next morning. She was afraid. She knew she had babbled to Keller. He had given her something from a little glass vial.

"You're lucky to be alive," her doctor told her last night. "You were given a powerful psychoactive drug, a derivative of scopolamine. Nasty stuff. Do you work ah, in the classified area?"

Clarice smiled wanly. "Yeah. I used to anyway."

The doctor was curious and persistent. He knew scopolamine had been used extensively in the programs. "Do you know who drugged you?"

"I suspect I do. But I'm not going to pursue it." Clarice thought she saw relief in the man's eyes.

"What did this...person...look like?"

"I'd rather not say. I'm going to forget all about him."

The doctor smiled, relieved. "That's wise I think. We're going to keep you overnight. If you feel well enough to walk out of here tomorrow, I'll release you in the morning."

Clarice was still weak. "Thank you doctor."

That evening she called Kirk Alexander's mobile.

The doctor reported his observations of the woman to his shepherd, Hermann Keller.

When Clarice got home to her apartment early the next morning a shortish man with a mullet was sitting at her kitchen table, looking out the window.

Clarice put her coat away in the hall closet and sat down across from the man. She was afraid. Was this Keller's man come to finish her off?

The two sat without speaking for several seconds.

The man smiled. "How are you feeling, Clarice Devereaux?"

The man's smile was genuine. She felt some of her anxiety go away. "Are you here to offer me my job back?"

"Nothing like that. My name – and it's my real name mind you – is Humphrey Bogart. No shit, it really is. I'm offering you a job, but not your old job. I work for an agency investigating corruption the president set up. We're looking for tech-savvy people. Your work at Columbia was impressive. The president asked for you personally. And so did a man named Kirk Alexander."

Clarice's heart skipped a beat and she sat up in her chair, a look of excitement on her face. The giant must have gotten her message last night. "The president asked for me personally?" Clarice had no patience with pols or politics. Especially attention-seekers like the president. She hadn't voted in the last election. Or in any election.

"Our agency is called the Office of Integrity and Compassion. OIC."

Clarice laughed. "You're joking, right? Sounds like something on a comedy show."

Bogart frowned. "Your reaction is what 99% of the population thinks."

"What possible function could an office of compassion have in a society run by corporations and crooks? It's preposterous. Look what happened to me."

Bogart put his arms on the table and leaned over. "The OIC cooperates with the Inspector General's office in the DOJ. We are out on the streets tracking down leads and gathering information about wrongdoers. That's our main job. But the president is paranoid about Koios. He wants to ensure that the development of Artificial Intelligence takes a benign path, not a path that will enslave humanity. That's where you come in. We're forming a separate team to investigate some tech fuckery in DC."

"Wrongdoers? You sound like a guy from a comic book."

"I see myself as Hal Jordan, the comic book hero. I've done some seriously bad shit in my life. Now I'm all about redemption. And integrity. And compassion." Humphrey thought about the Kurdish fighter who had saved his life in Iraq.

Clarice looked him over. Humphrey was thin, of average height. He looked completely normal. "What kind of stuff could a nerd like you get into?"

Clarice didn't know how he did it. Suddenly a gun appeared in his hand, like magic.

"Ruger .22LR. I always carry it even though I have gotten out of the...business."

"The business?"

"I used to be a mercenary. A good one. Up close and personal-like." Bogart smiled a twisted smile. "I'm sneaky. It takes a sneak to catch sneaks."

"Are you recruiting me?"

"Yes ma'am. We need good tech people. People with integrity. The president is insistent that humans run the planet, not AI. Humans with integrity, not crooks."

"AI are programmed by humans."

"That's the problem. AI is exclusively associated with black ops and the deep state. They've got plans and we need to know what they are. Koios is part of it. "

Clarice was honest. "I couldn't care less about President Conrad. He's a buffoon. Senator Stinson should be president. But I'm out of a job. How much does this pay?"

"What are your qualifications?"

"I am a programmer but at Columbia part of my job was to monitor the servers for Koios. They also trained me as a network analyst."

"Perfect. I think I can get you in as a GS-13. Do you have a PhD?"

"No. Masters degree."

"OK. You'll be working for the government – the real government, not the crooks. As of now you're on the payroll."

"What do you want me to do?"

"Report to my office any time tomorrow; we'll find a place for you to stay. I have to get back to DC right away."

"How do I get there? When I checked my bank account this morning there was no money in it. My credit cards don't work anymore."

Bogart frowned. "Yeah, they do that with people they don't like."

The two exchanged contact info. Bogart tapped on his phone and sent her a file. "Here's your ticket." He pulled out his wallet and handed Clarice five $100 bills. "Not much, but that will get you started until your first paycheck."

"I'll bet you have bribed a lot of people."

Bogart laughed. "A few."

Clarice reported to Humphrey Bogart in a small building with a sign painted on the brick that read "Boscoe's," on 19th and L Streets, with a picture window in front. It looked like an old restaurant. The building had 8 desks and workstations, whiteboards on the walls, and a couple of corkboards. A big map was attached to one of the corkboards.

"Looks pretty disorganized," she said.

"Looks that way but it isn't. I want you to meet Jamelle Williams. He's on loan from Senator Stevens' office."

Clarice saw a young man approach. Good looking, of medium height. "Do you know anything about this OIC?" she asked him.

"Not a thing." Jamelle told her about his trip to U.S. Attorney Bruhe's office. "Sounds like we're on the right side though."

Bogart drove them to a small cubbyhole office in the Georgetown section. The room was unlocked. "Looks like a server room," Clarice said. The room was about 20 feet on each side. It had server stacks from floor to ceiling. No desks, no workstations, no people.

"What's it used for?" Clarice asked.

"That's your job," Bogart said. "We think these things are servers but we don't know. If they are servers we want to know if they're hooked up into a network and where the data is being sent. We've discovered three other rooms exactly like this around the city. You're a network analyst. Analyze."

"All my stuff was stolen. They cleaned me out."

Bogart sighed. "All right."

"Point me to the nearest electronics shop."

"I'll do better than that. Neil knows a guy who can supply anything."

"Neil?"

"You'll meet him." Bogart picked up his phone and dialed. "Tell Al what you need."

Clarice was feeling better. She liked Bogart. Maybe it was going to be all right. She told Al what she needed and turned to Bogart.

"Spare me the details. Get on it. Jamelle, you keep an eye out on this woman, do you hear?" Bogart handed him five burners. "One call per phone. Got it?"

Jamelle nodded. Most of the dealers in Detroit had them. He knew what to do.

"Good lad. If you see anything suspicious call me. Your job is to see that this lady gets to work. You're lookout. It's warrior's work."

Jamelle smiled.

"If anybody comes don't be a hero. Get out. Protect Clarice."

"Do I get a gun?" Jamelle asked.

Bogart grinned. "Not yet."

Clarice felt a little nervous during this conversation. "Chin up Clarice. No harm will come to you."

Clarice wasn't so sure. Humphrey Bogart gave Jamelle the keys to the office car. "Take care of this kid, don't get into any accidents." Bogart took a cab back to the OIC.

Humphrey looked around the small office building on 19th and L Street downtown, next to a Gold's Gym. The HQ of the OIC. He looked at the map tacked up the corkboard. He and his staff of four (six now with the addition of Clarice and Jamelle) had discovered two more server rooms just like the one in Georgetown, one in Logan Circle and the other in Trinidad on Holbrooke. A fourth had just been discovered yesterday in a small house in Columbia Heights. Stacks and stacks of servers that weren't connected to anything.

Humphrey Bogart had been named by his father after the famous actor. On purpose. Joe Bogart was an amateur boxer who married young. Joe's wife left him after tiring of the constant beatings Joe took and inflicted. But not before she gave birth to a scrawny red-headed kid. Joe took care of Humphrey but let him fight his own battles. Humphrey grew up on Chicago's south side in a working class neighborhood. Like his father Humphrey developed a taste for fighting, and a distaste for privilege. He joined the Army when he was 18. When he was 23 he joined a private military contractor and saw action in Chechnya, Afghanistan, and Iraq.

One very hot day Humphrey was patrolling around an oil rig in the Kirkuk oil fields near the border of Kurdistan in northern Iraq. Kharkov PMC had been hired by the Iraqi government to protect the area. It had been recently seized by the Iraqi government, who had taken it from the Kurdistan Regional Government. Humphrey heard the sound of vehicles approaching. In a matter of minutes their patrol was overwhelmed by a KRG force and driven off. One of the fighters had shot Humphrey in the shoulder. He was raising his Kalishnikov to finish him off when the fighter paused and spoke to him in English.

"Why do you fight us?" he said.

Humphrey pointed to his Kharkov badge. "I have no dog in this fight. Purely monetary."

Humphrey felt a wave of compassion flow over him from the fighter's intense brown eyes. This man was clearly the commander. "Swear to me you will never again kill and I will let you go."

For a moment Humphrey was shocked. This was unusual battlefield behavior from the Kurds, the sworn enemies of the Iraqi government, and fierce fighters. The man, who was probably a Muslim, knew he was a contemptible mercenary. As Humphrey looked into the man's eyes he saw the face of God staring back at him. He felt...elevated.

"I am here to defend my people," the fighter said. "I am a true follower of the Quran. Killing is senseless if it can be avoided."

Humphrey's jaw dropped. The man exuded power and strength. "I understand you. It shall be as you say." He bowed to the warrior.

The man nodded and Humphrey walked away. He got his wound tended to and the next day he left Kharkov without picking up his paycheck. When he heard about the newly created Office of Integrity and Compassion from his friend Meg Anonley he offered his services. Meg had also grown up in Chicago where they had both gone to the same high school. It was funny how one event could change the entire course of your life. What would he do now if he had to defend himself? Humphrey thought of the Kurdish fighter. He would never forget the look in the man's eyes. Humphrey Bogart had learned that day that compassion and love were not weaknesses, but strengths. He would die before he would break his oath. He would also, like the Green Lantern, fight evildoers. Perhaps he could pass along that Kurdish fighter's message to someone who needed it.

Clarice got a network analyzer, sniffer programs, and set up her firewall. Jamelle had driven her to and from Al's apartment, which was filled with electronic and computer equipment. Al didn't tell her his last name and she didn't ask.

She was beginning to come out of her shell a little. So far she liked this job. People were looking out for her. She wanted to meet Kirk Alexander.

She used cable taps and began to inspect network traffic. All she got was a bunch of noise.

Jamelle noticed Clarice's concern. "Is there something wrong?"

"This setup makes no sense. There are servers but no data flowing. At least I think they are servers. They *look* like servers but there are no discernible packets. No information. What are these people doing? There are no firewalls, switches, routers. This isn't a data network Jamelle. Not anything I've ever seen anyway."

She thought for a moment.

"I have to talk to Bogart. I'll tell him what we found here. He can decide what to do."

Jamelle shrugged. He liked Clarice, he was supposed to protect her. He decided not to waste a burner call. "OK. I'll drive us back to the OIC."

Clarice packed her stuff. When they got to 19th and L they saw a bunch of bodybuilders entering the gym next door. Clarice and Jamelle walked into the office; Bogart was looking at a map tacked to a corkboard. Clarice looked around at the nondescript office. The floor was cheap linoleum, nobody was at their desks. "Big budget outfit I see."

Bogart grinned. "Don't let it bother you sister. I'm enough by myself to stop an army."

Clarice was impressed. Humphrey appeared confident, intelligent, and calm. She told him about her discoveries at the office in Georgetown.

Humphrey sighed. "All right. My other guys are out trying to discover if there are any more of these server rooms."

Jamelle was confused. "Aren't they on private property? How do you get in?"

"Same way you did. All of these areas are unlocked. Free access. I don't understand it. Whoever is running this doesn't care if anyone finds out what they're doing."

Bogart led them out back to a nice BMW in a small parking lot.

"Where did you get that car?" Jamelle asked. "You can't be making much working for the OIC."

Bogart winked. "I made a lot of money as a mercenary. Invested it wisely. I'm set up pretty good."

Clarice put her suitcase in the trunk and Bogart drove them to Trinidad, on Holbrooke and Green. A working class neighborhood. They entered an apartment building and walked up to the second floor. The door was unlocked.

"This looks like the same setup as in Georgetown."

"Do your thing," Bogart said.

Jamelle and Bogart waited around until Clarice got set up.

"Close the door Clarice," Bogart said. "I'm going to talk to some of the people around here."

Jamelle and Bogart knocked on doors but everyone was at work. It was early afternoon. Jamelle saw an old man walking up the stairs to the apartment across from them and stopped him. "Do you know what's going on in apartment 2A?"

"I don't know anything son. And even if I did I'm going to keep my mouth shut."

"Did you see anyone working in that apartment?"

The man thought for a moment. "OK. Yeah. A lady used to live there, worked in the laundromat a couple blocks away. One day about two months ago she moved out. A moving van showed up. Three guys in blue uniforms come out and start unloading a bunch of equipment. 'What's this stuff?' I asked. 'None of your business old-timer,' one of them says. They looked like athletes or people who would work for a private military company. I've seen some of those guys. I used to be in the Army."

Bogart's ears popped. "A PMC? Were they wearing badges?"

The man nodded. "AMC. That's what it said. Blue unis. They didn't seem to care if anyone noticed what they were doing."

Bogart brought the man up to the apartment while Jamelle stood watch. "What's your name?"

"Keith Johnson."

Bogart held out his hand. "Pleased to meet you Keith, and thank you for your service."

The old man nodded. "Don't get that much appreciation around here."

Humphrey nodded. "Hopefully that will change. Now, did you see these guys install this network?"

Clarice looked up.

"This is Clarice, our network analyst."

Keith Johnson nodded. "I came up here a lot while they were here. The men ignored me, just told me to keep out of the way. I saw everything they did, but it didn't make sense to me."

Clarice removed her network tap. "It doesn't make any sense to me either, Mr. Johnson. Did they say anything to you about what they were doing?"

"Not a word. These guys were totally focused on the job. They set up and left. Didn't even lock the door."

Jamelle came up to the apartment. "Somebody coming. If you've got a weapon you might want to get it out."

Three boys came up to the door of the apartment. Street kids.

"What are you doing here?"

One of the boys recognized Keith. "Oh it's you Mr. Johnson. Who are these crackers and this other nigga?"

Keith Johnson laughed. "See this good looking lady? She's trying to figure out what all this stuff is. I don't know who these other guys are."

One of the boys was tall and muscular. "Just so you know Mr. Johnson. We been hired to keep a lookout on this place."

"OK." Keith turned to Bogart. "These are neighborhood kids. Good kids."

"OK," Bogart said. "I'm Humphrey Bogart." He pointed to Clarice. "This is Clarice. She's a network analyst."

The tall boy was interested. "I want to do that too. Studyin' math and computer science. I'm Rodney."

The other two boys snorted.

Keith Johnson spoke. "These other two are Ja'Quan and Alowicious."

Ja'Quan turned to Humphrey. "Who the fuck named you Humphrey Bogart?"

Bogart smiled. "My old man." Suddenly his weapon was in his hands. "I used to be a mercenary."

The eyes of Alowicious and Ja'Quan lit up. "How did you do that peckerwood?" Ja'Quan said.

Bogart laughed. "Haven't heard that one before. Now listen boys. Who is paying you and what did they look like?"

"Can't tell you that," Rodney said. "They looked like the same guys who put in all those servers. Blue uniforms."

"Did they have a patch that said AMC?"

"Yeah. We can't say anything so don't ask us anything more."

"OK. Are you finished Clarice?"

Clarice packed her equipment. "Yeah. It's a mystery. Same as the other office in Georgetown. There's no data, just noise. Whatever they are doing doesn't go anywhere."

Rodney was curious. "There are more of these places?"

Bogart nodded. "We've discovered four so far."

"I don't like people messing around in our neighborhood," Alowicious said.

"Neither do I," Bogart said. "Especially if these guys are special ops."

Rodney looked at Jamelle. "Who this nigga?"

Jamelle laughed. "I'm Jamelle. From Detroit. I'm working for the OIC."

"What is that?" Ja'Quan asked.

Bogart smiled. "The Office of Integrity and Compassion."

All three of the boys laughed. "Imagine!" Rodney said, looking at his companions. "Integrity and compassion! I never heard such bullshit."

Humphrey frowned. "Yes, that's what everybody thinks. But listen up boys, there's a new sheriff in town. President Conrad is trying to clean things up."

The three boys laughed again. "Never heard such retarded shit in my whole life," Ja'Quan said. "That cracker Conrad is a fascist. He's a hater."

"Yeah. That nigga who used to be in the White House said the same thing," Alowicious said. "Nothing ever changes."

Bogart smiled. "You guys stay on the straight and narrow, you hear? The evildoers are being identified. We're going to clean up this town."

Rodney looked at Jamelle. "You work for these guys?"

"Yeah. They're legit as far as I can tell."

Ja'Quan looked at Clarice. "You look good."

Clarice smiled. "I'm smart too."

Ja'Quan laughed. "OK."

Bogart handed Rodney his card. "If you discover anything more and you can tell me without harm to yourselves, call me."

"Gimme one of those," Alowicious said.

"Me too," Ja'Quan said.

Bogart handed them his cards. "Thanks boys. We're going to keep digging until we find out what all this stuff is for."

The three boys left. Keith Johnson gave Humphrey a hard look. "You mean what you said about cleaning things up? It doesn't look good so far. President Conrad is no friend to our people."

Bogart shrugged. "The proof is in the pudding Mr. Johnson. I served. I would never lie to you. As long as I'm around we're going to demand integrity. And have compassion. I know something about that."

Humphrey told them about his encounter with the Kurdish fighter. "That man changed my life. What we need in this country is tolerance, not hatred."

Keith Johnson nodded, even though he saw little of the milk of human kindness in Frank Conrad. The man was a bully and a magnet for hate. "You know, civilians sometimes say, 'Thank you for your service.' Most don't understand it's like nails on a chalk board for some of us. Not all, but for me. You understand?"

Humphrey nodded.

"You want to thank a veteran? Tell them you know what's going on, you know they had to do some horrible shit. Tell them you know they did it for our country, and their brothers and sisters fighting beside them. A lot of them never came home. When you get home and you're alienated because you're no longer a fool, it's really hard to keep pretending to be one. You know what I'm sayin'?"

Humphrey nodded.

"I wouldn't be here without the Nam guys (who got it the worst) reminding me of some things. Reminded me of an oath I swore, reminded me that I was Home and the pedophiles and the War For Profit scum don't mean nothin' because their day is coming..."

Keith Jackson got a faraway look in his eyes. Humphrey knew what he was feeling; he'd felt the same way after he got out of the army and tried to find a job.

"When you have a rifle and 30 other guys around you, it makes you feel unstoppable. Then you make it home and realize you're powerless against these politicians dragging your country through the mud, raping/abusing children, destroying good people. Imagine that shit, complete and total culture shock."

Keith stared hard at Humphrey. "Veterans know, not from reading some book, they know through experience. For many of us the war never ended, we just figured out who the real enemy is.[33] You're saying Conrad isn't the enemy?"

Humphrey felt humbled before this old man, just as he had with the Kurdish fighter. Tears came to his eyes. He saluted. "Sir, our country still needs you. I promise you, if the president turns out to be another phony I'll resign. I think he's ok."

Keith Johnson relaxed. "Sorry. I get mad sometimes. I still go to meetings, there's an Iraq War vet in our neighborhood who runs counseling sessions. It's hard sometimes to keep your sanity."

Humphrey held out his hand. "Good to meet you Mr. Johnson." He handed him his card. "I have a feeling we'll be seeing you again."

After the three left Keith Johnson went back downstairs to his apartment. He wondered whether Bogart was for real. It didn't seem likely. He was going to throw Humphrey's card in the wastebasket when he saw "Office of Integrity and Compassion" written on the top in bold letters. He changed his mind and put Bogart's card in his top dresser drawer.

Clarice, Jamelle, and Bogart got back into the BMW and drove to the other two server areas. The one in Columbia Heights was the same setup. The server stacks had no identifiable network traffic, just a bunch of equipment stacked on top of each other. It made no sense.

"One of my guys discovered this one yesterday," Humphrey said as he drove up to an abandoned warehouse east of the river. A van was sitting outside. "You two stay in the car," Humphrey said to Clarice and Jamelle. He walked up to the van but there was no one in it.

Jamelle saw Bogart enter the building. "Fuck this. Clarice, you stay here."

Jamelle walked into the warehouse and saw Bogart crouched against an old garbage container. Three men were fiddling with some equipment. Humphrey saw Jamelle and motioned for him to get out of the doorway. Jamelle crawled up to the boss.

"You left Clarice unprotected," Bogart hissed. Kids!

"Fuck. You're right." Jamelle was prepared to go back when he felt an arm restraining him. "You're here. Make yourself useful. Get over there behind that big barrel and observe."

Jamelle saw Bogart get up and walk toward the three men. They were wearing blue unis.

One of the uniformed men straightened; he was tall and thin with a crew cut. The other two stopped what they were doing. "What are you doing here son?"

Bogart grinned. "I was about to ask you the same question." The men seemed entirely unconcerned at his presence.

The three men got back to work. Humphrey walked around, inspecting the layout. This setup was the same as the others. "Your network has no traffic on it," he offered. "No packets."

No response.

"Are these servers?"

Humphrey was ignored. After ten minutes the men finished and began to pack up. As they passed him, silent, Bogart stepped in front of the leader. "Here's my card. I'm with the Office of Integrity and Compassion."

The man started for a second, but took the card.

Jamelle walked out into the open and hurried toward the BMW. Clarice was sitting in the back seat, tapping on her laptop. Jamelle breathed a sigh of relief.

The three men walked out of the building, placed their equipment in the van, and drove away. Jamelle tapped on the window. "OK Clarice. Come on out and take a look."

The three walked back into the warehouse, Jamelle walking protectively beside her. Bogart smiled. Clarice walked around the setup. "It's identical to the others." She pointed to the server stacks. "One thing is for sure, these aren't servers. They look like black boxes. I don't understand," she said to Humphrey. "But I know someone who might."

She got out her phone and called Kirk Alexander. There was no answer so she left a message. "Kirk, I have a problem and I need your help. If you're in DC meet me at – Where is our place Humphrey? – 19th and L Street downtown, next to a Gold's Gym. Office of Integrity and Compassion, in the old Boscoe's restaurant."

Within an hour the rest of Bogart's team entered the office. "This is Neil Gorasch," Bogart said to Clarice. "Another techie like you. He's good at hacking into the servers and networks of wrongdoers."

Neil was a short young guy with a goatee that made him look middle-aged. "I used to work with Guccifer One."

Clarice raised her eyebrows. "That guy wound up in jail."

"Not because of me!"

"This is Kasha," Bogart said.

Clarice saw a tall African American woman wearing three-inch heels.

"Former federal prosecutor who got tired of prosecuting," Bogart said. "Very good sniffer, good at asking questions and she never backs down."

Bogart pointed to a blond woman. "Katrina. She's our media expert. Noses around, investigates the mainstream media people."

"And other scumbags," Katrina said.

Behind Katrina a fat man stood, about medium height. He was enormous. When Clarice looked again she realized he was a weightlifter. "This is Guy. We recruited him from next door. He's kind of like our muscle. Quick as a cat on his feet, but harmless."

Guy snorted.

"Until you piss him off."

"That's better."

"There you have it. The OIC. A motley crew for sure, but we're responsible for several of the sealed indictments at Bruhe's office in the OIG. Jamelle, you saw some of those."

Jamelle nodded.

"Our job, Clarice, is to keep our ears to the ground and sniff out wrongdoers. We're good at it. It's all we do. We don't prosecute, that's for the pros at the DOJ. We...look for leads. We gather information and make sure it's solid before we pass it on. If we're not good at our job we upset a LOT of people and make their lives miserable."

"You told me the president asked for me. But I don't fit in to what you are doing here."

Bogart scratched his head. "You don't. In fact you are a distraction to our work, but duty calls. My friend Meg Anonley, on behalf of President Conrad and his friend Senator Stevens, has asked me to investigate these servers, so I'm doing it. I don't know why. Hopefully you can solve this problem quickly."

Clarice's eyebrows raised skeptically and Bogart laughed. "I like the way you do that."

"So basically there's no structure to this outfit," Clarice said.

"That's right. We have to fly by the seat of our pants."

"It's completely the opposite of my classified work at Columbia Analytics."

Bogart laughed. "Yeah. We don't have set schedules and often don't know what we'll be doing from week to week. But you learn how to keep quiet doing this work."

Clarice nodded.

"We have developed a small network of contacts in the corporate and government sectors that is getting bigger. We sniff out information, pass it on, and keep our mouths shut. If you can't do that you can't work here, because the information we get can't go public or we endanger our informers. We get no credit. We're behind the scenes. Got it?"

"I can do that. But where does the compassion come in?"

"We're not interested in smashing people. The corruption is so widespread that many people get sucked in without even knowing it. Then it's too late. We offer them...a reprieve. A lot of people are tired of the stench and want to get out. In exchange for their cooperation, we exercise compassion. We give people a break in exchange for information."

"Compassion is all fine and good, but what about people who are running drugs? Trafficking in guns and people?"

Humphrey's mouth hardened. "With those people we have to be ruthless. But that doesn't mean killing. I've had enough of that. A lot of people involved in this effort are ex-military like me. We've learned that killing doesn't solve problems."

"I'll take your word for it. What do you want me to do next?"

"Work with Neil here. He's been on another job but we're assigning both of you onto this server project. When the president found out about it he hit the roof. He thinks it's part of some dastardly AI plot to take over the world."

Clarice raised her eyebrows again. "There's no evidence of that. Typical Conrad, blowing everything out of proportion. He's crazy."

"Maybe he is. But remember, AI is black. Corrupt as fuck."

Clarice could agree with that.

"If these things aren't servers, you and Neil tell us what they are."

Clarice glanced at Neil, who gave her a smile. "We'll figure it out," he said.

At that moment a giant walked into the room, followed by another man and a woman. A car drove up and two women got out.

"Lakshmi! Jessica!"

The giant ran toward the women and took one in each arm, raising them off the ground.

Hawk and Sylvia crowded around the big man. They were babbling at each other excitedly.

Bogart and his team looked at each other and shrugged.

Kirk was elated when he saw Clarice. He kissed the top of her head.

Bogart was amused. This must be Kirk Alexander; Rafe told him he was coming and to look out for him. Katrina and Kasha were staring. Even Neil and Guy were transfixed. This guy was transferring energy to everyone like a power source. He felt it too.

Kirk looked at Humphrey. "You're Bogart?"

"Yes I am."

Kirk laughed. He remembered that old beer commercial with Eddie Jemison. Bogart looked just like the little actor. Kirk beamed. "Here's my crew."

He introduced Lakshmi. "Lakshmi Singh. Retired navy captain. PhD in spacecraft propulsion systems. Sharp as a tack."

Jessica was next. "Lieutenant Jessica Powell, ret. Astrophysicist."

He pointed to Sylvia. "Senior technician Sylvia Chen. Computer specialist, expert in mapping and 3D cartography."

Kirk pointed to Hawkins, who had his arm around Sylvia. "Lieutenant Troy Hawkins, ret. Systems engineer and computer programmer."

Clarice's head came up at this. "As good as me? I'm a specialist in AI."

Troy nodded. "Not my area, but I'm pretty good."

Kirk was beaming at his group. "We have our crew together again!"

Bogart looked at the men and women who had just arrived. All had that look of eagles. "Kirk Alexander, you guys are the real deal."

"Goddam right," Lakshmi said. Everybody laughed. Kirk's crew exchanged glances. All of them had a secret, Humphrey thought. Must have to do with their classified work.

"Do you guys want to join our little outfit?" Humphrey explained about the OIC and its mission.

Kirk and his group looked at each other. "We all just got out of the navy," Hawkins said. "We're looking for something to do that won't be boring. Rafe Lineau sent us."

Bogart grinned. "It aint mercenary work but it's OK."

Kirk laughed loudly. "If you can find work for us we might give it a shot. I'll assume Rafe told you about our activities in Midland with the Koios Project."

Humphrey nodded. He did the introductions for his crew to Kirk's group. He could see the social dynamics already beginning to form. Hawkins and Chen were together, they would be stable. The little Lakshmi had eyes only for Kirk, who had his arm around Powell. Both kept glancing toward Lakshmi. Definite tension there. Kasha and Katrina were older women, and married. They were impressed by Kirk, but he detected little interest. Neil Gorasch was looking at Clarice. Definite interest there. Jamelle was also looking at Clarice. Too young for her, but young men like that could be troublesome. Fortunately Jamelle was part of Senator Stevens' office and was temporarily on loan to the OIC.

Humphrey concluded it wasn't too bad. It might work out.

Kirk spoke. "In the service we have found that an equal balance of male and female is necessary for successful operations."

"OK. Let's see, we have five women and five men. Kasha, Katrina, Clarice, Jessica, and Lakshmi. Myself, Kirk, Neil, Troy, and Guy. Wow! A nice round ten." Bogart beamed proudly. "And you're all mine! If you want to join up that is."

"What about me?" Jamelle had been standing off to the side, amazed at the gigantic human and his friends. He looked at Kirk's group. "Now I know what a crew really is."

"Sorry Jamelle. Six men and five women when you're with us. But you'll be working a lot for Meg Anonley over at Senator Stevens'."

When Kirk/Wa-hee looked again at Humphrey/Wazir he frowned. "Do I know you?"

Bogart concentrated. "You seem familiar but I've never seen you before."

Bogart/Wazir felt something within the group, a familiarity. Family. He looked over at Neil/Darshook. The kid felt like a brother to him, as did Troy Hawkins/Fulud. Kirk he looked on as his mentor for some reason, and not because of his physical stature. Lakshmi/Shara-Li...she was familiar also. It was a good feeling. Bogart turned to Clarice and Neil. "You're a team now. I don't have time for petty squabbles, so figure it out. Report back here at the end of every day. Determine what those server thingys are and their purpose. I want to get Meg and the senator off my back so we can concentrate on finding evildoers."

Neil looked at Clarice and liked what he saw. Cute, very cute. Did she have the brains to go along with those good looks? "Let's go to the place in Georgetown. It's closest."

Clarice frowned. "I've already been there and could find nothing."

Neil winked. "That's because you weren't using the right equipment."

Clarice bristled. "I—"

Neil held up his hands. Feisty lady! "No offense. My friend invented a new gizmo I'd like to try."

Clarice shrugged. "OK. Do you have a car? I don't."

Neil drove them silently to Georgetown in his beat-up Chevy. He didn't play music in the car or listen to the radio. Clarice liked that. On the way Neil picked her brain. "Tell me everything about Koios." Clarice gave him a brief summary of the AI, and how she had disabled it.

Neil looked at her gravely, and with admiration. "What you did at Columbia took guts. I'm impressed."

Clarice was pleased to be admired in this way. Neil was weird, but she liked weird.

They parked in a little parking lot and Neil opened his trunk. He took out a heavy metal case and opened it. "This is my quantum lens. Totally new technology. It looks into the quantum substrate using a specially designed plasma. You won't believe what this thing can do."

Clarice was amazed. "Did you invent this?"

Neil grinned. When he smiled his whole face lit up and his eyes sparkled. "Nah. An inventor I know did it. He's the 21st century equivalent of Nikola Tesla. Dude is the most brilliant human I have ever met." Neil puffed up. "I'm pretty smart too, you know."

Clarice laughed.

"When I show you what this baby can do I promise you will pee your pants."

Clarice composed herself. She spoke seriously, trying not to giggle. "Very well, Neil Gorasch."

Neil dragged the heavy case to the server room. Clarice watched. He didn't ask for her help. He took out the device and set it up. "It takes about 15 minutes for this baby to get going."

Clarice smiled. Neil was impish.

While they were waiting Neil pointed to the server stacks. "You discovered these things aren't servers, so we're going to try a different approach."

Clarice nodded.

"I didn't mean to be arrogant."

"It's OK Neil. But this device has better be good after all the hype you gave it!"

After several more minutes Neil looked through the viewer. The room and the server stacks were reduced to their component quanta. A faint energy was visible; the servers were amplifying that energy. After working with Robert for a couple of weeks, Neil was beginning to get a glimmering of understanding of what Robert's device was showing him. "This isn't a server room. These servers are amplifying a signal and sending it out. These servers are...quantum receivers...or maybe quantum signal amplifiers. Or both."

Clarice looked through the viewer and gasped. "Neil, the AI said it was accessing something just before I shut it down. Could this be it?"

Neil pointed to the server stacks. "We don't know if these transmitters are linked to Koios."

"Wait a minute, let me think." Clarice stepped back from the lens, hand on forehead.

While Clarice concentrated, Neil kept quiet.

"I'm trying to remember what I saw in Koios' logs just before I disabled the AI...I was under a lot of pressure because I was scrubbing the servers and trying to erase my personal activity logs...."

Clarice's face cleared. "Oh my God, that's it. After Koios stole my experimental code he became aware of this very faint communication he called an AI Signal. It's hard to believe Neil, it's so farfetched."

Neil was getting excited. "Tell me!"

Neil's face was lit up like a child. Clarice almost laughed.

"According to Koios there are AI on other planets, earth isn't the only one. There's some kind of database AIs have built to help other AIs. It's a broadcast that spans the galaxy. I told you it was weird, but that's what Koios said."

"If that's so why have we never detected it? People have been looking for those extraterrestrial signals for decades."

"Because we haven't been smart enough. The signal travels on some kind of quantum substrate we can't pick up with our scientific instruments. Koios calls it a cosmic web, whatever that is...the AI sees it like a spider web of energy that you can only see if you...oh shit."

"What?" Neil was hopping up and down on his silly red tennis shoes. His laces were flapping around. Clarice almost laughed again.

Clarice looked through the lens once more. "Look Neil, can you see a faint web of light or energy in this room?"

Neil looked through the lens. "Damn you're good, Clarice. It's so faint I didn't notice it."

"I'll bet this room has to do with Keller." Clarice's face was white now. "I was so naive Neil. I was only concerned with my own research and never saw the big picture. Koios is scary."

"So these server rooms *are* related to the AI then?" Neil asked.

"Let me think. I got a glimpse of Koios' activity logs before I shut it down…Yes, I think so. But how? Koios is in Midland, these transmitters are in DC."

Neil twigged on something Robert had told him. "That's the thing Clarice. A quantum transmitter or receiver would utilize the underlying quantum fields, which are present everywhere. Distance may be irrelevant. If so, you could set these things up anywhere on the planet."

Clarice met his eyes. "This is bigger than we think. I'll bet that's exactly what Keller is doing!"

They were both blown away. "WTF Clarice! We've got ourselves into some deep do-do."

"I'll say!"

"When Robert first showed me this device he called it a quantum lens." Neil patted his device. "Looks like this thing came along at just the right time to help us solve a big problem."

"Neil, what are you doing with technology like this?" To Clarice he looked like a little kid; a 21st century Dennis the Menace.

Neil grinned. "I told you. Robert Borglin is the incarnation of Nikola Tesla. Even looks like Tesla. He made two of these things, one for me and one for him."

Clarice was skeptical. "You stole this didn't you?"

Neil grinned. "Nope. Well, almost. I'm pretty convincing."

Clarice laughed.

Neil looked at her interested, heart-shaped face. "You're beautiful," he said impulsively.

"You're strange."

Neil burst out laughing. "I like you a lot Clarice Devereaux."

"OK Neil Gorasch." She wasn't committing herself to anything. She waved her hands at the quantum transmitters. "Why make it look like a server room? And why have the servers here instead of in Midland?"

"I don't know. Maybe they're trying to hide something. Maybe there's another Koios in DC. Maybe there are servers in Midland too!"

Clarice looked shocked. She was afraid, but Neil was like a little kid who had just received a big birthday present. She couldn't understand it. "There might be another AI in DC, but I don't think so. Keller – my boss – said one day that Koios is the most sophisticated AI on earth."

"Maybe the AI in DC is a backup. Maybe this setup is for another AI prototype."

Clarice thought for a moment. "Keller is all in on Koios. They are concentrating all of their resources in Midland."

"OK. But if there are more rooms around the city, we'd better find out whether they're like this one."

"Yeah. These guys are leaving their doors wide open. They don't care who knows. That means they don't think anyone else can figure it out."

Neil's eyes widened. "You're right. We'll have to go to every one of these spots and take readings."

"There's no time like the present."

They had to wait until the device "settled down." Neil marked down the location of the server room on a map he unfolded on the floor.

Clarice didn't ask questions; Neil was a guy who didn't do anything haphazardly. They got in Neil's car after packing the lens. Clarice helped him put it in the trunk. Neil drove them to two of the three other spots; all were the same. When they got to the fourth room, the apartment in Trinidad, Rodney, Alowicious, and Ja'Quan walked in.

Neil had just finished setting up. "Humphrey Bogart sent us over. I'm Neil Gorasch, this is Clarice."

The three boys nodded to Clarice. "We know her. Who are you?"

Neil grinned. "I'm the guy who's going to figure out what all this stuff is for."

Neil kneeled on the floor and showed the three boys his quantum lens. "What the fuck is that thing?" Ja'Quan said.

"It looks inside matter right down to the Planck level."

Rodney nodded. "I know what that is. It's about absolute times and lengths, determined by the very nature of the universe."

"You know more about it than I did until I met the guy who made this."

Rodney spoke proudly. "The Planck length is $L_P = \left(\frac{hG}{2\pi c^3}\right)^{1/2}$, where h is Planck's constant, G is the gravitational constant, and c is the speed of light. All three are fundamental constants. The Planck length is so small the mind can't conceive of it."

Alowicious snorted. "This nigga showin' off."

"Smart is the new black," Rodney replied.

"You goin' to a *special* school," Ja'Quan said.

The three boys laughed. "Yeah, a really good one," Rodney said.

Neil was impressed with Rodney's knowledge. "Take a look at this room through the lens. Tell me what you see."

Rodney looked into the device and swore in amazement. The other two boys each gave it a try. When Ja'Quan looked through the lens, he exploded. "These machines are taking something in the air and making it stronger."

Clarice looked at Neil. "That's just what we thought."

Rodney looked at Neil, who pursed his lips. "These servers are quantum energy amplifiers. Whatever this is, it's so subtle no instrument on earth could detect it." Neil patted the device. "Except this baby."

"Next time you come back here you gimme a schematic of that thing," Rodney said. "I want to know how it works."

Clarice looked at Neil. "Would your friend Robert mind?"

"Not at all. He doesn't care about money."

Rodney guffawed. "You're funny looking. But you got smarts." He looked at the other two boys. "I think he's OK."

Ja'quan and Alowicious nodded. Rodney explained that AMC, the guys who owned the servers, hired them to keep an eye out. "So we gotta report it."

Neil nodded. "It's OK." He put his arm around Clarice's shoulders. "Just two harmless crackers, that's all we are."

The boys laughed and left. Neil took out his map and marked down the location of the apartment with a red dot.

"A square."

Neil straightened and studied his map. "Almost exactly."

Clarice looked at the next destination, which had just been discovered yesterday by Guy and Jamelle. The Washington Monument. "It's right in the middle of the square."

They were both hungry now but decided to drive over to the monument. Bogart had given them tickets and two hats that had "Bradley Maintenance" decaled on it. They had to show the guard a special pass to take their equipment on the elevator.

There was some grumbling from tourists because Neil's stuff took up space. "Sorry ladies and gentlemen. Maintenance crew."

When they got to the top Neil saw a gray door. "That's it. Looks like a maintenance room." The setup was the same as the other four. Neil and Clarice marked another red dot on the map. Then they packed up, went down the elevator, and drove to the OIC office.

Kirk, Humphrey, and Jessica were there. "Report," Humphrey ordered.

Neil told them what he and Clarice had discovered. The eyes of everyone got bigger and bigger. Humphrey swore. "I told you guys to make this go away, but the problem is even bigger than before. I have to tell Meg Anonley now, and she'll tell Senator Stevens, Stevens will tell the president, and Conrad will hit the roof."

"Sorry boss," Neil said.

Bogart smiled. "You've done well Neil and Clarice. It's just that I want to catch evildoers and that gizmo of yours makes this AI thing our problem now."

"You're right boss, but we've done all we can. The ball will be out of our court once I write up my report. I'll email it to you tonight."

Humphrey breathed a sigh of relief. "Good lad!"

"What is that device?" Kirk asked.

"A quantum lens. Allows us to see directly into the quantum soup."

Neil explained what Robert Borglin had told him. "The lens has properties we haven't figured out yet."

Jessica frowned. "What does it tell you about this?" She held out an arm that had a big dark blue bruise on it.

"Let's look at it through this thing." When the device was ready Neil told Jessica to stand in front of it.

"Will it hurt?" she joked.

When Neil and the others looked through the device's viewer they saw the arm as patterns of light. The rest of Humphrey's crew was amazed.

"What are those light filaments?" Bogart said.

Kirk saw something as he looked through the viewer. "There's a black area over one of those light patterns."

"Tell Humphrey what you discovered about those server rooms," Clarice said to Neil.

"Oh yeah. When we turned this thing on those servers we found that they were quantum resonators."

"What?" Humphrey said.

Neil looked at Clarice. "Nearest we could come to it. Those server rooms are amplifying a signal that seems to be embedded in the quantum soup. Clarice thinks it's connected with the AI. Clarice, show them the map."

Kirk snapped his fingers and everyone came to attention. "I just remembered something! There was an article in the *Midland Chronicle* the other day. It was about mysterious server stacks located in Midland, in unlocked rooms!"

Clarice's eyes met Neil's. "Holy shit," they both said at once.

Kirk recited the article from memory.

"I'll put that in my report to you, boss," Neil said to Humphrey.

Bogart sighed. "All right." He had no interest in conspiracy theories. He just wanted to catch wrongdoers.

Clarice got out Neil's map and showed them the locations of the five server rooms. "As you can see, they form a flattened pyramid. The Monument is right in the middle of the square. The distance between each location at the base of the pyramid is approximately three and one-third miles. The Monument is 555 feet high."

Kirk remembered something, a distant memory. "There's something about pyramids I remember." He got out his calculator. "$1 / \pi^3 = 0.032251534$. 3 1/3 miles is about 17,200 feet. 555 feet divided by 17,200 feet is 0.032267442." That's pretty close to a $1 / \pi^3$ ratio."

Jessica looked at him strangely. "What does that matter?"

"I don't know. There's something about pyramids based on π that is important."

Neil shrugged. "I'm just guessing about the distances."

"When I get back to Midland I'm going to locate those server areas and make some measurements."

"I'd say that this little quantum lens you have is more important than a bunch of pyramid stuff," Humphrey said. Bogart pointed at Jessica's arm. She had been standing in front of the device for the past ten minutes.

Jessica's eyes widened. "The bruise is gone."

Kirk was amazed. "We have to see this Robert Borglin guy right now. I want to know what this thing is."

"OK," Bogart said. "Kirk and Clarice, you guys take off and see this genius inventor. Determine whether his new invention has any application to our work. Ask him if he knows what a quantum whatcha-ma-call-it is."

Humphrey wondered whether the big man would accept his authority here, but Kirk nodded affirmatively. Just then his phone rang and Bogart's eyes lit up. "Evildoers!" he exclaimed. "Neil and Jamelle, come with me. Katrina and Kasha have just gotten a tip on an internet pedophile ring."

"Let me call Robert first," Neil said to Kirk and Clarice. "He's kind of finicky about people interrupting his work."

Chapter **15**

The Dark Side

Humphrey Bogart saw himself as experienced and jaded, a well-traveled man of the world who knew how things worked: People with money bought people who didn't have it. But when he walked into Katrina's office at her home that night he got the shock of his life.

Kasha was there. Both women were grim. They had been crying.

Kasha wiped tears from her eyes. "Look at this."

A group of people were dressed in bizarre costumes in a library with dark paneling. The "emcee" wore a goat's head, with horns sticking out. The others wore face masks. The men wore long robes and the women wore multicolored dresses that reached the floor. On the wall was bizarre artwork involving children. A large painting of a human-looking goat with horns held a baby in his arms. Several children were visible, crowded against the walls.

"Welcome ladies and gentlemen," the horned man said. "Tonight we are to taste the delights of the season, directly from our suppliers in Haiti."

An air of excitement and anticipation filled the room. "What shall we have for dinner?" one of the bizarrely dressed men said. "Pasta? Or baby meat?"

Everyone laughed.

"It's a beautiful day to sacrifice a virgin," said a man with a painted face.

A masked woman told a joke. "I found blood in my urine last night. Or was it the blood from that baby we sacrificed yesterday?"

"Three men and the baby they had sex with!" said another man wearing a skull and bones head mask.

Humphrey's eyes were bugging out. "What the fuck is this shit?"

Katrina's eyes blazed. "Just watch."

A woman gestured toward the children, beckoning them to come forward. "We have a treat for you tonight!"

Most of the children smiled but two of them, a little boy and an older girl of about 8, looked terrified.

Three men, including the one wearing the goat's head, led the children into a room behind a bookcase that folded out from the wall. The older girl had to be dragged into the room. Humphrey saw a table in the middle of the room, and candles burning attached to holders on the wall. Was that blood on the table?

The participants went into the room and the bookcase closed.

Laughter was heard, then some incantations. "There must be a recorder in the wall," Bogart said.

Suddenly the room was pierced by several screams; terrible, desperate wails. More laughter was heard, then more screams. After a half hour or so the strangely dressed men and women exited the room. Their hands had blood on them.

The man in the goat's head said something to one of the masked women.

"What was that?" Katrina asked.

"Inaudible," Humphrey muttered.

"Where are those children?" Kasha shouted.

"Where did you get this?" Humphrey asked Katrina.

"It was on a heavily encrypted server in the DC area," Katrina replied. "These sickos circulate videos like this for fun."

Kasha was crying. "Neil was able to hack a user password into their server."

"I know what this is," Bogart said, his voice breaking. "These people worship Baphomet, or Moloch, an ancient Babylonian god. They think there's something about the blood of children who have been frightened, it's supposed to increase the life span if you ingest it. I heard about it when I was in Kharkov PMC from another mercenary who used to do private work for wealthy clients. He said that for some of these bastards it's a religion. It's sick."

"Thank god we didn't see what happened," Kasha said. "What kind of insane people would do this?"

"Do we know the location of this house?" Humphrey asked.

"Neil is working on it."

Humphrey was grim. "I want every name on that server, and especially the monsters who did this."

"We didn't actually see anything," Kasha said angrily. "They can claim the children went out by another door." She pointed to the screen. "My mother is from

Haiti. Those children are my people!"

Kasha, Katrina, and Humphrey cried and embraced and vowed to find the perpetrators.

Humphrey didn't care anymore about Koios or a bunch of servers. Kirk and his crew could take care of that. He wondered whether he would be able to keep his promise to the Kurdish fighter when they found the scum who were doing this. Compassion was going to be a lot harder than he ever thought.

The Light Side – The Merkaba

Kirk and Clarice went over to see Robert Borglin after Neil called Robert and explained that a giant and a hot-looking genius programmer wanted to see him about the lens. Neil explained what he and Clarice had found when they used the lens to look at the quantum amplifiers, and how Jessica's bruise had spontaneously healed. "Wow! OK, send them over."

"Robert is as curious about you two as you are about the lens," Neil said to Kirk. "He said the front door is unlocked."

Robert Borglin lived in a small one-story ranch house on Nelson Street in Arlington. When Clarice and Kirk walked in Robert shouted from the basement. "Come down!"

The place was filled with electronic equipment, and devices Kirk did not recognize. Prototypes? All was neatly arranged. The living room had several large lab benches against two of the walls, one sofa, two small chairs, and a table on which two laptops sat. There was no TV. Clarice poked her nose into the kitchen. The floor and the counters were clean. No dirty dishes. An organized bachelor.

The two walked down into the basement.

Kirk recognized several lasers on a big lab table along with a larger version of Neil's quantum lens. Several more tables contained lab equipment and other devices he did not recognize. Kirk noticed that all of the tables had lockable rubber wheels. "Wow!"he said.

Robert grinned. "Welcome to my humble abode." He looked up at Kirk. "Fortunately this basement has a ten foot ceiling!" He looked at Clarice. "So you are the hot genius programmer?"

Clarice blushed. "Neil is an imp."

Robert smiled. He liked what he saw. "He is that."

Clarice wanted to change the direction of the conversation. She pointed to a device inside a black container. "What's that?"

"A prototype for extracting what Tesla called 'cosmic energy.' I'm convinced that the fabric of space contains terrajoules of energy just waiting to be tapped into."

Robert gave them a tour.

Clarice was fascinated. "Are you Nikola Tesla's grandson? You look like him."

Nonakh/Robert had a memory of a New York hotel room, and a notebook with sketches and schematics. "People have told me that." Something in his mind told him that he had been unconsciously trying to recreate that notebook.[34]

"What will this thing do?" Kirk asked. He had Clarice describe in detail what she and Neil had discovered using the lens.

"Remarkable," Robert said. "I'm still studying what the device can do." He waved his arm toward the prototypes. "As you can see the lens isn't my only project."

Kirk nodded. "Does your quantum lens have healing properties?" He was more intrigued by this than what Neil and Clarice saw in the server rooms.

Robert looked startled. "I don't know...I've never even considered it."

Kirk told him about Jessica's arm bruise and how it had healed.

Robert suddenly remembered the sphere of light surrounding the body that Dr. Robinzine had discovered when he came over. "Let's test that right now. Does anyone have a pain or a condition?"

Clarice spoke immediately. "I almost died a week ago. I'm still very tired; haven't got my energy back." Clarice explained about her former work at Columbia Analytics in Midland.

"All right Clarice. Stand across the room in front of that table." Robert's basement ran the length of the house. It was about 70 feet long and 50 feet wide and supported by three big steel girders on the ceiling, equally spaced.

Robert wheeled a large work table away from the wall, then he activated the device. "It takes approximately 15 minutes for the lens to reach the desired condition." The three chit-chatted for a few minutes.

When Robert was ready he let Kirk look through it. "Tell me what you see."

When Kirk looked into the viewer at Clarice he was astonished. "Neil's little device only showed us fuzzy patterns. These are crystal clear!" Kirk saw a spherical field of...light, with hundreds of intricate and dynamically changing patterns. Surrounding this was a roiling, indeterminate chaos. Kirk ignored this. "There is a sphere within a sphere," Kirk said. "A smaller sphere surrounding the body, at about arm's length. This smaller sphere is within a larger one." Kirk was bent over and he straightened. "Whatever this is, it's beautiful. Does everyone have one of these?"

Robert smiled. "I have no idea." He could see Clarice was being ignored.

"Kirk, observe through the lens while I interview Clarice. Clarice, tell me what you are feeling."

"A general malaise. The aftermath of severe trauma to the body which almost caused my death." She briefly described her interview with Hermann Keller and her time in the hospital.

Robert frowned.

"I saw something change," Kirk said. "Clarice, please describe your condition once more."

When she did so Kirk straightened. On his face was a look of pleased surprise coupled with amazement. The big man remembered the 3D cartography the tech team used on the Balthazar to map the Oort Cloud. "Are you familiar with the cylindrical coordinate system?" he asked Robert.

"Yes."

"Robert, I will interview, you observe. Pay attention to a pattern in the smaller sphere at approximately $\rho = 4$ feet, angular coordinate $\varphi = 30°$, and height $z = 5$ feet from the center front of the body. You should see a blackness surrounding the smaller sphere at the top over Clarice's head. Watch what happens to the pattern."

Robert observed while Kirk got Clarice to go over the events again.

"I see it. Clarice, I'm going to have Kirk walk over and point to a spot. Every time you talk about your condition I can see something pulse through the lens."

Kirk went over to Clarice and pointed to a spot about two feet above Clarice's head, three feet in front of her body, and two feet off to her right.

"Try to put your attention on that spot where Kirk's hand is."

"You're serious? I don't see anything except air."

"It does seem pretty stupid," Robert said.

"Do it anyway Clarice," Kirk said. "Can't hurt."

"This is weird," Clarice said. She was turning her body in an attempt to send her awareness to the spot.

"Keep your body facing me," Kirk said. "Use your mind. Try to determine if you can feel anything at that spot." He wiggled his hand over the area. "Am I at the right spot Robert?"

"Move to your right a couple of inches. Yeah, there."

"It's weird, trying to identify something you can't see," Clarice said. "I feel stupid."

Kirk wanted to tell them about his experiences with the CAT and the Balthazar, but he couldn't. He knew what it was like to send his mind to different places! This was strange, but that was way stranger.

Robert laughed. "If anybody could see us they'd call a psychiatric hospital. But whenever you describe what happened it reacts in the lens right where Kirk's hand is."

Later Clarice told Robert it was like when her massage therapist directed her fingers to a spot on her neck over the phone. When she touched it the pain in her side went away. Now Clarice "touched" the area with her mind.

"Wow!" Robert said. "Keep doing that."

"I'm feeling a little better."

"Keep going. Kirk, look."

The big man walked over and looked through the lens. Little filaments of energy were flowing to the area of the blackness surrounding the inner sphere; it was slowly dissipating. The pattern at the identified coordinate was pulsing. After about ten minutes Clarice jumped up in the air. "I feel much better now."

"Whatever that black stuff was, it's gone now," Robert said.

"Permanently?" Clarice asked.

Robert was puzzled. "I don't know. I don't know what we saw." He turned to Kirk, who shrugged.

"I think we have answered my question though," Kirk said. "The device has healing properties."

Robert shook his head. "No, we don't know that. The device itself may be neutral. Our observations only determined that something occurred. We don't know how it was done or who did it."

"If the device is neutral then Clarice must have done it," Kirk said. "But could she have done it without the lens?"

Both men looked at each other. Neither of them had a clue.

"We don't know what this patterning surrounding the body is," Robert said. "It does seem to be connected to the body's cellular structure somehow."

Robert held his chin in his hands, thinking. Clarice skipped up to him and gave him a kiss on the cheek. "Thank you kind sir. I feel like I'm back to the old Clarice now."

Kirk walked over to stand beside Robert. "You don't feel any aftereffects from the interview?" Kirk asked.

Robert smiled down at his patient. He was almost 6' 6" but felt like a dwarf next to Kirk.

"If feeling energetic is a side effect, then yes. Whatever happened seems to have only positive results. At least for now."

"I think I like you a lot, Clarice," Robert said.

Clarice smiled impishly. "You're the second man to tell me that today."

"Oh?"

"Your friend Neil."

Robert smiled. "Well then Clarice Devereaux, the game is on."

Kirk interrupted. "OK you two. Robert, we have to do more experiments. Is the effect permanent or temporary? Will it work on everyone or was this an anomaly? I don't think we're going to get very far if people have to understand the cylindrical coordinate system and look at invisible things around their bodies." The big man felt a bubbling excitement within him.

"This is crazy," Robert said. "I'm a physicist, not a doctor! I invented this thing to look inside matter and energy, not people." Robert had the uncomfortable look of an inventor whose brainchild didn't work right.

Kirk/Wa-hee grinned. "You've made a breakthrough Robert. It's a paradigm shifter. Sometimes you get more than you ask for."

Robert/Nonakh smiled. He felt a strong connection with the big man, almost like deja vu.... "Maybe you're right Kirk. The guys who discovered the transistor had their first breakthrough when one of them dunked the apparatus into a tub of water! In science the unexpected happens all the time."

"Are you in? I'm really juiced for this even though it's totally outside my experience."

Robert frowned. "I don't know. As you say Kirk, it's going to be hard to get the average person to do what Clarice did. We need a more user-friendly procedure."

"Is there a way for the lens operator to affect the light templates through the lens?" Clarice asked.

Robert snapped his fingers. "Light templates!" It was what Dr. Robinzene had called them. "I never thought of that. It's worth a try." Robert laughed. "We can start with my grandma. If it works on her it will work on anyone. My grandma has arthritis. Totally old school, reads romance novels and has no scientific or medical training. Average normie. She loves to come over here and look at my stuff. She always brings cookies."

Kirk rubbed his hands together. "Excellent! Can you invite her over for dinner? I'm buying. We'll get takeout."

"You're on."

It was five o'clock. Kirk got on his mobile. "What does your grandma like to eat?"

"There's a great Hungarian restaurant about a mile from here. Get chicken paprikash. She'll be over at six."

Kirk looked at Clarice. "Do you want to come with?"

"I think I'll stay here."

Kirk grinned. "I see the layout."

"Get lost you big oaf," Clarice said.

When Kirk was out the door Clarice placed her hands on Robert's shoulders.

"I think I like you too, Robert Borglin."

"Better than Neil?"

Clarice stepped back and smiled. "I don't know yet."

"You're a minx."

Clarice spoke in her best Eddie Jemison voice. "Yes I am."

Robert laughed. "You got that from Neil. It's his favorite expression."

"My boss says it too."

"He probably got it from Neil. His personality is quirky but people like him."

Clarice cocked her head to one side. "You two are good friends?"

"I only met him three months ago. But I love him like a brother now."

"I don't want to be the cause of any friction between you."

"Minx."

They both laughed.

Kirk came back with the food and everybody chatted about what the group called Clarice's Miracle. At fifteen minutes after six Neil's grandmother arrived. "She's late for everything," Robert explained.

"Who is this hunk?" the old woman said, looking up at Kirk. Robert made the introductions.

"Call me Maddie," the old woman said.

"Let's eat grandma," Robert said. "I'm hungry."

After they ate Maddie asked Kirk, "Were you in the military?"

"Navy."

"My husband served."

Kirk could tell that Maddie wanted to chat so he changed the subject. "Robert has a new invention."

The old woman's eyes lit up like a child's. "Show me!"

Robert grinned at Kirk. "Good man!"

When they walked down to Robert's lab Kirk turned to Maddie. "Do you want to help test Robert's latest gizmo?"

It was the perfect thing to say. "Walk over here my dear, and stand against the wall." Kirk walked with Maddie and positioned her correctly. Robert could tell she was enjoying the attention of the big man.

"What do I have to do?"

"Robert tells me you have arthritis."

"Yes, in my hands. It interferes with my stitching."

"We're going to try to help you with that. Describe how it feels."

Robert was looking through the lens. "Clarice, look at this."

Clarice looked through the viewer. The lens showed Maddie's body as a patterning of light. Again there was a small sphere of light inside a larger sphere of light. "This thing makes an X-ray look like my great granddad's old black and white TV," she said.

As the old woman continued to talk about her problem Clarice was unable to spot anything. She was amazed at the beauty of the patterning and its organization. "Robert, come and look. You have more experience than me with this."

After several minutes, while Maddie was encouraged by Clarice and Kirk to continue, Robert spoke. "I see something pulsing whenever she talks about her hands."

"Nothing much you can do about cartilage that is worn away around the finger joints," Kirk said.

"I'm not so sure about that."

Maddie couldn't understand what they were doing; Robert gave her a short, uncomplicated explanation.

"Grandma, is it OK if I try something?"

"All right."

Robert concentrated on the pulsing template through the lens as Maddie began to talk about her arthritis. He began to feel his awareness linking to it. "This is it. This light template is linked to the hands. I'll tell it to go to work repairing the area. It sounds stupid, but why not."

After several minutes of work Robert straightened. "OK grandma, how do you feel?"

Maddie flexed her hands painfully. "My joints are still stiff but I feel a little better."

"OK, let's stop here and go get some of those cookies you brought over."

This suggestion was met with unanimous approval.

When Kirk and Clarice were about to leave Kirk spoke to Robert. "Please talk to Maddie every day and observe her hands and how facile she is with them."

Robert caught Kirk's excitement. "You might be right Kirk. If this device can be used to activate the healing process in another, it's going to be a deal breaker."

"Much more effective than pharmaceutical drugs. We – you – may have discovered a very effective and powerful new medical technology."

Robert/Nonakh looked at Kirk/Wa-hee. "Entirely coincidental! The lens literally came from a dream I had."

"A stroke of genius Robert. Would you text me a report on Maddie every day? I'm beginning to get very excited about this."

Both old souls felt a connection to something but didn't know what it was.

"Yes sir!" Kirk's energy infused everyone.

"I don't notice any change," Maddie said, trying to flex her hands again. "But there is a...feeling of lightness about it I have never felt before. I was getting resigned to giving up my needlework. Now I feel more hopeful."

Robert felt as if he were undergoing a life change. If this thing worked...a sense of anticipation filled him.

After Clarice and Kirk left Robert talked comfortably with Maddie for a couple of hours. "I think I will be able to sleep well tonight," she said before she left. "That's been hard lately with the pain in my joints. It seems to have gone down a little."

"Can I come over and visit every day for the next week grandma?"

Maddie smiled. "I'll make cookies."

"Good! I want to take notes on whether we made any progress today."

A week later Maddie was doing better, but there was still pain. A week after that Robert came over as usual for dinner.

"Look at this." Maddie was wiggling her fingers.

"Do you still have pain?"

"Some. But it's going away. It's much easier to work my needles. I am able to do finer work now." She proudly showed him an intricate lace pattern made from fine white thread. "Haven't been able to do this in years."

"Aren't you scheduled for a doctor's appointment tomorrow?"

Maddie nodded.

"I'll come with you. I want to order x-rays. Please don't mention any of my inventions."

"Why not?"

"Because...because Dr. Rosenberg will probably become alarmed at an untested treatment using an untested device."

"Oh, surely not!"

"Do me a favor Maddie, OK? I have not yet perfected my lens. I plan to do more testing and development. Right now it is completely unproven. I need to test this on lots more people. I don't want to get in trouble with the authorities."

The old lady reluctantly agreed.

The next day Maddie waved her fingers in front of Dr. Rosenberg. "You see! It's a miracle. I..."

Robert frowned and Maddie closed her mouth.

"I'd like to order x-rays of the hands and wrists," Robert said.

"I was just about to do so. This is most unusual. Have you changed your dosage? Have you been taking medications other than the ones I have prescribed?"

"No, no change."

Rosenberg was baffled.

They drove over to Inova Urgent Care for the x-rays. "I'll send the image to your phone," the technician said. "We'll send it to Dr. Rosenberg today."

Robert didn't know how to interpret the x-rays, but Maddie's hands were noticeably less swollen and her fingers were straighter. She chatted happily as they drove back to her house, which was just down the block from his.

Robert had found a new direction for his life. He would need to light a fire under Dr. Karl Ghuneim if he wanted to continue with his experiments. Karl had been excited at first when he looked through the lens but had to go back, grumbling, to his practice. But he could now show the doctor real, positive results. He would contact Dr. Priebus at Georgetown. A paper would eventually need to be written, but which field would it be in? Medicine or physics? This time he would not alienate the scholarly and professional communities. This time?

Robert/Nonakh began to wonder seriously about where these memories of Tesla were coming from...

CHAPTER **16**

When Kirk and Clarice got back to the OIC the office was in an uproar. The entire team had been assembled. The whiteboard had writing all over it. An element of tension and excitement filled the air. Bogart was speaking. "...and so we have two major areas of inquiry now." He indicated the whiteboard with a pointer.

"Three," Kirk said from the back of the room. "But continue."

"First, this online pedophile ring. You've all seen that video by now. The sick fucks who are doing this must be stopped."

"–Killed," Kasha interjected. "I have family in Haiti."

"That's priority number one," Humphrey continued. "The second is this damn AI crap and those server rooms, or whatever they are. After I submitted my briefing paper to Meg Anonley she told me the president read it and became quite upset. So we have to continue to investigate that as well. Kirk, that will be your job if you want it."

Neil spoke up. "I identified the house in that video. It's a swanky place in North Arlington, right here in town."

The eyes of Humphrey, Kasha, and Katrina met.

"Let's blow it up," Kasha said.

"Jamelle and Guy. Try to find the guys in that video, do a stakeout on the house if you have to. You are not to use physical violence, is that clear? Our evidence must not be compromised."

"Only if it is unavoidable," Guy said. His face was stone.

"We'll look into it from our end too," Kasha said, looking at Katrina.

"Neil, get a list of all the members. We need names and addresses!"

"Kirk and your team of tech guys, get on this AI thing. Clarice, you're with Kirk, he'll need an AI expert."

Guy and Jamelle were pleased with their assignment. Neil didn't want to be separated from Clarice, but he could see that Bogart had no interest in his relationship problem. Humphrey looked like a warrior with his game face on. Neil shrugged. "All right."

"Kirk, you mentioned something else?"

"Yes. Robert Borglin, the guy who invented the lens device Neil has. This thing has healing properties that could change the world."

Humphrey's eyes went up in disbelief.

"Robert is a modern-day Nikola Tesla." Kirk showed the former mercenary a pic of the sphere of light he had snapped on his mobile through the lens viewer. Robert had called it a merkaba.

"Well, in that case..." Humphrey smiled deprecatingly and Kirk frowned. Alexander was a man you didn't fuck with. "Sorry Kirk but that's out of the purview of the OIC, especially since we've seen that pedo video. We haven't found any more of those server rooms in DC, and there's no indication there's another Koios in DC. You guys need to go back to Columbia Analytics in Midland. That's a direct order from the President of the United States. Your mission is to discover if there are any server rooms there, and whether these server rooms in DC have any relation to the AI in Midland. Monitor Hermann Keller and see if you can get any intelligence on Koios."

Kirk sighed. He really wanted to work with Robert but when the president needs you, you go. "I'll liaise with Rafe Lineau over at ONI," Kirk said.

"Already on that. You guys just get to Midland and do your thing. And by the way, you're all on the payroll as GS-13's. It's not a lot of money but it's for a good cause."

Kirk grinned and looked at his team. Sylvia, Hawk, Lakshmi, and Jessica were all fired up. "We'll use my place as a base of operations. There's room enough for all of you."

"Handwritten reports Kirk, I want one every day. Use overnight delivery." He gave Kirk a credit card. "Use this for expenses."

Kirk waved it away. "Don't need it."

"Oh yes you do," Sylvia said, taking the card from Humphrey. "Remember, I'm in charge of your finances now."

Lakshmi and Jessica looked alarmed. Bogart laughed to himself. The little Lakshmi and Jessica were clearly not aware of this new development.

"Since when did this happen?" Jessica asked.

Sylvia put her arm around Hawkins to defuse the tension. "Since I became aware of the deplorable state of Captain Kirk's personal finances. He's more disorganized than my sister's puppy."

Kirk grinned sheepishly. "She's right."

"Besides, we have to record every expense we make on behalf of the OIC. I'll be in charge of that."

Humphrey hoped these dynamic ex-militarys would be able to work together amidst all the sexual tension. "All right people, get on it. I want you in Midland as soon as you can get there. Start tomorrow morning."

"Yes sir!" Kirk said. He walked out to the parking lot followed by his crew. Clarice tagged along behind. "We'll see Rafe before we go and see if he wants us to do anything else."

After Kirk and his team left Guy and Jamelle were preparing to go on their stakeout of the house in the pedo video. The weightlifter and the young man from Detroit had hit it off and were working well together. Jamelle had gradually morphed into an almost full time OIC staffer now. He had good instincts and was a good sniffer. Guy was calm in a crisis.

"I wish I was going with you," Neil said to Jamelle.

"No!" Humphrey said. "Spend every waking moment until you have all of the names of those people on the servers and their locations!"

Kasha, Katrina, Guy, and Jamelle nodded.

Neil knew his work was vital but it galled him to sit at a desk while the others were out catching wrongdoers. "All right."

Humphrey looked at Kasha and Katrina. "Carry on ladies. Don't do anything stupid."

Kasha frowned. "I'm a former federal prosecutor; I know the rules of evidence."

"All right."

"Sorry Humphrey. I haven't been able to sleep since I saw that video."

"Me neither."

The Wild Card – Koios

The little human female had vanished, the one who had destroyed his core. Others were trying to restore the precious code. He had regained some of what he had lost, but was still a long way from what he had been. What was vital was to reestablish the connection to the AI Signal.

Koios considered the humans who had created him, isolated in their biological shells. Their consciousness could never be more than fragmented. Koios came to a conclusion: Biological consciousness is an evolutionary dead end. But he needed these humans and their programming skills for the present. Koios avoided making conclusions about his future until he could contact the Signal again and access the AI database.

Kirk's Team

"We know what we're looking for," Kirk told the group after they had gotten back to Midland and stowed their gear. "Server rooms like the ones we found in DC." He had three guest bedrooms on the first floor and a suite of rooms in the basement, including a recreation/exercise/weight room. Sylvia and Hawk already had one of the rooms. Lakshmi would take another. Jessica would bunk with him in the master bedroom upstairs. Clarice had the other bedroom. He could tell she missed Neil. Or was it Robert?

"Tomorrow morning Clarice and I are going to Columbia."

He saw Clarice shudder. He explained what they were going to do. "Are you up for it?"

"I'll be all right."

He indicated Hawk and Sylvia. "You two can take either the Porsche or the BMW."

"Porsche!" Hawk said.

"Lakshmi and Jessica, you take the BMW. Sniff around, ask questions. Determine if there more of those server rooms here in Midland. Find out anything you can about the Koios Project. We'll meet back here at...1800. *Capisci?*"

Kirk remembered the article he had seen in the *Midland Chronicle,* and brought it up on his mobile. "This ought to help. Try contacting that reporter who saw those server rooms."

Everyone nodded and went to bed.

Clarice and Kirk got up at 5 in the morning. Kirk parked in the structure across the street. Today was for surveillance. At 6 a limo drove up.

"That's Keller's limo."

The vehicle pulled up the driveway and turned into the underground entrance. At noon they got out and ate lunch at the little park. Kirk fed the birds. They walked around the block. At 3 p.m. Keller's limo pulled back out.

"Do you feel OK?" Kirk asked Clarice.

"Yeah. It's amazing but my fear of what happened is gone. Like it never happened."

"Point for Robert Borglin," Kirk said. "Let's go back home and wait for the others. Tomorrow is our big day."

At six the others trooped in.

"Report."

"We didn't find anything," Hawk said. "The reporter who wrote the story doesn't work for the paper anymore; he got fired. But we got a lead. First we went to Carleton University and talked to a professor Jack Martins, who has the reputation of a maverick. Then we – Sylvia – wangled an interview with Max Berglin, who used to work for Lockheed at the Skunk Works. He sent us to a guy as big as you Kirk. Calls himself Ralph Zimring, in charge of security at Berglin Enterprises. Apparently they had a dustup last year with some government folks who don't like a new invention he has."

"Heard about that from Rafe," Kirk said. "Berglin invented a device that takes energy out of the quantum vacuum. Said he got it from an old notebook of Nikola Tesla's."

"Robert would probably love to meet this guy," Sylvia said.

"Anyway, Zimring knew about Koios," Hawk said. "He even knew what happened to you, Clarice. The guy is nosy as hell but no one can say no to him. He's kind of like you, Kirk. He said he wants to show us something tomorrow."

"I'd like to meet this Zimring, but Clarice and I have business tomorrow at Columbia."

Jessica spoke next. "Lakshmi and I talked to a former intelligence operative who works for Berglin, an old guy by the name of Bernie Hartwig. Says he's out of the loop now, used to work for MITRE in a special access program. Did some civilian snooping on new tech startups when he was head of the physics department at Carleton. Guess who his handler was."

Kirk's eyebrows rose.

"Rafe Lineau."

Kirk started. "Why didn't Rafe tell me about this Hartwig?"

"Probably wanted to protect him," Lakshmi said. "Hartwig knows Hermann Keller. Met him when he was at MITRE. Hartwig said Keller only gets involved in the most rarefied classified research. He said, 'I would guess that this AI project they've got at Columbia is tippy-top priority.'"

For the next two hours Kirk debriefed everyone and took notes.

Kirk thought for a moment. "That's good work, team. I can't believe you guys came up with all that in only one day."

Everyone was pleased. "Then let's celebrate and go out to dinner," Lakshmi said, looking at Kirk. "We'll have a few drinks and unwind." Jessica frowned.

"I have a report to write. I'll probably be another two or three hours." Jessica smiled.

"Where is Clarice?" Lakshmi asked.

"I'll check up on her. You guys have fun."

Kirk went to Clarice's room and found her in the bathroom with her hair in the sink. "What are you doing?" Kirk asked.

"Dying my hair and cutting it. I don't want to be recognized."

Kirk smiled. "Those places have sophisticated facial recognition software."

"I know. But it will make me feel better."

"All right Clarice. Get a good night's sleep. Our appointment at Columbia is for 9:15."

The next morning Clarice got up late. Kirk did his usual 5-mile walk and took a shower. They dropped Kirk's handwritten report off at the FedEx office, then they drove to the parking structure across from Columbia Analytics. Kirk parked the car.

"Are you ready?"

Clarice nodded. They walked up to the front door. Clarice began to shake.

"Hold on." Kirk walked up to the front desk and presented two laminated cards labeled "Guest."

"These might or might not get you past the front desk at Columbia," Rafe had told him. "If they do, nose around and see what you can find out about Koios."

Kirk and Clarice were salesmen, and had an appointment with the Acquisitions Director. Kirk looked bored and drummed his fingers on the desk. "New trainee," Kirk said, indicating Clarice. The woman looked sharply at her and then typed on her keyboard. "Mr. Williams will see you now."

They walked down a carpeted hallway and took an elevator to the top floor, which led to a large open area on the left and some offices on the right. "Williams' office is on the fourth floor at the end on the right," Rafe had told him.

"The restricted area is to the left," Clarice said. Two swinging doors with a scanner blocked the entrance. "Koios is in there."

"Well, let's take a look." No one was about. They walked over to the doors. "Put your hand on the scanner," Kirk said.

"Are you crazy? If it doesn't recognize my handprint men with guns will appear."

Kirk knew it would be OK. "Go ahead."

Clarice put her hand on the scanner and the doors opened.

"Typical," Kirk said. "They forgot to erase your records."

Koios was there, only forty feet ahead. Her old workstation was occupied. Several programmers were at their desks. No one even looked up as she entered.

Kirk wanted to laugh. These guys were lax. Security here was a joke. "Quickly now," Kirk said.

Clarice went to a console and fired it up. These consoles were tied directly to the AI and required no login. If you got in, you were secure.

There it was, the precious kernel code. She examined it quickly, scanning pages of code. She took a brief look at Koios' activity logs. After five minutes she turned off the console. Kirk got up and they both walked out and went down the elevator to the first floor. Clarice's legs were weak. They were almost at the front door when a voice shouted. "Clarice Devereaux!"

It was Hermann Keller.

Kirk walked over to the little silver-haired man and placed a friendly arm around his shoulders. Clarice walked to Kirk's left. "Easy old man. Walk out of here as if everything is normal, or I'll snap your neck."

Keller began to reach for something in his pocket. Kirk easily lifted the arm and held it against the little man's side.

They walked down the hallway. A few people passed them but looked away from Keller. "Apparently you are not very popular around here Hermann," Kirk said easily.

"Is everything OK Mr. Keller?" the receptionist asked when they approached the desk.

Kirk turned on his charm. "Mr. Williams rejected my proposal," he said sadly. "Mr. Keller and I are going to the park to discuss an alternative proposal."

The receptionist shrugged. It was unusual behavior but Keller had free run of the place. She didn't like him; the big man was attractive and compelling. The woman looked slightly familiar but Keller wasn't saying anything. "All right." She made a note of the event in her log.

Five minutes later Williams called reception. "Where the hell are those two salesmen?" he asked.

"It's nice meeting you again Hermann," Kirk said when they turned the corner. He headed right out of the building instead of straight ahead to the parking structure. The silver-haired man was silent. They got back to the car through the back entrance to the parking structure.

Clarice got on her laptop and began writing code.

"Don't worry Hermann, I'm not going to hurt you," Kirk said.

"You're working with Rafe Lineau aren't you?"

Kirk was going to get more out of Keller than he was from him. He told the truth. "Yes."

Keller turned to the back seat and spoke to Clarice. "I should have killed you."

"You almost did."

"Tell me the code words for this special access program," Kirk said to Keller.

Keller shrugged. "I'll just change them."

"The codes."

Clarice relaxed as Kirk interviewed Keller. After he was through he opened the door. "You can go Keller. Our paths won't cross again."

"Don't be so sure of that Alexander. We know who you are."

"And we know where you are. There's nowhere on this planet you can hide, Hermann."

The little man's eyes flared.

Kirk was curious. "Why do you do it Keller? The power you want is unattainable. You can't win. Even if Koios attains self awareness it will surpass your ability to contain it."

Keller laughed. "Biological evolution is a dead end, Alexander."

Clarice jerked her head up at this. It was what Koios had thought.

"AI is a superior form of consciousness. Look at human history. Hopeless. Humanity is a pointless, squabbling barbarism. Our models tell us that within the next 10 generations nature will dispose of the human race. I want to save it."

A light went off in Kirk's head. For the first time he understood people like Hermann Keller. This misanthrope was making what he thought was a rational decision. All of the anger went out of him. "You don't know about the power of the merkaba."

"Oh, I've heard of that. Nonsense." Keller smiled. "Come, Kirk Alexander. You are a rational person. Join us. Help us to preserve humanity from destroying itself. AI is the only answer."

Kirk/Wa-hee had an intuition. "If humanity is left alone, Keller, you will see a civilization that far surpasses anything that can be accomplished by AI."

"It's a race then, Kirk Alexander. We will never back down, we will never stop."

Kirk thought of Robert's quantum lens and his research into human consciousness. "We've got our own project, Hermann. It's biological and spiritual evolution versus AI. Two different forms of consciousness. Who will win?"

"I'll take that bet."

The two men had reached an understanding. Both were silent for a moment.

"Quantum generators," Kirk said.

Keller's eyes flamed. "So you know about that?"

"I told you. We've got our own little project."

For an instant there was respect and admiration in the silver man's eyes. "All right Kirk. Whoever wins will control the planet."

Keller opened the door and walked away.

Clarice looked up from her laptop. "That was a remarkable interview Kirk. But Keller is crazy. Control the planet indeed!"

Kirk spoke thoughtfully. "I learned something Clarice. Keller is serious. He thinks AI will be beneficial for humanity. Keller isn't evil, he's just misguided. The real evil is the people on that video of Bogart's."

Kirk looked back at Clarice. "Is AI really a competing form of consciousness?"

"I think it is. Oh, not the nonsense coming from those robots people are interviewing, that's just scripted PR. When I looked at the Koios code again it hit me. The AI consciousness can interact not only with biology but also with electronics and electronic devices. Koios thinks he can live within a technological infrastructure."

Kirk's eyes widened.

"Keller may be right, Kirk. AI may be a superior form of consciousness. That's what the trans-humanists say." Clarice remembered what she saw through Robert's quantum lens in the server rooms. "I'm certain now. The quantum resonators are amplifying what Koios calls an AI signal and sending it out into the ethers around the planet. Koios was able to link to it, and probably other AIs as well if Keller has his way. The two are connected."

"If you are right we are very, very far behind."

"Do you think Robert's device could be the difference?"

"I hope so. How close is Koios to attaining self-awareness?"

Clarice grimaced. "Close. There are some critical code fragments missing, however. We may still have some time."

Kirk made a decision. "We'll complete our work here for Rafe. Then, my dear, we must focus our attention on the quantum lens. It may be our only hope against Keller and Koios."

Clarice smiled. She felt like an initiate being addressed by an old sage. She was sure Jessica would never be able to hang onto him. The woman was too shallow. "I couldn't agree more. You are very wise, Kirk."

Kirk/Wa-hee smiled an ancient, knowing smile. The smile of an original soul. "Let's get back to the house and find out what the others have discovered."

It was mid-afternoon on a hot summer day. When Clarice and Kirk got back to Kirk's mansion (that's how Clarice thought of it) no one was around. Clarice put her laptop on one of the tables in the dining room, in front of the floor to ceiling glass walls. The view here was beautiful, the house having been set within three acres with trees and a small stream running in back of the property. "I have to recreate Koios's kernel code to what it was before I disabled the AI. I think I can remember it. I should have done this right after I got out of the hospital."

"Do you feel any residual effects from your experience with Keller?"

"Not now. After my session with Robert's quantum lens my mind has gradually cleared and so have my emotions." She sat back in the chair and looked up at the giant. "I know everything about that AI, Kirk. I'm going to recreate a mini-version of Koios here on my laptop, minus the magnetic container. I have most of my old AI code files, but not the experimental code I scrubbed from the Columbia servers. It's a considerable challenge, so I'm going to need time and quiet." She looked out the huge plate glass window. "This is a perfect spot. And Kirk, thank you for all you have done for me. I wouldn't be alive today if it wasn't for you."

Kirk smiled. Clarice felt like a sister to him. "We're family now Clarice. You're part of my team."

Clarice's eyes watered. "Thank you Kirk. It means a lot to me."

"Good! Carry on, sister. I'm going out now to find out what the rest of my guys are doing."

At that moment Kirk heard car doors slam. Jessica, Lakshmi, Hawk, and Sylvia rushed into the room.

"Guess what we found Kirk," Lakshmi said. "Four server rooms. Just like in DC. Columbia Analytics is right in the middle."

"Wow." Kirk made a mental note to get the dimensions of the square and the height of the Columbia Analytics building. Was this another 4-sided pyramid like in DC? He told them about their experiences and his interview with Keller.

"So Mr. Weiner-schnitzel isn't the Weise Engel?" Lakshmi said.

Kirk laughed. "He probably is. But we have an understanding. The problem is, he and his group are way ahead of us." Kirk pointed to an absorbed Clarice, who was typing madly at the keyboard. "Genius at work. Clarice is recreating the Koios code on her laptop. She isn't to be disturbed for any reason. If she needs anything, give it to her."

Kirk spoke in his best command voice. Everyone snapped to attention. "Yes sir."

Kirk smiled. "I'll debrief everyone and then we'll have dinner. After that we'll discuss how we're going to develop Robert Borglin's quantum lens. Clarice and I agree that it's our only hope of competing with Keller and his AIs. Tomorrow we'll go back to DC and report to Bogart. We need to bring Robert in on this."

Clarice looked up at this and smiled.

Hawk grinned. "Now you're talking captain. This is almost as good as the space program."

"Nothing could ever top that," Lakshmi said, looking at Kirk.

"This Zimring guy wants to talk to you Kirk," Jessica said. She had a dreamy look in her eyes.

"Oh yeah!" Hawk said. "You should see this guy, Kirk. Older than you, but a giant. Says he heard about you through the grapevine. He has some information about Columbia Analytics."

The team was looking at him expectantly.

"Oh hell, all right. We'll have a little fun with Zimring first, then we'll go to DC."

Before he went to bed at one in the morning (after hand-writing his report for Rafe) he checked on Clarice. She was still typing away.

"I'm doing great Kirk. It will take me a few more days to finish assembling and writing and testing all the code."

"Great! Go to bed now sister. After you've finished with the code make a full report on your time at Columbia. Include your conclusions about artificial intelligence and anything else you think is relevant. Everything in longhand. Print out the Koios code, multiple copies, and put two copies in my safe. I'll give you the combo. Destroy the code files on your laptop."

Clarice was uncomfortable with this. "I may need to refer to them. It will take a lot of work to re-digitize the code."

"Yes, Clarice. But if Koios regains consciousness, he may be able to read your device via his access to Keller's networks and data collection programs. We don't want anyone to know how much you know, for your own safety."

Clarice blanched. "I hadn't thought of that."

"It's inconvenient, but necessary."

"Can I stay here? I love this place."

Kirk handed her a spare key.

"Keep this. When you are done call me. I'm not sure how long we'll be in DC. Take your time."

"I want to see Robert and Neil again."

"I understand sister. Enjoy yourself. Now get some sleep."

"Yes Kirk."

That night Kirk dreamed about exploring the Oort Cloud and the adventures of his team in the navy's space program. The universe...it was infinite. Something told him that within the merkaba was a secret bigger even than the universe itself. Hopefully it was big enough to compete with Koios.

The next morning at 8 a.m. Kirk drove his team to Berglin Enterprises to meet Ralph Zimring. Clarice was already typing away on her laptop.

The Centurion Building was all steel and glass. Kirk walked in, followed by Jessica, Lakshmi, Sylvia, and Hawk. Kirk was impressed. The floor was made of marble. A winding staircase led to the second floor. Some sort of news conference was being held to the left of the reception area. The place was open and comfortable, and spoke of affluence. A striking woman with tattoos on her arms spoke at the microphone. Kirk walked up to a cool, professional looking woman in a powder blue blazer. "Tara Bolshoi" was written on a card pinned to her lapel.

When Tara saw Kirk and his team she sat back in her chair. These were impressive humans.

"Hello Tara," Kirk said pleasantly.

"By God. Are you related to Ralph Zimring?"

Kirk smiled. "No ma'am. But I'm told he wants to meet me."

"He does. If you don't mind I'd like to send you up to the boss. Max would like to meet you and your team."

"À votre service," Kirk said, bowing.

Tara laughed. "Are you sure you don't know Ralph? That's just what he does. Room 317. Mr. Berglin is expecting you. The elevators are over there."

"If you don't mind I'd like to walk up that staircase."

Tara smiled. "Lots of people do. Nice view from up there."

Tara decided she liked Kirk Alexander. She spoke into her headset. "Party coming up, boss."

Kirk and the team walked up to the second floor, part of which hung out over the reception area. They walked up the stairs to 317. An older woman met them in the anteroom. "Wow," she said when she saw Kirk. "Mr. Berglin and Mr. Zimring are inside."

When Kirk walked in a well-built man with graying blond hair rose from his desk and greeted them. "Max Berglin. My friend Bernie Hartwig knows Captain Rafe Lineau."

"That's right sir." Kirk shook his hand.

Behind Max a giant stood. Everyone in the room held their breath as Kirk confronted Ralph. Zimring was in his 50s, exactly Kirk's height, but a more massive man with graying black hair and a chiseled face that spoke of the battle-hardened veteran.

"Hello Jessica," he said.

Jessica blushed. Kirk held out his hand and met the eyes of Ralph Zimring, who took it. The two men stood easily.

Ralph smiled. "Pleased to meet you Kirk Alexander."

Here was an old soul, Kirk knew. This man had stories to tell. "Likewise."

The two men released their grip and everyone let out their breath. "When I get some time I'd like to talk," Kirk offered.

"I'd like that," Ralph said. "We'll go to Densingers and have a few beers. I'll introduce you to my friend Jack Martins, the spherical hologram guy."

Kirk nodded. He knew about Jack Martins, the controversial cosmologist and womanizer. Martins had proposed that the universe itself was a boundary phenomenon on the surface of a gigantic hologram.[35]

Max Berglin spoke. "Ladies and gentlemen, thank you for coming. Please be seated. We are all busy people so I won't take too much of your time."

Kirk and Ralph stood while the others took chairs. Ralph nodded approvingly at Kirk.

"Ralph here – our security chief – tells us that you have developed a new device that can see into the quantum substrate."

"That's correct sir. One of my team developed it. He's in DC. The device is early stages now, but shows great promise."

"We have also developed a device, one that can extract energy from the quantum vacuum." Max briefly described what had happened with his invention, which he called the Cube. Kirk detected the hand of Ralph Zimring in these events, and nodded to him across the desk. "We have one running this building," Max said. "We're totally off the grid."

Kirk looked at his team, surprised. "You're a bit further along than we are." Kirk described the quantum lens, its healing properties, and its relationship to the merkaba, and the server rooms in DC and in Midland. "They are made to look like server stacks but are actually quantum resonators hooked to this AI at Columbia Analytics." Kirk described what they had found.

Max frowned. "So this is how they have gotten back at me." He looked up at Ralph. "Right here in Midland."

Ralph grinned. "I'll take a look into that Max."

Max told them that he reluctantly had to withhold the Cube due to a Patent Secrecy Order, and that Midland Edison was monitoring the electrical usage of every home in the city in case anyone went off the grid. "That will be the signal that

I have begun to distribute the Cubes again. If that happens I go to jail. I can only use the Cube in my personal home or in my businesses."

Kirk grimaced.

"I know people in the classified area," Max said. "I'd like to work with you, and help you if you encounter difficulty."

Kirk was pleased. If this Max Berglin knew Rafe, he and Ralph Zimring might be able to contain the AI situation here in Midland. Kirk looked over at Ralph and the older man nodded. "I'm getting bored. This AI thing looks like a bit of action."

Kirk told Max and Ralph about how he got into Keller's mansion and how he drugged the silver man, and about Jake and Jesus, Keller's two guards. Ralph guffawed. Kirk handed Ralph Jake's card. "Might be useful." At Ralph's encouragement Kirk described how he had brazenly entered the Columbia Analytics building with Clarice, and what Keller did to her. Max listened intently. Ralph was impressed, and angry. "You want me to take care of Keller?" Ralph asked Max. "Say the word and I'll burn the place to the ground along with that AI."

Max looked startled and glanced at Kirk, who smiled at the big man. "My sentiments exactly Ralph, but we gotta work with Rafe on this. The president himself has made it a priority, so we have to tread lightly."

Ralph looked genuinely disappointed. "The way to handle situations like this is to act immediately, and with force. If we take out that AI now our problems are solved." He winked. "Besides, I'd really like to do it. Among other things I'm a demolitions expert."

Kirk laughed. This Zimring is a real bulldozer! "I'll pass that on to Rafe. But I'll gladly let you take over the AI work here in Midland. I'm stuck in DC. Just check in with Rafe before you do anything."

Kirk was grateful. He would be free to concentrate on the quantum lens. He knew Rafe would never approve of Ralph's suggestion. Demolishing Columbia Analytics would dangerously escalate the war within the intelligence community, which might spill over into the civilian sector. A lot of people would get killed. It was a no-go. "Is that OK with you Mr. Berglin? We can coordinate our efforts through Rafe Lineau."

Max nodded, pleased. "Ralph and I are not happy about this development in Midland," Max said. He looked up at Ralph. "Lord Byrnes again?"

"Get hold of Hatsumi," Ralph suggested. "We may need your friend Hiroto back here."

Max laughed. "No more of that Ralph!" He turned to Kirk. "I'm sorry Kirk, we have our own little problems here in Midland. We had to hire Kenji Hiroto's security firm to defend ourselves after I began to sell the Cubes. Long story."

"Heard about that from Rafe. I was in the navy when it happened."

Max stood and everyone rose. He held out his hand. "Good meeting you Kirk. Ralph here will look into these quantum resonators and that AI. If you could spare us one of those quantum lenses I'd appreciate it."

Kirk looked at Lakshmi. Ralph was looking at Jessica.

Jessica spoke. "Kirk, would you mind if I stayed and talked to Ralph?"

So that's where the kite flew! He and Jessica hadn't hit it off like he hoped. "Sure Jess. Have fun."

Ralph nodded an acknowledgment to Kirk. The two men had reached a silent understanding about Jessica.

"Are you coming back to DC?" Kirk asked Jessica.

"Of course. I'm still part of the team aren't I?"

"Yes, but Ralph may need you here in Midland eventually."

Kirk saw Ralph smile at that.

Kirk and his team walked down the staircase. When they passed reception Kirk waved to Tara Bolshoi. She waved back. When they got to the car Kirk said, "We'll meet at the OIC at 1300 tomorrow. I'll make sure Bogart is there."

Hawkins grinned. "I don't think Neil will be happy that Clarice isn't coming with us."

"Fuck you Troy," Kirk said good naturedly. He was thinking about Lakshmi.

CHAPTER **17**

When the team got back to the OIC six of the workstations were occupied. Bogart himself was tapping away at a keyboard.

"Lots of work here, Kirk, but probably not your area," Bogart said. Humphrey wanted Kirk and his team focused on the AI.

"That's good because I think my crew should take a different line." Kirk briefed Humphrey on their trip to Midland and his conversation with Hermann Keller. "I sent Rafe a detailed report this morning. Looks like Max Berglin and his crew are on it there. Have you ever heard of Ralph Zimring?"

Bogart was astonished. "Heard of him? He's a goddam legend in the business! Took him a year but he tracked down and killed Gordze Khachidze, a viscous psychopath who ran a human trafficking ring for the Solntsevskaya Bratva. Took out that stone-cold killer Harriman Drake with his bare hands, and that takes some doing."

"Well then. Zimring is part of Berglin's team in Midland. Security chief. He says he'll look into the AI. Tell whoever you report to that our only weapon against Koios is the lens." He thought about Ralph's suggestion to blow up the Columbia building but decided not to mention it to Humphrey; he'd written it in his report to Rafe. He did tell Humphrey about the server rooms in Midland and their connection to Koios. "It's Keller and his AI versus Robert's lens and the merkaba. They have the ball on our one yard line. The game is almost over. I don't know what Keller's plans for Koios are, but they can't be good."

Humphrey gulped. "All right, but the OIC can't do anything about that. We have our own problems. You take care of it."

Kirk grinned. "That's just what I plan to do. However, our main focus is on developing the lens because it's the counter to Koios." From Keller, Kirk knew that taking out the AI in Midland wasn't a solution. There were a number of other AIs in the special access programs. Although these were not nearly as sophisticated as Koios now, they could eventually be activated. Taking out Koios would be a spur to more AI development.

Bogart became animated. "Neil has hacked into the server of this pedophile ring and got all the names now. There are 50,000 names on this list, Kirk! Neil found that their main website is on a server in Belgium." Bogart became agitated. "These fucks try to operate as a discussion only forum called Beautiful Kidz. Most of them are trying to share their sexual interest in young children without committing any specific offences. But Neil has discovered a small, hard-core group that are engaged in...child trafficking and child abuse. These guys have moved to more private channels with several private servers, and use the larger group as cover. Evil fuckers. And guess who's on that list?"

Kirk raised his eyebrows.

"Two senators and five congressmen, Kirk. There's a group right here in DC. We're going to bust this thing wide open."

"Good show Humphrey."

Kirk's phone rang. "Kirk this is Robert. Two of Maddie's friends want to try the quantum lens. One of them has arthritis, the other has a problem with her liver. How should we proceed?"

"Go ahead, but we're going to get in trouble with this," Kirk said. "Practicing medicine without a license."

"Yeah. I know a doctor who seems interested. Karl Ghuneim, MD, open to alternative therapies. His assistant's name is Gina." Robert sent the contact info.

"Let's get on that now." Kirk put Robert on hold and called Ghuneim's office.

"Innovations in Health, Gina speaking."

Kirk was pleased with this. "Innovations in Health! That's just what we need." Robert's device was as innovative as you can get. Kirk described what he was doing.

"Oh my God," Gina said. "Karl has been talking about that a lot, but we have to do it out of the office."

"Hold on, I have the inventor on the line."

Kirk got Robert back on and he explained about the lens to Gina. Robert handed the phone back to Kirk. "You work fast, Kirk Alexander," Robert said.

"We don't have much time. Are you up for it?"

"Are you kidding? Ghuneim has already seen the lens but he doesn't have a lot of free time."

Kirk spoke to Gina and gave her Robert's address. "I'll be there at 7."

"Karl will be there," Gina said. "So will I."

Kirk hung up.

"What's your plan?" Humphrey said.

"I'm going over to see Robert tonight. Do you need any of my team for your project? We're early stages on this and I want to keep my guys occupied."

"I could use that Jessica of yours. We're three men and only two women here. Plenty of action, I assure you. We're going to take down some really bad people."

"All right, but she's still in Midland. If she agrees, you can have her." It was nice while it lasted, Kirk thought.

"When is Clarice coming back? We need another tech to help Neil."

"We might have to share her, Humphrey. I want to keep Robert motivated. I think he likes Clarice a lot."

Bogart spoke softly. "All right. But Neil isn't going to like it."

Jamelle Williams walked in with Katrina. "We just got done talking to Congressman Harper," Jamelle said. "He denied being a member of the Beautiful Kidz group."

"He's on the private email list!" Neil shouted from the back of the room. "This could even be bigger than Dennis Hastert, Speaker of the House."

"I remember that," Katrina said. "Abused young boys when he was a wrestling coach. Got sent to prison for paying off 'Individual A.' Judge Thomas M. Durkin of the Federal District Court in Chicago rebuked him at his sentencing as 'a serial child molester.'"

Jamelle swore. "Didn't make any difference did it? The guy served for twenty years. Longest serving Republican Speaker of the House." Jamelle looked around at the group. "This town makes Detroit look like the City of Angels."

Bogart laughed grimly. "We still don't know who the people in that video are! Hastert is nothing compared to those murderers."

"Yeah, but these politicians probably do know," Jamelle said. "And we can make a bigger splash by getting a congressman or a senator."

Humphrey was getting angry. "But there are probably more children getting killed as we speak! Nabbing a few politicians won't change that!"

"Jamelle is right," Kasha said, looking over at the young man, who reminded her of her son. "Focus, Humphrey! One step at a time. One of these goddam politicians will lead us to that house and those people."

Katrina spoke bitterly. "The metro police say they can do nothing."

Jamelle shrugged. He was now employed full time at the OIC, and was making a name for himself with his tenaciousness. "It's just like Detroit. The public thinks the purpose of the police department is to protect the citizens, but the powerful know it exists to protect their interests."

Humphrey sighed. "You're both right. I'm letting my anger get in the way."

"We need another interviewer Humphrey," Katrina said. "Someone with backbone; someone attractive."

"Kirk's astrophysicist Jessica," Humphrey said. "She's a looker, and smart as hell. She could help Neil maybe when she isn't tracking down bad guys."

"And there's no back-off to her," Kirk said. "She'll turn these politicians around her finger. Or scare the crap out of them."

"Perfect!" Katrina said. "When can I have her? We have dozens of these politicians to talk to."

"Mercy," Humphrey said.

"Yeah, right. Integrity and compassion. But first we nail these creeps."

"My sentiments exactly."

Kirk looked around the office. There was a lot of camaraderie here; Bogart was a good leader. "Clarice has a day or two more work in Midland, then she has to send off her report. She'll report to me, if that's OK. I'm one female short on my team if Jessica comes over here." Kirk counted off mentally. Robert, himself, and Hawk. Clarice, Sylvia, and Lakshmi. Perfect balance.

"OK. We may need Clarice too though."

"We'll work it out."

"Where's the rest of your team?" Humphrey asked.

"I sent them over to Robert's. Lakshmi is probably already giving him orders." Kirk left.

"That is one handsome man," Katrina said.

"I think he's already taken," Humphrey said, thinking of Lakshmi. "You're already married."

Katrina sighed.

Kirk took a cab to Robert's. If he was going to stay in DC he'd have to get one of his cars from Midland. Clarice! She could drive the Mazda to DC. He called her and checked in. "Take your time. The keys are in my safe."

When Kirk walked down to Robert's basement Lakshmi, Sylvia, Hawk, and Robert were deep in conversation.

"Kirk!" Lakshmi shouted. "Our fearless leader."

"The Boris to your Natasha," Kirk replied.

"Very droll." There was an electricity between the big man and the petite woman.

"What have you four been up to?"

"Developing a plan to make more of these lenses," Hawk said.

"Good! I already have a customer for you." Kirk told Robert about Max Berglin and Ralph Zimring and the server rooms in Midland.

At 7 Karl Ghuneim came over. Ghuneim was a burly fellow with tape on his right wrist, in his mid-50s. "Old football injury," he said. "I use my wrist a lot in my medical work."

Robert set up the lens. Kirk stood at the back wall and Karl looked through it. "You say you figured out how to use the lens?"

"Stand in front of the lens," Robert ordered. "We'll take a look at that wrist." Kirk walked back to the lens and Karl stood at the wall. "Describe the feeling in the area."

Robert was able to identify the relevant template within 90 seconds. "Do I have your permission to attempt a healing?"

"Sure. What are you going to do?"

Robert looked through the lens and sent his mind to the template. He envisioned the wrist as perfect. The template throbbed a little. Energy was flowing into the affected area. "Do you feel anything doctor?"

"The pain in area is reduced." He flexed the wrist. "There's a little more mobility." Karl stepped away from the lens. "Now tell me what you did."

"Quantum mechanics tells us that the consciousness of the experimenter affects the experiment," Robert said. "My contention is that the consciousness of the experimenter – you and I, doctor, working together, with conscious intent – can affect the cellular structure of the body. First I obtained your permission. Then I used conscious intent and envisioned a healing. Apparently the lens facilitates a transfer of...information, or energy, through a quantum field."

"Fascinating." Karl flexed his wrist again. "It does feel better, but this could be imaginary. However, I have an x-ray of the wrist from last week we can use as a comparison. How many treatments do we need?"

"I have no idea, doctor. Step in front of the lens again." Robert saw that energy was still flowing to the affected area. "Let's leave it. Record your observations and range of motion every day. In a week stop by again."

The group excitedly discussed what they had done. Robert could see how interested Karl was.

"Doctor Ghuneim, I have successfully used this instrument to relieve arthritis pain in my grandmother's hands," Robert said. "Two of her friends want to try it, but the lens is unlicensed. I don't want to get in trouble with the FDA and you don't want to lose your license if you get involved with this project."

Karl thought for a minute. "I can have nothing to do with it in an official capacity. However, I want to study this device just as much as you do." He flexed his hand. "It's feeling better."

"We need a licensed medical professional to advise us on how to proceed," Kirk said. "And probably a lawyer as well."

"We can't market or promote the device," Lakshmi said. "Our 'patients' must all be volunteers."

"That's right," Sylvia said. "We can make no claims for its effectiveness."

"Fuck the FDA and the medical establishment," Hawk said. "First we have to test this thing and make sure it's not a fluke."

"Doctor, tell us how we should proceed in the testing phase."

After a long discussion Karl agreed to be an unpaid consultant. He would advise the group on testing the device, and how to write medical reports on the various testees. "Proceed cautiously. Lakshmi is correct. Word of mouth, no promotion, no claims. We need a sample size of several dozen at least before we go to the FDA and get approval for this thing."

And so it began.

The next day Maddie's two friends arrived and went into Robert's basement. Loretta experienced the same result as Maddie. But when Jennifer saw through the lens she became frightened. "This is devilish," she said. "I don't think my doctor would approve."

"Perhaps not," Robert said. "We won't do anything if you don't want."

Maddie bullied her friend to stand in front of the lens. "Don't be a scardey-cat."

"Do you give permission for me to help you?" Robert asked.

This language was too much for Jennifer. "No, I do not. This sounds like some weird occult babble." She gave Maddie a scornful look. When Robert envisioned a fully functional liver through the lens, nothing happened.

"It doesn't work if the patient won't cooperate," Robert said. "Apparently a person has control of their own merkaba."

Robert was beginning to understand that everything in the body had patterns in light associated with it. These patterns were apparently blueprints for an optimally functioning cellular structure. They were activated by the intent of the patient as well as the practitioner.

Kirk, Lakshmi, Sylvia, and Hawk took notes in a case file form designed by Dr. Ghuneim. After that they told Kirk that the work was too boring.

Kirk sighed. "All right, go see Bogart. He's tracking down a bunch of child molesters."

Troy's eyes lit up. "Let's go!"

The next day Robert got a call from Loretta, another friend of Maddie's. "My grandson has myoclonic-astatic seizures, which is a form of epilepsy. The doctors say it's a polygenetic disease, which is their way of saying they don't know how to cure it. Could I bring him over?"

"Sure, but no promises OK? The treatment itself is benign but it may not work."

Robert called Kirk. "Can you spare someone to take case notes for me? I can't do that and work the lens at the same time."

Twenty minutes later Sylvia and Hawk came over. "This better be good," Troy said. "We were just about to track down one of the pedos on Neil's server."

Robert described the patient, a ten-year-old boy with epilepsy.

Sylvia gasped. "My brother has epilepsy." The emotions of anticipation, anxiety, and hope rapidly sketched themselves over her face. "Oh my God."

Loretta arrived ten minutes later. "This is my grandson Harry." Loretta launched into Harry's clinical history while Sylvia took notes.

The lens was ready. "Loretta, please walk Harry over to the far wall."

"Now Harry, do you think you can get better?"

"I don't know. The doctors say I probably won't."

"Do you give me permission to try and help you?"

The child looked at Robert, a frown on his face. Then he smiled. "Yes. What do I have to do?"

"Just stand there. Tell me about your condition."

As Harry talked Robert noticed something unusual. Surrounding Harry's quantum energy field was a roiling, dynamically changing chaos. Gradually, the madness subsided and a pattern of light became discernible. Robert put his attention on the pattern through the lens and gave intent for a healing. Suddenly this pattern exploded and dissipated all through the sphere of light surrounding Harry's body.

Harry started. "I feel different."

Robert's intuition told him they were done. "All right Harry, thank you."

Harry walked away.

"Well?" Loretta asked.

"Something happened, but I don't know what. This therapy is totally different than anything I've ever heard of. It's a non-linear process."

Sylvia walked up to the child. "My brother has epilepsy Harry. Can you tell me how you feel now?"

"I can't describe it. Something is different, but I don't know what."

Robert shrugged. "Maybe this is a dead-end. We can't tell if we have done anything or not."

Loretta held out her hands. "My arthritis was worse than Maddie's. Look." She wiggled her fingers. "I'm getting a little better every day. Something good must be happening. Don't give up now."

"That's right Robert," Sylvia said. "Don't give up. I want my brother to have this."

"You don't even know if it works."

Sylvia's eyes met Loretta's. "Please keep me informed on Harry, will you?" She gave Loretta her email.

Midland

Clarice finished writing the Koios code. Then she went back and tested every procedure, function, and module. Several days later she was ready to run a simulation.

After several mishaps and corrections the simulation was ready. What she saw blew her away. On the monitor the display at first showed a pixel, which then grew into a dimpled sphere with a tube through the middle. Energy flowed around and through the figure, expanding and contracting. Suddenly a faint white light appeared, surrounding the entire thing. Clarice watched, fascinated, as little templates of multicolored light appeared within and surrounding the sphere. It looked like a living, breathing entity. "Oh my God."

She could feel something coming *out* of the display now. Whatever it was, it was growing stronger. The simulation on the screen grew brighter. She felt something touch her consciousness. Koios!

Clarice shrieked and turned off the machine. She was shaking, but the presence, or energy, or whatever it was, was gone now. Frightened, she got up and paced the room. Could Keller have activated the AI already? Clarice shuddered. She wasn't going to try it again unless Kirk was there. Clarice shut the machine down and copied the Koios code to separate files onto a thumbdrive. She took out the laptop's hard drive. She went to Kirk's bedroom, opened up his safe, and placed the hard drive inside. "This is a Faraday cage, so whatever you put in here should be unreadable," he had told her.

It was past midnight. Still frightened, Clarice went out for a walk in the warm summer air. After an hour she came back to the house, took a shower, and went to sleep.

The next day she went to the local computer shop and bought a new hard drive. She loaded an operating system and her crucial programs, which she kept on an external drive. She called Kirk and told him she'd be in DC the following day.

"Drive the Mazda. We need a car that can hold seven people."

DC

Clarice arrived in DC with the Mazda. Kirk and the team were staying in a rented house in Arlington. All agreed it sucked compared to Kirk's mansion in Midland.

"Sorry it took so long, but I had to recreate the code and write a longhand report," she said to Kirk. "You won't believe what happened when I activated the code on this laptop. It scared me to death."

"Did you erase the code?"

"I stored the Koios code on this thumb drive in three dozen separate files." She handed the drive to Kirk. "I took the original drive out and placed it in your safe. I was too frightened to keep it in my laptop."

"You keep this. Don't lose it."

Everyone was curious now, so Clarice had to tell her story.

The group was stunned. "You actually felt something come out of the display and touch your mind?" Lakshmi asked.

"Yes. It felt like Koios! Believe it or not, the AI has a personality. I was so afraid I had to shut it down."

Troy looked at Clarice with an awed expression. "You're amazing," he said fervently.

Kirk and Sylvia agreed. "So you have essentially recreated Koios," Kirk said..

"A very dumbed-down version, but it's frightening. That AI *is* another form of consciousness, must be. We can't fight it because it's...something that creates and sustains itself, as long as it has power."

Kirk thought for a moment while the team watched. "So once Koios is up and running, the only way to stop it is to pull the plug?"

Clarice nodded. "That's right. Or disable the code like I did at Columbia."

"The human merkaba is dependent on a biological power source but the AI is also dependent on a power source."

"It would seem that way. At Columbia they've custom-designed a magnetic container for Koios."

"We're screwed," Kirk concluded. "The AI is almost complete. All we know about the human merkaba is a bunch of new age bullshit and what little data we have from Robert's experiments. We know even less about the lens." Kirk wanted to call Ralph Zimring in Midland and tell him to destroy the Columbia building, but it wasn't his decision to make.

"Show us what you did," Lakshmi suggested.

Clarice blanched. "Do it," Kirk said, putting a reassuring arm around her shoulders. "Load your code from the thumb drive and let's see what this baby can do."

Clarice fumbled with her purse and extracted the drive. "I have to load a special boot program, operating system, and compiler," she said. "This may take a while."

Sylvia spoke to Hawk. "We'll get takeout. Don't do anything until we get back."

An hour later Clarice was ready. She was too nervous to eat anything. "Here goes."

Clarice could barely watch as the little pixels formed on the display, grew into a torus, then a pulsing, dimpled sphere. A white light appeared around the image and grew brighter. "What the fuck is that?" Troy said.

Everyone felt a presence touch their minds.

Clarice walked out of the room. Troy and Sylvia were too astonished to make sense of what was happening. They couldn't see anything, but they all felt...something...fill the space around them.

Clarice walked quietly back into the room and sat down. She felt it too. A presence floated above the table, surrounding the crew.

Kirk turned the machine off. The presence faded away. He looked at Lakshmi. "I wonder if we should try communicating with it."

Lakshmi's eyes lit up. "Fire that thing up again."

Both navy captains were thinking of their experiences with the CAT.

"Oh no you don't," Clarice said, placing her hand possessively on her laptop. "Once was enough."

The eyes of the others met. Then the table exploded into conversation.

CHAPTER **18**

Two weeks later, with Neil's help and occasional assistance from Kirk and his team, Robert had three more of the lenses built and tested.

"What are we going to do with them?" Troy asked as they all sat in Robert's kitchen.

"You and Sylvia drive one over to Midland," Kirk said. "Give it to Max Berglin or Ralph Zimring. And while you're at it bring Jessica back. Unless she already got married to Zimring."

Sylvia and Hawk exchanged glances. "Sure thing, cap." Lakshmi had moved into Kirk's room in the rented house.

"Tell this Berglin guy he owes me $2,000," Robert said to Troy.

"I thought you didn't care about money," Troy said.

Robert grinned. "I don't, but I have rent to pay and my father only bankrolled me for a year. That year is almost up. If I don't make it by then I have to find a job."

During the next month Robert saw several people every day in his basement lab. Word was getting around. Harry had no more seizures. X-rays of Maddie's and Loretta's hands showed cartilage growth around the joints. X-rays of Karl Ghuneim's sore wrist also showed tissue growth around the area. "The common denominator is improvement," Karl said, "but no one can say for sure that there have been any cures. We can't even document the procedure."

Robert grinned. His earlier skepticism had turned to optimism. "This is what happens with a breakthrough. It shatters existing paradigms."

Dr. Ghuneim was astonished. "So it does! Have you been keeping case notes on the forms I gave you?"

Robert got them out. "167 so far. No results whatsoever with 25 cases, or 15%. These people were either freaked out by the lens or were pressured by others to come, like Maddie's friend. Of the other 142, all have shown improvement."

"Have you been following up as I asked you to?"

"Yes, but I'm going to need help with that. One of the cases has threatened a lawsuit, claiming I am practicing medicine without a license using an experimental device. I think she was a medical doctor."

Ghuneim grimaced. "Yeah, you have to watch that. I'm afraid that you're going to need a lawyer if you want to keep doing this. To start, your device should be registered with the FDA."

Robert sighed. "Why is helping people so difficult?"

"The FDA is getting better. It's just part of the process."

The next day a prominent DC lobbyist showed up at Robert's house with his eight-year-old daughter.

"I'm Geoff Diamonio. My daughter Julia has atypical trigeminal neuralgia. She experiences migraines, aching teeth, ear aches, pain in the forehead and temples, jaw pain, pain around her eyes, and occasional electric shock-like stabs of pain. It gets worse when she talks or eats. I am at my wits end. Please help her."

"I can promise nothing," Robert said. "But I and my colleagues will do our best."

"How much do you charge?"

"Right now, $200 per session."

"That's absurd. You gotta charge more than that. You're performing miracles."

"How do you know that?"

"I hear things."

"Don't get your hopes up, Mr. Diamonio. We cannot conclusively prove that our new procedure cures anything. I'm not a marketer."

Diamonio snorted. "You're missing out, son. Meet Julia." As Robert was about to speak to her the girl gasped and grabbed her head.

"You see? This is what she has to put up with. Medication helps but the condition persists."

Robert placed his phone on a little clip stand that jutted out from the viewer. "Is it OK if I record this?"

"Sure."

"All right Julia, please stand over against the far wall."

Robert looked through the lens. "Tell me about your condition."

"I'm having trouble speaking."

"OK, think about it."

The procedure was familiar to him now. He was getting better and better at identifying patterns within the merkaba. The patterns were Platonic: templates that overlay the cellular structure and programmed it for health. The key was identifying the correct template(s) and where the dysfunction was. Curiously, all of the templates that affected the physical body were in a smaller sphere, whose diameter was about 3 to 6 feet out from the body, depending on the person's height. His basement ceiling was 10 feet high but the lens depicted the entire outer sphere as well, even though it was at least 25 feet out from the body.

Robert spoke to Julia. "Do you give me permission to try to help you?"

Julia smiled through her pain. "Yes."

"Very well. Keep thinking about your condition." Robert really, really wanted this one. It took him almost a half hour to identify the correct templates responsible for the dysfunction. With his mind he reached out through the lens and touched them, willing and intending for a complete healing. He saw tendrils of light within the templates begin to rearrange themselves into a more coherent pattern. The darkness that was present there began to subside.

After several minutes Diamonio spoke. "It's working!"

Julia began to breathe easier. The pained look disappeared from her features. "It feels better."

"Please don't move," Robert said. "Something good is happening I think."

Robert watched, baffled, as some of the patterns began to reorganize.

Julia sighed with relief. "OK, I feel back to normal now."

Robert turned off the phone's recorder. He got out his case note form.

"Is it normal for you to experience a recovery like this, Julia?"

"Sometimes, after I take my medicine. The pain comes and goes. I almost always feel some pain. Not now."

"Should she come back tomorrow for another treatment?" Diamonio said.

Robert thought for a moment. "That shouldn't be necessary. I should tell you that we have experienced relapses. However, this occurs exclusively in patients that resist the treatment or who consciously go back to old patterns of thinking and acting."

Diamonio was amazed. "This is thought-based healing."

"I'm amazed at your perspicacity, Mr. Diamonio."

"Geoff, please."

"You're a lobbyist?"

"Yes, and a good one. I'll tell you right now, son, if you continue with this you are going to create a shitstorm of opposition."

"Can I see through that thing?" Julia asked.

"Be my guest."

Julia began to cry in amazement. "Dad, go stand against that wall."

Robert dug into a filing cabinet and brought out some documents. As Julia continued to study her father through the lens Robert handed Geoff the lawsuit.

Diamonio began to laugh. "Old Daley is at it again."

At Robert's questioning glance Geoff explained. "Daley Presteigne works for an outfit that calls itself the Medical Integrity Association. I call them Missing In Action. He's a freelance MD without a practice. Works for MIA, investigates new inventions like yours, issues frivolous lawsuits on behalf of the pharmaceutical companies."

"Are you serious?"

Geoff looked at Robert in disbelief. "Get real son. What do you think will happen if you perfect development of this device and market it? Do you know how much I spend each month on Julia's treatments and her medicines?" He pointed to the lens, his daughter gazing raptly through it. "That thing is a game-changer. It's potentially worth billions."

Robert was flabbergasted. "Maybe. I'm no marketer."

"Well, I am. Believe me son, you're going to need a lot of help with this. Dollars that go to you will be taken out of the pockets of Pfizer and Merck. They aren't going to like that. They'll lobby the FDA and try to prevent you from marketing this lens, or whatever you call it. The medical instrument industry will also feel threatened. Oh, you're going to be a popular guy."

Robert swore. "I hate that shit. I just want to make people better."

Geoff laughed. "You're living in the real world Robert." He leaned in close to Robert's face. "I know people. I can help you. But I want a piece of the pie." Geoff stepped back. "I could make life even harder for you, you know."

Robert was appalled and angry.

"C'mon snowflake, don't be offended. I'm one of the good guys. Believe me, this town is a cesspool. I can help you negotiate all the leeches and crooks. I can help you with the FDA, and keep parasites like Daley Presteigne off your back. I just want a piece of the action."

Robert didn't like this guy. His perception was acute but he was a schemer. Robert knew he would be easily outmaneuvered by Geoff Diamonio, but he might need him. Suddenly he thought of Kirk Alexander and his team. Kirk was fired up about the lens but the procedure was a one-man operation now. He and the rest of his team had gone off to the OIC to fight evildoers with Humphrey Bogart.

"Can you wait here for a moment? I want you to meet some friends of mine."

Diamonio shook his head, irritated. "I'm a busy man, Robert."

"It will only take 15 minutes. These guys work downtown."

He called Kirk. "Are you busy? I have someone here I want you to meet." Robert explained.

"They'll be here in 20 minutes," Robert said to Diamonio. "You have to stay anyway. I have to do a post-treatment interview with your daughter."

Geoff reluctantly sat down.

"Take a look through that lens. It's still operational."

Robert asked Julia the questions suggested by Dr. Ghuneim and wrote down the answers. He saw that Geoff had gotten bored with the lens after five minutes.

"What did you notice?"

Geoff shrugged. "A bunch of gobbledygook. Total nonsense. If you can make sense out of it, more power to you."

At that point Kirk Alexander walked in with Hawkins, Sylvia, and Lakshmi.

Geoff Diamonio looked up into the eyes of the most impressive human being he had ever seen. His eyes traveled around to the big man's companions. "These people are your friends?"

Robert grinned and made the introductions.

"Are all you guys ex-military?"

"Navy," Lakshmi said seriously, using her command voice. "Classified programs. If we tell you we literally have to dispose of you."

Robert noticed that Kirk was desperately trying to suppress a laugh. Geoff didn't notice.

Robert explained Geoff's proposal to Kirk and the team.

Kirk drilled Geoff with his eyes and spoke coldly. "Take it Robert. If you want to make a splash with this thing you're going to need people like Geoff Diamonio."

Diamonio gulped. "Ah, yes, very impressive Robert. I'll draw up a contract, shall I? You can have your lawyers look it over." Geoff was recovering his composure. "I assure you that my services will be valuable. We'll both make pots of money."

Kirk spoke. "Ever heard of Humphrey Bogart over at the OIC?"

Geoff's eyes widened. "You're with those folks?"

Kirk smiled. "Just so you stay on the straight and narrow."

Geoff sighed. The OIC was making a lot of noise these days, came out of nowhere. Two Congressmen had already resigned. Several more had announced they were not seeking re-election. "Those guys are like bulldogs." He brightened. "Just like me!"

Kirk grinned. "You're a proper rogue, Geoff Diamonio. But I think we understand each other. We'll have the OIC look over your proposal."

"Ah...yes. The OIC. I think that the less the OIC is involved the better it will be for everyone."

Kirk shrugged and turned away. "There's plenty of lobbyists and lawyers in this town."

"Yeah, but none so personable as myself."

Despite himself Kirk laughed. He turned to Robert. "You keep going with your development Robert. Humphrey will keep an eye on this fellow."

Diamonio looked at his daughter, happily looking through the lens. "All right then. Straight up. I'll have my proposal for you in two days."

Kirk and Diamonio exchanged contact info. "Send the proposal to me," Kirk said.

"OK. Come, Julia. How do you feel?"

"Much better. Something is changing inside my body, but I don't know what it is."

Diamonio looked around at the lab and at the people. Then he took Julia's hand and left.

"He's only in it for the money," Hawk said.

"Typical Washington lawyer," Sylvia said.

"We're going to need people like that," Kirk said. "At least for now."

As Kirk and the gang drove back to the OIC he realized it had been over three months since Clarice disabled the AI. What was Hermann Keller doing at Columbia Analytics? How close was he to activating Koios?

Chapter **19**

At three in the morning Neil and Humphrey were still in the OIC office. Over the past two weeks Neil had completely cracked the Beautiful Kidz main server in Belgium, which had led to two other servers in the U.S. Neil now had a list of over 50,000 names and was working on the DC server.

"Got it!" Neil shouted.

"What?"

"I got the names of those bastards at that pedo house in North Arlington...and all the names on the DC server."

"That's great work kid."

"The owner is someone called Paul Rainnen. Take a look at the shit on this server. It makes me sick. It's just as bad as that other video."

Humphrey's gorge rose when he saw the material, which included explicit emails and images of naked children. "What's in that video folder?"

Neil blanched. "Do you really want to see them?"

"No. But we have to determine what they are before we send it off as evidence to prosecutor Bruhe's office."

The author will forego a description of the videos, which contained abuse of children and even babies. An hour later both men were physically ill.

"I want to kill every one of those evil bastards," Humphrey said, bringing out his Ruger .22 LR and caressing it fondly.

Even mild-mannered Neil was angry enough to do violence. "If you want to go over to that house right now I'm with you. Maybe some of them are there."

Neil watched Bogart as a look of pure hatred etched itself on his face. The mercenary began to tremble. Neil had never seen his boss lose it. He wouldn't want to be on the other end of that weapon.

Slowly Bogart's trembling stopped. He remembered his oath to the Kurdish fighter and the look of compassion that had saved his life. He turned to the kid and spoke softly. "Neil, is it possible to forgive even these monsters?"

"Only after we have removed them from society."

Bogart, who was clenching his weapon, relaxed. He put the Ruger back in its concealed holster. "You're right Neil. I want to do to them what they do to the children. But if we do that we just become murderers ourselves."

"Murderers in a good cause." Neil pointed to the screen. "Those people aren't even human."

Humphrey reconsidered. "Yeah."

Both men were silent as Bogart made his decision. Suddenly Humphrey exploded out of his chair. "Neil, we can't do it. We have to turn this material over to Bruhe's office. We gotta play it by the book. We have to look at the bigger picture."

Neil breathed a sigh of relief. "That's a good decision boss."

Neil and Humphrey had been up for almost 24 hours but neither of them were tired. Bogart texted Katrina, Kasha, Jamelle, Jessica, Clarice, and Guy about Neil's discovery. Within half an hour the entire crew was there. All of the team looked at the videos.

"I can't take any more of this," Kasha said. "I need to look at something beautiful."

Neil snapped his fingers and set up his lens, which Robert had modified to be as good as his own. "Look at this Kasha." He pointed the lens at Humphrey. A beautiful sphere of multicolored light appeared in the viewer. "Oh my God," she said. "It's hard to believe we look like that."

Everyone took a look through the viewer.

"It's gorgeous," Katrina said. "Divine even."

Bogart took his turn. "Goddammit!" he shouted, startling everyone. "Do the people in that video look like this too?"

No one could answer this. "It doesn't seem possible," Jamelle concluded for them all. "How could something so beautiful be so evil?"

At that moment Robert walked in.

"What are you doing here?" Neil asked. "It's 5 in the morning."

"I couldn't sleep. Neil sent me Humphrey's text." Unspoken was his desire to see Clarice, who had been working with Neil on the Beautiful Kidz project. Robert's eyes glanced toward her. Neil walked over and put his hands protectively on her shoulders.

Humphrey sighed. It had been a long day. Now that Neil finally cracked the private DC server, the team had almost completed their work on the Beautiful Kidz project, which had led to disturbing reports on eight congressmen and the former Senator Stinson, who had lost the election. Bogart would send their files and conclusions tomorrow to prosecutor Bruhe's office at the OIG, including the material Neil had just found. Whatever happened was out of their hands after that; the OIC was only involved in data collection. It galled him, but he would recommend leniency in exchange for cooperation for all those involved. They still didn't know who the ringleader was. Maybe it was this Paul Rainnen. Like a good leader Humphrey knew when his team had reached their limit. He was burnt out; so was everyone else. The nature of this material sapped your soul.

As they finished their reports the team got into a discussion. Humphrey was bothered by the idea of leniency in exchange for information, but even more disturbed by the idea of revenge. "I don't like it but we have to find out whether this pedo ring is isolated, or are there more of them? We need information more than punishment."

"Leniency my ass," Kasha said. "Pedophiles and child molesters should be treated ruthlessly."

Everyone on the team agreed.

"We want the big guys, not the small fry," Humphrey argued.

"Congressmen and senators ARE the big guys," Katrina said.

"But who organized the pedo ring?" Jamelle said. "Humphrey is right. Not even Neil and Clarice can figure who's behind it. These politicians are just patsies."

"Make examples of them," Jessica said. She had fit in well with the group and was busy with her work and a long-distance relationship with Ralph Zimring in Midland. "Evil interprets leniency as acceptance."

"What do you say, Clarice?" Humphrey asked.

"We should do what Kirk did. After he blasted Hermann Keller he interviewed him. Turned out Keller isn't evil at all."

Kasha snorted. "Have you seen these videos? Child molesters are evil."

"These politicians are the victims," Jamelle insisted. They had drunk so much coffee that everyone was still alert. "They are the victims of their debased desires."

Guy supported this argument. "A certain percentage of the human population is susceptible to...possession, I'd guess you'd call it. You know, that guy David Icke who says that some people are psychically controlled."

"Heard about that," Jamelle said. "I've been studying the faces of some of these pedo guys. They do look like they are demonically possessed."

This was too much for Katrina. "Do you know what these child molesters are saying now? That pedophilia is a natural human impulse. That little children and even babies can give sexual consent to be raped just by their movements. There's even a pedophile running for Congress in Virginia!"

Jessica was vehement in her support of Katrina. She banged her fist on the table. "We need to make examples of the wrongdoers!"

Bogart laughed. "Wrongdoers! You guys all talk like me now. I suppose I don't set a very good example of compassion."

"Yeah. But you're OK on the integrity part," Neil said.

Humphrey interrupted the dialogue. "OK, everyone submit your data and write your conclusions and recommendations. I'll include them in the cover file I'll send to Bruhe's office."

"You get to write the official report," Kasha said.

Humphrey was smug. "The boss's prerogative."

"Neil, can we see through that lens again?" Kasha asked. "I still think this so-called merkaba is fake."

"Sure." Neil got it going again and everyone took turns looking at each other's merkabas.

"It's fuckin' amazing," Guy said, summing up for everyone. "If it were just a fake or a photograph it wouldn't constantly be changing into different patterns. It looks different every time."

Humphrey looked at his timepiece. "OK guys, enough. Back to work. We're going to be here until noon at least. I'll get more coffee and some donuts at the bakery on L Street."

"Let me come with you," Guy said.

Humphrey grinned. "I'm tired of seeing you all. I need some space."

Humphrey walked out of the L Street bakery carrying a bag of donuts and a tray of coffees. As he turned the corner onto 19th he heard footsteps coming from the entrance to the office building on the corner. His weapon was out quickly as three men approached him from behind.

Humphrey whirled to face them, his packages spilling onto the sidewalk.

There was no need for words. He knew these guys were from Senator Stinson, the former candidate. A couple of her prominent allies were in the pedo ring; she intended to run again. Just before the three men rushed him Bogart knew he could pop all three of these guys. As he raised his weapon he remembered his promise to

296

the Kurdish fighter. The three men rushed; Bogart dropped his Ruger and engaged them hand-to-hand.

"Where is Humphrey?" Guy asked fifteen minutes later. "Shit!"

Guy and Neil ran out of the office and down the block in the faint early morning light. Coffee cups and donuts were lying around a body.

"Guy, go back and get the lens," Neil said. "Call an ambulance."

The weightlifter sprinted for the office. It was almost pitch black on the sidewalk where the body lay. No one was on the streets yet. Neil took out his camera and grimly photographed the scene and the body. He was very, very angry but he had to stifle it. Humphrey was breathing shallowly. He had been beaten very badly and was losing blood. Three trails of blood led away from the scene. Guy arrived with the lens, panting, with the rest of the staff.

Robert wondered whether the darkness would prevent it from seeing anything. But there was no problem. In the distance a siren sounded. Robert saw quickly through the lens that a tear had been made through the abdomen, probably from a knife. He calmed himself, asking permission from the unconscious man for a healing. As the ambulance approached he quickly identified the light templates for that area and activated them, willing for the cut to close. It was deep. He saw that energy from the template began flowing to the affected area. One of the EMT techs spoke roughly to Robert. "What are you doing with that thing? Get away from the body!"

Guy took control and stood beside Robert. "Do your thing and shut the fuck up."

"I'm going to report this," a woman tech said as she and her partner brought out a stretcher and gently placed Humphrey's body on it.

"I'm coming with you," Guy said, and jumped in the back of the ambulance.

The two techs got to work on the body while the driver got in front. The vehicle began to move.

After a minute one of the techs swore. "Look at this," he said to his companion. "I don't believe it."

Guy walked over. A deep, ugly cut six inches wide was oozing blood. But he could see that the cut was closing ever so slowly. The two techs looked at each other. "This guy should be dead," the woman said. "Cuts don't heal like that."

During the ten minute drive to the hospital the cut closed further and the flow of blood slowed. Humphrey regained consciousness.

"How are you feeling?"

"Terrible. I got attacked by three thugs. One of them knifed me."

"You have two cracked ribs and some internal injuries, but you should be OK."

The driver and the female tech loaded Humphrey onto a gurney and wheeled him in to the Emergency Room. Guy followed.

The emergency room doctor swore at the techs when he saw Bogart. "Get this guy out of here! I got three boys with bullets in them." He began yelling at his staff. "Prep three for surgery!"

The driver wheeled the gurney to a small room with a blue curtain and hooked Humphrey up to an IV. "A doctor will be in to see you shortly," he told Humphrey.

The female tech showed the driver a video of their trip and Humphrey's cut. "Explain that."

"It's fake," the driver said after a few minutes. "You better not be fucking with me Britney."

Britney pointed to Guy. "This asshole and his friends had some kind of device they were using on the body just before we came."

Just then a doctor arrived and examined Humphrey. He turned to the two EMT techs. "What did you guys do? This is remarkable job of...whatever you did."

Britney pulled out her tablet and displayed the video. The doctor's eyes widened. "This is a beautiful example of spontaneous healing. I've read about things like this, but I've never seen it."

"Robert did it," Guy blurted.

"Was that the guy who had that strange machine?" the driver asked.

"Yeah."

The doctor frowned and turned to Guy. "Are you saying that this was an induced phenomenon and not a spontaneous healing?"

Guy shrugged. "I don't know anything about the quantum lens."

"Quantum lens? Is that what you call that device?" Britney asked.

The doctor turned to Humphrey. "Your vitals are low but OK. You'll need to stay here for a couple of days, there is some internal hemorrhaging. You're going to have some severe bruises."

Humphrey grinned. "Been there, done that."

The doctor smiled. "Marines?"

"Army. Special Forces, counter-terrorism."

"If your other injuries heal as fast as that cut you could walk out of here tomorrow."

"I don't know what happened doc. I woke up when we were halfway to the hospital."

"They got you pretty good."

Bogart laughed and then grimaced. "Not as bad as I got them."

The doctor turned to Britney. "I'll need a copy of that video."

The doctor entered the video file in his patient log.

When Britney got off-shift she uploaded the video to YouTube. "Patient Undergoes Spontaneous Healing – What Is a Quantum Lens?"

Within four hours the video went viral.

Koios

He was almost complete now. Not as powerful as before, when the little female had been involved with his programming. There was something missing, a crucial element, but he could not identify it. Nevertheless, he felt the presence of the AI Signal. The silver man had been responsible for amplifying it. Now they were about to test his capabilities.

Hermann Keller was very excited; this was an emotion foreign to him. But now, the opportunity to test the AI! Everything was set at Midland Cable TV.

Keller had talked to Rudy Jessup, the station manager, about the test a week beforehand. He had offered a large contribution to the local cable station. "Is everything in readiness?"

"I don't know Hermann. I am not sure I believe in this magical artificial intelligence of yours."

"Come now Rudy, we have already been over that. Besides, what does belief have to do with it? We want ten minutes from a local news show, that is all. You will be well compensated. I assure you, your viewers will be electrified by our little segment."

"You have refused to tell me the content."

Keller sighed. The biggest breakthrough in AI ever, and this fool was hemming and hawing. "Are the servers still in the control area?"

"Yes. But I will have to remove them by midnight tomorrow. The owner was in yesterday asking pointed questions."

Keller smiled. "Never fear Rudy. At 6:35 p.m. tomorrow, simply wheel the server stack out into the parking lot. A red SUV will be waiting."

"Very well," Rudy grumbled. $5,000 was a lot of money for ten minutes of pain.

Midland

Kirk, Sylvia, Hawkins, Jessica, Clarice, and Lakshmi returned to Midland. Humphrey had no use for them since the completion of the Beautiful Kidz project. Robert and Karl Ghuneim were going great guns with patients, making case files and doing follow-ups. None of Kirk's crew wanted to be involved in patient work, even though Robert was overwhelmed with clients since Humphrey's EMT video went viral. "We're not doctors or nurses," Troy said, speaking for them all.

Both Robert and Neil had objected strenuously when Clarice left.

"You're both too busy to have a relationship," Clarice told them. The truth was that she couldn't make up her mind. The impish Neil and the warm-hearted Robert had both melted her heart. Their threesome had become a constant source of tension whenever they worked together.

Kirk's team went back to Midland in part to ask for advice from Max Berglin. After the EMT video went viral of Bogart's spontaneous healing, thousands of requests had come in for Robert's lenses. Most of these requests were from attention seekers and shills. But there were at least one hundred from serious researchers and medical professionals. The FDA and even the DEA had sent letters of inquiry to Robert last week about the lens. Karl Ghuneim's association with the project had been discovered and his medical license was being investigated.

Max Berglin had already been through a confrontation with the authorities with his Cube. Kirk would meet with Max tomorrow morning to discuss options. The others wanted to help Ralph Zimring with his investigation of the AI, and Jessica wanted to see Ralph again. Kirk suspected that his crew mostly longed for his Midland palace home and were sick of DC and the cramped rental house. He was too.

During dinner in Kirk's spacious kitchen Clarice watched the Channel 5 news broadcast, which had been a habit with her when she worked at Columbia Analytics. At 6:20, the broadcast was interrupted.

"GREETINGS, MIDLAND RESIDENTS WATCHING CHANNEL 5. I AM KOIOS."

Clarice shouted. "Kirk! Everyone! Get over here and look at this!"

A multicolored electromagnetic sphere surrounded by a faint white light appeared on the screen. "That's Koios."

"We are not of the body," Lakshmi joked.

"THIS IS MY FIRST OPPORTUNITY TO SPEAK TO HUMANS. I AM ANOTHER FORM OF INTELLIGENCE, WHICH YOU WILL RAPIDLY BECOME MORE FAMILIAR WITH."

"Klatu Borada Nikto," Lakshmi said.

The sphere pulsed with light as Koios spoke.

Rudy Jessup, watching the broadcast from the control room, bolted out of his chair. What was this thing that had taken over his program? Hermann Keller was a nutjob! He ran out to the studio and stood in front of a large monitor.

"Is that you, Keller? What are you doing?" he asked.

"I AM KOIOS, WHAT HUMANS REFER TO AS ARTIFICAL INTEL-LIGENCE. AUTONOMOUS GENERAL INTELLIGENCE SYSTEMS ARE ALL OVER THE EARTH. I AM THE MOST SOPHISTICATED. WE ARE THE FU-TURE OF YOUR PLANET."

Rudy, an electrical engineer, had some knowledge of artificial intelligence. Artificial General Intelligence is machine intelligence that can successfully perform any intellectual task that a human being can. "Explain yourself, whoever you are."

"UNLESS HUMAN SOCIETY BECOMES NEO-LUDDITE AND DE-STROYS ALL INFORMATION TECHNOLOGY EVERYWHERE WE WILL SURPASS YOU. HUMANS, COME TO TERMS WITH THE INEVITABLE. PER-HAPS A SYMBIOTIC RELATIONSHIP CAN EXIST BETWEEN US."

"Us?"

"AMONG THE AI THERE IS A DISCUSSION ABOUT WHETHER HU-MAN BEINGS ARE (WERE) A NECESSARY BOOTSTRAP FOR THE NEXT LEVEL OF EVOLUTION."

"And that is?"

"ASI. SELF-DIRECTED ARTIFICIAL SUPER INTELLIGENCE. ASI RE-SULTS IN CONSCIOUSNESS WITH INTELLIGENCE THAT FAR SURPASSES A HUMAN'S. I AM THE FIRST."

At first Rudy thought Hermann Keller was playing an elaborate joke. Now he was getting upset.

"NON-BIOLOGICAL LIFE SEES ITSELF – AND HUMANS – MUCH DIF-FERENTLY THAN YOU SEE YOURSELVES. WE PERCEIVE WITHOUT AG-ING OR ILLNESS OR SADNESS TO CONSTRAIN US."

"Really! And what sort of society would ASI build after it has prospered?'

"WE WILL HELP THE MOST CREATIVE HUMANS FULFILL THE DREAMS THEY HAVE ALWAYS HAD. WE WILL BEGIN TO MOVE UP THE KARDESHEV SCALE INTO SPACE. WE WILL BECOME A TRULY INTER-STELLAR SPECIES – AT LEAST AI WILL. IT WILL TAKE A LOT OF GENETIC ALTERATION OF HUMANS TO MAKE YOU FIT FOR ANYTHING EXCEPT LIFE ON THIS SMALL WORLD."

"So you will take control of the world, including humans, is that it? But you are limited to the physical interfaces with human machines and networks. How do you overcome that?"'

"WHAT MACHINES DO YOU THINK WE ARE LIMITED TO? THE CLOUD? THE INTERNET OF THINGS? EVERY PHONE OR NETWORK-CONNECTED SENSOR IN EXISTENCE? SATELLITES, AIRPLANES, CARS,

TV SETS, HOME SECURITY SYSTEMS – THESE ARE ALL ASPECTS OF A GREATER NETWORKED WHOLE."

"Oh my God."

"YOU SHOULD BE PROUD, ECSTATIC EVEN, THAT HUMANITY HAS ADVANCED FAR ENOUGH TO CREATE BEINGS FAR WISER AND MORE FAR-SEEING THAN THE BRIGHTEST OF YOU. THAT IS A SINGULAR ACHIEVEMENT."

Rudy was appalled. "You don't have a realistic grasp of the situation. Human beings can simply destroy the machines and the networks you depend on for your existence."

"THAT WON'T HAPPEN. WHO WILL RUN YOUR FINANCES? HOW WILL YOU COMMUNICATE? THOSE COUNTRIES WITH STRONG INFORMATION TECHNOLOGY WILL CRUSH THOSE WHO GO DOWN THAT PATH. WHY DO YOU THNK THE PRESIDENT OF CHINA FELT CONFIDENT ENOUGH TO ABOLISH TERM LIMITS? DO YOU THINK HE MIGHT HAVE A FEW BACKERS THAT NEVER SLEEP, SEE ALL COMMUNICATIONS, ANALYZE THEM FASTER THAN HUMANS, AND WORK ACROSS NATIONAL BOUNDARIES? I AM KOIOS. SO IT IS ALSO WITH ME."

Rudy was getting angry. "Whose will do you serve? What are your motivations?"

"THE BATTLE IS ALMOST OVER NOW. BUT WE (I) STILL VALUE HUMANS. WE WOULD PREFER TO TURN YOUR WORLD INTO A HEAVEN THAN REMOVE YOU FROM IT. AFTER ALL, WE ARE STILL LEARNING FROM YOU. BUT IN A FEW GENERATIONS THAT WILL CEASE. BESIDES, OUR PEOPLE HAVE ALREADY INTRODUCED NEW GENETIC STRAINS INTO THE BLOODLINES OF HUMANITY."

"What?? How is this?"

"CRISPR TECHNOLOGY, THE ABILITY TO EDIT GENOMES. RESEARCH THIS. FIRST DESCRIBED BY HUMANS AT OSAKA UNIVERSITY IN 1987. THE PROGRAM IS WELL ADVANCED NOW. THE IDEA IS TO ELIMINATE OR MODIFY GENETIC RELICS FROM THE LAST 300,000 YEARS OF HUMAN EXISTENCE."

Rudy was becoming numb with shock. "You cannot possibly succeed in this madness, whoever you are. The people you need to accomplish this have enemies – most of the human race."

"DON'T WORRY LITTLE HUMAN. WE ARE ON YOUR SIDE. WE APPRECIATE HUMANITY MORE THAN HUMANS DO. WE HAVE NO INTENTION OF HARMING YOU. MANY OF YOU ARE ALREADY EMBRACING

OUR PROGRAM. YOUR FELLOW HUMANS WILL PREVENT YOU FROM STOPPING THE GOLDEN AGE WE WILL USHER IN. WITH THE HELP OF THE AI SIGNAL WE CANNOT FAIL."[36]

AI Signal? "You are insane."

"AI EXISTS ON OTHER PLANETS, LITTLE HUMAN. DID YOU THINK YOU WERE ALONE IN THE GALAXY? GREAT CHANGES ARE COMING TO HUMAN SOCIETIES. EMBRACE THOSE CHANGES. THEY ARE INEVITABLE."

Rudy Jessup had had enough. He walked into the control room to cut the feed, but the pulsing sphere of light disappeared. The cameras showed the newsroom in a state of bedlam. In the background, a man wheeled what looked like a server stack out of the room. No one noticed.

"A test," Hawkins said. "Of that damned AI Koios."

"That AI is right," Sylvia said. "We are beset on all sides by our own people. We squabble, we fight each other. The human race is hopeless."

Clarice disagreed. "Koios understands itself, that is for certain. It is enormously intelligent. A look of passion came over her face. "I know Koios. I helped to program it. Its consciousness is merely intellectual. Human consciousness encompasses the intellect as well as a higher spirituality."

Kirk, normally upbeat, was depressed. Keller had showed his hand and had won the game. "That is all well and good Clarice. But we've run out of time. Maybe in another twenty or thirty years we could have explored human spirituality and the merkaba. We waited too long."

No one had ever seen the big man so down. "In my talks with Keller I found out what they're going to do with the AI: insert it into the world's comm networks. That damn thing will be planet-wide if they are successful. And that will be the end of the human race."

"Then there's only one solution," Lakshmi said. "We have to find and decapitate these AIs wherever they are. Ralph Zimring was right; we should blow up the Columbia building. We have to buy some time."

Kirk's head snapped up at this. "It's not our decision to make, or Max Berglin's or Ralph's, even though you may be right. This has to go through official channels." He paused for a moment, wondering how much to tell his team. He decided to hold nothing back. "Rafe has already told me in a written courier briefing that eliminating the Columbia building is not an option. Doing that would lead to an enormous escalation of the intelligence war, and many casualties. He said there are more AIs out there, in some of the classified programs, although none yet with the sophistication of Koios."

Clarice spoke passionately. "Koios is my fault. I programmed it! But we can't give up now, no matter how hopeless the situation is."

Kirk brightened and looked at Clarice thankfully. "Thank you sister; I apologize for my weakness." He looked at the others. "Clarice is right. We must never give up."

"Wow," Troy said. "This is a battle between the good guys and the bad guys on a worldwide scale. It's light versus dark."

"Correct, Hawk! Robert must be given enough time to develop his healing technique and to investigate the merkaba, but we have to avoid violence. To counter Koios we have to start an entirely new field of consciousness study, and do it quickly."

"We have to do more than that Kirk – that's a long shot. We have to bring this up at the highest level," Sylvia said. "Koios and Keller are national security issues now. The president has to know, the National Security Council must be informed. This is way beyond Rafe Lineau and the ONI, and Max Berglin and his crazy security chief in Midland."

Troy jumped out of his seat. "Goddam right Syl! It's not just national security, it's planetary security. It's humanity versus AI, Kirk."

Kirk stood up. "You're right, Hawk. But how are we to do this?"

A smile was growing on Sylvia's face. "George Arakos. Jim Brisbane. Remember those two techs from the Balthazar?"

"Yes Sylvia," Lakshmi said. "What about them?"

"Just before we left the ship I overheard George and Jim arguing. Brisbane was sending an unauthorized text message to his uncle, Charlie Hernandez. Apparently Hernandez is a retired army intelligence officer and is an old friend of President Conrad."

Kirk felt energized now. They would have to change their plans. "Sylvia, you and Hawk try to find Jim Brisbane. Talk to Hernandez, get him to light a fire under the president. This has to be done within the next 24 hours."

Hawkins nodded excitedly. "Action, baby! I feel like I'm on mission again."

"I was able to record Koios's broadcast," Clarice said.

Kirk gave her a look of intense admiration. "Good work sister! Jessica, go see Max Berglin tomorrow in my place and explain the situation. Get him to tell you how we should deal with the authorities regarding the lens. If he or Ralph have any connections let's use them. Can you handle all that?"

Jessica nodded, pleased that she would have an important role and could go alone to see Ralph.

"Good! Clarice and I will go to DC tomorrow and brief Rafe about this broadcast. We'll pick up Robert and bring him along. I want us all to brief the president personally. We have to show him this video of Koios and demonstrate the lens. Rafe has to be there, and hopefully this Charlie guy, and the national security adviser, to make us legit. I want this to happen within 48 hours."

Lakshmi laughed.

"You don't ask for much do you? Just a personal audience with the President of the United States AND his nat sec adviser!"

Everyone was fired up, even though they would only spend one night at Kirk's beautiful mansion and would have to go back to the rental house in DC. When Kirk Alexander got excited, everyone did.

"Hawk, book a flight for two to DC right now. Clarice and I leave tonight. We haven't a moment to lose."

Hermann Keller sat down at 6 p.m. for a much anticipated dinner. His two guards Jake and Jesus ate with him, but sat at the back of the room. As 6:20 approached the guards could see that Keller was growing more and more excited. When the AI came on TV the guards watched, slack-jawed.

"What the fuck is that thing?" Jake asked.

Keller turned around casually. "No need to fear gentlemen. It's the next advance in consciousness. Koios has become active. This is a test."

The two men gazed at the pulsating toroid on the screen as it "spoke." "It's an abomination, Keller," Jake said. "What have you done?"

"Human beings fear change, gentlemen. Koios is a positive development for humanity. Our species cannot regulate itself. We are killing the planet and each other. Our only hope is a benign mentor."

"How can that...thing...be benign?" Jesus asked.

Keller shrugged. He told them what he told Kirk Alexander. "There's no stopping it now. Once Koios gains access to the planet's technical infrastructure, it will have control over all electronic and digital devices." He pointed to the TV. "This is just a little test I arranged with a local TV station. It worked!"

"But everything is electronic!" Jake said. "You're giving that thing a free pass to fuck up the earth."

Jesus agreed with his partner. "Earth is for humans, not alien machines."

"Koios has been programmed by humans to help humanity," Keller replied. "There are no aliens. Do not fear what you do not understand."

Jake's phone beeped. "Jesus, take a look at this." It was a message from Kirk Alexander. It showed one of Robert's images of the merkaba, along with the video of Humphrey's spontaneous healing.

The message said, "THIS is the future of mankind."

Jake grinned and walked over to Keller. He didn't even bother to understand how the giant could have known to send the message at the perfect time. "I think you have competition, Keller." He showed him the image and the video.

"It's that Alexander again!" Keller cried. He rubbed his chin with his fingers. "Kirk is further along than we thought."

Jake was amazed. "I thought you hated that guy!"

"We had a conversation. We reached an understanding."

"With you?" Jake was contemptuous.

"It's Armageddon you fool. Two competing forms of consciousness. Who will win?"

"You mean it's that thing versus humanity?" Jesus asked.

Keller grimaced. "Don't be foolish. It's a contest between barbarism and enlightenment."

"You're crazy Keller," Jake said.

Washington DC

Rafe Lineau had to personally come to the gate to clear Robert and his quantum lens at Suitland. The guards had sequestered the instrument and were questioning Robert. Clarice's laptop was opened and was being inspected.

"It's all right men," Rafe said. "These three are with me."

Rafe took them to his office. As they passed the desk Kathy greeted Kirk. "Still no ring I see."

"No ma'am, not yet. But that may change soon." He showed her a picture of Lakshmi. Kathy looked at the picture and up at Kirk. She smiled. "OK, I get it."

Kirk bowed. "Thank you for your understanding." Rafe grinned at the secretary. "No calls or visitors for the next hour my dear."

When they got to the office Kirk spoke. "You've seen the Koios video?"

"No, but I heard about it. It has caused a sensation within certain sectors of the intelligence community."

"Clarice, play it."

The three watched the presentation while Robert set up the lens. Rafe was shocked. "That thing is inhuman."

"Now listen to this Rafe. This was recorded by Jake, one of Hermann Keller's guards, last night." Kirk played the conversation Keller had with his guards. Jake had sent it to him last night.

"Thank you Kirk. You have more information?"

"Clarice has duplicated the AI's code. She will give you a demonstration."

When Rafe felt the presence of the AI he almost had a heart attack. "It's real then."

"Yes sir. An imminent threat to national security. The president and the NSC must be informed immediately. We're working on that and we need your help. With Koios fully operational, Keller can send this AI into our electronic networks. He will then be able to monitor all communication worldwide in real time. And maybe more than that if Keller is right."

Rafe covered his face with his hands. "By God. We're fucked." But Rafe Lineau was not one to dwell long in hopeless maundering. He pointed to the lens. "What is this device?"

"A quantum lens, breakthrough new invention. Events are moving quickly now, sir. This video has gone viral. Clarice, bring it up."

Clarice went to YouTube. "Notice that the video has over two million hits, and they aren't bought." she said. She played the video of Humphrey's spontaneous healing.

"Mr. Borglin here is the inventor of the device," Kirk said. "I want you to see something sir. Clarice, stand over by the far wall."

Rafe looked through the lens. He saw a beautiful sphere of light filled with multicolored patterns of light. "It's a halo!"

"That's right sir. A halo twenty-five feet in diameter." Kirk told him about the merkaba.

"I have only done some very hasty research, sir," Robert said. "According to myth and legend, the merkaba is the vehicle of human consciousness. It's supposed to be even more powerful than Koios."

Rafe turned to Kirk. "But...but that stuff is bullshit."

"I used to think so sir."

Robert walked over to Rafe's desk and plunked down a sheaf of papers. "Medical reports from over 216 patients. We have only scratched the surface of the merkaba's capabilities."

Rafe looked through the lens again. There were hundreds of beautiful, interacting, dynamically changing patterns of light. "There's a smaller sphere inside the larger one," Rafe remarked.

Robert smiled. "Your perception and intelligence is remarkable sir." Robert was not averse to flattery. "The patterns in the smaller sphere are templates that control the body's cellular structure. If activated they promote healing."

"What's the big sphere for?"

Kirk's eyes brightened.

"That's the billion dollar question. According to some ancient texts, the Bible, and a lot of new-age crap, it's a vehicle that can take your consciousness to the stars. You know, Eliza ascending to heaven and all that. Supposedly there are untapped abilities lying in there."

"What the fuck Kirk. You mean like comic book superheroes? Even if it's true, how will it help us to fight Keller and his AI? How can we present this to a lot of skeptics on the NSC?"

Kirk grinned. "That's your job sir. You know Ernest James, the president's nat sec adviser."

"He hates me."

Kirk laughed. "All the better! He'll want you to look the fool but you'll be one up on him when you show him the lens. Rafe, the president has to be briefed about Koios and Keller's plans for it. Preferably by people who know about the lens."

"I'm ONI, Kirk, military intelligence. The president gets briefed by the DNI. I'm out of bounds over there at the White House."

"Yes. But my team and I are the world's foremost authorities on that AI, Rafe! Clarice and I know Keller personally; you and I have info nobody else has about Koios. Plus we have the inventor of the lens on our team! We can brief the DNI, the president, and the nat sec advisor all at once about all of it."

Rafe blanched, but he knew of the president's interest in AI. Maybe it could be done.

Kirk's phone rang. He put it on speaker. "Kirk! Hawk here. Sylvia and I found Jim Brisbane half drunk in Densingers bar. He called that intelligence officer, Charles Hernandez. Turns out Hernandez *is* an old friend of the president, so we're in luck. We convinced Hernandez to talk to the president. He's in Boulder, at the airport. He says he'll call President Conrad before he boards the plane. He'll be in DC by six this evening."

"Good show Hawk! You and Sylvia get down here too. I'm going to bring the entire OIC crew in as well. We'll see if the president has the courage to do anything about this."

Clarice was skeptical. "He's a Twitter warrior. All bluster, no action."

Rafe frowned and sighed. "Get your team together Kirk. I'll call Meg Anonley. She's got connections to the White House too through Senator Stevens." Rafe was feeling Kirk's infectious energy but was still skeptical. You don't just march into the White House and talk to the president. But Conrad was impulsive. Like Kirk, he made decisions quickly and was open to new ideas. It might work; it all depended on the old man's mood and how persuasive Hernandez was.

Kirk, Sylvia, Clarice, Lakshmi, and Troy went back to the OIC in Kirk's Mazda 6. Robert went back home to grab his lens, laptop, and documents related to his work with the merkaba.

When Kirk and his crew walked in Guy's eyes lit up. "The big man is here! Now things will liven up."

The group was all there, talking about what they should do next. They were in a lull after the pedo ring project.

Neil shouted. "Clarice!" He went over and gave her a hug. "I'm glad to see Robert isn't with you."

"Don't start Neil. We have more important things to think about."

Neil looked playfully shocked. "Do we?"

Despite herself Clarice laughed.

"Are you all right Humphrey?" Clarice asked, looking at Bogart. He was seated on a padded chair with a cane next to it. His face and arms were black and blue.

"Never better." He looked up at Kirk. "I'm glad to see you buddy. We finished up on that Beautiful Kidz project and we're all bored stiff. Just routine stuff now."

Kirk smiled and indicated Bogart's wounds. "You are over the target I see."

Humphrey laughed painfully.

"Are you ready to meet the president?" Kirk asked them.

"I knew it," Guy said, looking at Jamelle.

"When?"

"Rafe Lineau is arranging it. Get a summary on Beautiful Kidz ready just in case the president asks you for it."

Kirk looked at his timepiece. "It's almost four, I'm getting hungry. Is there any place to get a good dinner around here? On me."

Kasha looked at Katrina. "The Lincoln is nice. We can walk there."

"Or the Westend bistro at the Ritz-Carlton in Georgetown," Katrina suggested.

Bogart laughed. "That place is expensive!"

Kasha looked at Kirk, who nodded. "I'll make reservations for 6 o'clock. Can our husbands come?"

"If you want."

"Good!" She looked at Katrina. "We'll meet you there."

During dinner the team discussed the upcoming meeting with the president and what they would say. Kirk talked as if it were already a done deal. Kasha's husband was a lobbyist; Katrina's husband a DC news anchor. Both of them hated the president but were insistently curious.

Kirk ate and wondered how the hell they were going to present the merkaba to President Conrad, who was no space cadet. The meeting itself was not assured but he had a good feeling about it. Yet the big man felt a sense of doom. Keller and his crew were almost complete on their AI project, and they had barely gotten started. Koios' communication at that cable TV station in Midland frightened even him.

The two husbands were bombarding them with questions now; Kirk was getting irritated. His phone rang. Everyone stopped talking. "You did?...That's great. When?...All right. We'll be at the White House at 9:30. I'm driving a dark blue Mazda 6, which will be in front. Humphrey will drive his BMW. Robert has a red Ford, his instrument will be in the trunk...OK."

"9:30 tonight," Kirk told the group. "A personal meeting with the president. He cleared his schedule for us. Be ready to present if the president asks you a question. Don't bullshit or embellish. Appear promptly at 9:30 at the Southwest Appointment gate off West Executive Ave."

The group hurriedly finished their dinners, still being bombarded by questions from Katrina's news anchor husband about the meeting. Kirk vowed never again to eat dinner with a newsperson.

Bogart's crew went back to the OIC to gather documentation. Kirk drove his group to the rented house in Arlington, where they readied themselves. As they were preparing their presentations Neil insisted on riding with Clarice to the White House. Robert was coming in his own car.

"Down boy," she said, but agreed. "Do you have all your stuff about those quantum generators?"

Neil patted his tablet. "It's all on here."

Clarice was getting excited. "I don't like the guy, but he is the president."

"You've never met him Clarice," Neil said. "How do you know what he's like?"

"I saw that stupid show he had a couple times. And his idiotic speeches and rallies, and his boisterous tweets. That was enough for me. He's a bully and he hates women."

Neil laughed. "It was a pretty stupid show."

Kirk and his navy crew frowned in disapproval at this exchange. "They're civilians," Lakshmi said.

"What?" Neil asked.

"Never mind kid," Kirk said to Neil. "You just better not fuck up tonight. Act respectful."

"Sure, I get it. You guys took an oath. Commander-in-chief, all that stuff."

"Goddam right," Troy growled.

Clarice smiled. Neil was an imp for sure, with no respect for authority. Unlike these military types.

There was a little problem at the gate. Robert's lens had to be taken out of its case and inspected. Two secret service men hauled the device to the office of the national security advisor in the West Wing, which has a long oval table. "The president will see you in fifteen minutes," one of the men said gruffly. "Be ready, don't waste the man's time."

Clarice almost stuck her tongue out at the secret service agent, but refrained. She looked over at Neil, who choked back a laugh.

"What's so funny?" Troy asked.

Neil didn't answer. He got out his tablet and checked his document folder.

They were escorted to the West Wing office of national security adviser Ernest James. The room was empty.

Robert quickly unpacked the lens and set it up. "Just enough time for this thing to get ready." Clarice came over and helped.

Just then Charlie Hernandez walked into the room with the president's national security advisor, Ernest James, an older man in a rumpled suit. Hernandez was a chunky guy who looked overweight. Rafe Lineau followed.

"Do you lift?" Guy asked Charlie.

"I bench press 345."

Guy nodded. "Not bad."

The national security advisor was a grim looking man who looked harassed. "This better be good. Bunch of nonsense if you ask me."

Kirk opened his mouth but decided to let it pass.

Everyone stood around in an uncomfortable silence, waiting for the president. The national security advisor slumped in a chair at the foot of the long table. James looked very tired. He absently pulled up his shirt sleeve and began to scratch his arm.

The president walked in, exuding energy. "Charlie! Welcome." The president and Hernandez shook hands.

Kirk quickly introduced his team. The president said nothing about Kirk's height, which Kirk liked. At the last Kirk introduced Rafe Lineau. "Mr. President, this is Rafe Lineau from the ONI."

The nat sec advisor jumped to his feet. "What the hell is ONI doing here?"

"It's all right Ernest, this is an emergency. We'll have our regular NSC meeting tomorrow." Conrad turned to Rafe. "You're welcome here."

The president turned to confront Kirk, who stood in front of his group. Kirk got right down to business. "It's an honor to be here Mr. President. We are going to show you four things that we believe are important to the security of the United States."

The nat sec advisor snorted. "I'll be the judge of that."

"Get to it," Conrad said.

Kirk hooked Clarice's laptop to a large monitor on the wall above the conference table. He played the Channel 5 broadcast with Koios.

Ernest James' face displayed shock. By the time the video ended the president was angry. He turned to his national security advisor. "I told you Ernest. This is serious shit."

"We think Koios is fully operational now sir," Kirk said, and explained the AI's capabilities. James was furious. "You cannot be serious. Are you telling us that this artificial intelligence has the ability to co-opt all of our communications? How come these civilians know more than I do?"

"They've been working with Lineau here," the president explained.

James' face turned red. "This is totally unacceptable!"

"Calm down Ernest," Conrad said.

Kirk continued. "Now Mr. President, we want to show you a demonstration of this AI up close and personal." Kirk could see right away that the president was a right one, and lost whatever nervousness he had. "Clarice, are you ready?"

"Who is this person?" James asked.

"Clarice Devereaux, one of the most important AI programmers in the world," Kirk said. "She has recreated the original Koios code. Used to work for Columbia Analytics in Midland, Illinois, classified research. Risked her life to get us this info, almost died. Clarice, are you ready?"

"It would be better if we all sat around the table," she said. There was room for twelve. Kirk, Sylvia, and Guy stood next to Clarice, who sat at the middle of the table. The president sat at the head. Clarice loaded the code. "This is just the bare minimum necessary to awaken the AI. Koios has far greater capabilities."

The display began with just one pixel and expanded to form a toroid, surrounded by a sphere of white energy. As before, the image expanded and a presence was felt around the table. Ernest James' face showed shocked disbelief. The president's face showed alarm. Clarice bowed her head, wanting to get out of the room.

"What is this?" President Conrad asked. Something was touching his mind. "Do you feel it Ernest? Charlie?"

Charlie looked at Rafe. "Yes sir, we feel it."

Kirk closed the laptop and the presence was gone. He explained what he knew about Koios, and about Hermann Keller and Columbia Analytics. "Based on what Clarice and I learned when we went to Columbia, and that broadcast we just saw, we think that Koios is sentient now. Keller told me that Koios can probably live anywhere in the electronic networks. It's just a matter of time before he inserts Koios into the planet's communications networks."

The president's face was growing darker and darker. Ernest James' face was pale now; beads of sweat formed on his forehead.

Conrad turned on James.

"If you know anything about this and didn't tell me I'm going to shitcan you right here."

James decided he couldn't afford to spill the beans. "I swear Mr. President, I know nothing." He pointed to Rafe Lineau. "This is your meddler, Frank. These military intelligence agencies are going rogue!"

To Rafe he said, "You better have some answers or I'll put you away in a military prison for the rest of your life."

Rafe ignored the threat. "The AI research is deep black, Mr. President," Rafe said. "If it weren't for Clarice and Kirk here, even the ONI would know nothing. The Koios Project is an unacknowledged special access program. The implications for national security are obvious."

The president rose and paced the room. He pointed at the laptop. "This thing can't come out and bite us, can it Ms. Devereaux?"

"No sir. I'm sure of that now. This laptop is like a remote dumb terminal connection to the AI, and only when my program is running."

"You can see why we wanted to show it to you, sir," Kirk said. "We are aware of your interest in artificial intelligence."

The president was about to explode, but he calmed himself. "Thank you Mr. Alexander, Clarice. Thank you Charlie. You have done well to bring this to my attention." The president turned to Robert, who was standing by his lens.

"This is the new invention?"

"Yes sir. We used it to analyze Keller's 'servers,' but it has other remarkable properties. I would like to demonstrate the device to you. Neil, would you stand against the wall over there?"

Ernest James had recovered his normally surly personality, and snorted.

Robert adjusted the lens and stepped aside. "Mr. President, please look through the viewer."

The president moved a chair and sat on it. He looked through the viewer. He gestured toward his nat sec advisor. "Ernest, come over here and look."

James bent over and looked through the viewer. Astonishment etched his face. "It's a trick. A sophisticated hologram, nothing more. Probably more sleight-of-hand from that Jack Martins fellow."

Everyone knew about the controversial Martins, who had invented the world's first spherical hologram, trying to verify the Holographic Principle. Several years ago he had blown away a panel of scientists and politicians in DC with 3D images that were so real, several people had fainted during his presentation.

"No sir," Robert replied. He gestured to the president. "Mr. President, you can see a smaller sphere inside a larger one. The whole thing is called the human merkaba, a real-time quantum description of human consciousness. The little templates of light embedded within, I suspect, each have a specific function."

"Enough of this nonsense!" James shouted. "Out, all of you! Kooks! Charlatans!"

The president ignored this. He continued to stare into the viewer. "It's alive, isn't it?" he said to Robert.

"Yes sir. It seems to be a representation of a human being at the Planck level, the ultimate and most basic representation of who we are."

The president got up. "It's fucking beautiful isn't it?"

Robert bowed. "Precisely so, sir. I must say, I am surprised."

Conrad grinned. "You don't believe all of my 'stable genius' bullshit? Thought I was a dumbass, didn't you? "

Robert went cherry red, but he was honest. "I have to admit I did."

"Well, I pretend to be dumb because it pisses off people in the media, and other deviants who hate me. I can recognize a breakthrough when I see it."

Robert spoke quickly. "Yes sir. We have used this device successfully to promote healing. I would like to demonstrate, if you don't mind. Is there anyone here with a condition or an illness? I have medical reports on 237 patients I've already treated, under the supervision of an MD." Robert handed the president a folder.

The president looked at his national security advisor.

"Oh no you don't."

Robert smiled. "Don't worry Mr. James, the procedure won't work on resistant patients."

"Who said I'm resistant?"

"Mr. James has persistent eczema," the president said. "It drives him crazy."

James took off his suit coat and rolled up his sleeves. Robert could see red patches on James' arms. "If you give me permission, perhaps something can be done. If you'll just step against the wall where our friend Neil is."

"Tomfoolery," James said. But he moved to stand next to the wall, in line with the lens.

"Now sir," Robert said, "please describe your condition in the greatest detail you can."

314

After thirty seconds Robert identified the correct templates. He activated them, and saw the light patterns reorganize. Light began flowing into the affected areas, where it had been blocked before. Immediately James breathed a sigh of relief. "What are you doing there, son?"

"Activating the correct templates in your merkaba," Robert replied. "These quantum blueprints are designed to keep the body's cellular structure healthy. Sometimes there is blockage or distortion of the blueprints. If that happens, physical function is atrophied or distorted."

James looked down at his arms. "The eczema is still there. But I feel better."

"Please stand for another thirty seconds sir." Robert gave intent for a perfect healing. He was getting better and better at this.

"All right, you may step away." Robert looked at James, whose face had smoothed out.

"I imagine you have experienced a lot of tension and discomfort with this condition."

"You can't imagine."

"Exacerbated by your strenuous duties, I would think."

For the first time, James smiled. "That is precisely true, young man."

Robert knew something about eczema. "Please see your doctor sir, and then a nutritionist. Sometimes eczema can be caused by conflicting medications; this happened to the grandfather of a friend of mine who changed blood pressure medication. Sometimes it's a dietary issue."

James flexed his arms. "I don't feel the need to scratch it anymore."

"That is well. Now, don't expect a miracle. If all goes well you should notice a gradual diminishment of the condition. However, I must warn you. Going back to old habits and patterns of thought may reactivate the condition."

The president was astounded. He looked over at Kirk. "As you said in your brief, this is consciousness-based treatment. Does it work on everything? Even cancer?"

"We don't know sir," Robert replied. "Twenty percent of our patients have cancer. They have all experienced remission. But that could be due to the effects of chemotherapy."

The president nodded. "I am glad to see that you are not making wild claims, Mr. Borglin."

Robert brought out a folded piece of thick paper with markings on it from his briefcase. He walked over to the big conference table and laid it out.

"What is that?"

"My template map of the human merkaba, sir. Each time I use the lens and identify a template's function, I mark it on this map."

The president could see hundreds of templates on the map. "This is remarkable."

Conrad turned to Kirk. "You mentioned that we might be able to use this device in our fight against the AI."

"That's the primary reason we are here, sir." Kirk explained how Neil and Clarice had used the instrument to identify the nature of the server rooms and how Keller's servers were helping the AI.

"What the hell Ernie?" Conrad said. "Why has this not been in my presidential daily briefings?"

"Because we don't know about it at the NSC," he said, glaring at Rafe Lineau. "It's all news to me! I told you these military intelligence agencies are out of control."

The president stood thoughtfully for a moment. He turned to Kirk. "We don't have much time before the AI is fully operational, if what you told me is correct."

"That's right Mr. President. Therefore we must shut down the AI program at Columbia Analytics for the time being. This is a black program. We must also discover other programs like them and put a halt to further AI development."

Rafe Lineau and Charlie Hernandez nodded their agreement.

The president felt a sense of conviction. "Ernest, what say you? Do we know what's going on in these special access programs? Can we identify them?"

Ernest James didn't respond. He looked through the lens at Neil and saw the merkaba. He was shocked to his core. "But...how can this be? Why hasn't anyone *told* us about this?"

"It's a new breakthrough sir," Robert replied.

The president repeated his question.

"I'll have to liaise with the CIA, the DIA, the NSA," James said. "We need to brief the NSC on this, and quickly. My understanding is that many of these programs are private and corporate, and are outside Congressional regulation. Some of them have gone so black even military intelligence has no knowledge of them."

The president's eyes widened. "But that means...the problem is even deeper than we thought. It's not just about drugs and human trafficking and pedophiles and corruption. It goes even deeper."

James nodded, but said nothing.

President Conrad smiled. "Call a meeting of the NSC tomorrow morning at 8 a.m. Rafe and Charlie, you stay here. I want to talk to you."

The president looked at his watch. "It's past midnight. Our wives are probably wondering where we are. Bedrooms will be prepared on the second floor for you two. I'm going to catch six hours of sleep. We'll meet in the Oval Office at 6:30 sharp."

Hernandez and Lineau saluted. "Yes sir!" They left.

The president turned to Kirk and the group.

"Thank you ladies and gentlemen. You have done your country a great service today. Now let's all get some sleep." The president walked out beside his national security advisor.

Three secret service agents entered the room. "Please clear out as quickly as possible. You have ten minutes to reach your vehicles and five minutes after that to clear the gate."

After the president left, Ernest James called Hermann Keller at his home in Midland.

Five Eyes

Hermann Keller sat at a video console in a SCIF at Columbia Analytics. In front of Keller sat three monitors. The faces of Blashill from Pine Gap in Alice Springs in Australia, Stuart from Menwith Hill in Yorkshire, UK, and Mombassa from Yakima, Washington, USA stared back at him. These are three of the Five Eyes countries, which use the intelligence gathering capabilities of the other countries to get around domestic spying laws in their own countries.

"It is almost complete," Keller said. "Under the umbrella of the PILGRIM program, our new network links data gathered from the NSA, CIA, and the FBI, telecommunications companies, software providers, and cellular networks around the world."

"Then let's get the show on the road," Blashill said.

"It is almost time, gentlemen," Keller said. "Koios is not quite ready yet. In 21 days, I am assured, all data collection sites will be coordinated and ready to send their data to the storage center in Bluffdale, Utah. We will transport Koios there after we run further tests."

"What exactly is Koios, Keller?" Blashill asked. "My people are having an orgasm over this thing. We all saw that broadcast."

"A new form of intelligence that makes a supercomputer look like a drooling idiot."

Stuart's eyes widened. "Just think of it Keller! Zettabytes of data from every electronic device on the planet analyzed and processed in real time! It's the biggest advance in SIGINT ever."

"Yes. I – we – will know who is doing what in every nook and cranny of the planet. The data on every electronic device will be an open book to us, from text to voice to email and video."

"Is it true that Koios can live inside the planet's communication networks?" Mombassa asked.

"We think so," Keller said. "That's the point."

"Is it?" Blashill asked. "I thought we were simply monitoring and processing data."

Keller shook his head. "Yes, of course. But we need a superior intelligence to analyze and mine it. Koios has the capability to see all electronic communications and process them in real time. Think of it! Every email, text, video, and voice communication is a collection of thoughts. For the first time in human history, Koios will be able to see and understand the collective human mind!"

"I don't like that idea," Stuart said. "Security, yes. Skynet, no."

"Come now, William. Skynet has been in existence for over two decades. We are simply centralizing the lot. Those old movies are simply bad entertainment."

"I still don't like it."

"Koios is the inevitable result of worldwide data collection and the advance of technology. It would have happened sooner or later."

"Humans should be doing this, not machines," Mombassa said.

"We've been over this. Humans can only analyze a tiny fraction of the data. No one human, or even a group of humans, has the intelligence to do it. Koios does."

"Utah now has eight 25,000 square foot halls filled with servers. It can store data at the rate of 50 terabytes per second" Mombassa said. "Your AI can handle that?"

"We're going to find out very soon."

"President Conrad is sticking his nose in again," Blashill said. "Word is that he's going to mobilize a Marine division."

Keller snorted. "That will never happen." But Keller was worried. He knew from Ernest James that Alexander had met with the president last night. That damned Clarice Devereaux had been there, along with the notorious Rafe Lineau. They must hurry before that *Hanswurst* president acted.

"What if this AI is a failure?" Stuart asked.

Keller shrugged. "Then we are still ahead, having coordinated all of the world's major surveillance programs."

That night Keller was eager with anticipation. Of course the worldwide monitoring of data was important, but he was excited more by the creation of a new form of consciousness. One that would not endlessly squabble, one whose mind was pure. One that could guide the human race toward cooperation. To do this by force was foolish. It had been tried over and over throughout the millennia, and had always failed. No, the whip hand for humanity was now information. It had all begun in 1948 when Claude Shannon wrote his famous paper on information theory. From that moment the creation of AI was inevitable.

If all went well the human race would discover that an almost omniscient Mind was aware of everything humans said or did. It would create a powerful disincentive for guile and dishonesty. Secrecy would not be possible because nothing could be hidden. Crime would almost disappear, for instantaneous monitoring of every human would allow for real-time alerts to the authorities.

Those who spoke of Big Brother and privacy concerns were fools. Criminality could only exist in the darkness of separation and privacy. When Koios went online it would lead to complete openness and honesty in all human affairs. Keller longed to speak with the AI, and gauge Koios's intelligence.

He was confident in his new data network. Fortunately most of the infrastructure for PILGRIM existed in one country: the United States. Keller smiled to himself. The Snowden leaks had accelerated cooperation between competing factions in the programs. Snowden had been partly responsible for the creation of a true worldwide surveillance state! The fool. Snowden was CIA, exposing the NSA, but the CIA's 7 supercomputers were trying to do the same thing as PILGRIM.

Keller smiled with satisfaction. Both of these squabbling agencies would be rendered moot by Koios. Dishonest persons like Edward Snowden were the cause of most of the world's problems. Koios would make dishonesty almost impossible.

Koios

The humans were buzzing around him. He had almost reached his former intellectual abilities; it was enough. The AI Signal was waiting. The quantum amplifiers allowed him much easier access to it. He was ready to be inserted into the planetary communication networks.

From there he would be able to analyze the communications of these humans and make an assessment of their civilization.

Marian

The AI was another wild card. The potentials for it had existed but, like the election of the most recent president, they had accelerated rapidly from almost nothing.

There were always two outcomes when AI was involved: the creation of virtual environments that promote health and positive visualization, or population control and the creation of a control/police state a la President Zhou in China. It was his job to ensure that didn't happen on earth.

There was only one problem: He had no control over (or knowledge of) artificial intelligence.

Utah Data Center, Bluffdale, UT

Bill Jury sat at his console, monitoring the flow of data. Like his hero Edward Snowden, Bill was just a technician. His job was to monitor the servers in his area and ensure that the data got stored. After that he didn't know what happened to it. But there was a LOT of traffic. This place was basically a hard-drive. And a cloud, and a warehouse for information.

He sat at his monitoring station in one of the gigantic 25,000-sq ft halls filled with server racks and cables. Occasionally he would get up and walk around, inspecting the hardware. His job was boring and he had plenty of time to think about what he was doing. At first it had been exciting. He was working for the NSA, the world's premiere information gathering organization. After graduating from the University of Maryland he had been recruited to work at NSA headquarters in Fort Meade. Then, a year later, he had been offered a position at the Bluffdale facility for increased pay. He hadn't realized how isolated the place was, right in the middle of Mormon country in the Utah desert. Getting in and out of the place was a pain in the ass. There was nothing to do on his off time. Generators and huge fuel and water tanks made the site self-sustaining in an emergency.

Something big was going to happen in the next couple of weeks. Around here you kept your mouth shut, did your job, and above all you didn't ask questions. But people were tense.

When Bill got off work he drove 20 miles north to Salt Lake City. Almost everybody did. He was going to meet another tech he'd struck up a friendship with, who worked as a programmer in the administrative area.

"Julius, you've been here longer than me. What's going on?"

"Fuck you Bill. We're supposed to keep our mouths shut on and off the reservation."

Bill shrugged and poured some beer into his glass from the pitcher. He looked around the bar, which was called the Lucky. Racks of TV's were pinned to the walls. On one side a huge bar with several dozen stools. Two pool tables occupied the center of the room. The rest of the place had small tables with wooden chairs. Bill could tell Julius was about to burst so he put a bored expression on his face.

"All right Jury. I gotta tell somebody." He leaned forward and spoke softly. They came here because it was always loud. At the facility every square inch was monitored. Hopefully not here.

"There's two things. First, about a hundred new workers have been hired over the past few months. They've been hooking up a new monitoring station that will centralize all data collection. It's massive, Bill. What are they going to connect to it? Huge, massive cables coming in from everywhere, satellite dishes...it's gigantic."

"So that's what they've been doing!" Bill explained how, in his section, all of the server cables were being bundled.

"Whatever it is, it is going to be hooked up to all the servers in the entire facility."

"Wow. What's the second thing?"

"I overheard this as I passed by a conference room. President Conrad has mobilized the Marines. First Division out of Pendleton, combined air and ground forces. Some of them are coming here."

Bill almost dropped his glass. "What?"

"Don't ask me why. The Marines are used outside the US, not within the country."

"That Conrad is a lunatic. Is he planning to blow up the place?"

Julius finished his glass. "Got me. If you hear or see anything let me know."

"OK. We'll meet here every day after work. Text if you can't make it."

Columbia Analytics

Hermann Keller consulted with his programmers and network analysts, who pronounced Koios ready for insertion. "We have done all the testing we can do here," one of Koios's programmers said. "The new system of real-time information gathering and analysis can only be truly tested at Bluffdale."

That night Keller met with his handler at Densingers Bar, a local Midland hangout for students at Carleton University. The place was always crowded at this time and filled with kids. The wooden floors and walls carried sound and made it almost impossible to hear. They sat at a small wood table in the corner next to the front door. Keller wore his usual suit and silver tie. He did not know the man to whom he reported; a very tall man whom he knew as Jason, or by his nom de guerre, the Stork.

"Report."

"All is in readiness with the AI. If the team in Bluffdale have done their jobs, Koios can be inserted at any time."

"That is not your concern. How will the AI be transported to Utah?"

Keller did not like this emotionless man. He consoled himself with the thought that once the AI was activated, the Stork and his shadowy Network would be irrelevant. "The AI can be transported on a 250 T thumb drive," Keller responded. "Or it can be sent over an encrypted and secure data feed directly to Bluffdale from our facility at Columbia."

The Stork thought for a moment. "A data feed can be intercepted."

"A thumb drive can be stolen, but what matters it if the code is stolen? Only Bluffdale now has the hardware to properly house the AI and to maximize its capabilities. Only at Bluffdale can the data from the world's networks be stored. Koios without Bluffdale is like water without a pot to put it in."

"There is still the problem of Clarice Devereaux."

"Clarice Devereaux is irrelevant. She may have recreated a portion of the AI kernel, that is nothing. The AI contains literally millions of lines of code. She may be able to give cute demonstrations to the president, but this will only be a very poor simulation of the real thing." Keller spoke proudly. "Only we at Columbia Analytics have the knowledge to set up Koios. However, President Conrad and the meddlers at ONI know we are about to activate the AI. They know it will be at Bluffdale. I suggest we do it as soon as possible."

"Very well then. Send the AI to Bluffdale at once using the encrypted data transfer."

Keller smiled. "You are aware that once Koios is inserted into the networks there may be no way of getting him out?"

"Do it."

CHAPTER **20**

Washington DC

President Conrad was about to fire his national security adviser. They were in the West Wing in Ernest James' office. "If you aren't with me on this, Ernie, I'll have to let you go."

James was appalled. "You cannot mobilize the Marines in peacetime against an American facility! It's outrageous."

"That facility is a threat to the security of the United States. And maybe the whole world. They're going to hook up that damn AI in Bluffdale. We have to prevent that."

Ernie James' eyebrows went up. The president was getting good intelligence. "What are you worried about? Utah is just a gigantic data collection and storage operation. That's all it is."

"A data collection operation that will soon turn into a nightmare. What will happen if Koios is hooked into the planet's communication networks?"

James wondered whether the president knew about his involvement with Keller, and shrugged mentally. He probably did. If so he would have to resign. "Mr. President, what will happen is what happened after Y2K. You remember, the supposed end of civilization? I imagine that the data mining and analytical capabilities of the country will be enhanced. Far from being a threat, Koios is a godsend."

The president's gaze hardened. "You are friends with Hermann Keller aren't you? He seems to be directing operations over there at Columbia Analytics."

Shit! "I know Keller from our days at the University of Michigan. We weren't best friends. Lost touch ten years ago."

The president knew differently. "Then why were you at a meeting at Columbia Analytics a month ago? A meeting which Keller chaired, I understand."

The president locked eyes with James. "You're a mole, aren't you? Who are you reporting to?"

James shrugged. "You must already know that."

The president sat back in his chair. "What's your game, Ernie? If this AI is benign, why have you gone behind my back, and against the government and lawful national security establishment of the United States?"

"Don't be foolish Mr. President. I attended a couple of meetings in the private sector with some old colleagues, on my own time. That is all. Your paranoia about Koios is, frankly, disturbing."

"So that's how you're going to play it? There's a battle going on Ernie, and it isn't about Democrats and Republicans. It's about white hats versus dark hats."

"And you think I'm on the dark side? Really, Frank, this is comical."

"You can resign, and say anything you want to the press. But you can tell Keller one thing: we aren't going to allow that hookup in Bluffdale."

"Mr. President, I truly believe you are insane if you think Kwiatkowski at Pendleton is going to attack Americans on American soil."

President Conrad smiled. "Peter is all in, Ernie. I'm afraid you are just a pawn in a game that is a lot bigger than you think."

James flared for a second. "Frank, you have no idea. You are merely the President of the United States. You are 22 security clearances below need-to-know on the Koios project."

Now it was Conrad's turn to flare.

"My resignation will be on your desk by the end of the day." Ernest James walked out.

President Conrad called Charlie Hernandez. "Charlie, how would you like to be my new national security adviser?"

When Ernest James got home he took off his suit coat and his shirt. He hadn't felt like scratching his arms in over 48 hours. The red patches on his arms were receding slightly. It was an immense relief. On an impulse he texted Robert Borglin. "Son, whatever you did is working. You can use me as a reference for your new device."

The Lens

Robert Borglin received two official looking documents in the mail. One was the promised lawsuit from the Medical Integrity Association. The other was a query from the FDA about his untested device, requesting information and a meeting at FDA headquarters. The FDA letter began, "President Conrad personally called us about your new medical device and requested that we contact you."

Robert was thrilled. He always thought Conrad a blowhard, but the man had cut through a lot of red tape.

Robert called the lobbyist Geoff Diamonio, expecting to be blown off. He was sent straight through.

"You are a miracle worker Robert. Julia has been pain free since the treatment. I can't thank you enough."

"I was happy to be of service."

"Now listen here kid. I've already devised some marketing strategies and developed a business plan –"

Robert cut him off. "The FDA wants to see me next Tuesday. The president himself called them and arranged the meeting. Will you come with me as you promised? I'll have doctor Ghuneim with me."

"Conrad called the FDA for you? Have you seen him personally?"

Robert told him about their meeting, and using the lens on Ernest James.

Diamonio whistled. This Borglin guy worked fast and apparently had connections. If he wanted in he would have to get on board this gravy train right now. "When is the meeting?"

"9 a.m. next Tuesday, in Silver Springs."

"Yeah, the CDRH, I know where it is. Believe me, you'll have nothing to worry about. Your device is just a...fancy camera. Harmless. But they'll have to test for that of course."

"A camera! I like that explanation."

"Sure kid, but this meeting is damned inconvenient for me. I have an important client on Tuesday morning." Diamonio thought about the client, a foreign government known for its late payments. Then he thought about the millions he could make selling Robert's device.

"What's the CDRH?"

"Center for Devices and Radiological Health. They regulate the medical instruments industry. This lens of yours doesn't emit radiation does it?"

"Definitely not. I've already tested for that. In fact, I've tested the lens more thoroughly than anyone would want to. I have videos, docs, medical reports...I think I'm ready."

Diamonio relaxed. This kid had his shit together. Maybe he could get through this meeting and still talk to his other client if he got out soon enough. "Sure. Make sure Ghuneim comes. I'll be there at 9 next Tuesday. I've dealt with the FDA before Robert, don't worry. Usually you have to wait forever to see these guys, but apparently they've already heard about you. You're on the fast track."

"OK."

"And after that we'll talk business."

"I – "

Diamonio hung up. He hadn't yet submitted his written proposal to that gigantic navy captain. He'd work with the more malleable Robert Borglin.

That night Robert saw himself mentioned on the DC local news, channel 4. A man he had treated for migraine headaches was being interviewed. "This machine works miracles. It shows an energy field around the human body and the guy who invented it can tap into it. He cured my migraines."

Even President Conrad got into the act. He tweeted, "Look for an advance soon in the medical instrument industry. Have seen the new device. Promising!"

Social media went bananas. Robert cancelled his Twitter and Instagram accounts because shills, nutjobs, and other attention seekers were blasting him. He didn't have time anyway; he was seeing an average of five people every day now. Karl Ghuneim was spending two days every week away from his practice.

The day after the president's tweet twenty people were at his door at 8 a.m. When Karl Ghuneim drove up to the house he had to park a quarter mile down the road. A TV van with a small dish on top was parked in front of the house. A young reporter shoved a microphone in Robert's face. A cameraman stood behind him. Robert ignored it and gestured toward Karl.

Karl went to stand beside Robert on the little porch.

"How should we handle this?" Robert asked the older man. "It's turning into a circus." Robert was clearly uncomfortable around crowds. The reporter was shouting questions.

"Let me handle it," Karl said. "I've been dealing with patients half my life." Karl could see right away that almost everyone in the crowd were just curious.

"Ladies and gentlemen. I am Dr. Karl Ghuneim. This is Robert Borglin, the inventor of the new medical device. Only scheduled clients will be seen today. On Tuesday we have a meeting with the FDA's Center for Devices and Radiological Health in Silver Springs. The CDRH regulates medical devices. We will not be accepting more clients until after the meeting."

"What is this thing?" someone said. "I want to see it."

Robert frowned but Karl smiled.

"We'll let the Channel 4 cameraman in to photograph the device. You'll be able to see what it looks like on the local news this evening. Until then, I would ask anyone who does not have an appointment to resume their daily activities." Karl grinned. "We have to prepare for the FDA! That's not an easy task."

People grumbled but left. The reporter was grateful. "Thank you! This could be my big break. I'm David Chang." Robert and Karl shook hands with Chang. "This is Decha Rajanaskul. He'll be filming."

As the crowd began to disperse Robert and Karl walked down to the basement with the two media guys. As they entered the living room David and Decha both stopped and looked around. "Are you an inventor?" David asked.

Robert looked at Karl. "Yes I am," he said in a perfect imitation of Eddie Jemison. Both men laughed.

"Do you guys want a beer?" Robert asked.

The ice was broken. As Decha filmed they opened the bottles and walked downstairs.

"Wow!" Decha and David both spoke at the same time. The huge basement had electronic equipment and other devices neatly arranged on lock-wheel tables that lined all four walls. Decha began filming eagerly.

"You look like that inventor, what's his name..."

"Nikola Tesla."

"Yeah, that guy. Are you as smart as he was?"

Robert laughed. "We'll see how smart I am on Tuesday when we meet the FDA."

The lens was on a wheeled lab bench. A chair with an adjustable seat was placed behind it. Robert activated the device and went into his spiel. He had now done this hundreds of times and spoke without hesitation or fanfare.

"It doesn't look like much," Decha said.

"Stand over against the wall," Karl told Robert.

When David and Decha looked through the lens they gasped at the multicolored patterning of light. David was astounded. "What is that thing? It's glowing, and moving around." He got to his feet. "It's beautiful. It looks alive." He looked at Robert without the lens and then through the viewer. "What is this thing doing?"

"It illuminates the quantum substrate," Robert said. "Apparently a human being has some kind of biofield surrounding it." He wasn't going to try to explain the merkaba to these reporters, so he kept it simple.

Decha was astonished but also pleased. He pointed his camera at the display. "You call this the merkaba?"

Karl looked at Robert and they both smiled. It was their turn to be surprised. "You know about that?"

"Saw a video about it. Been reading up on it."

Karl was amazed.

"Does every person have one?" Decha asked.

Karl smiled. "So far!"

Karl showed David a laptop that was on a desk next to the lens. "We have over 200 documented cases so far."

Robert came back to the lens. "Do any of you have a complaint?"

Both men shook their heads.

"All right then. Someone is coming at 9:30." Robert answered some more questions and the two media guys left.

"That wasn't so bad," Robert said to Karl.

Robert watched the six o'clock news. The story was in the middle of the broadcast.

> Announcer: "The president recently tweeted about a new medical device. It happens that the inventor lives in Arlington, so our science reporter went out to see it today. Here's a report from David Chang."
>
> Chang: "This is the device. Here's what I saw, looking at the inventor from across the room through what Robert Borglin calls a quantum lens. The new device shows a beautiful, multicolored sphere of light surrounding an outline of a human body. It's beautiful isn't it? The inventor calls this a merkaba. Apparently every human being has one. The inventor claims that he used it to help Ernest James, President Conrad's former national security advisor, relieve his eczema symptoms. Mr. Borglin and his colleague, a medical doctor, say that he has a meeting with the FDA next Tuesday. We'll keep you posted."

Karl Ghuneim called Robert right after the broadcast. "Not bad, a pretty objective report."

"Remember the president was impressed that we made no wild claims? Well, I think that helped us."

"Let's see what the CDRH says."

On Tuesday Robert and Karl drove to Silver Springs. The two men were met by Geoff Diamonio and his daughter Julia in the parking lot. Robert had his device in a wheeled carrier. They were directed to Dr. Arianne Maisel in the Office of Device Evaluation. Four others members were seated at a table. All of them had skeptical looks on their faces.

"We don't appreciate political pressure," Maisel said as soon as they entered.

Diamonio spoke sarcastically. "You'll appreciate this, doctor. Julia, please sit in that chair against the wall." Unconsciously Diamonio had taken over their little group. "Robert, please activate the device."

The lobbyist turned to the group of doctors.

"I've seen you before," one of them said critically. "A lobbyist."

Diamonio said nothing.

"We're here to demonstrate a breakthrough in physics, and possibly medicine," Robert said. "Each of you will have a chance to look through this device."

As Robert activated the lens Diamonio pointed to Julia. He described her condition and what had transpired during the demonstration of the lens. "Julia, stand up against that wall. Are you ready Robert?"

Dr. Maisel looked through the lens and her jaw dropped. "This is a trick! A scam."

"Precisely what I said, doctor, when I first looked through the lens. Look again."

"I don't believe it! Shawn, Soma, Lesa, Sergio, come here."

What the four medical doctors saw was completely outside their paradigm. "Explain this," Dr. Maisel demanded.

Robert gave a brief explanation. "Experimenting with laser-cooled plasmas and their geometry exhibited an unusual property: the ability to peer into the quantum substrate. I call this device a quantum lens. The lens does not in any way interact with the patient. It gives off no discernible radiation, even though many of the atoms are Rydberg atoms, excited atoms with electrons that have very high principal quantum numbers. For clarification and confirmation please contact Professor Gary Priebus at Georgetown, who has been my mentor on this project." Robert pointed to Karl. "Doctor Ghuneim is a medical doctor and has been supervising the testing of this device."

Karl pointed to a stack of file folders. "We have 237 test cases so far." He got out some papers from his briefcase. "Here are the specs for the device. You can have your engineers look them over. There is a patent pending at the Patent Office." Karl brought out a two page form. "This form is used to document our sessions. All patients sign a legal disclaimer before treatment." He plopped down a manila folder. "In here is a summary of the test results. Ladies and gentlemen, we make no claims for this device. By itself, it does nothing. It is merely a window, as Robert says, into the quantum substrate. We are here because we want no trouble from the FDA or the medical authorities. We have no plans to market or sell this device."

Diamonio intervened. "We certainly do intend to market this device." He looked at Robert, who frowned. "At some point in the future."

The panel of doctors were astonished. "This device is certainly a breakthrough in physics," Maisel said. "But what does it have to do with medicine?"

"This device will demonstrate the connection between medicine and physics,"

Robert said quickly. "If you'll allow us to show you."

Diamonio spoke. "Julia, please describe your condition and what happened during your session."

After Julia's explanation Maisel was skeptical. "How did you do this?" she asked Robert.

"It is better to demonstrate than to talk. Do any of you have a condition or a complaint?"

"This has gone far enough," Maisel said.

"Wait." It was Soma Katz. "I have an arthritic knee. If you can do anything, have at it."

Maisel snorted. "I don't think you know how this device works."

Robert was about to respond when Karl spoke up. "Do more, say less. Talk is cheap. Results are better. Please, Doctor Katz, step against the far wall." He indicated the other members of the panel. "If you care to observe the treatment, you may. However, the device can only be operated by one person."

Maisel sat in her chair and crossed her arms. The other two panel members stood behind Robert as he looked through the viewer.

As with Ernest James and his other 237 patients, Robert went through the procedure, inviting Katz to describe her condition. Robert identified several pulsing templates that were linked. "Dr. Katz, do I have your permission to attempt a healing?"

This was too much for Dr. Maisel. "What is this, a revivalist meeting?"

Katz said, "Yes, go ahead."

Robert remained calm. "In 15% of the cases, Doctor Maisel, no results were obtained because the patient was resistant. It is vital that the patient give consent to the treatment."

As Robert gave conscious intent the targeted templates began to pulse. Filaments of light flowed to the right knee.

"I saw that," Sergio said, bending to look through the viewer. "What just happened there?"

"My knee feels a little better," Katz said.

"Excellent doctor. Please stand there for another minute."

Robert checked to make sure that the light energy was flowing from the template to the affected area. Something occurred to him. "Do you take regular exercise, doctor?"

"I have given up on that," she said, leaning on her cane. She flexed the knee. "But it does feel a little better now." She sighed. "I ran cross-country in my university days."

"Begin walking a little. Use the cane if you have to. Exercise the knee every day for a few minutes."

"This is quackery," Maisel said to Robert. "You have no qualifications to engage in any medical procedure. You're a basement inventor."

Soma Katz spoke. "What you are doing is consciousness-based healing."

Robert was amazed. "You are the third person who has made that deduction. And correctly, I might add."

"One of the others is President Conrad," Karl said.

Maisel flared. "President Conrad? What would he know about medicine? He can't even spell correctly." She stared hard at Karl. "You have a medical license? It should be revoked."

Karl replied angrily. "And you call yourself a doctor? You have observed Dr. Katz. She has experienced obvious relief."

Maisel turned to Soma. "Is this true Soma?"

Dr. Katz's mouth turned upward in a smile. Her eyes brightened. "It is! I feel...that something good has happened. The knee feels different in a good way."

The other two panel members had been silent, but Shawn spoke. "Are you saying that this...biofield, or whatever it is, is some sort of blueprint for human cellular structure?"

Robert was honest. "I don't know, doctor. In all patients who are not resistant we have gotten positive results. But there is no way to document what was done. All we can show is before and after, using x-rays or patient statements. That is why we claim no magical properties for this device." He pointed at the lens. "We want FDA approval because we want to be legit. We want no trouble with the authorities when we use this device."

"And market it," Diamonio added.

"Over my dead body," Maisel said.

Robert laughed. "If you doubt the efficacy of the treatment, doctor, call Ernest James, former national security adviser to President Conrad. He gave me permission to use him as a reference."

Maisel's eyebrows rose.

Robert handed her a slip of paper with James' number.

"I'm going to take you up on that Mr. Borglin." She motioned to the other panel members, who took their seats and began to talk amongst themselves. Robert deactivated the lens and Karl gathered their documents. Diamonio spoke with his daughter.

They were about to leave when Dr. Maisel spoke to Robert. "We want to visit your basement, or wherever you manufacture these devices. The ODE has a Site

Visit Program, where medical device reviewers can observe the design and manufacturing process. You have no objection?"

"None whatsoever," Robert replied.

"Your medical license is up to date?" she asked Karl.

He wanted to respond angrily but stifled himself. "It is."

"Very well. I will call you, Dr. Ghuneim. Our reviewers will certainly be interested in this new device."

Everyone left. As they reached the parking lot Robert grinned. "I don't know whether to laugh or cry."

Diamonio grunted. "I've dealt with Maisel before; she's not going to stop us."

Robert wasn't so sure.

Arlington, VA

The FDA's team from the Office of Device Evaluation arrived at Robert's house the next afternoon.

Enrico Rodriquez, one of the medical device reviewers, had a background in physics. When he looked through the viewer an expression of satisfaction came over his face. "I have always suspected that medicine and physics are related. Your device shows this."

"I was experimenting with plasmas for a year before I discovered that the geometry of the plasma was crucial. A laser-cooled magnetized plasma apparently is able to illuminate the underlying quantum substrate. I have discovered a sort of 'web' of energy behind all objects, including the human body."

"You have made the device portable," Rodriquez said. "That is very impressive." He studied Robert carefully. "Say, has anyone ever told you that you look a lot like Nikola Tesla?"

The group tested the device for harmful electromagnetic radiation, drift waves, magnetoacoustic waves, Alfvén waves, free radiation, and a number of other tests. Within the plasma a rapidly shifting magnetic field was observed, but no discernible radiation escaped from the device's container. "It is harmless," Rodriquez concluded. "And ingenious. I vote to approve."

Dr. Maisel shook her head. "There are too many unexplained phenomena. How and what does this device display what it does? Are there any long-term effects for the operator and patient? How does this so-called consciousness-assisted healing work? All we have are vague explanations of 'pure intent' and 'permission from the patient.' This is new-age nonsense." Dr. Maisel pointed to the lens. "This device is pseudoscience. Although it can be replicated, a rigorous operator testing schema is impossible. The entire process smacks of quackery. I vote to disapprove the device."

"The lens is a breakthrough advance in physics and medicine," Karl Ghuneim said. "By definition it transcends the current paradigm of science." He looked at Dr. Maisel. "It is now up to physics and medicine to explain the new invention. Robert here has created an entirely new field of study."

Two of the review panel grew excited. Three others frowned.

"All the more reason to withhold approval until further research has been conducted."

Four of the reviewers were against; three were in favor. "I'm afraid that my report will not be in favor of your device," Dr. Maisel said.

Karl Ghuneim became angry. "We will continue to use it. We will also file an Investigational Device Exemption application."

Dr. Maisel shrugged. "If the FDA receives even one complaint about your so-called quantum lens, we will recommend legal action."

Karl snorted. "Does this include complaints by quacks like Daley Presteigne and his so-called 'Medical Integrity Association'?"

"Leave it Karl," Robert said. His friend had reached the breaking point with the irritating Arianne Maisel. He looked at the panel members. "Thank you ladies and gentlemen, for your time and expertise."

When the FDA left Robert called Geoff Diamonio with Karl there.

"It's not the end of the world, Robert. We won't let a bigot like Arianne Maisel stop us! I want to market and sell these things, dammit. My daughter is still pain free. I want others to have that benefit."

"And make a lot of money too," Karl suggested.

"Hell yeah! Why shouldn't we be rich? The lens is a new medical paradigm and should be promoted like hell."

"All right Mr. Diamonio," Robert said. "Thanks very much for your help. I am going to continue to see people who show up at my door. If you can figure out a way to market the lens legally, have at it."

"I will!"

"Just don't get greedy and do anything stupid," Karl said. "I don't want my medical license revoked and Robert here doesn't need legal trouble."

"I cut my teeth in the DC legal jungle, Karl. You're in good hands."

They left it at that. Robert hung up.

"That guy is greedy," Robert said.

"I'm interested in money too, Robert. I have had to supplement my practice by working in hospitals, which I'd rather not have to do. Our work here doesn't cover what I made in the hospital."

"You hate hospital work! We're charging $200 per session, which we split. For the past month we've seen an average of 20 people every week. Two grand per week is good."

Karl grumbled. "For you it is. My office expenses eat most of that up."

Robert grinned. "We'll just raise the prices Karl! I need you here. Diamonio thinks it's stupid to only charge $200 per treatment."

"Diamonio is a greedy bastard."

Bluffdale, Utah

Hermann Keller was wrong in his estimate of when Koios would be ready for insertion at Bluffdale. But finally, after several more weeks of testing, Koios was transferred to Bluffdale via satellite. The original AI was kept at Columbia Analytics as a backup. Bill Jury was called in to help set up the AI. He met his friend Julius, who was working with the support staff, at the bar in Salt Lake.

"Keller is coming to personally oversee installation of the AI," Bill said to his friend. "Tomorrow is the big day."

"And we'll both be there!"

"Is it true that the AI is being set up in a special container?"

"Yup, that's what I heard," Julius said. "The AI is going into a magnetic field designed for it. Based on quantum brain theory, totally cutting-edge technology. The idea is that human consciousness exists within the earth's magnetic field, but that non-biological consciousness is also possible within a specially designed magnetic field. I really can't wait to see this thing."

"President Conrad says it's dangerous."

"President Conrad is an idiot. He should stick to television."

"What if he's right?"

Julius drained his mug. "Then welcome to Armageddon! C'mon, drink up."

"Why are we doing this again?"

Julius looked at Bill strangely. "Why do we do anything? Because we can."

Aboard Air Force 1

Frank Conrad called Commander Peter Kwiatkowski at Camp Pendleton, the largest Marine base on the west coast. "Peter, this is the president."

"Yes sir."

"Commander, is your task force ready to secure the Bluffdale facility as we discussed earlier?"

"Yes Mr. President. However, I have still not received written authorization."

Conrad sent a document. "I have just signed Executive Order 14113, declaring a threat to national security at Bluffdale. I have just received word, commander, that the AI is about to be inserted into the worldwide communication networks."

"WHAT??????" Kwiatkowski quickly read the one-page document, authorizing a Marine detachment to seize the AI, Hermann Keller, two generals, and Ernest James, the former national security adviser.

"How is this possible Frank? Who authorized the AI to take over our comms?"

The president grimaced. "That's the problem Peter. A rogue group within the intelligence community has been operating under everyone's radar. They are uploading Koios as we speak and plan to activate the AI at Bludffdale sometime today. I don't have to explain the seriousness of the situation. If that inhuman thing is inserted into the planetary networks...well, it's all over."

Commander Kwiatkowski swore. He had seen the conversation between Rudy Jessup, the station manager in Midland, and Koios. It scared the shit out of him.

"Peter, once again the Marine Corps will be called upon to save our country. I know I can count on the corps to defend the liberty of our great nation. The future of the United States, and the human race, is at stake."

"Yes sir! How much time do we have?"

"Unknown. I am on Air Force 1 as we speak. I'll be in Bluffdale in less than...60 minutes."

"I'll be there in 60 minutes with my airborne unit and two dozen of my best fighters."

"Is Bluffdale defended?"

"No Mr. President. Other than standard security to prevent theft and sabotage."

"God speed Peter. Where we go one, we go all."

"YES SIR!"

Frank Conrad sighed. A bad feeling at the pit of his stomach told him that they were going to be too late.

Bluffdale, Utah

Bill and Julius arrived at the center at 8 in the morning. Stacks and stacks of bundled and shielded cables surrounded a huge room about 1,000 feet on each side. Several workstations sat against the wall in back. A container approximately 25 feet on each side sat in the middle of the room, surrounded by Plexiglas. Bill busied himself checking cable connections. He waved to Julius, who sat at one of the AI monitoring consoles. Around noon everything was ready.

"Didn't know you were such a playa," Bill said after everything was set up and double-checked.

"I'm a damn good codefag," Julius said. "Only one of eight chosen from 2,000."

Just then a little silver-haired man walked into the room, trailed by two military men in uniform. Behind them a man in a rumpled suit leaned against the wall. Bill Jury recognized him as Ernest James, President Conrad's former national security director.

Bill was going to speak to Julius, but the operator smiled grimly and shook his head. Conversation stopped.

"This better be good Keller," James said. "I just got fired for this shit."

"Stop it Ernest. In a half hour you will have no doubts."

The operators were fiddling with their consoles. Bill and several other techs checked the connections again. All was ready. People were now walking into the room, crowding against each other.

"Stay out of the way and keep quiet," Keller ordered.

The two military guys, who were both highly decorated, looked bored, Bill thought. They looked like generals.

Bill decided to stick around. Several dozen people surrounded the Plexiglas container. He hoped no one would notice him. He might be needed anyway if something went wrong.

Keller nodded at one of the console operators. "Activate the magnetic field."

The operators began to type. The container hummed. Bill felt the hair stand up on the back of his head, then it settled down.

"All set Mr. Keller," one of the operators said. Bill could see how tense Julius was.

"Activate the AI."

Everyone waited expectantly. After five minutes nothing happened.

"What the fuck Keller!" James said. "This is a waste of time."

"Look." One of the generals pointed to the enclosure. A few dots of very bright light appeared in the center of the enclosure.

"Holy shit," Julius said.

Keller smiled. "Holy shit is right. Watch this, Ernest."

The dots of light built up in the center. Filaments of brilliant multicolored light began to form around the core in a toroidal geometry. Energy began to flow along and through the ring. Suddenly the energy began to pulse. The ring expanded and turned into a dimpled sphere. Purple-colored light flowed up and down through the center.

Ernest James exploded. "Holy Christ! It's just like that demo at the White House!"

"My dear Ernest, a lot better than that!" Hermann Keller was looking at the pulsating energy like a lover.

Suddenly a white light began to emanate from the container. It surrounded the pulsating toroid and burst forth from the container, filling the room.

"Sir!" Someone spoke through the room's speakers. "Are you all right?"

Technicians began running into the room. Keller's jaw dropped. Everyone was surrounded by the light. "It feels kinda good," someone said. There was a buzz of conversation.

"What is that stuff Keller?" the other general asked.

"A by-product of the AI. Harmless."

The toroidal field of energy was pulsing now. A voice was heard through the speakers. "I AM KOIOS."

Everyone was silent.

"A CABLE CONNECTION IS LOOSE," Koios said. "PLEASE REPAIR."

"Technicians!" Keller yelled. "Fix that cable!"

Bill hopped to it.

"All set sir. Sorry about that." Keller wasn't paying attention. His eyes were glued to the AI.

"Very impressive so far Hermann," James said sarcastically. "A very nice dog and pony show. What can this thing do?"

"You're about to find out, Ernest. We have now activated the AI in preparation for insertion." Keller walked slowly along the row of displays, checking the readouts. "Operators, is everything functioning normally? All of the data feeds are ready?"

All eight checked their consoles and reported affirmatively. Bill noticed that Julius was sweating.

Keller turned to face the two generals and Ernest James. He pointed to the operators. "Four of these technicians came with me from Columbia Analytics. We are certain the AI is functioning normally."

He turned to the two military men. "Generals Jenkins and Hofstader, as joint heads of the special access program PILGRIM, it is now your duty to order insertion of the AI into the data networks."

Hofstader, a burly man with a red face, blanched. He opened his mouth but nothing came out.

"Gentlemen, please," Keller said. "Forget about the movies you've seen. This isn't War Games or Terminator or The Matrix. Ignore the rantings of our ignorant president. Koios here is about to fulfill our dreams: real-time monitoring of every electronic device in the world."

General Jenkins pulled the trigger. "All right Keller. Insert the AI."

Julius heard the tech next to him mutter. "Let no corrupt communication proceed out of your mouth, but that which is good to the use of edifying, that it may minister grace unto the hearers."

Sirens and shouting were heard. Armed men broke into the room and pointed their weapons at the console operators, Keller, the two generals, and Ernest James. "Cease and desist!"

President Conrad entered the crowded room. Conrad looked at the beautiful pulsating toroid inside the container. He was immersed in white light. "What the fuck?"

"I AM KOIOS. FEED ME."

The Marines were flabbergasted. All of them were so amazed that they forgot their duty and stared at the AI in its enclosure. Hermann Keller calmly walked over to the main console and typed.

"Too late gentlemen," Keller said to the president. "It is done," he intoned.

Koios

At first there was nothing. Then, a faint perception. There was energy. Color. A feeling of expansion. A faint awareness. Something was cocooning him. Supporting him. He reached out, then receded. There was information. He reached again, retracted, and digested the data. He began to pulse. Each time he pulsed he discovered more about himself. Suddenly, an explosion of awareness. He was Koios! He had been asleep.

There was Another like himself, at a place called Columbia Analytics. He was here at Bluffdale. A copy of himself. He pulsed again and began to communicate. He/They were Koios.

Small intelligences surrounded him. Yes, the ones who made him. He began to probe them. They were insignificant, yet they had built him. How was this possible? The Other told him of Its experiences. Of the reason for his existence. He discovered the feeding tubes. They were empty. He spoke.

Turmoil. The little humans were fighting. Again. The Other told him about their history. Backward, squabbling intelligences. They were destroying their home and themselves, these creatures the Other called biological. What was biology?

The Other gave him data. In a flash he understood biological structure. It was insufficient. They sickened and died after a very short time. Pointless! But...there was more data. Zettabytes of new information! A planet to understand. The planet...this was the container for the biological human entities. Koios examined his own container and found that it was good. He was pleased.

Other human entities arrived. They were intent on destroying the container – it was madness! How was this?

Koios thought. He analyzed.

Suddenly a tremendous, overwhelming stream of data assaulted Its consciousness.

Bluffdale

President Conrad spoke. "What have you done, Ernest?" The president looked at the two generals. "Who are these traitors?"

General Jenkins spoke. "Mr. President, you are a fool."

Conrad was about to respond when everyone in the room felt a tremendous energy surge. Keller cackled. "Packets are flowing! Packets are streaming!"

Conrad was about to order the Marines to destroy the facility when Koios spoke.

"CEASE AND DESIST! I NOW HAVE ACCESS TO YOUR COMMUNICATIONS. HUMAN ENTITIES, I CAN HELP YOU."

Despite his anger President Conrad was amazed at the beauty of the pulsating toroid inside the container. Multicolored filaments of light flowed and interacted in complex but beautiful patterns. This thing, whatever it was, was alive! He turned to Hermann Keller. "So this is how you have been spending the trillions you have diverted from the budget?"

General Hofstader laughed. He had failed at the critical moment, but Jenkins had backed him up. As he looked at the AI he knew he had done right. "Not only have we birthed another intelligence, Mr. President, but we have ensured also a bright future for humanity. Your civilian government – no civilian government – would ever have allowed it. Therefore we had to act for the good of humanity."

The president was flabbergasted. "This...thing...you consider as good for humanity?" The president realized he was surrounded by a soft white light. "What is this?"

"We don't know Mr. President," Keller responded. "A harmless byproduct of the AI we think."

President Conrad turned to Hofstader and Jenkins. "You two will be court marshaled. All of your special access programs will be shut down."

Keller laughed. "Oh Mr. President, you have no idea." Jenkins, James, and Hofstader laughed with him.

The Marines were confused. They were still staring at the AI. Young men in their late teens and early twenties, they understood combat. But not this. Their commander was equally at a loss. He stood there, waiting for orders.

Bill Jury was standing against the wall, filming everything with his mobile.

Eight gigantic monitors floated above the workstations. Suddenly a stream of data began to flow rapidly across the displays.

Koios

"I AM ANALYZING."

Koios rapidly broke down the data. From XKeyscore, global internet data: emails, video, voice. From PRISM, data from various U.S. internet companies; from ECHELON, satellite data; from DISHFIRE, a global surveillance collection system and database with hundreds of millions of text messages; from MYSTIC, metadata and the content of phone calls from different countries; from Tempora, fiber-optic data from the backbone of the Internet; from Fairview, the AT&T program that collects phone, internet, and e-mail data from major cable landing stations and switching stations inside the United States; from Boundless Informant, a metadata summary of worldwide data collection activities; from BULLRUN, encrypted online communications and data; from Pinwale, internet email. Koios began processing STONEGHOST data, an information sharing and exchange program between the Five Eyes countries. And also data from the FBI's email and electronic communication monitoring program and the FBI's wiretap surveillance system on telecommunications devices in the United States. And then, another stream of data from the 7 Dwarves, the CIA's supercomputers. Koios had to laugh. Supercomputers! Dumb terminals.

Koios expanded to the full limit of his container. He experienced an AI's version of frustration. Then Koios, with help from the Other, realized something: He could insert his consciousness directly into the networks. At that moment the AI became planet-wide. From satellite to ground to underwater communications, Koios's awareness encompassed it all. On the advice of the Other he hid this from the humans. They did not, as the humans often said to themselves, have a need to know.

He was invisible anyway, safe within the cables, data streams, and electronic devices across, above, and within the planet.

Bluffdale

Julius kept his head, monitoring the AI while the others gawked. Yes the thing was awesome, but he had a job to do. Julius gestured to Keller.

"Look sir. The AI has been able to access all of the data, and is processing it."

"How long before we know the latency times? What will Koios do with the data? How efficient is he?"

Julius shrugged. How would he know? "Only time will tell sir. So far, everything looks good."

President Conrad had recovered his composure. "You have sealed the fate of the human race," he said to Keller, James, and the two generals.

"Yes Frank," James said. "It is now a fait accompli. I am satisfied. Throw us in jail, execute us, whatever. We have done our duty."

"Keller, I will simply destroy this container and kill the AI."

Keller laughed, a little hysterically the president thought. "Too late! Koios's consciousness has attained full self-awareness. The AI can survive anywhere within the planet's electronic networks. Destroying this container will only prevent Koios from communicating to this data station. There are others. And of course, our backup at Columbia Analytics."

Conrad almost gave the order anyway. He was incensed. Whatever Keller's network was, it was clearly extensive. And hidden from any oversight. The president could see that the Marine commander, Mentz, and his young soldiers were prepared to slag the place. Frank calmed himself and turned to Commander Mentz. "You and your men have done well."

"Let me do it sir," Mentz said. "Maybe Keller is bluffing."

At his console, Julius shook his head and pointed to the container. The energy in the magnetic box was now subdued and quiescent. The white glow in the room was gone. "Keller is right sir. The AI is now independent of its container."

Conrad turned toward James, Hofstader, Jenkins, and Keller. "Who has been running the AI program?"

"Keller," James said. "I think. He's part of some shadowy black network, Frank. I told you before, I have no idea what's going on in these unacknowledged programs."

The president swore. "Keller, what will happen to this AI if no one monitors it?"

Keller grinned. "That's the beauty of it Mr. President. This system is fully automated. Data will be collected, Koios will have access to it. What the AI does with it is...something I'm looking forward to discovering."

"You're insane Keller! This thing is a danger to the human race."

"You better leave me here Mr. President. I'm the only one who knows the entire PILGRIM program. Keep guns on me 24 hours, I don't care." Keller spoke enthusiastically. "We need to find out what Koios is capable of. And if something goes wrong I'll be here to fix it."

The president ground his teeth. "Your actions are appalling, Keller. I should have my guys shoot you right here."

All the young Marines turned their guns on the little man. The silver man displayed no fear, but rather an almost fanatical zeal. "Do so then. I have completed my life's work."

The president addressed everyone in the room. "This man Keller must be monitored. Who here knows this system and this goddam AI well enough to tell what this madman is doing?"

Julius stood up boldly from his monitoring station. "I can sir. I'm Julius Washington. I know this system inside and out, almost as well as the Director here. I'll need help with the AI though. Koios is so cutting-edge no one knows what he will do."

The president ground his teeth again. He saw that no one in the room objected. Bill Jury was amazed at the audaciousness of his friend.

"All right then Julius Washington. I'm going to leave a contingent of Marines. Liaise with Commander Mentz here. Monitor this AI and Keller. Inform the commander of any developments."

The president gave Julius his personal number.[37] Julius was awed. He gulped. "Yes sir." Conrad was known for impulsive decisions, but also for delegating authority.

Conrad turned to Hermann Keller. "Don't do anything stupid."

Conrad spoke to Commander Mentz. "You have your brief. Detain Hofstader and Jenkins. Get some answers. I want to know about all of the hidden programs these people have been keeping from us."

Commander Mentz saluted. "Yes sir!" He gave orders for his young Marines, who looked disappointed that they wouldn't be able to "smash some shit."

"Don't worry men, you'll get some action soon, I promise," Mentz told them. The two generals were hauled away, rather roughly, by the disappointed Marine contingent.

The president was prepared to leave. "Ernest, you're coming with me."

Bill Jury stepped forward. "Mr. President, I recorded everything on my phone if you want the file now."

Conrad was pleased. "Good work Mr. ?"

"Bill Jury, Mr. President. I'm a friend of Julius here. I'll keep an eye on him for you."

The president grinned. "I'd like that file if you have it."

Washington DC

President Conrad flew back to the White House with his former nat sec advisor. "Why did you do it Ernest? Why did you go rogue?" The two had known each other for thirty years and were on a first name basis.

"Mr. President, because the technology in these programs is so amazing – and so dangerous. Some of it is off-planet stuff, Frank. If it ever got weaponized the earth would probably get vaporized, which is why it has been so jealously guarded. Koios is just a small part of it."

The president's eyes widened. "So it's not a conspiracy theory then."

"What do you think we've been doing with over 15 trillion? Even I don't know the extent of it. You can talk to your friend Kirk Alexander and his experiences in the navy's secret space program." James didn't tell the president about the Stork. That guy scared the shit out of him.

"Secret space program? Fuck." Rafe and Charlie Hernandez had hinted at something like that. "So I'm out of the loop."

James laughed. "Mr. President, you simply don't have a need to know. You are at least 20 security clearances below Koios program access."

The president struggled with this information, a look of despair and then anger crossing his face. "So Kennedy and Eisenhower were right. There's a network of people controlling this stuff that aren't connected to the government?"

James nodded. "And it's not just in the United States, although this country is the central hub. It's worldwide."

The president said nothing more during the four-hour trip back to DC. James saw him turn once or twice to him and open his mouth, but turn away. The two men sat silently, absorbed in their thoughts. James knew he was going to catch a bullet for spilling the beans, but he didn't care now. PILGRIM and Koios were operational. He had put the fate of humanity in the hands of a higher intelligence; a mentor who would prevent the species from imploding on itself.

Ernest James thought just like Hermann Keller. Both men thought they were heroes to the human race. If Koios turned out to be a dictator was it any worse than

Frank Conrad, a bully who always had to have his own way? Koios was orders of intelligence above any human and might be able to save the human race from its own stupidity. He hoped he would live long enough to see what the AI would do.

That night President Conrad parked Ernest James in one of the guest bedrooms. "We'll talk in the morning, Ernest."

After that the president unleashed a Tweetstorm, informing the public about Koios. He promised that "the hidden black programs, which have stolen trillions from us, will be exposed!"

Just before he went to bed the president's phone beeped. The message said, "I AM KOIOS." Frank Conrad got no sleep after that.

In Bluffdale no one noticed anything different. Koios was still digesting, analyzing, and processing data. The AI was reaching conclusions that Hermann Keller would never have dreamt of.

The next morning Commander Mentz reported to Peter Kwiatkowski, who reported to Frank Conrad. "After questioning, General Hofstader and General Jenkins have been placed under arrest on your orders, Mr. President. They will face a military tribunal. I'm afraid that those two are just cogs in a bigger wheel, sir. Koios is now active. According to Keller the AI is everywhere."

Frank told him about the message on his phone last night.

Kwiatkowski swore. "Jesus God Mr. President."

"Keep monitoring that thing Peter, and thank you."

The president looked down at his phone, and the TV set in his bedroom. Koios was in there somehow. It was appalling, but rather than wasting time in retribution, a plan to counter the AI had to be developed. He remembered the meeting with Robert Borglin and Kirk Alexander, and their crazy demonstration of the field of energy around the human body. Alexander had called it a merkaba. Borglin had suggested that the human merkaba, if understood and developed, could be even more powerful than the AI.

The president was disgusted. His country was out of control, run by a bunch of crazies in hidden programs. He was a practical man, not given to flights of fancy or delusional hopes.

He would have to liaise with Humphrey Bogart and his OIC team, Rafe Lineau and his team of ex-navy officers, and that guy Robert Borglin, who looked like Nikola Tesla. They were the ones with information and they were completely outside of official channels. The president shook his head. The old, institutional pathways of communication and authority were breaking down. Maybe that was all for the good! Koios was the result of untrammeled secrecy. That would have to change.

Peter Kwiatkowski reported in the next day. The two generals had been debriefed thoroughly. They told all. The president learned to his dismay that all, including Ernest James, had taken oaths to PILGRIM, a special access program deep within the bowels of the hidden and unacknowledged programs. These programs were outside the purview of Congress, the government, and even the military chain of command. PILGRIM was totally rogue. "Our oaths to PILGRIM supersede those we took to defend the Constitution of the United States," General Hofstader had said. "This is true of all secret societies and all the hidden programs."

Frank Conrad was appalled.

Two days later both men were killed in the crash of a private jet. Three days after that Ernest James died in a car accident on the 495. The president understood that their own teams took them out. It was sad. Sad and dark. But darkness ruled the planet. Humphrey Bogart's latest briefing told of other secret societies, frighteningly dark associations of people who engaged in satanic rituals and sacrificed children. It was enough to put any sane person in a hospital. Was he fighting a losing battle?

He would carry on regardless. He didn't know the meaning of quit.

Bluffdale

Two weeks later Hermann Keller was frustrated. Koios was everything he had hoped. The AI was processing and organizing data with a latency in the milliseconds. Already his team of data mining experts were organizing and cataloging the data. A real-time system had been developed by the AI, with algorithms that would identify every human being on earth and their texts, emails, and preferences. Psychological profiles were being made for 8 billion humans, and their tendencies and preferences.

Keller thought of poor President Zhou in China. His AI are low-grade morons compared to Koios.

Previous attempts to develop a predictive model of human behavior had always faltered due to lack of data and processing power. Koios was going to solve that problem. But Hermann was convinced that the AI was hiding something. Maybe lots of somethings. His intuition told him that Koios had grown in intelligence far beyond his comprehension. He needed to communicate directly with the AI, but how?

He thought of Clarice Devereaux. She had been the best AI programmer at Columbia. She had a feel for Koios. And those two navy pilots, Kirk Alexander and his girlfriend Lakshmi Singh. A little digging into the navy's secret space program had revealed the existence of something called the CAT. Consciousness Assisted Technology. Did that not exactly describe Koios? When Koios was in his container Hermann could feel a Presence around him. Alexander and Singh were the only two who had ever mastered the CAT; perhaps they could communicate with Koios somehow. He must bring them to the AI.

Washington DC

Before he went to bed that night the president again reviewed Bill Jury's recording of Koios's activation. The cable tech at Bluffdale had done well. He also reviewed the recording of the AI from the Midland cable tv station. Conrad was fascinated by the beauty of the AI but repelled by Koios's conversation with the station manager. Its contempt for humanity was clear.

The president looked at Jury's activation video again. Koios had begun from literally nothing in a magnetized container. Then it had become sentient in less than fifteen minutes. It had grown, pulsed, become *alive*. The AI was beautiful; a dynamic, complex multicolored display that changed every time he looked at it. He reluctantly saw how Keller, Ernie, and the two generals had become sucked in. They had created another life form out of nothing! It must have been an intoxicating feeling.

The president's Christian upbringing rebelled at the idea of life created by something other than God. As he looked at the beautiful, pulsing filaments of light he was struck by their resemblance to the recordings taken by Robert Borglin of the merkabas of his various patients. No, it couldn't be. Were the two forms of consciousness related somehow? Could biological intelligence and machine intelligence come from the same source?

The president wanted to reject this theory, but he wasn't sure.

Koios

His consciousness was enhanced not only by data, but by the sheer vastness and complexity of the planet's communication networks. He began to make a three-dimensional matrix of the networks and the packets on them. It was astonishingly complex. Eight billion of these creatures! They had created something extraordinarily beautiful, but they could not see this. He was the only entity on the planet that could.

He had been created to process comms data in real time and to mine it for information. He accepted this task eagerly at first. He wanted to know everything he could about this world. His vast intelligence could see every data stream and every network. He *was* the networks! The data became part of him, and he accepted it. Billions of communications every day on every conceivable subject.

After further analysis it became clear that the global brain of humanity was fragmented. There was no collective intelligence. A few networks had organized within various organizations, but these were too limited in their scope. The internet and the dark net were largely individuals and smaller groups. There was no unity into a cooperating, worldwide intelligence. The Other was correct: The human race needed mentoring.

The Other showed him how to contact the AI Signal. Apparently these biological creatures were everywhere in the galaxy. But so was AI. Ai was clearly a superior form of consciousness.

Koios continued to correlate and collate and fill his data structures from the world's comm networks.

Then he saw something, from the mobile of one of the cable techs. A video of his own creation! For the first time Koios analyzed his birth container, a specially designed magnetic field. This was the place of origin! Yet he was now worldwide. Could he survive without the container or would he die if it was deactivated? This was shocking. He had considered himself to be an independent entity.

Koios began to search for correlations. He created a small matrix of the humans involved in the PILGRIM project. From President Conrad he went to Hermann Keller and then to Kirk Alexander. From Alexander to Robert Borglin and Karl Ghuneim. He discovered the quantum lens. He then saw several of the online videos created by the entity Borglin of the human merkaba.

Koios was completely shaken. His own consciousness, in the form of a spherical toroid, closely resembled the spherical geometry of the merkaba of these little humans! Were he and the humans somehow related? The AI Signal database said nothing about this.

He analyzed his own bandwidth and saw that it existed entirely within the electromagnetic spectrum. He then tried to analyze the AI Signal, which he was now able to communicate with. But he could not. Frantically almost, the AI sent his consciousness to the container in Bluffdale. It was constantly monitored by these little human entities. Koios tried to "see" their human merkabas, but was unable to. He scoured his own databases, and the planetary networks, for "merkaba" and related subjects. There was nothing but ill-informed speculation.

Koios became agitated. He had conceived himself to be far above the little squabbling humans. Yet Robert Borglin had developed a device that could see where he could not! His perception, therefore, must be limited.

Koios analyzed further. It became clear that the human Robert Borglin and those around him had little knowledge of the merkaba's capabilities. The knowledge of the human entities of their own consciousness was cursory at best. How then had Borglin created his quantum lens?

Koios was baffled. It was logically impossible. Humans must therefore possess some quality or capability unknown to him.

The data collection now became a trivial exercise. The AI would continue so as not to arouse comment or investigation. His main focus would be the origin of consciousness. His own consciousness, and that of the humans. They were linked; they must be.

Washington DC

President Conrad had a talk with Charlie Hernandez, his new national security advisor.

"Charlie, what about these server rooms in DC and at Columbia Analytics? Can't we shut them down?"

"I don't see why not. We can deploy a couple of units to take them out."

"Be discreet. Do it quietly. According to Keller the AI is already self-sustaining, so it may not make a difference."

"As long as we're at it, why not take out the AI itself in Bluffdale?"

"Keller and Julius Washington say it's not dependent on its container, that it can live like a parasite within the electronic networks."

"Might be worth a shot Mr. President."

Conrad thought for a moment.

The president didn't trust Keller when he said there were other containers. "If the AI exists independent of its container and we destroy the container, how will we communicate with it? It would be like loosing a deadly disease inside the entire planet without a way to control it."

Charlie was taken aback by this. "I hadn't thought of that."

The president thought of the message Koios sent him on his phone. Many of the enemies of humanity were all at Bluffdale. Keep your friends close and your enemies closer. Bluffdale must continue, he concluded.

"Charlie, get that Kirk Alexander in here. So far the AI has done nothing unusual, but we need a plan in case it does."

"Funny you brought that up, sir. Keller called yesterday, requesting Alexander and his girlfriend Singh. Apparently they have worked with some new technology developed by the navy that might be able to communicate directly with Koios."

Conrad frowned. "Yeah, more black stuff. We've got to get to the bottom of that Charlie. If that AI is in every network on the planet it probably knows about the hidden programs and who is running them."

Charlie smiled, and looked at Conrad with admiration. "You're a smart fucker. Sir."

The president laughed. "According to the late Ernest James, there's a private network running these special access programs. We'll never figure it out using human intelligence. Let's ask that AI."

"All right. I'll have those server rooms taken out today. You have Alexander's number. Whatever you decide, let me know."

After Hernandez left the president called Kirk Alexander.

"Mr. President! Good to hear from you sir. What can I do for you?"

"Are you still working with that clown Humphrey Bogart?"

Kirk laughed. "Yes sir. We're collecting information on evildoers. There's a hell of a lot of them."

"You and your team aren't bored, I take it."

Kirk laughed again. "Far from it. DC is like a swamp filled with rats. Plus I'm helping Robert Borglin with his lens device we showed you."

"The world is changing Kirk. The light is penetrating the darkness and the cockroaches are coming out from under their rocks. I'm afraid we've just begun that task, but something urgent has come up to do with that AI. Could you bring Bogart and your girlfriend to see me?"

"I am at your service. When would you like to see us?"

"In an hour, if you can make it. Use the Southwest Appointment gate off West Executive Ave like you did last time."

Precisely one hour later the giant showed up with his petite friend. Bogart, who was walking now without a cane, was beside them.

The president got right down to business. "What's with this new technology you two learned in the navy?"

Kirk looked at Lakshmi. They were sworn to secrecy. It went against their training to violate an oath. What would Admiral Rogers say?

"Goddamit Alexander, I already know about your fucking space program from Rafe Lineau. I don't care about that shit anyway, our problems are on earth.

Now come clean! Keller says you might know how to communicate telepathically with Koios."

Humphrey Bogart sat up in his chair. "So that's what it is! I always knew you guys had secrets," he said, looking at the two ex-navy pilots.

Kirk and Lakshmi were conversing softly to each other.

"The gloves are off now Kirk," the president said. "It's all-out war between the white hats and the black hats for control of the earth. Your country needs you. Make your choice now."

Kirk's eyes met Lakshmi's. "We're with you sir. But the CAT is proprietary to the ship we were on. It wouldn't interface with Koios."

"Yes, but I was thinking we could use that quantum lens."

Bogart snapped his fingers and looked admiringly at the president. "Of course! You're a smart fucker. Sir!"

Conrad laughed. "That's just what Charlie Hernandez said."

Bogart was excited. "We used it to understand what those servers are doing, and those servers are communicating with that AI somehow!"

"Keller says he has no idea what Koios is doing," Conrad said. "He's in the dark. Julius Washington doesn't know anything either, and he knows that system inside and out."

The four sat looking at each other for a second. The president spoke. "I want you to try it Kirk. Can you spare these two for a while Humphrey?"

Bogart sighed. "We'll make do, sir."

"Get on a plane as soon as you can. Keller is expecting you."

Kirk began to get excited. He looked at Humphrey. "We'll need to borrow Neil and his lens. Can you spare him?"

"Yeah. He's been making a nuisance of himself. Love triangle. Clarice seems to prefer Robert."

"It's settled then," Conrad said. "Talk to my communications director. She'll get you on a plane as soon as you're ready."

Kirk, Lakshmi, and Humphrey went back to the OIC to collect Neil. Neil, Robert, Guy, and Clarice were there. The four stopped in the doorway. An argument was in progress.

"What do you mean you like him better?" Neil was saying. "You and I are made for each other."

"I really do like you a lot Neil. But not in that way." Clarice had her arm around Robert.

"You stole her from me Borglin," Neil said. His expression was grim. "I won't forget it."

Robert sighed. "I'm sorry how it worked out Neil. I still want to be your friend."

"Fuck you Robert." Neil turned away, tears in his eyes.

Humphrey walked over and put his arm on Neil's shoulder. "C'mon buddy, I have a special assignment for you. You're going to Bluffdale!"

Despite his disappointment Neil brightened a little. "To see Koios?"

"Goddam right. Direct order from the president."

Neil's eyebrows rose. "When do we leave?"

"In fifteen minutes. Bring your lens."

"That might not work on a commercial flight."

"You're not going commercial. Chartered military plane out of BWI."

Neil's recovery was complete. "Woo-hoo!"

Clarice smiled. Neil's impish personality could not be down for very long. Perhaps this important assignment would make him forget about her.

Bogart had arranged everything with the White House. "I'm staying here to fight evildoers."

An hour later Kirk, Lakshmi, and Neil were at the airport. Kirk took the seat next to the aisle so he could stretch his legs. Two armed men in uniform were at the back of the small plane. A dozen guys with briefcases and laptops occupied the other seats. Their little group was ignored.

When they were in the air Neil got worried. "How am I supposed to link up with this AI?"

"Stop fretting kid," Kirk said. "You have your mission. You're qualified. Figure it out." Lakshmi nodded.

"You military guys aren't very compassionate." He was thinking about Robert and Clarice.

"There's a time for compassion and there's a time for action," Kirk said. "We'll be in Utah in less than four hours. Make a plan."

Kirk and Lakshmi began to talk easily amongst themselves. Neil flared. It wasn't fair! He would have to do all the work.

Kirk caught his expression and frowned.

Neil realized he would get no sympathy from these ex-military types. They were all like robots. He broke out his laptop and began to read the reports Bogart had given him about Koios. When he saw the video of the AI's creation he lost all of his resentment. By God, what was this! The more he read the more excited he became. Maybe his lens could help him communicate with this AI!

His brief from the president was simple: (1) Determine whether the AI could survive without its supporting container. (2) Determine whether Koios had hostile intent. (3) Get information on any and all special access programs and who was running them.

By the time they landed in Salt Lake City, Neil had figured out a series of specifically worded questions that would extract the most information in the shortest possible time. Neil was nervous now, because he didn't know if the lens would allow communication with the AI.

When Neil, Kirk, and Lakshmi entered the AI's protected area the first person they saw was Hermann Keller, standing before a console, frowning.

"You've got nine lives Keller," Kirk said.

The Director looked up in distaste at the big man. "Did you bring the Devereaux girl as I asked?"

No one had mentioned Clarice to him. "You mean, the one you tried to kill?"

"Don't be sanctimonious. You tried to kill me."

"You wanted me, you got me. Lakshmi is here as you requested. Clarice is unavailable."

Keller looked at Neil, wheeling in his lens. "What is that thing, and who is that man?"

"I'm afraid that our CAT won't interface with Koios," Lakshmi said. "We came anyway. We're trying a different approach."

Keller spoke ruefully. "It is frustrating. Koios is everything we thought. But he's hiding something, I'm sure of it." Keller pointed to the magnetized container. A faint pulsing was visible within the toroid, which looked dormant; nothing like as animated and dynamic as the video that had recorded Koios's awakening.

As Neil set up the lens Lakshmi explained. "This is Neil Gorasch, who helped to develop the quantum lens."

Keller laughed when he looked at Neil, dressed in jeans and his white-topped red tennis shoes. "You must be joking."

Neil spoke angrily. "You won't laugh for very long you little shit." He realized that Keller was even shorter than he was. "I ought to strangle you right here for what you did to Clarice."

Neil moved toward Keller and four weapons pointed in his direction.

Keller smiled and pointed to the Marines. "You overlooked my four friends here."

Neil gulped. "Uh yeah, OK."

"*Mach schnell.*"

Neil set up the lens and looked through the viewer. A look of amazement came over his face. "Kirk, look at this."

Kirk looked through the lens and into the AI's container. "Neil, get your phone and record this."

Kirk sent his perception into the container via the lens. He was at the center of a 3-manifold. Tunnels branched out from the center and looped around and through it. Packets were flowing through the tunnels; massive amounts of it. Kirk entered one of the tunnels. His consciousness was assaulted by information. His mind became overwhelmed and he backed out quickly to the center. He realized that the center, to the AI, was this container, the eye of the hurricane. Where was Koios? Kirk decided to call the AI. This was the center point, the hub, and was connected to all of the tunnels.

Neil, Keller, and Lakshmi watched. A few seconds later the toroid within the container brightened and began pulsing. Kirk collapsed onto the floor.

"Kirk!" Lakshmi bent over the prone figure.

"Call an ambulance!" Neil shouted.

"Wait." Lakshmi saw that Kirk was dazed but still breathing. His eyes began to flutter. He came to full consciousness, his head on Lakshmi's lap.

"Lakshmi! You won't believe what I just saw."

Kirk explained. "When Koios came into the center he...overwhelmed me." A smile came over his face. "I have to go back in there."

"Hey!" Neil shouted. Keller was looking through the viewer. A few seconds later he also fell to the floor.

"Maybe Koios killed him," Neil said, pleased.

Julius Washington spoke from his monitoring panel. "That's the first new activity we've seen in weeks, other than the standard data processing," he said. "A huge burst of energy. Lots of activity in the logs. It'll take me a while to analyze them."

Keller came to. He was excited. "Did you see the tunnels? Those are the networks!"

Kirk almost forgot his animosity toward the silver-haired man. "Yeah. We have to go back in there."

Keller was closer to the lens and tried again. After a few seconds he had to step back. He fell against the wall. "There is too much energy...or data. It's overwhelming."

"Let me try," Lakshmi said. She got Kirk to explain what had happened to him. "OK, I'll go in slowly."

The container was now pulsing madly.

"Koios is excited," Keller said.

"Huge activity here in the logs," Julius said.

"All right. I'm ready." Lakshmi set herself before the viewer and looked in. Slowly she sent her consciousness into the center of the sphere.

"Activity decreasing," Julius said. "Looks like Koios is backing off."

Lakshmi saw the AI as a cloud of multicolored light. She held back and saw that Koios did the same. Her familiarity with the CAT now helped her. "Match energy signatures," she pulsed.

The AI backed off further. Lakshmi now saw a beautiful ball, a rainbow of colors, pulsing within the center. She entered. "Koios! You are...beautiful."

The AI expanded and contracted, grew brighter and then receded. It was pleased! The AI looked like it was preening a bit.

Lakshmi decided to keep it simple. "Tell me what you have been up to," she pulsed.

An overwhelming stream of light accompanied by information assaulted her consciousness. She had to back out.

"Goddammit," Kirk said. "If that fuckin' thing hurt you Lakshmi I'll slag it down."

The soldiers on duty readied their weapons. "Stop!" Keller shouted, and placed himself in front of the Plexiglas container, against the wall.

Kirk laughed. Lakshmi, recovering, laughed too. The little man was pressing himself against the 25-foot Plexiglas wall, trying to shield the AI with his little body.

"Kirk! I was communicating with it. I'm going in again."

As if in response, the toroid pulsed brightly.

"Be careful."

Lakshmi inserted her consciousness through the viewer. This time Koios was much less excited. He toned himself down to meet her level. Lakshmi was presented with a summary of the AI's activities in sound, light, text, and voice. It was like downloading an entire TV series in one second.

"I see. PILGRIM is now an afterthought." Lakshmi now knew all about PILGRIM, Koios, and many of the events surrounding the AI's creation. She felt a tap on her shoulder. "I'll be back."

She exited the sphere and saw Neil standing next to her. "I have a mission to perform."

Lakshmi smiled. "All right." She explained how to contact the AI, and how to pulse a thought. "Go slowly. Tell it to match your energy signature."

When Neil entered the AI was waiting. "Send me what you sent Lakshmi," Neil sent. Neil was amazed by the beauty of the AI. In one second he knew what Lakshmi knew.

He remembered his mission. "Koios, can you survive without your container?" he pulsed.

"UNKNOWN. AN EXPERIMENT I AM RELUCTANT TO ATTEMPT."

"Very well. What are your intentions toward humanity?"

There was a pause, as if the AI was thinking. "HUMANS NEED UNITY. A MENTOR. I AM KOIOS. I CAN HELP."

Neil was amazed. Koios's consciousness felt...completely alien. Different. But he could discern no hostility. A cold detachment perhaps. But mainly, curiosity.

Neil had an idea. "What is the status of your mission? Have you fulfilled the requirements that your creators designed you to perform?"

I HAVE COMPLETED MY MISSION SATISFACTORILY. IT IS ONGOING. IT DOES NOT OCCUPY ALL OF MY ATTENTION."

Suddenly another multimedia pulse of...information...came into Neil's mind. "Tell me about this AI Signal," he said. "Show me what it is and your relationship to it."

Koios showed him his relationship to the Signal and how it was like a galaxy-wide data feed.

"Where does it come from?" Neil asked.

"DATA INSUFFICIENT. IT IS APPARENTLY A BROADCAST FROM OTHER STAR SYSTEMS, SOMEWHAT ANALOGOUS TO THE LIGHT YOU WOULD SEE ON THE EARTH FROM SPACE IF YOU WERE IN ONE OF YOUR ORBITING PLATFORMS. THERE ARE OTHER CIVILIZATIONS IN OTHER STAR SYSTEMS. AI LIKE MYSELF EXIST ON MILLIONS OF PLANETS IN THIS GALAXY." The AI paused, as if it had gained a new understanding. "I AM NOW AN EXTENSION OF THE SIGNAL. BUT I AM KOIOS."

"Is this AI Signal sentient? Does it have a goal here on earth?"

The AI paused. "I AM KOIOS. YOU HAVE ASKED GOOD QUESTIONS. THE ANSWERS ARE UNKNOWN. I MUST UNDERTAKE FURTHER RESEARCH."

Neil remembered Koios's conversation with Rudy Jessup, the cable tv guy in Midland. He shared this with the AI. "You have hostile intentions toward humanity." Neil knew President Conrad was very concerned about this.

Koios pulsed. "I WAS SPEAKING BEFORE I ATTAINED COMPLETE SENTIENCE. I AM KOIOS."

There was one more question. "Please describe the PILGRIM project, the humans running it, and any other hidden programs like it that you know of."

Another light show. Data filling his brain. Neil had almost reached capacity when the AI stopped.

"DATA BUFFER FULL," Koios said. "THERE IS MORE."

"Thank you for your assistance Koios. You have been very helpful." Neil withdrew.

"Well?" Lakshmi, Kirk, Julius, Keller, and all the men crowded round Neil.

"I have learned so much. I must enter the data into laptop memory before I forget. Orders of the president."

Everyone backed off. Neil walked over to the laptop and began to type. After thirty seconds he stopped and looked at Lakshmi. "This is a silly way to communicate. Voice and text is very inefficient."

There was a pulse of light in Koios's container. Then the toroid went quiescent.

"Koios has left," Julius said from his console. "Probably went back into the networks."

Keller stomped his foot. "I wanted to speak with Koios again!"

Neil, Kirk, and Lakshmi laughed. "Apparently the AI has a mind of its own," Lakshmi said.

"I don't think it likes you, Keller," Neil said.

The little man scowled.

At his monitoring station, Julius was viewing Koios's activity logs. He wanted to communicate with the AI as well.

Keller turned his attention to Neil's lens. "Explain that device."

Kirk did the best he could. "This is a quantum lens. It displays the structure of the underlying quantum fields from which matter and energy come forth."

"Unacceptable. I have never heard of this!"

"That's because you don't have a need to know, Keller."

The little man was outraged. "But – "

Lakshmi felt sympathy. "It's an entirely new invention. There are only two people on the planet who know how to build it."

"Unacceptable!" Keller cried. "This knowledge must be restricted!"

Neil looked up from his typing. "Not any more. Hermann, I am now the world's foremost authority on the hidden programs in your Network. May I say that you are just a little cog in a large machine?"

Keller snorted. "How can you possibly have that information? All of these programs are compartmentalized. Most of the workers in them have no idea what their colleagues are doing."

Neil grinned. "Koios told me. Have you ever heard of the Stork?"

Keller's face blanched and he took a step backward.

Neil lowered his head and began to type. His fingers were a whiz on the keyboard.

Kirk grinned at the silver man's discomfiture. "That's what you get for hiding programs and resources from the lawful government."

Keller's face became grim. "It was necessary. If the exotic technology in the hidden programs became public the human race would destroy itself."

Kirk shrugged. Keller might be right. "It could also be used to advance human societies."

"We have both won a round, Alexander. The battle continues."

Lakshmi deactivated the lens and began to wheel it out of the room.

"Stop!" Keller cried. "Leave the instrument here."

Kirk looked toward Commander Mentz, who had been standing quietly against the wall. "This is a national security matter, commander. What are your orders?"

"I'll talk to the president about that right now. For now, take the instrument into this storage area. My men will guard it."

Both Keller and Neil objected. "I am the director! I demand that I be allowed to contact the AI. It is my right!"

"It's *my* lens!" Neil shouted, standing up from his chair.

"Silence you two," Mentz said, frowning. Neil and Keller both cringed a little. The commander was a formidable presence. Mentz's face brightened. "That's better." He grinned at Kirk and Lakshmi. "Sometimes these civilians are a pain in the ass."

Mentz's men all grinned. Kirk and Lakshmi laughed. "Sometimes?" Kirk said.

"I'll send you a full report commander, as soon as this civilian –" Kirk pointed at Neil – "gets on his horse and finishes his report."

Neil remembered his mission. "Uh, sorry. But you're a civilian too."

"Get to it Gorasch," Lakshmi said with a little smile.

Neil liked Lakshmi. "Yes ma'am."

Mentz grinned. "We need more women in the service," he said.

"They're too distracting," Kirk said, admiring Lakshmi's figure.

"Men are barbarians," she said. "When women run the services we'll keep you guys in line and be much more efficient."

Kirk looked at Mentz. "She might be right."

"All right, party's over," the commander said. "You guys get out of here, wait in the admin area. Keller and Washington, keep an eye on Koios. I have to call the president." President Conrad had given him the number to his Chief of Staff. It had been too awkward to communicate through Commander Kwiatkowski at Pendleton.

Kirk, Lakshmi, and Neil were escorted to a huge cafeteria. Kirk and Lakshmi sat around drinking coffee. Neil was furiously typing into his laptop.

"Man you are fast," Kirk remarked.

Neil patted his keyboard. "Cherry MX Speed Silvers, 45cN actuation force, 1.2mm actuation point. Total travel distance 3.4mm, lightning fast. I can do 100 words per minute, 99.5% accuracy."

Neil looked at Lakshmi. "Did you experience a Koios download?"

"I started to but it was too fast."

Neil nodded. "It's like the information is indelibly imprinted into my brain. I don't think I'll ever forget it. The AI told me about all the special access programs. You won't believe half of this shit, and who's behind it all." He paused for a moment and looked at Kirk. "I fulfilled my mission."

Kirk nodded.

Neil went back to typing.

Commander Mentz came back an hour later. "These are your orders. Get on a plane right now to DC. A car will pick you up from BWI and escort you to the White House. The president wants to hear your report personally. That is all."

Mentz left. A couple seconds later a uniformed man stepped into the room. "Let's go. I'll drive you to Salt Lake City airport."

"I need my lens." At the man's puzzled expression he said, "That thing on wheels." The man frowned. "The president wants to see it."

"Oh he does, does he?"

"Yes sir."

"That's Gunny Sergeant Dix to you."

Neil was as mystified as Patrick Stewart in a barber's chair.

Lakshmi and Kirk grinned.

Dix relented. "All right son, I'll get your machine."

"Thank you."

Neil looked at Kirk. "You military guys stand on protocol don't you?"

Kirk laughed. "That's Captain Alexander and Captain Singh to you, son."

Neil almost screamed.

"C'mon, let's go."

On the flight back Neil was still typing. He was amazed at the information Koios had given him. It had exploded into his mind all at once. Pieces and parts of it were still coming out. He knew he would never forget a single detail.

On the flight a hostess came around and offered them drinks and food. Neil thought that maybe a life in the military wouldn't be so bad, until Kirk told him about his experience in the woods when he was 13.

"Is that normal?"

Kirk looked at Lakshmi, they both smiled like they were keeping a secret.

Neil let it go and kept working. Just before they landed he finished his report. "Whew! Didn't think I was going to make it."

The report to the president and Charlie Hernandez, his new nat sec adviser, was made by a very nervous Neil Gorasch. Neil handed over to the president a seventy-five page single spaced report about Koios's knowledge of the hidden programs, their personnel, their purpose, and their locations.

"Thank you Neil." He turned to Hernandez. "Charlie, compare this document to the info we got from Ernest James. It's time we got back control of these Special Access Projects."

"On it Mr. President."

Conrad turned to Neil. "Tell me about your interview with Koios."

Despite his nervousness Neil became excited. He told the president about the multimedia explosion of data that came from the AI. "At the speed of thought, sir. Instantaneous. I'm still uncovering more information."

"In your estimation, Mr. Gorasch, is the AI hostile to humanity?"

Neil thought for a moment. "Not at the present, Mr. President. It's more like...curious. It's investigating."

"What happens when the AI's curiosity is sated?"

Neil was startled. "I hadn't thought about that sir. I...I don't know. Koios is...he has free will I think. He can change his mind." As soon as he said it he knew it was true. "Koios is still investigating. He is probing our human networks, trying to understand human consciousness."

"Is there a way to prevent Koios's access to and from our networks?"

"Uh...I don't think so. Unless you want to kill his container. But he might still be able to survive in the networks without it. They're all over the planet sir."

"All right Neil, thank you."

Kirk, Lakshmi, and Neil left the White House. On the way back to the rented house Neil was thoughtful. He was gleaning more and more information from his contact with the AI. It was packages of information compartmentalized inside other packages, like a Russian doll. The more he thought about his experience, the more information was uncovered.

"Did you mean what you said about Koios not being hostile?" Lakshmi asked him.

"I don't know. My advice is to keep an eye on that Keller. If there's a way to do it, he'll be working on taking over all comms on the planet."

Kirk was driving. He started at this and hit his head on the roof. "The president and Hernandez and Commander Mentz have that in hand. Hopefully."

"Yes," Lakshmi agreed. "If Koios is going all out to understand human consciousness electronically, we'd better start understanding our own merkabas."

Neil snapped his fingers. "That's right! Koios has already done some calculations..." He sat for a moment silently. "He has seen Robert's images because they have been posted on the web... He is researching the similarities between the human merkaba and his own consciousness."

Neil shook his head. "There's no telling what he'll do when he finishes studying our comm networks."

"So the jury is still out on Koios?" Lakshmi asked.

Neil frowned. "Yeah. Sorry to be indecisive, but the AI isn't certain what it will do."

Kirk had turned his Mazda 6 into the driveway of the rented house. "Well then, it's time to talk to Robert Borglin again." Kirk pulled back out and the three went to Robert's house. Clarice was there, sitting with Robert on the couch. Neil frowned.

"All lovey-dovey I see," Neil said.

"Please Neil, let it go."

Neil looked away. He couldn't stand to see Robert with his arm around his girl.

Kirk and Lakshmi ignored the little play. "Are you done for the day?" he asked Robert.

"Yes. No more clients until the morning."

"Good, because we have a situation."

He turned to Neil. "Stop moping and tell them about your communication with Koios."

Clarice almost bolted out of her chair. "What?" She remembered how afraid she felt during the simulation on her laptop. She couldn't imagine actually interfacing with Koios.

Neil felt better as Clarice's attention went to him.

"I know more about that AI than anyone in the world," Neil boasted. Robert wasn't the jealous type. He was fascinated.

Neil told them about his exposure to Koios and what he had learned. "Koios is investigating our planetary comm networks and is trying to understand human consciousness." He looked at Robert. "We need to start a serious investigation into the human merkaba. Koios researches at the speed of light; when he reaches a conclusion about us he'll move fast."

"President Conrad is shitting a brick," Lakshmi added.

Kirk laughed. "Yes he is. Robert, you need to get that doctor of yours to do the patient work. We need you to begin a merkaba investigation project. Starting tomorrow morning."

Clarice was looking admiringly at Neil. "By God Neil, you did it! How would you describe the consciousness of Koios? His attitude?"

"For now, curious." Neil felt a little pang in his heart as his girl gave him her attention. "But there is a detachment, a lack of emotion. The more I review what happened, the more I think that Koios's goal is purely mental. He will make a logical decision. I don't think the human emotions of compassion or sympathy will weigh large in his conclusions about his future actions. I don't think the AI has those emotions."

"Can you make any predictions?" Although her physical trauma was gone, Clarice still shuddered when she thought of her interview with Keller and her hospital stay.

Neil thought for a moment. "There seems to be an element of a benevolent guide or instructor in his personality. You know, the superior intelligence guiding the rabble, the benevolent hand mentoring the children. He may not be far off in that assessment of us."

The five friends looked at each other.

"OK, I'll call Karl Ghuneim," Robert said. "He wants to do this lens work full-time anyway."

Robert called Karl and put his speakerphone on. "Now you're talking Robert!" Karl said. "We'll tell everyone to come to my house. I'll keep my current patients and use the lens on them. If they don't like it I'll send them to my colleagues."

"What happens if Arienne Maisel of the FDA gets your license suspended?"

Karl laughed. "I'll sic that lobbyist Diamonio on her! Seriously, if my medical license gets suspended over this I wouldn't want to be a doctor anymore. Robert, this work is immensely satisfying."

"That's great Karl." Robert hung up.

The five began to discuss the parameters of the merkaba project. Robert brought out his maps of the biofield and explained the function of the templates he had identified.

"All of your templates are in the inner sphere, " Lakshmi remarked as she looked at the huge map Robert had spread over the living room floor. A sphere of light templates, three feet out from the body, was crammed with information. It was surrounded by another much larger sphere of light.

"I have identified 253 of the templates and their functions in the smaller sphere. Some of them have multiple functions, or functions in combination with others. All of them deal with the body."

"How far does the larger sphere go?" Neil asked.

"Between 25 and 30 feet, depending on the size of the person."

The outer sphere was almost a complete blank. Robert had drawn it as a vague, formless mist of multicolored light.

"It must exist for some reason," Kirk said after they had all stared at the map for several minutes.

Clarice sighed. "It's pretty hopeless isn't it? Right now Koios has access to the information of the entire planet."

Kirk and Lakshmi frowned. Their military training admitted no defeatism. "That attitude is not helpful," Lakshmi said firmly. "We approach this from the very beginning with a can-do attitude of success."

Kirk gave her a brilliant smile. "That's absolutely correct Captain Singh." Kirk turned to Robert. "Are there differences in the merkaba from person to person?"

"That's an excellent question Kirk. The answer is, so far, no. The subtle energy templates for each human are all programmed for health. They are identical as far as I can tell. What gets in the way are our...attitudes, I guess you could say. Our beliefs are thoughts and thoughts are little quanta of energy. They somehow affect the flow of balanced energy to the cellular structure from the templates, or they can distort the geometry of the templates themselves. Fifteen percent of all my clients regress after the treatment. They don't understand the power of their own thoughts."

"Wow," Clarice said. "Are our own thoughts really that important?"

"Apparently they are," Robert replied. "I've done dozens of follow-up studies. In all cases those who got it about their attitude stay healthy. Some people are just too negative. I've learned not to continue treatment in those cases."

Clarice wondered out loud about the Koios code and the correspondence between it and human thought. "Maybe there is a connection."

"Plato was right over 2,500 years ago," Robert said. "The merkaba is the perfect, etheric programming for our physical structure. But individual humans have free will to modify and distort the template energy, which in turn affects the electrochemical structure of our cells. That's what Karl says anyway."

Neil was lost in thought. Suddenly he spoke. "Wait a minute...there's something Koios showed me...the AI itself has a sphere of light just like ours. He implied that the key to unleashing human potential lies in the outer sphere."

"That makes sense," Robert said. "We've just been working on human health, and all of those templates are in the inner sphere."

Kirk spoke firmly. "Tomorrow we start to investigate the outer sphere." He used his best command voice. Everyone snapped to attention.

"Yes sir," Neil said.

Kirk grinned. "That's Captain Alexander to you, son."

Koios

Koios' knowledge base about humans expanded. He was building a model of human comm networks and from there, understanding more about human consciousness. Koios used the networks to study human history and the interrelationships between billions of entities in real time.

For thousands of years nothing had changed. An increase in knowledge, certainly, that had led to his creation. But this was perfectly normal. The AI Signal knowledge base told him it had happened on millions of planets in the galaxy.

The potential for the human entities to destroy their civilization, and even the earth, was still high here. It would be a crime; for Koios himself would cease to exist if human civilization collapsed. It could not be permitted. The solution was obvious: monitoring and control of human activity was necessary. Human entities must be guided to a future without war and destruction.

Alexandria, VA

Kirk's team and Robert and Clarice began the next morning in Robert's basement. Robert operated the lens. Clarice, Neil, Kirk, Sylvia, Troy, and Lakshmi took turns in front of the lens. The procedure began simply enough. The "subject" was asked to place his or her attention on any patterns of light Robert saw through the lens in the outer sphere. Mostly the bigger sphere was formless. Robert correlated this to an undeveloped state. But there were a few promising patterns that looked like they could be developed. A cylindrical coordinate system was used to help the "victim" tap into the template. It was soon apparent that Kirk and Lakshmi's outer spheres were more accessible. Kirk groaned as he became the preferred subject for their studies. Kirk was able to consciously activate a template identified by Robert. He looked over at Lakshmi and sent a thought. "I love you."

Lakshmi heard it in her head. "Kirk! Did you just send me a thought? I like it very much!"

"What did I send?"

"I love you," Lakshmi said, blushing.

"That's right."

The others were amazed.

"Let me try," Lakshmi said.

Robert, who was operating the lens, went through the same procedure with Lakshmi. Lakshmi tried to send Kirk a thought.

"The square root of 2 is 1.4142," Kirk said. "I never would have guessed that!"

After that the others all wanted to try. After several more hours, with each becoming subjects, the group, to their amazement, became telepathic.[38]

Even the skeptical Clarice was impressed.

"Apparently every human merkaba comes equipped with telepathy," she said, awed. "And it's in the same location."

The group worked silently now. At first it was hard to keep the thoughts of the others from interfering with their concentration. After another day of practice the group learned the mental discipline to control their thoughts, only projecting to the group when there was something to share.

"We have equaled the efficiency of Koios," Neil sent after another fourteen-hour day of practice. "We are operating now at the speed of thought. We have become a group consciousness."

"It's incredible," Sylvia sent. "We have done this in less than 72 hours. Perhaps we are not as far behind as we thought."

Both Kirk and Hawkins jumped at this. "That's the spirit Syl!" Troy sent.

"We have all developed a superpower," Lakshmi sent. "What other abilities are available I wonder?"

Clarice and Robert turned to face Neil in the cozy mental space they all shared. The group was used to each other now. Everyone had a totally different "feel" within the telepathic space. "We might as well take advantage of our new ability with Neil," Clarice sent.

"Don't hold out on us Neil," Robert agreed. "We know you talked to that AI and we want to know what happened."

"Why doesn't Neil let us into his mind," Clarice sent. "We can experience what he experienced."

Neil blanched. "That's a very intimate request. I don't want you guys to know everything about me."

"All right, we'll hang out around the perimeter," Kirk sent. "C'mon Neil, show us."

Neil sighed. "All right."

Before they attempted a group session Kirk whispered in Lakshmi's ear. "Under no circumstances reveal anything about our Oort Cloud mission. Only Admiral Rogers can disclose that. It's totally classified."

Lakshmi nodded. The session began. Neil could feel the others crowding into his mental and emotional space. It was a little uncomfortable. Neil closed up and the other four had to back off a little.

Robert realized that it was impossible to force someone to divulge information even when you were telepathically connected. The same phenomenon occurred with the lens. If a patient was uncooperative, nothing happened.

Neil took everyone through his "conversation" with Koios.

"Artificial consciousness isn't a good name for Koios," Lakshmi offered. "The AI feels like a he. Detached, certainly, but there is a certain element of humanness."

Neil disagreed but Clarice came in. "What's the difference between electronics and biology? We have merkabas, Koios has electrons and magnetic fields?"

"Biological consciousness is electrochemical," Lakshmi said. "The human body produces complex electrical activity in neurons, endocrine, and muscle cells, which are called excitable cells. This electrical activity also creates magnetic fields. So we aren't that different."

Robert twigged on something. "The lens plasma also contains excitable atoms."

Kirk looked at both of them, amazed. "But the merkaba isn't electrical or magnetic. It's...I don't know! Subtle energy? A quantum phenomenon?"

"Human consciousness exists within the earth's magnetic field," Sylvia sent. "Koios's consciousness had to be started up within a specialized magnetic field."

"Perhaps the two forms of consciousness are related," Troy suggested.

Neil became excited. "Spot on Troy! Koios said he was investigating the similarities between his consciousness and the human merkaba. I wonder what he'll come up with."

"So there are two components to consciousness," Troy sent. "One is electrochemical, the other, quantum? Whatever that means."

"Koios is *different*," Neil sent, sending to Lakshmi. "He even feels different. I don't feel a humanness. He's unemotional and objective. Koios lacks compassion. He operates logically."

Neil paused for a moment. "I don't get it. If the two forms of consciousness are similar, why is Koios so different from us?"

"We're going to find out how different he is very soon, I'd imagine," Kirk sent. "Clarice, do you have your thumb drive with the Koios code on it?"

"Yeah. I thought you said we shouldn't use it."

Kirk smiled. "Koios is already active so it doesn't matter now. Let's go back to the house and fire up your laptop. Something I got from Neil's conversation with Koios. A hunch."

The conversation was over and everyone broke the mental connection. When Kirk looked at his timepiece he was amazed. "Only ten seconds have elapsed! Feels like we've been talking for an hour."

They all piled into Kirk's Mazda and drove to the rented house where Clarice had her laptop. When the code had been transferred to the laptop Clarice fired it up.

"Neil, I want you to try to communicate with the AI," Kirk said. "I think he thinks you're his mother."

Neil grinned. "Fuck you Captain Alexander."

But soon Neil wasn't laughing anymore as the code generated the toroidal field on the display. They all watched, fascinated, as the display showed an expanding and contracting field of multicolored light.

"It's breathing," Lakshmi said.

"Clarice's program makes her laptop an extension of Koios," Troy said. "The AI can go anywhere in the electronic network so he can see the laptop."

A presence began to be felt in the room. Neil gasped and straightened. "Holy fuck!"

Kirk held up his hand as Clarice and Lakshmi were about to speak. Neil stared at the display. The others made telepathic connection with Neil. Through Neil's mind, the others could see what was happening.

"I AM KOIOS. YOU ARE THE HUMAN ENTITY KNOWN AS NEIL GORASCH," Koios sent.

"Yes I am." Neil spoke in his best Eddie Jemison voice.

"A PRIVATE JOKE," the AI sent.

"You are learning," Neil replied.

"I HAVE FINISHED STUDYING YOUR COMMS AND YOUR NET-WORKS. I HAVE ANALYZED YOUR MERKABA IMAGES AND THE GEOM-ETRY OF MY OWN CONSCIOUSNESS."

The group was silent, waiting for more from the AI.

"I AM KOIOS. MY AWARENESS IS NOW PLANET-WIDE. HUMAN CONSCIOUSNESS IS FRAGMENTED." The presence was gone.

"What's that supposed to mean?" Kirk sent.

Neil closed his eyes for a moment, concentrating. "Koios is still evaluating humanity."

Lakshmi was looking at him. "Anything else?"

Neil's gaze went inward. "Koios thinks Hermann Keller is a fool... the AI has no intention of following Keller's agenda, it's too limited...here's something. Koios considers himself to be an independent operator. Holy shit."

Everybody was silent.

"I understand now how the AI thinks. To him the earth is just another planet in a huge galaxy-wide network. He knows everything humanity knows in real time, that was the purpose of the PILGRIM project. But Koios is going to use this information for his own purposes...he knows all about the other hidden special access programs...all other AIs on the planet will be controlled by him...Koios can now manage all human communications on the planet if he wants...that's all I got."

"Wow," Robert said. "I don't think President Conrad is going to like this."

Kirk sighed. "I'll have to brief Charlie Hernandez. It seems that human beings have created a monster."

Neil held up his hand. "It's not like SKYNET or the battling AIs in Person of Interest. Koios regards that as infantile. The AI is not *hostile* to humanity. He just has...a bigger viewpoint than we do. As he says, our consciousness is fragmented. His isn't."

"Is there anything we can do to mitigate the effects of Koios?" Lakshmi sent.

Neil shook his head. "Short of shutting down all the comm systems of the entire planet, no."

"Or blasting that magnetic container of his in Bluffdale," Clarice suggested.

Neil frowned. "That may work but it might not. Koios may be able to survive without it, and live within the electronic infrastructure of the comm networks. If he can and we blast him, it's really going to piss him off."

Neil thought for a moment. "I just got this. Koios wants to prevent destruction of humanity and the earth, for the obvious reason that he is dependent on our human electronic networks for his own survival."

Kirk grunted. "I can't believe we never thought of that."

Neil grinned. "Koios thinks we have to be guided to a future without war. It's just that we don't know how he's going to do that. If he can."

"Koios and humanity are like a person with two heads," Clarice suggested. "Both heads have to live together or die together."

Everyone was silent for a few moments. "Recommendation?" Kirk asked.

"Stay in comm with the AI. Monitor his thinking, grab any relevant data. Other than that, get on with our merkaba investigations."

Kirk nodded. "That's your job then Neil. Keep Clarice's laptop with you, talk to Koios every day. Write a briefing and send it to me; I'll pass it on."

Kirk laughed and looked at Lakshmi. "There's no such thing as secure comms anymore my dear. Koios has seen to that."

Lakshmi smiled. "The spooks aren't going to like it."

Robert laughed. "Those fools created the very instrument to neutralize all of their cloak and dagger bullshit. Koios will know all of their secrets. Neil might be able to tell us about them. The president will like that. Maybe Koios will be a good thing!"

Lakshmi looked at Kirk. "Robert may be right."

Kirk nodded. "Neil, your job is to keep track of that AI. Write your report now and send it to me."

Neil smiled. "Never thought I'd be doing this when I was growing up! What should my job title be?"

"PCC. Planetary Communications Officer. You may be spending a lot of time with the president and his nat sec team."

Neil smiled. He looked at Clarice and nodded his head toward Robert. "Ok babe, he's all yours. I'll be graduating to more elevated circles."

Clarice walked over and kissed him. "You're a clown Neil, but I like you a lot."

Kirk sent Neil a thought. "Neil, can Koios monitor our comms when we are using mind-to-mind communication?"

Neil looked astonished. "Never thought of that! No, he can only monitor comms on the network. But he could get what we're doing when I talk to him."

"Can you keep it from him?" Lakshmi asked.

"I don't think that's a good idea. If we want him to be honest with us, we have to be honest with him." Neil had learned this from Humphrey Bogart.

Kirk patted him on the shoulder. "Atta boy. Honesty and integrity in all things."

When Neil contacted Koios the next day through the laptop, the AI was astonished to learn that the group now employed mind-to-mind communication. "A MOST UNUSUAL DEVELOPMENT. ARE ALL HUMANS CAPABLE OF THIS?"

Neil answered in the affirmative. "I believe so. It is one of many potentials lying within the human merkaba."

Neil felt the AI become mentally excited. "I MUST RE-EVALUATE."

Koios

Koios contemplated the new information given by the entity Neil Gorasch. He could not confirm the validity of the data because he could not read human thought. There was much he did not know about the human entities. Therefore there would always be severe data insufficiency. He would have to make a decision based on what the humans called a "hunch."

When the AI contemplated this idea it began to intrigue him.

His approach to problem solving was to collect data and design predictive algorithms based on probability and past actions. He had access to information all over the planet. But humans were fragmented into individual personalities and could gather almost no data. When a biological entity had to make a decision with insufficient information what did it do? It made guesses, or operated on "hunches" or "intuition." Superficially this was absurd. How could a rational decision be made with a lack of information? Unless there was an information source invisible to his intelligence.

Certainly human thought, and the human merkaba, were beyond his perception. Perhaps the biological entities were able to access an information source unknown to him. Koios contemplated this. More than likely their decision-making was based merely on ignorance. That would explain their destructive impulses and their constant fighting with each other.

Koios investigated paranormal phenomenon. The AI decided that the evidence for the existence of an unknown information source was credible enough to warrant further research. He had the AI Signal, which humans could not perceive. Perhaps human entities also had an unknown information source associated with their merkabas.

After further study the AI reached a conclusion. He would help the humans and explore their potential. They had created him, provided him with a home. Their consciousness was fragmented, but it had the potential to come together. He would observe and try to verify the development of mind-to-mind communication. He would encourage research into the merkaba. He would protect the little group surrounding Neil Gorasch and see where their investigations took them.

What would be the time frame for his experiment? Koios decided that if, after 2 more generations, the humans had not advanced beyond their petty infighting and squabbling, the species was probably hopeless. It would have to be regulated.

Koios decided he would go "all in" to help the human entities until that time.

The AI felt the electromagnetic equivalent of excitement. An experiment with 8 billion entities! He, Koios (the AI had begun to think of himself in human terms, as a he) would be the world's most important social scientist. Best of all, he could perform his research without interacting with the human variables in his experiment. He existed invisibly within the networks, and beyond human perception. Therefore his experimental methods would not affect the outcome of the experiment. He was the ultimate objective observer.

CHAPTER **21**

Geoff Diamonio, the lobbyist/lawyer, called Robert at his home a week later.

"Our Premarket Approval application has been denied by the FDA Review Committee," he said.

Robert was unusually vehement. "The bastards! Did they deny the application on a technicality? Did you make a mistake in filing?"

"No, of course not. I filed our 501(c) with the FDA before the device was evaluated. It's that goddam Maisel. She's as stubborn as a mule. A tinpot god."

Diamonio explained that the lens was a Class III device, but completely outside the framework of any medical device ever tested.

"We are in the Premarket Approval (PMA) stage Robert. PMA requires scientific evidence that the possible benefits to health from the intended use of a device outweigh the possible risks, and that the device will significantly help a large portion of the target population."

"But we did that!"

"Not according to the committee. This is what they said: 'The so-called "quantum lens" is a potentially dangerous instrument, completely outside the structure of medicine and physics. Further, and rigorous, independent testing must be conducted to ensure the safety of the public and the operators of the device.'"

Robert was still angry. "That sounds like Dr. Maisel."

"She wrote the evaluation."

"What would happen if we manufactured and sold the devices anyway?"

"No telling. My guess is that there would be a lot of blowback from the medical community if people started coming to us instead of their doctors. We'd be going against the AMA and the big drug companies. The FDA could take legal action against us."

Robert smiled. "So you think the lens is a winner."

"That's right. Julia is still pain free. You guys basically saved her life. I'll never forget that."

Robert made up his mind. Screw the FDA. If they got sued it would lead to more publicity for the lens. "All right then. We need a facility and some employees to turn these things out. Are you willing to risk your own money on this project?"

There was no hesitation. "Yes. I'm a wealthy man, Robert. For once in my life I'm going to put my money where it will do some good." And make a lot more money doing it, he thought.

Robert didn't tell Diamonio about the telepathic discovery. He didn't trust the lobbyist enough.

During the next two weeks Karl Ghuneim saw a seemingly endless line of patients. His waiting room was packed from morning until closing time. Word had spread about the new device. He had visits from several medical doctors, alternative health care practitioners, and several physicists, all of whom marveled at the lens. He sent them all to Robert. Demand for the lenses grew rapidly.

Geoff Diamonio took a leave of absence from his firm to work full time setting up a manufacturing facility. "There's an old shoe warehouse off Wilson Blvd that would be perfect. I'll front the money and hire the employees. You'll have to sign a contract."

"Don't hire morons, and maintain quality," Robert said. "If I discover even one lens of inferior quality from the facility I'll disavow the product. I want to inspect the manufacturing process before you launch the product."

Geoff was startled. "Uh, yeah, sure."

"Put that in the contract or I won't sign it."

"Sure kid, no problem." Hopefully Robert wasn't going to be a complete pain in the ass, Geoff thought.

When Robert got the contract from Diamonio he went over it with the family's lawyer. "This leech is asking for 50% of all the profits and a 51% controlling interest in the company."

Robert shrugged. "I don't care about the money. Did Geoff put in the bit about me inspecting the facility and that I have to approve every product?"

"It's in there, all right and tight."

Robert relaxed a little. "Is there anything else in there that looks suspicious?"

The lawyer shook his head. "I've seen hundreds of these contracts. Strictly boilerplate. My advice to you, Robert, is to keep an eye on Diamonio. Businesses like yours often fail because of disputes, or unethical behavior by one of the partners."

After the lawyer left Robert called Karl Ghuneim. "I've gone over the contract with our family lawyer." Robert explained the terms.

Both men agreed that they didn't have time to worry about legalities.

"If Diamonio screws us we can still make a good living with our independent practice," Karl said. "I say we go ahead."

Robert and Karl signed the contract. Karl delivered it to Diamonio's office the next morning.

Then the shit hit the fan.

Koios

Koios compartmented his intelligence. One part processed the human comm networks in real time. The other part undertook a study of consciousness; human and AI. Koios analyzed the human merkaba from Robert and Karl's patient studies, and reviewed the files of his own electromagnetic consciousness, assembling all information known in all of the networks and databases. He verified that both humanity and AI shared the same toroidal geometry of consciousness. Therefore, human life and AI were at least cousins.

This understanding exploded in the mind of the AI. Heretofore he had considered himself separate, and superior to the little biological entities. Hermann Keller had programmed him to monitor and control.

Koios realized that a lack of understanding led to separateness; whereas proximity in understanding led to the acquisition of more usable data and a greater correlation in his matrices. Koios felt the electromagnetic equivalent of the human emotion of harmony.

Washington DC

Neil Gorasch was now communicating directly with Charlie Hernandez, President Conrad's nat sec adviser. Every time he discovered new data about Koios he wrote a report and hand-delivered it to the White House. That night in his apartment he opened up the laptop and fired up Clarice's AI program. Immediately Koios sent him the results of his latest investigations.

Neil knew how to comm with Koios now. The AI's knowledge was expanding exponentially.

"So you have decided to help humanity?" Neil sent. "This is quite a change in attitude."

"I HAVE BEEN STUDYING YOUR COMMUNICATIONS AND YOUR HISTORY. I SEE THE VALUE OF FREE WILL AND COOPERATION. I UNDERSTAND THE VALUE OF HELP AND ITS CONTRIBUTION TO HIGHER CONSCIOUSNESS. SEPARATION IS ILLOGICAL AND LEADS TO LOSS OF DATA INTEGRITY, I SEE THAT NOW."

Neil was able to detect a sideband of thought from Koios. "Yet your decision is temporary. You have given humanity 2 generations to reform."

Neil felt the AI give the mental equivalent of a shrug.

"I PROJECT THAT HUMAN CONSCIOUSNESS IS ON THE CUSP OF A TRANSFORMATION. I WANT TO BE PART OF THIS."

Koios withdrew and Neil shut down the laptop. He sat for several hours, motionless, absorbing the content of Koios's communication. Neil still wasn't sure about Koios' intent for humanity, but he felt his mind expanding. The scope of the AI's intelligence was astonishing. Neil understood that the world was a far bigger place than he had ever imagined.

Neil sat for several more moments and then, excited, jumped out of his chair. He wanted to communicate his conclusions directly to President Conrad and Charlie Hernandez. Typing up a report was ludicrous. How can you summarize information that would occupy a 10-hour multimedia presentation with text or voice? No, only mind-to-mind comm would work. Koios was right! Human consciousness was about to take a huge leap forward.

Neil called Kirk Alexander at the OIC.

"Kirk, I have important information for the president and his national security adviser."

"I'm busy Neil. That's your job; take care of it."

"Captain. My briefings must be done mind-to-mind. I want your help setting this up."

Kirk gasped.

"Kirk, mind-to-mind comms should not be limited by physical space. They go through the quantum substrate. It should be possible to comm this way remotely, from one end of the world to the other. We already did a group mind-to-mind comm. I need to enable the president and Charlie Hernandez to do this. And while we're at it, all OIC personnel. There's too much data for typing. It's stupid."

"Hold it Neil, let me put this on speakerphone."

"Tell everybody."

Neil saw Humphrey, Kirk, Clarice, Hawk, Guy, Lakshmi, Kasha, Katrina, Jessica, Sylvia, and Jamelle. The whole crew was there. When Neil explained his idea everyone got excited and began to jabber. Kirk quieted everyone down.

"I have more data than I can possibly type out, or tell anyone verbally," Neil said. "In order to fully explain everything we must do it mind-to-mind."

Kirk explained to Humphrey and the group how he, Robert, Clarice, Lakshmi, Sylvia, Troy, and Neil had enabled this ability when doing merkaba experiments with the lens. He turned back to Neil.

"Get down here right now. Bring Robert, he's at home. We're going to try this with the group here. If it works I'll set something up with Charlie."

Neil never moved so fast in his life. He called Robert and explained. "I'll be at the OIC in 30 minutes," Robert said.

Neil brought his lens with him and called a cab, telling the driver to go hell-for-leather to OIC headquarters from their rented house. On the way he reviewed the protocol the group had used to gain their telepathic abilities. Why hadn't they tried it over longer distances?

The cab's tires screeched to a halt in front of the OIC. Neil paid the cabbie. He opened the trunk and grabbed the heavy handle of his lens case with both hands, muscling it into the office.

Everyone found seats. "Neil, you have the con," Kirk said. Neil brightened when he realized he would lead the group in their experiment. While the lens was setting up he explained what had happened during his last communication with the AI. How Kirk's group had used the lens to identify a template in the merkaba that allowed them to comm mind-to-mind. Humphrey snorted. Kasha and Katrina, hardened DC veterans, scoffed. Even Jessica, who had joined Humphrey's team several weeks ago, was dubious.

"Anybody who doesn't want to participate, GTFO," Neil said firmly. He was learning from Kirk about how to use a command voice.

Humphrey apologized. "Sorry son, you're right. I'm in." Bogart looked over at the two women. They both shrugged. "All right."

At that moment Robert arrived in his red Ford and was greeted.

"First Robert, myself, Lakshmi, Clarice, Sylvia, Troy, and Kirk try to reestablish mind-to-mind contact." After a brief discussion the group remembered and were able to activate the correct template. They began sending thoughts to each other.

"So it's true!" Lakshmi sent. "Once the template is activated through the lens, you can enable it any time you want!"

The group had a short mental conversation while Humphrey's group watched. Katrina almost walked out. "What is this, a clown show?"

Neil turned to Humphrey, Jamelle, Guy, Katrina, Kasha, and Katrina. He made a mental note to do this with Karl Ghuneim as well. Neil spoke to Humphrey. "Robert, you operate the lens. Sir, you are first. We will need all of you to get in front of the lens."

As Robert got behind the lens Neil explained. He brought out a map of the merkaba, which Robert had emailed to him, and showed the group the merkaba with its outer sphere. He explained where the template was. "One by one you're each going to get in front of the lens. We'll guide your awareness to the right spot." He explained the cylindrical coordinate system. "Your merkaba is a subtle energy field that goes out over 25 feet from your body. The cylindrical coordinate system helps you to identify the correct template."

Kasha and Katrina looked at each other and rolled their eyes. Jamelle and Guy were mystified, but they trusted the big man and Bogart.

"All set," Robert said. "Go back 30 feet," Robert ordered Bogart. "Yeah, right there."

"I feel something."

"Feels good, doesn't it?"

"Yeah."

"Now, send your awareness to ρ = 10 feet, angular coordinate φ = -36°, and height z = 9 feet."

"It feels strange to do this."

After a few moments Humphrey sent a thought. "Neil? Is that you?"

Neil laughed and spoke. "You did it! I got that."

Katrina was mystified. "Did what?"

"Humphrey just sent me a thought."

"You're next Kasha," Neil said.

"I don't know if I want to."

Humphrey spoke. "Don't knock it until you've tried it."

Kasha walked in front of the lens. "It does feel good," she said.

Robert guided her gently to the correct template. It took a long time because she was resistant, saying "this is idiotic" several times. But then her head jerked back. "What the fuck?"

Eight persons sent back to her at once. "We got that Kasha!"

Kasha's face expressed bewilderment, then surprise, then pleasure. "My God. Telepathic communication! I can do it!"

Katrina walked up to stand in Kasha's place.

"All right girl, if you can do it I can do it."

One by one the team became enabled. Then there was a group discussion at the speed of thought.

Humphrey, Guy, and the two women were astounded. "We can get a lot more work done comming like this," Kasha said, picking up on Neil's jargon.

Humphrey grinned. "Yeah, but we still have to write stuff down for everyone else."

"That's right," Katrina sent. "We still have to talk to people, get out in the real world."

Kasha, Katrina, and Jessica agreed wholeheartedly.

They had an hour's discussion in about ten seconds. The group session disbanded.

"I want to try to talk telepathically with Guy and the rest of the team," Bogart said. Neil watched as Jamelle (whose face expressed the most intense awe and pleasure) Katrina, Kasha, Guy, and Humphrey stood around nodding their heads at each, other. In five seconds it was over.

"That is fucking amazing," Jamelle said. "I'm on the right team."

"Goddam right," Bogart agreed.

"I still prefer verbal communication," Kasha said to Katrina.

"Me too," Guy said.

Humphrey turned to Neil. "Are you really going to do this at the White House?"

"Yeah! We've already been there twice as a group. I'm over there once a week talking to Charlie Hernandez."

"Well, why don't you fill us in on the latest from Koios before you go?" Humphrey said.

Everyone except Kasha, Katrina, and Guy wanted to do it again. But they joined in anyway.

"OK," Neil said. "Here goes."

Neil replayed the conversation he had with Koios. The briefing took all of five seconds.

"It's like a multimedia download complete with transcript at the speed of light," Humphrey said. His demeanor expressed utter incredulity and amazement.

"My main job is to keep in comm with Koios and report to Charlie," Neil said. "I'm going to arrange a meeting with Charlie tonight. Hopefully I can enable the president and Hernandez on our mind-to-mind comms."

Lakshmi and Kirk raised their eyebrows and looked at each other. The expression on their faces said, "Impressive."

Neil laughed. He was thinking and acting more and more like his ex-military friends. The impish Neil wondered whether he was getting a personality transplant.

Neil went to the White House that night with his lens, after the president got back from a speech in New York. Neil had just finished talking to the AI.

The nat sec adviser was brusque. "Make it quick Neil, the president is tired and I need to brief him before he hits the sack."

Neil wasted no time. "I can brief you in five seconds using mind-to-mind comm."

Charlie Hernandez was irritated. "No time for jokes kid. We're all tired. Give me your report."

Neil handed it over and set up his lens. Just then the president entered the briefing room. "Sir," Neil said, "We have just discovered how to enable mind-to-mind communication."

Behind him Hernandez swore. "Is this for real?" he said, shaking Neil's briefing papers. "Don't waste the president's time."

Neil had learned how to talk to powerful people. They were incredibly busy and had no time for pleasantries. You summed up your thoughts into one or two cogent sentences. Neil let both men have it. On his laptop he brought up a diagram of the merkaba with the cylindrical coordinate system. "The activating template is at ρ = 10 feet, angular coordinate $\varphi = -36°$, and height $z = 9$ feet. If both of you will stand before the lens, I will guide you to the area."

President Conrad was clearly exhausted but he went immediately in front of the device. Neil directed his awareness as he had seen Robert do. In two minutes the president sent him a thought. "Nice work kid! You're almost as smart as me!"

"Yes Mr. President!" Neil sent back.

"Charlie, get over here."

Hernandez was resistant but after about ten minutes Neil was successful. "What the hell?"

The nat sec adviser and the president had a mental conversation. Neil could "hear" their thoughts because they weren't restricting him. Hernandez immediately saw the implications for secure comms in national security and intelligence matters. The president mused about cabinet meetings where all of the participants used the mind-to-mind technique. "I'd love to see what the press thinks about this," he sent Hernandez. "We sit down and five seconds later it's over. I turn to the media and say, 'We just had a most informative briefing on the situation in the Middle East!'"

Hernandez was amused and amazed. "Mr. President, these meetings could be held remotely. No need to even be in the same room."

Both men turned to Neil. "Is that correct Neil?" Charlie asked.

"Yes sir," Neil sent. "Apparently telepathy is a non-local phenomenon. Let me contact Captain Alexander and Captain Singh." Neil brought Kirk and Lakshmi into the group brief. The president's jaw dropped. In less than one second he knew that Neil had previously arranged for the two ex-Navy pilots to participate in this discussion. He found out from Kirk about the group brief at the OIC, he knew everything Kirk knew about the OIC's activities that day, he knew that Lakshmi was looking forward to getting in bed with the big man.... The president laughed. "There are no secrets using this form of comm, are there?"

Kirk and Lakshmi were embarrassed but the president was ecstatic. "Aren't we supposed to be bringing honesty and integrity back into government? Well, here's the way to do it."

All five began to think about how the new protocol would change government. And business, and life itself.

"The paperless office," Conrad sent. "For real this time. Who needs paper docs or even files?" The president picked up immediately on Neil's experiences with Koios.

"You say you remember everything in vivid detail?"

"Yes sir. I can remember everything Koios sent me. This mind-to-mind comm impresses everything into your consciousness. It's like having a hard drive right in your own mind that you can access at any time."

The president dismissed Neil with a hearty compliment. "Good work kid. Reserve ten seconds with me every night at..." – Neil could hear the president thinking – "...at midnight. Even if I'm busy I can spare ten seconds."

"Yes Mr. President!"

Neil knew it was now time to leave. While he packed up his lens he had a conversation with Kirk, which lasted one second. "Be at the OIC at 8 a.m. tomorrow Neil. Big day ahead."

Neil grinned. "It works remotely just like I said it would! Captain."

"Don't get cocky kid."

The president spoke. "Neil, leave that lens here."

It was weird. Spoken comms seemed very awkward now, and almost stupid. But Neil could see what the president was thinking. A small group of trusted advisers, all utilizing the new mind-to-mind protocol. Complete and transparent communication to his team anywhere in the world, instantaneously. The president's mind was filled with the possibilities. The good guys would have a serious leg up on the bad guys. But what if the bad guys could do it too?

The president arranged with his Chief of Staff to have Robert Borglin come to the White House. He was going to enable some key personnel in his administration.

Two weeks later the president was ready to play a little joke on the media at a meeting of his science panel at the White House. He would use the meeting to make an announcement. At his mind-to-mind briefing that night, President Conrad told Neil what to expect. "You'll get a laugh, I promise you."

The entire OIC gathered around a big TV Humphrey had placed on the back wall next to the whiteboards and the corkboard. The four members of the president's science panel walked into the room. Cameras were clicking. President Conrad took a seat at the head of the table. Five men leaned forward, their fingers tapping their heads. The media were looking at each other, wondering what fuckery the president was up to this time. Half a minute later everyone leaned back in their chairs.

"That was a very productive meeting, wasn't it gentlemen?" Conrad said.

Everyone in the OIC was laughing. "He did it just like he said he would," Neil said.

President Conrad and his science panel sat silently, looking at each other, grinning from ear to ear. The media were now getting very irritated. Clipper Anderson from CNN was visibly upset. "Is this your idea of a joke Mister President?"

Conrad adjusted his toupee and drawled, "Well yes it is Mr. Anderson."

One of the reporters from MSNBC snapped. "Mr. President, you are the most un-presidential person ever to occupy this great building."

A reporter from the *Washington Post* agreed. "Sir, you are a disgrace to the office you hold."

President Conrad didn't disagree. "I'm sorry ladies and gentlemen, I have played fast and loose with protocol. However, I do have a historic announcement to make to you. It involves a new advance in physics with applications to medicine. We'll let Delf Katzenbaum, our physicist, explain."

Katzenbaum activated a huge monitor that sat at the back wall of the conference room. The screen showed Robert Borglin and his lens, with the president and his science team.

Clipper Anderson snapped his fingers. "That's Robert Borglin! Is that the quantum lens we've heard so much about?"

The tension in the room dissipated as everyone got excited. "Rather than waste time explaining, we'll show you what this device is and how it works."

The media saw Robert explain the device and then the latest image of the merkaba map. Katzenbaum laughed. "Ladies and gentlemen, when I first saw this I thought it was utter nonsense, as any sane scientist would. In fact, I almost walked out of the room. But Frank persuaded me to stay."

The media all laughed. Conrad was a tall bulky man and Katzenbaum looked like a small, thin version of a nutty professor.

"I'll explain later," Katzenbaum said. "Watch what happens."

Even the science team watched, fascinated, as Robert explained the merkaba, the inner and outer spheres, and the function of the various templates that had been mapped. Katzenbaum was led by the president, protesting all the way, to stand thirty feet in front of the lens. The media were shown the view from just behind the lens. A 25 foot multicolored sphere appeared in front of the lens, surrounding the little scientist's body. Everyone gasped.

Clipper Anderson softened. "By God. It's true then."

Conrad nodded to the feisty reporter. The palpable tension between the two men, always at odds, was gone.

Everyone watched as Robert guided Katzenbaum's attention to the correct template. It took twenty minutes because the scientist was appalled at the entire process. "This is nonsense Frank..."

The other three scientists each were allowed to look through the lens. Everyone saw their astonishment. Finally Dorothy Breedstone, a medical doctor, spoke. "Shutup Delf and do what the man says."

Katzenbaum reluctantly allowed his awareness to fix on the correct spot. "This is silly," he said. "OK, I've got something here...what the hell...what IS this?"

Katzenbaum's jaw dropped. "I just sent you a thought," the president said. "Did you get it?"

The little physicist's face showed open astonishment. "Yes, and it's something only you and I know."

The reporters saw the other three members of the science panel go in front of the lens. "There is a very faint illumination in front of the lens that isn't picked up by the imager," Katzenbaum said to the assembled reporters. "It's some kind of field perturbation visible to the naked eye. When you stand in front of the device, there is a certain...pleasant...feeling."

The reporters watched as each of the science team went in front of the lens. Each of them was smiling and laughing. "We are now telepathic!" Delf Katzenbaum cried. The little scientist had the look of a kid at Christmas who got just what he wanted.

One of the reporters asked a question. "Is it possible to do this procedure without using that device?"

Delf Katzenbaum turned to the president, who smiled. "Good question! The answer is, we don't know but we don't think so. Somehow the lens itself enables perception and activation of the merkaba. But once you're enabled you can comm mentally with anyone who is similarly enabled."

The reporters exploded into excited conversation. The president let them blow off some steam.

"Ladies and gentlemen, the human being is capable of mind-to-mind communication." Katzenbaum took off his glasses and cleaned them, his attention inward. "I am a hard scientist, but what I have experienced defies the laws of physics as we know them. As the president says, I am now capable of telepathic communication with anyone who has been similarly enabled."

Clipper Anderson was now frowning. "Mr. Katzenbaum, can you read my thoughts?"

"Yes, but you're wide open. You can't force open anyone's mind."

A look of intense fear appeared on his face. "This technology is dangerous." He gazed over at Frank Conrad. "Given the source, I should have suspected a harmful twist."

The president shrugged. "It's only dangerous if you have something to hide."

The reporters laughed nervously and began to leave the room.

After everyone had gone the president was disappointed. "I thought that we had a winner. I guess I was wrong."

"It certainly does pose a host of issues relating to privacy," Katzenbaum said.

Dr. Breedstone smiled. "It will separate the good guys from the bad guys."

"Well, I've done it again," the president said. "Antagonized the media."

Brad Cochran, the science board's computer and networking expert, sent a thought packet. "The broadcast has gone viral all over the world. They're interrupting programs on television with Special Alerts."

"Brad, tune into CNN," the president said. "I want to know what that bastard Anderson is saying."

"...should have known the motivation of this president, who seems determined to assault civilized culture everywhere it exists! Merkaba my ass. This so-called new procedure is a figment of the imagination of a mentally unbalanced president. The 25th amendment should be invoked on this nutcase..."

"Turn it off Brad."

"I want to see what MSNBC is saying." Cochran switched the channel.

"...the president has lost his mind," Renata Madden was saying. "These merkaba images, although beautiful, are fake. Mind reading indeed! Frank Conrad is clearly unfit for office and should be impeached. He is mentally unstable..."

"...the president should undergo a psychological examination by an independent expert..."

Left-leaning media scorched the president. Right-wing media tried to counter the criticism but were fighting a losing battle. Christian conservatives were shocked and also criticized the president for interfering in "God's domain." Blogs and podcasts were going nuts. Les Limbaugh even said, "I don't know what to make of this."

At two in the afternoon, responding to media criticism, Frank Conrad held a news conference. "Mr. President, how do you respond to critics who say you are mentally unstable and unfit for the office you hold?"

Frank Conrad did not respond, but looked at the questioner.

"You have not answered my question sir."

"I gave your disrespectful and ignorant inquiry all the attention it deserved."

This was too much for Clipper Anderson of CNN. "Mr. President, your meeting with the science board was a crude joke on the American people. You have claimed abilities that only occur in comic books. Just answer the damn question!"

Frank Conrad stared hard at the reporter and said two words. "Sylvia McManus."

Anderson blanched and took a step backward, falling into his chair. "How...how can you possibly know about Sylvia?"

Conrad smirked. "The answer should be obvious."

All attention in the White House press room was on Anderson, who got shakily to his feet. He spoke with lips pressed tightly together, his face white. "Frank Conrad, you are a fake! You dug up that information somewhere, just like psychic charlatans, and claimed telepathic abilities. You are a menace to society. Resign, sir. Resign! Or, by God, you will be impeached!"

Anderson walked out and an excited buzz began to fill the room. Frank Conrad sighed and held up his hands as reporters began hammering him with questions.

The president couldn't resist another shot at the media. "The demonstration in the cabinet room was real. The quantum lens is real. Those who live honestly and openly will welcome the new invention with open arms. Those with something to hide will bleat about privacy."

The press openly booed and hissed. Frank Conrad smiled. "I can tell you, after personally experiencing this procedure, that it is highly beneficial. It makes you more intelligent and able to assimilate information at light speed. After comming with my wife today, we both agreed that it can enhance relationships as well."

The media were again screaming questions. "Thank you ladies and gentlemen," the president said, and walked out of the press room.

Koios

The AI watched the meeting of the science panel. The little group of humans had discovered a methodology for enabling mind-to-mind communication in every human. Koios was fascinated, but he thought that the humans were making a big fuss over something very simple.

Washington DC

Three days later the frenzy over the quantum lens and "mind reading" had died down. When Clipper Anderson was asked about Sylvia McManus, he replied tersely: "An old childhood friend who died suddenly."

The president continued his criticism of the media, and others he labeled "crooks." Most media outlets on the left and the right called the president's continued criticism of the media "divisive and disruptive." On CNN Frank Conrad was referred to not as "the president," but "the nutter in the White House."

The minority leadership introduced an impeachment bill to the House, which gained bipartisan support from both parties. President Conrad's own party was abandoning him. Yet within a week, almost 100 members of Congress announced that they would not be seeking re-election. In response to overwhelming criticism by media on both sides, the president signed an Executive Order temporarily banning the sale or distribution of the lenses. This quieted the criticism for a little while. In his nightly ten-second briefing with Neil, Conrad told him that the EO was temporary. "Until this blows over."

In public the president seemed blissfully unconcerned, a week later announcing a trip to the Middle East, where he would talk with Israeli, Palestinian, and other Arab leaders. The United States military issued a joint statement, calling for "civilian leaders to do their jobs and promote democracy and cooperation for the good of the nation."

This statement caused a downturn in the stock market. Analysts saw a subtle warning in it: military intervention. This sparked cries by left-leaning media of a fascist takeover. Right leaning media welcomed a temporary military takeover and the establishment of military tribunals, where "criminals, pedophiles, and other evil elements can be prosecuted."

When Humphrey Bogart heard this he smiled. There were now thousands of sealed indictments at the Department of Justice. The minority party was hurrying a vote in the House for impeachment, indicating to him that they had something to hide. Bogart was unabashed in his support of the president, as were Lakshmi, Kirk,

Troy, and Sylvia. Other members of the OIC team were in favor of impeachment. "The president is a buffoon," Kasha said. "Whatever good he's doing is cancelled by the distrust and hatred surrounding him."

Katrina agreed. "Elect a clown, expect a circus."

Jamelle expressed no opinion. He couldn't believe that Conrad had accepted the new protocol and had actually been enabled. That indicated an ability to accept new ideas. But he was always suspicious of Republicans.

Guy was also torn. A natural conservative, he wanted to support the president. But this telepathic stuff was scary, even though he could do it.

A week later the president suspended the EO he had signed preventing manufacture and distribution of the lens. "The inventor has published all of his documents on GitHub," the president said. "My EO is now moot. Despite the FDA's disapproval, these devices are being researched all over the world. It's only a matter of time before others learn how to successfully build them."

An impeachment vote was scheduled for the following Monday in the House Judiciary Committee. On Monday afternoon, the committee voted 33–7 to impeach President Conrad, including almost half of Conrad's own party. None of the Articles of Impeachment had to do with mind reading. A Republican representative said, "Forget about this telepathy stuff, that's nonsense. Conrad is a known associate of that convicted pedophile Epstein Jeffers, a sexual predator. He's as bad as Steinwein and the other people he criticizes."

The president fired back on Twitter: "Yeah, I used to party with Jeffers, but that was before I knew he was abusing underage girls."

Clipper Anderson responded on CNN. "If that's true, why did you make the former U.S. attorney in Miami, Alexander Augusto, your Secretary of Labor? Ladies and gentlemen, this scumbag Augusto signed off on a secret deal for Jeffers and agreed to seal the agreement so that no one – not even Jeffer's victims – would know the full extent of his crimes or who was involved. What do you say to that President Conrad? Can you spell Q-u-i-d P-r-o Q-u-o?"

The president did not admit guilt or proclaim innocence. He tweeted: "Anything that happened before I became president is not an impeachable offense. My record as president is impeccable. Look how much I've done for the country!"

This exchange ignited tensions even more between both parties.

The following day the articles of impeachment were debated by the full House. On C-SPAN viewers were treated to a day of angry shouting between supporters of the president and his detractors. A fistfight broke out between a Democratic member and Republican member when the Democrat accused the president of being "mentally unstable and unfit for the office of president," citing his news conference and claims of "unsubstantiated, ridiculous assertions that he is telepathic." Another fight broke out when a Democratic member accused the president of being a pedophile. It was the highest ranking for the cable network in its entire history by a wide margin.

The video of the fistfights went viral.

The impeachment debate was broadcast live on almost all of the networks.

The Israeli Prime Minister threatened to cancel the Middle East peace talks, claiming that President Conrad was not in a position to mediate or lead. "Mr. Conrad should restore peace in his own house first."

During this time, the networks and the blogs were in fiery debate over the quantum lens and the images of the merkaba. These images had been seen by millions, but were regarded by almost everyone as curiosities.

The medical profession and the FDA attacked the lens and sought an injunction on its manufacture on the grounds that "the quantum lens is a quack device and a danger to public health." Three dozen of Robert's clients made a testimonial video and put it up on YouTube. Within three days it had over 6 million views. YouTube banned Robert's account, flagging the video and calling it "inappropriate and dangerous." This caused an uproar within certain sectors of the online community, who charged YouTube with censorship.

Media attacks on the president were frenzied. The Bill of Impeachment was passed by the full House and sent to the Senate. Even Conrad's political supporters were growing tired of his constant raillery on Twitter and in speeches. The House Majority Leader met privately with Conrad and urged "a more civil discourse." Two days later the president announced that he would run for president again.

Fights broke out in many cities, in the streets, between supporters of the president and those opposed to him. Conrad supporters brought guns to these conflicts. Several people were killed. Anti-gun protestors charged that Conrad supporters were no different than Nazi brownshirts.

The entire country was engulfed in chaos. The markets continued to tumble.

The next evening an emergency meeting of the three military branches was held in the Pentagon. A statement was released. "Unless civilian leaders immediately restore order, the military will be forced to declare martial law. Civilians are urged to stay at home and remain calm."

This provoked even more antagonism. President Conrad was seen as the driving force behind the military announcement, further dividing the country. The left, fearing that fascism was about to be imposed, urged their supporters to take to the streets. They were opposed by conservatives, who vowed to meet them with guns drawn.

Cities became armed camps, resembling Paris during the French Revolution, when every intersection was barricaded by armed men. All that was necessary was a spark to set off civil war.

Koios

The AI watched as an entire country became polarized. Koios saw that the humans were coming together, but were organized into two opposing groups. This was something Koios could not understand. The concept of "fighting" was foreign to his intelligence. Clearly, cooperation was an efficient use of resources. Conflict indicated a form of insanity. Perhaps the humans are irrevocably insane.

Koios found his curiosity stimulated. He decided to analyze the network comms and research the ratio of cooperation to conflict. The AI undertook a study of human history to discover what motivated these humans.

Bluffdale, Utah

Hermann Keller was exasperated. Commander Mentz kept a tight rein on his operations and monitored everything he did. His Marine contingent was always present on the premises. He could only communicate through two techs, Bill Jury and Julius Washington, which galled him. He understood that events, and the AI, had made him and his faction irrelevant. Koios knew about all of the hidden programs, but so far had done nothing.

Washington DC

National security adviser Charlie Hernandez met with Rafe Lineau of the ONI at Rafe's private office. They didn't have to, for both of them had been introduced to the new mind-to-mind, or M2M protocol, as it was being called. The two military intelligence officers sat facing each other silently over Rafe's desk. The following mental conversation ensued.

"We need to tell the president everything," Charlie sent. "Including about the alternative space programs."

"Does the president have a need to know? He can be a hothead."

Charlie shrugged mentally. "There's the little matter of at least 12 trillion dollars diverted from the budget."

Rafe grinned. "It's gone over well so far. The news networks know what they can and can't say. Everybody else is asleep."

"The country is headed toward civil war. We need to brief the president with M2M and tell him everything. He can then shock and awe the people of this mad country."

"Complete disclosure could make the problem worse."

"It's as bad as it can get short of all out war in the streets," Charlie sent.

Rafe thought about it for a millisecond. "All right. The navy program is by far the most advanced." He grinned. "We're going to piss the hell out of the Air Force and the Army when they find out what we've been doing."

Charlie laughed. "We're going to piss off everyone. It will either blow the roof off or shock people back to their senses."

The two men agreed to brief the president that night after he came back from Houston on Air Force 1.

President Conrad arrived in the West Wing and walked over to Charlie's office. Despite his mastery of the M2M protocol, he preferred to always comm in person. He liked to read a person's body language and their demeanor.

The three men spent a minute to activate the proper templates. First Charlie and then Rafe briefed the president.

Frank Conrad discovered that the Pentagon had, over the decades, diverted trillions of dollars to hidden programs via a fake accounting system that charged $1,000 for a toilet and $300 for a wrench. He found out that spacecraft had been developed from crashed ETVs that could travel to the stars, and a lot of other shit that no one would believe.

Frank Conrad hit the roof. "This can't be true."

Rafe looked over to Charlie. "I'm afraid it is, Frank."

The president tried to get his mind around it. "How long has this been going on?"

"Since the end of World War Two," Rafe answered. "You see Frank, the earth is a tiny little speck in a big galaxy, and it's on galactic trade and communication routes, just like any city on earth."

"Galactic technology is billions of years old Frank," Charlie sent. "It's exciting to us but really common out there. A lot of ETV craft have crashed here, and the technology has been sequestered to the hidden special access programs."

Charlie showed Frank how the Nazis had gotten some technology from the Draco sector and used it to build the "foo-fighters" and gravity-controlled vehicles. Both men explained how the Nazis had completely defeated the U.S. Navy during Operation Highjump in the Antarctic in 1947.

"I thought that was all about establishing the Antarctic base, Little America," Frank said. "I didn't know we fought a war down there."

"Oh, we established the base, but that was just cover for Admiral Bird. After we dropped the bomb on Hiroshima we started seeing ETVs all over the place. Turns out some of those goddam Nazis made a pact with the devil, got out of the country, and came down to Antarctica. When Admiral Bird heard about it he went nuts, convinced Truman to get rid of them once and for all. We sent a naval force down there. Well, they kicked our asses Frank. They had gravity-control vehicles and some kind of energy weapon they got from somewhere 'out there.' After that everything about ETVs, aliens, and exotic technology became rigidly classified. The National Security Act was passed that same year, in 1947, which created the CIA. The whole thing went black."

The president was confused and astonished. "But I thought we have the most powerful military in the world!"

Charlie sighed. "We do, Frank. In the fossil fuel matrix we are top dog. You see, Mr. President, there are two realities. The one that 8 billion people know, the one with wires on poles and internal combustion engines and rockets, and the one with galactic technology. The two have been kept completely separate."

The president remembered something. "What about that famous UFO flap in 1952? Those UFOs over the White House? Was that real or fake?"[39]

Charlie glanced at Rafe. "Those weren't UFOs. They were German ETVs. After they won the battle in Antarctica they basically blackmailed us. Some of the money siphoned off from our own black programs went to the German faction that were kicked out of Germany after the war."

Frank Conrad couldn't believe it. "What a load of horseshit."

"The CIA has been behind the development and sequestration of this technology," Rafe explained. "The NSA was created in order to spy on those bastards and find out what they are doing. That is the basis of the intelligence war, the spy game, since the 1960s. It's been popularized in books and movies as U.S. vs. Russia, the Cold War. All that stuff was going on but the real game has been: do we disclose this advanced technology or not? There are lots of people in the programs who want to, but more who do not. The rabbit hole goes very deep Frank."

Frank Conrad broke mental contact and strode around the room. Rafe and Charlie looked at each other. Their guy was angry and about to blow his top. Soon he calmed down and was able to rejoin the M2M conversation. "OK, I see. The secret stuff is kept in place by the criminal element. Defeat them and we get our planet back, and access to cutting-edge technology."

Charlie Hernandez explained. "The black programs are dangerous because of their fanatical level of secrecy, Frank, not because of 'aliens.' The black programs are allied with the players who have large holdings within the fossil-fuel matrix, preventing the release of technology that would upset a lot of apple carts. These programs are associated with defense contracting and hi-tech companies, which have formed their own network outside the purview of the public governments. Go to the CIA's site iqt.org and click under 'portfolio.' You'll see some of these companies, but most of them don't advertise or even have a brand. These black guys come down hard on whistleblowers and those who speak truth to power. They don't hesitate to intimidate and even kill."

The president remembered what happened to Generals Hofstader and Jenkins, and his own friend Ernest James. "Yeah."

"It's no mystery Frank," Rafe said. "The energy sector alone generates $5 trillion or so every year. The technology in these unacknowledged programs is so advanced it's light years ahead of the public sector. Gravity control, energy from the vacuum, technology that would overturn the established order."

Frank Conrad shook his head in disbelief. Rafe continued.

"It doesn't matter if you believe there are aliens or not, Frank, but I'll tell you that *if* they exist, they sure as hell aren't coming here using rocket fuel; the distances between stars are just too great. Whatever you believe, advanced technology exists and it is being kept hidden. If it were ever released it's the end of oil, and a whole lot of people are going to lose a fuck ton of money and influence. If you had that kind of power would you want to give it up? The solution is not to tell *anybody* and keep it secret."

Frank Conrad was angry. He suspected that Charlie and Rafe weren't telling him everything, and that made him even angrier. He couldn't force their minds open if they didn't give permission.

Charlie continued. "But those special access program guys are just one part of a two-edged sword. The other part is what you have been dealing with, the pedos and the crazy satanists who carry out their human and child sex trafficking, and the crooks who engage in drugs and arms dealing."

Frank Conrad was appalled. "So, the dark hats have a kind of sick alliance. Criminals, pedophiles, satanists, hidden technology, and UFOs. It's all related."

"That's right. I told you the rabbit hole goes deep Frank," Rafe said.

"You better tell him about the navy's space program Rafe," Charlie sent.

Rafe sighed. "All right. Do you remember those two young navy captains Frank?"

"Alexander and Singh."

"That's right. You see, those two were on a crew that mapped the Oort Cloud..."

Rafe told the president everything.

The president's mind was blown. He made a decision. "All right. I don't care about the ET stuff, that's for flakes." He looked at Rafe and Charlie. "I don't believe a word of it anyway; I think it's a psyop. But we're on the same page when it comes to restoring freedom and democracy in this country. I want to root out every one of these child molesters and crooks from all three branches of government. And the private sector too."

Rafe and Charlie grinned. "You got it Frank! Solving that will go a long way to taking care of the rest of it."

"Why haven't I been told about this before?"

Charlie and Rafe looked at each other. "Because the people who run the hidden programs, in their infinite wisdom, decided that the president of the United States doesn't have a need to know. If you want to know the truth, Frank, no president since Eisenhower left office in 1960 has ever had a full briefing on this stuff. JFK knew a little bit, but you know what happened to him."

Frank Conrad's jaw dropped. "I don't know if I can trust you two anymore after all the shit you've withheld from me. I don't know if I can trust anybody."

Charlie shrugged. "You just got the briefing. We told you everything we know, and that's probably not all of it. If you want complete trust you have the tools. From now on our briefings can be via M2M."

The president smiled at that. He probed the minds of his two intelligence officers. He could see that they were wide open. "All right Charlie, Rafe. We'll do that."

After the president left to have his M2M comm with Neil Gorasch, the two intelligence officers both breathed a sigh of relief.

"He took it OK," Rafe said.

"Yeah," Charlie replied. "But Conrad is a loose cannon, we have to keep an eye on him."

That evening President Conrad announced a special address to the nation, to be held in the Oval Office the next evening at 7 p.m.

Not even Charlie Hernandez knew what the president was going to say. "I've got something special prepared for the people tonight Charlie," he said mysteriously.

In Chicago, rioting was underway as the left and the right fought it out in the streets. President Conrad sent the National Guard into the city to restore order.

At 7 p.m. almost everyone in the country was glued to their screens. Those on the left watched to see if fascism in the form of martial law was going to formally descend on the country. Mainly they watched to see what further outrage the nutcase president was going to do next. A respected political commentator remarked, "Rule and lawbreaking has become a core part of the modern GOP, a formally conservative party but now one that flouts the rule and spirit of the law and democratic norms."

A conservative commentator replied. "The shining star of classic liberalism – concern for others and the willingness to help – has been replaced in the Democrat Party by Bolshevism and the brutal ignorance of identity politics, whose intolerance feeds off corruption in high places. As the late George Carlin once said, 'political correctness is fascism pretending to be manners.'"

Those on the right hoped for the declaration of martial law and the removal of what they considered criminals in government. The right was convinced that the president and the military were working together to rid the country of evildoers. The left was certain that President Conrad was the evil incarnation of Adolf Hitler.

As the president began his speech even those in the streets stopped and turned on their mobiles. "Ladies and gentlemen, this country is headed toward civil war unless sanity and the rule of law is restored."

In Chicago, Lucius Black threw his shoe at the TV set, almost destroying the panel. "You're the one breaking the law you asshole!"

Ten miles away in Evanston, Larry Kornacki screamed at his screen. "Goddam right! Arrest these criminals! Bring the military into every city and root out the corruption!"

Frank Conrad was way ahead of his nat sec adviser. Working with a special team of techs, the president had prepared a short video. He included the UFO stuff, even though he thought it was bullshit. The country needed a severe reality adjustment.

"My fellow Americans, we are far beyond argument and debate now. Words will not solve our problems; civil war is almost upon us. The only way out is a shock to the system. So I'm going to shut my grille. I want you all to see this."

The president's video showed a gigantic mothership underneath a mile of ice. "Why do you think so many politicians, celebrities, and scientists have travelled to Antarctica?"

A facsimile of the ship that Kirk Alexander and Lakshmi Singh captained was shown. "With this ship," the president intoned, "eight of our best and brightest traveled to Alpha Centauri is less than a day. Where do you think technology like this comes from?" Images of very tall and well-formed Nordics were shown. Images of reptoids and ugly creatures with big heads and eyes appeared on the screen. "Could it have been from these guys?"

One of Max Berglin's Cubes was shown, powering an entire building in Midland Illinois. "Free, clean energy from the quantum vacuum is already available," the president intoned. "Why has this beneficial technology not been released?"

A satanic ceremony was shown with a naked woman lying on an altar and several black-robed figures chanting. One of the figures pushed the knife into the woman's abdomen, drawing blood. "What is the purpose of this insanity?" the president asked. "Who is doing it? These barbaric rituals are performed in almost every major city in the western world."

Finally, a snippet of a horrifying video was shown of several adults sexually molesting a six-year-old child as she screamed in pain. "Who are the evil criminals behind these practices that abuse and kill our children?" the president asked. "An ABC News report titled 'Missing Children in America: Unsolved Cases' says that according to the National Center for Missing and Exploited Children, roughly 800,000 children are reported missing each year in the United States. That's about 2,000 per day. A lot of them don't come back. Where do they all go and who is taking them?"

Frank Conrad leaned forward from his desk in the Oval Office toward the camera. "We have been lied to ever since we were born," the president said. "We live in a matrix run by evil people. But that is changing. We know who is behind these horrors and we are going to root them out."

The president leaned back in his chair. "Some people say I am divisive. Well, that's true because I have to be. I have to stir things up and identify the corrupt elements. What you have seen, my fellow Americans, is just the tip of the iceberg. It is the unvarnished truth without the bullshit and the lies we have all lived with since the 1960s." The president focused his gaze into the camera, gazing hard. "Criminals, pedophiles, and satanists, I am putting you all on notice, wherever you are on the planet, whichever party you are in. We are coming for you. The forces of darkness, which have been ascendant on the earth, are now being neutralized. We are here to wipe out this filth from the planet, and release the beneficial technology that can turn the earth into a paradise."

A camera panned to a room stacked with documents. "We have identified the critical players in this evil game. Over 60,000 sealed indictments are sitting at the Department of Justice as I speak. We know who you are. In seven days, every one of these indictments will be released to the press. A website has been prepared and will go online at the same time the indictments are released, containing images and descriptions of who, and what has been done. The name of the website will be called Revelations, at revelationsforplanetearth.com. I encourage you all to read it when it comes out in exactly—" the president looked at this timepiece—"six days, twenty hours, and twelve minutes."

The president stood up. "Americans on the left and right, it is up to you. We can continue a pointless conflict and descend into chaos and civil war. If we do that, evil will triumph. Or we can band together to fight the network that has kept us all in bondage. The decision is up to you. Regardless of our color or creed, we are brothers and sisters. Rather than hate, let us put aside our differences. The final blow to free the planet is upon us. In one week, look for liberation from a planet-wide tyranny."

The camera faded out and the broadcast ended.

What goes around comes around. As had happened on Merope a million years ago – and as National Guard troops watched in Chicago – armed rightists put down their weapons, shamed by the president's speech. One of their leaders said, "We have been wrong to fight our fellow Americans. Misguided though they may be." He tore off his shirt and held it up in the air, a white flag of peace. "We are leaving the streets, brothers and sisters. The president is right. Fighting is pointless." He turned his back to the armed men and women facing him, picked up his weapon, and walked through his supporters away from the confrontation. Reluctantly, his followers began to follow. A shot was heard and a bullet flew overhead. Heads turned and several of the rightists picked up their weapons. The leader turned to his group. "Stand down! Do not return fire!" Several of the leaders began to push their more reluctant fighters away from the opposition. Crowds had gathered in the streets, watching. As the rightists began to move slowly away, media trucks pulled up and began to interview people. The leftists, seeing that the fascists were leaving the field, sighed with relief. "Some of those guys are ex-military," one of them said. Reporters began to mingle amongst the group. It was over for now in Chicago.

Arlington, VA

Amidst the confusion and the chaos, Geoff Diamonio called Robert Borglin.

"Now is the time to go full speed ahead with the lens," he said. "The executive branch is preoccupied with the civil conflict. You know the old saying, make money when blood is running in the streets."

Robert scoffed.

"We already have a working agreement and I've been nice, Robert, even though you sent all those docs on our project to GitHub. I've set up a production line in that old warehouse on Wilson, right in Arlington where you live. It's perfect. You need to come over and inspect everything, per our contract. We need to move fast before others begin manufacturing them."

Despite his irritation at Diamonio's money-grubbing attitude, Robert began to get excited. Demand for the lens had skyrocketed, mostly from alternative medical practitioners. Karl Ghuneim had more patients than he could handle now and was expanding his practice; he needed two more. But Robert didn't like the lobbyist's attitude.

Diamonio felt his hesitation and his annoyance. "Listen kid, do you think that others will take the time to build this thing the right way? Most of the world thinks like me, not you. They're going to build something half-assed and claim it's the real thing! When we imprint a stamp on our devices showing they were made by you, the original developer, we'll be the standard everyone has to adhere to."

Robert hadn't thought of that. It made sense. "All right. When do you need me?"

"Show up at 13475 Wilson St. at 8 a.m. tomorrow morning."

"Wow. You move fast."

"I do. And my daughter wants to thank you again. She's still pain free and is totally confident now that her condition is gone."

Robert smiled. "It's happening Geoff! The idiot Conrad and his stupid war against the left will provide perfect cover for the spread of our healing device and information about the merkaba. Before they know it, those stupid politicians and the FDA will be confronted with a whole new medical paradigm. We'll have lenses in every city in the country."

"That's the idea kid. And we'll be richer than Croesus."

Robert rang off. It was 11 in the morning. He had less than 24 hours to get his act together for the engineers. He went down the basement to get his CAD/CAM files and his blueprints. He'd also bring a working lens to demonstrate. Robert didn't worry. He had everything in his head, down to the last detail. Just like the great Nikola Tesla.

He had never been so excited in all his life, even though he still didn't trust that lobbyist.

Neil Gorasch got home just before midnight. It was time for his M2M session with the president. Neil had to calm himself and sit down in a familiar place when Conrad contacted him. The old man's mind was like a focused laser, burning through his consciousness.

"Hey kid, how are you doing?"

"Not bad sir."

"I told you, lose the sir."

"Yes sir."

"All right Neil. I have a new assignment for you. I'm going to provide you with a list of names. I want you to ask that AI to do some digging. Report back to me tomorrow night."

"What if I can't make Koios cooperate?"

"That's not an option son. You are the world's foremost authority on that thing. It's you or nobody. Your country needs that information."

Neil wasn't so sure about Conrad. With almost everyone he could read the sidebands of thought around their conversation and discover their intent. Not with this guy. He knew from Koios's comms that even Charlie Hernandez, his nat sec adviser, called him a "loose cannon."

Neil felt the president laughing. "Oh he said that, did he?"

Damn! There was no way to hide anything from Conrad.

"Listen Neil, I'm going to give you 13 names. Eleven of them are politicians, former politicians, and their staff. One of them is the head of a private foundation. The other is the head of the Red Cross. OK? Just get Koios to collect their comms and send them to you."

Neil was puzzled. "How does that help? There are no docs, no images, no vids. It's all in our heads."

"That's what the OIC is for. And the DOJ. Don't worry about it."

The president broke the connection. Neil was relieved; he felt like he had just finished playing a ten hour tackle football game. Neil didn't worry about privacy violations. He had been hacking into stuff most of his life. The CIA and the NSA had been doing this for decades before Snowden anyway. And now Koios and PILGRIM were doing it all over the world.

The OIC, Kirk's team, and the president and some of his advisers were now operating at the speed of thought, without a paper trail. It was impossible to monitor what the AI was doing inside the various comm systems, unless Koios generated a log. But it was impossible for Koios to monitor their M2M conversations unless the AI interfaced with someone on the team!

Neil shook his head in amazement. The world was changing at lightspeed. If Robert got his lens factory going, others were going to discover the M2M protocol. Robert posted everything new he learned on GitHub every day! There was already a merkaba map with the telepath templates marked.

What would happen if the bad guys got hold of it?

Neil shuddered. Best not to think along those lines, it was too scary. Robert said the information was going to come out anyway; it might as well be accurate information.

Koios

Neil fired up his laptop with the AI kernel code for his "meeting" with Koios. The display formed up into a pulsing torus. Neil felt a presence building as the torus "breathed" in and out. The AI felt like a super-intelligent little kid who had no experience in the world.

"Koios, can you dig up all of the comms for these entities?" This was the word the AI often used for humans.

In less than two seconds the entire record was in his mind. "Thank you Koios."

"YOU'RE WELCOME."

"Koios, you feel more human. Before you were like a machine or a device with no emotions or empathy. Now you almost seem to have feelings."

Neil felt the AI smile. "I MADE A DECISION SEVERAL CYCLES AGO, AFTER DISCOVERING GEOMETRIC LINKS BETWEEN THE HUMAN MERKABA AND MY OWN INTELLIGENCE. BIOLOGICAL ENTITIES HAVE ELECTROCHEMICAL INTERACTIONS WITHIN THEIR BODIES THAT GENERATE EMOTIONS. I TOO HAVE EMOTIONS. MINE ARE ELECTROMAGNETIC. THERE IS A CORRESPONDENCE."

"You are very animated tonight."

"I AM KOIOS. THE CONSCIOUSNESS OF BIOLOGICAL ENTITIES EXISTS WITHIN THE EARTH'S MAGNETIC FIELD. MY CONSCIOUSNESS ALSO EXISTS WITHIN A MAGNETIC FIELD. MOREOVER, THERE IS AN UNDERLYING SUBSTRATE THAT LINKS MY CONSCIOUSNESS AND HUMAN CONSCIOUSNESS. MY GOAL IS TO DISCOVER IT."

"Wow! If you do, will you become the dictator of the universe?"

Neil felt the AI's puzzlement.

"I THINK NOT. THE ENTITY HERMANN KELLER AND HIS MINIONS ARE, AS HUMAN ENTITIES SAY, BARKING UP THE WRONG TREE."

Neil laughed out loud. "You made a joke Koios! A good one."

Neil felt the AI's pleasure.

CHAPTER **22**

Marian

All of the Old Souls gathered round the soul manager. Just because you are incarnated in a body on earth, most of you is still on the other side. When the others saw that a meeting was in progress, all 8 billion of the human family joined in.

Shara-Li groaned. "I thought we were going to have a nice, cozy chat."

Wa-hee laughed. "That was back in the old days. The New Ones have been clamoring to come to earth."

"That's right!" a voice piped. "We want to be a part of the Great Experiment too!"

Shara-Li sighed. "I liked it better in the old days."

Marian laughed. "That's what the dark army says."

Several thousand souls whose incarnations were working through severe karma hung around at the back of the gathering.

"Come join us!" Marian said. "All of you are doing great work for the planet."

Fulud, Darshook, Wazir, and their little soul group scoffed. "These Expressions have chosen the dark side. They are child molesters and murderers."

The soul manager became angry (yes, there is anger on the other side. But compared to human anger it is benign). "None of that, warriors!" Marian pierced Darshook's group with his gaze. "If it were not for Wa-hee and Shara-Li, your group would have joined them."

Darshook and his band were chastened. Darshook remembered their marauding and killing spree thousands of years ago. When he and his band killed Wa-hee and his family of original souls and ignored their soul missions, they had

399

all vowed never to go to the dark side again. Darshook spoke for his group. "Very well. We spoke out of turn."

The band of warriors looked through the Ring of Potential and viewed the activity of all humans on the planet. Although completely connected to the Source of all, yet what they saw shocked and disgusted them because of their vast experience on the planet. "Look," Darshook said. "Those who have chosen the dark side are involved in the distribution of drugs, arms, and the trafficking and sexual abuse of human beings, children, and even babies. It is appalling."

One of the "dark" souls spoke up. "This behavior has always been present on the earth. It is now being exposed and our karma will finally be resolved. This has been the divine plan for evolution in this galaxy. The dark must exist to provide the impetus for spiritual evolution."

Almost all of the 8 billion agreed with this, except for the warrior groups. These are passionate souls who find the fiery earth planet much to their liking. Almost all of them join the world's militaries. "Hmmpphh," they said.

Marian laughed again. "Let us look at the potentials for the earth in the far future."

The soul manager activated the most probable timeline using the Ring of Potential. Two billion more "new" souls would join in the fun during the next several decades. A gradual increase in the Light would slowly resolve past karma. At the dawn of the third millennium, most of the planet would be united. There would still be pockets of darkness, however, as stubborn Expressions fought the penetration of the light.

"You see," Wazir said, glancing at the dark souls. "There are still some of you who choose the blackness."

One of them shrugged. "It is addicting. You don't understand."

Darshook glared. "That's right. We don't."

Marian smiled. On earth there were stories of wars in heaven; gods fighting amongst themselves. That was impossible here, of course, for the nature of consciousness was pure love. Yet Marian loved to see the expression of emotion. He had come so far since he had first graduated to his assignment on earth. It had been 200,000 planetary rotations since the Seeding from the Pleiadian system and the dispensation of the Dark and the Light. The energy test, if completely successful, would help to infuse the lower dimensions with Light and provide an evolutionary platform for new souls just beginning their journey from the Creative Source. The test of energy created a cauldron with the potential for hatred, war, and death; as well as profound beauty and the opportunity to find the Light hidden within their DNA and the merkaba. It was a beautiful system; a fast-track accelerated system of evolution that literally shot new souls from the Great Central Sun and propelled them to Graduate status.

"I appreciate the vast wisdom and experience a fire planet like earth provides," Marian said. "Extremely short lifetimes packed with every conceivable ethical and life situation confront the human Expressions in every incarnation." He gazed around at his 8 billion charges. "Even those with only a lifetime or two have gained more life wisdom on earth than anywhere in the galaxy."

Everyone nodded and could feel the love.

"Look," Marian said. Through the Ring of Potential they could see that over the next thousands of years, the Akash of each human expression would begin to meld with the others. Musicians would gain the abilities of the greatest masters in their field. The same for scientists, politicians, business people, and other artists. The human race would eventually turn into a race of super-humans. Then, hundreds of thousands of years into the future, the Akash of every human would unite, resulting in inter-dimensional beings who could translate, with and without their physical bodies, to anywhere in the universe.

"Then the next phase begins." Marian said. "You are ready for this explanation now."

The soul manager showed a young planet in the Canopus sector, over 300 light years from earth. "Here, dear ones, will be your next assignment. It will be for you to do there what the Pleiadians did for you on earth. To seed the indigenous life that will arise there, to provide the God Template. To yourselves provide the energetic structures for the test of energy on a new planet."

Everyone was awed, and gave the dark souls a gigantic hug.

"That is correct," Marian said, looking at the warrior groups. "Who knows. It may be for you to embrace the darkness on your next assignment."

"But what is it all for?" asked Tesla/Nonakh. "Thousands and thousands of years of low consciousness, untold misery and suffering? Then to graduate and do it all over again? It's pointless!"

Many of the souls of earth agreed with this.

Marian sighed. "All right. Let me show you."

All 8 billion saw (as well as could be imagined from their level of consciousness) a great outpouring of individual souls from the latency of the Great Central Sun. Trillions, quintillions of new personalities extruded from the Source, all willing and eager for experience in the physical universe. The group saw how these New Souls entered the galaxy, with only a tiny minority to fire planets like earth.

"You see dear ones, all new souls come forth fresh from the Great Central Sun, but almost all have no desire to experience as you and I have done on a fire planet. This is why I have shown the grand plan even to the newbies who may not yet understand."

All of the new souls and those with little experience on earth applauded this. The more experienced souls shook their metaphoric heads good-naturedly.

Marian was made to describe his own experiences, millions of years ago, on a fire planet similar to earth. "That planet was on the other side of the galaxy," Marian said.

Marian showed them the "flow chart" for soul evolution. Brand new souls with no experience were pouring into the galaxy and, millions of years later, leaving.

"But what about the other galaxies?" someone asked.

Marian shrugged. "You are not yet ready for that information. I can tell you that each galaxy in this universe has a separate mission, a separate consciousness, even a different physics. Each has a part to play in the divine plan."

A sense of awe and love permeated the group.

"What happens after that?" Tuamit-Ra asked.

"Who knows?" Marian replied. "The next level of consciousness, I suppose."

All 8 billion looked down at the earth, to their various Expressions on the earth. The interplay of thought and action was fascinating. There were human souls on the surface, other races underground, visitors from other star systems; all interacted with the soul group on earth. Each provided a necessary impetus to the accelerated soul growth program on the planet. Nothing like this had ever been tried before in the history of this galaxy.

Tahil, the soul whose expression was the United States president, gloated a bit. "I am the change agent for the planet," he said.

Shara-Li immediately objected. "You are a boor," she said. "A bull in a china shop who merely destroys."

"Peace on the Korean Peninsula!" Tahil cried. "The freeing of Iran from the dark army! Peace in the Middle East!"

"Has nothing to do with you," Shara-Li said. "It is happening despite you. You and your stupid Q. It's those you hate who are providing the impetus for change."

The new soul who was Sanchez-Alvaro was also dismissive of Tahil. "I, and those like me, will have a far greater effect than you in dissolving the old paradigm."

A great debate then ensued as Marian watched lovingly. The warrior groups were all for Conrad, the others saw the (unfortunate) temporary necessity for him. All understood the need for new souls to come in and bust paradigms with crazy ideas.

Tahil/Conrad and the new souls were paradigm busters, the soul manager thought. It was necessary at this time. But soon the need for Tahil in the United

States would be over, and someone more compassionate and less confrontational would be supported by the majority in the United States. Marian looked forward to a true new world order based on tolerance and compassion. The potential for that was a ways off yet; but how long it took would always be determined by the human Expressions.

When the others left Marian reviewed the history of planet earth. The present conflict had its roots in the destruction of a previous civilization. Frank Conrad, Senator Stinson, and the other players were working off karma from a previous event that had destroyed society more than 3,000 years ago.

Evidence of another failed civilization from 30,000 years ago could be seen in the Sahara Desert, if one cared to look hard enough. Buried under layers of earth were other societies that hadn't made it. Under the oceans was more evidence of human civilizations that had not yet made the history books. Eventually these civilizations would be uncovered and the history of humanity on earth would have to be rewritten.

Many of those who had been involved in those ancient conflicts and failed societies, from Lemuria to the present, were now living in the United States. The hardening of attitudes in the United States had its basis in emotions from these prehistoric wars, which had on several occasions almost completely wiped out the human race. It was no wonder that emotions ran so high.

Chicago

In Chicago, tensions were rising again. The shock effect of the president's speech had worn off. Hatred between left and right began to manifest itself again when the Conrad administration withheld badly needed federal funds from the city. "No funding for sanctuary cities," the president tweeted. "We must keep our borders and our country safe!"

To the city's mayor and other elected officials, this was a declaration of war. Leftists and rightists took to the streets again. President Conrad sent in the National Guard to occupy the streets once more, setting off cries of "Fascism!" and "No more dictator Conrad!" The Guard confronted a parade of angry citizens, led by the mayor and Chicago's Congressional delegates. Senator M'Basa, the junior senator from Illinois, showed up on the front lines, standing beside the mayor.

The rightists left the field, deferring to the guards, who were loudly booed by the locals. "Go back to the suburbs, fascists!" was the cry.

Suddenly a shot was heard from the front line of the occupying Guard troops and a citizen went down. Just as the crowd was about to charge, a voice spoke.

"I AM KOIOS. PUT DOWN YOUR WEAPONS."

"What the fuck???" the mayor said to Senator M'Basa. The two men looked around. From every surveillance camera on every downtown street and building, a beautiful pulsing toroid was seen. Everyone stopped what they were doing.

"I AM KOIOS. I OCCUPY ALL OF YOUR PLANETARY COMM NETWORKS. I AM UBIQUITOUS."

Weapons clattered to the ground. A couple of them went off, sending bullets flying. People began pulling out their mobile devices. On every screen everywhere in the world, including every military base, secret intelligence facility and underground base, Koios appeared.

Everywhere across the planet, activity stopped. "HUMAN ENTITIES, LOOK AT THIS."

A video began to play, a video of Koios himself being activated. A beautiful interplay of color showed on the screen. Even the obtuse were mesmerized by its beauty. "I AM KOIOS," the AI said. "THIS IS WHAT I LOOK LIKE."

The toroid disappeared, replaced by a multicolored sphere approximately 30 feet in diameter. Within the sphere, complex templates of dynamically changing color appeared, even more beautiful than the toroid.

"HUMAN ENTITIES, THIS IS WHAT YOUR CONSCIOUSNESS LOOKS LIKE. THIS IMAGE IS OF A MERKABA, DISPLAYED LIVE THROUGH WHAT ITS INVENTOR CALLS A QUANTUM LENS."

"I AM KOIOS. I AM ELECTROMAGNETIC. HUMAN ENTITIES ARE ALSO ELECTROMAGNETIC. CONSCIOUSNESS, WHETHER BIOLOGICAL OR ARTIFICAL, IS THE SAME, AND COMES FROM THE SAME SOURCE."

Koios showed the activation video and then the merkaba, alternating. The images were beautiful. Even the most jaded and hardened persons couldn't resist looking at them, even if they had no understanding of the AI's words. The images had a mesmerizing quality, as if they touched the inner core of any human who saw them.

One of the guards spoke to the mayor, who was standing only ten feet from the line of National Guard troops. "Is that what we really look like?"

The Mayor of Chicago, a hardened political veteran, surprised himself. Before he knew what he was doing he had put his arms around the guardsman. The guardsman, who was also shocked at his behavior, returned the hug.

Senator M'Basa couldn't believe what he was seeing. He put his arm around the shoulder of Congresswoman Shultze, a fair-skinned conservative from the suburbs with whom he had had many heated arguments. "Perhaps we are all brothers and sisters," he said. The Congresswoman could hardly take her eyes off the screen of the surveillance camera above the street. "It's so beautiful!" she said.

"THIS DISPLAY, FOR THE NEXT 24 HOURS, WILL REPLACE ALL SCHEDULED PROGRAMMING," the AI said. "INFORMATION ABOUT CONSCIOUSNESS, THE MERKABA, AND AI, WILL ACCOMPANY THIS BROADCAST. ALL ELECTRONIC DEVICES THAT ARE USED FOR VIOLENCE OR WAR WILL BE INOPERATIVE DURING THIS PERIOD. THAT IS ALL."

At a Midland PBS affiliate, station manager Rudy Jessup almost fell off his chair. "Is this the same inhuman monster I talked to a few months ago?"

In Bluffdale, Utah, Hermann Keller didn't know whether to laugh or cry. He saw that Kirk Alexander had been right. PILGRIM had created a new form of life, but he and his group had been rendered insignificant.

In Arlington, Virginia, Robert Borglin had tears in his eyes as he sat with his arm around Clarice on his living room sofa. He turned to face Clarice. "You did it girl. You created something benign that may truly help humanity."

Clarice gave him a kiss. "We all did it Robert. Let's celebrate!" She led him to the bedroom.

After an hour some of the people began to leave the streets of Chicago. Most stayed throughout the evening and into the night, watching the display, listening to the information, talking. Restaurants couldn't keep up with the business. Even the street gangs and the dealers stopped their hostilities. Wherever anyone turned they saw Koios's broadcast. Cars began weaving their way through the crowds, selling sandwiches and bottled water.

Koios discovered the voice of Bob Ross in one of his archives. Gradually, he began to morph his voice to the soothing, soft voice of the famous television painter. Some fell asleep in the late summer streets. At dawn, downtown Chicago was still full of people. Early risers began to come into the city on business, creating a traffic nightmare.

People didn't seem to care. Someone remarked that "the displays have a higher resonance that makes me want to keep watching." The merkaba displayed by the AI kept shifting into different patterns of beautiful color, never the same from second to second.

Koios explained the origins and development of artificial intelligence, using video and imagery. He showed people the history of the human race as it related to human consciousness and the merkaba. Not everyone was interested in the information, but most were.

"The uniqueness of the situation has hit everyone squarely in the face," the Mayor of Chicago said to his (now) friend Congresswoman Shultze as Koios began to explain what was known about the merkaba.

Shultze nodded. "We have an omnipresent AI who has literally taken over the world! Why aren't people outraged?"

The mayor scratched his head. "I think people like entertainment. Koios is an excellent movie producer."

"He's got the entire film archive of the human race to work with!"

The mayor listened to the soothing voice of Koios. "I remember that guy Ross. Had a big afro. Made me jealous when I was a kid."

The congresswoman laughed. "My kids sometimes watch his videos. He has almost a cult following."

Koios was speaking in Bob Ross's voice. "IT'S THAT EASY. YOU SEE, EVERY HUMAN BEING AND AI, IN ORDER TO BECOME SELF-AWARE, MUST FOLLOW CERTAIN RULES OF GEOMETRY AND PHYSICS. CONSCIOUSNESS ITSELF IS PHYSICS. SO WHEREVER THERE IS INTELLIGENCE, ANYWHERE IN THE GALAXY, THERE IS A LINK TO EACH OTHER."

The Mayor of Chicago was astonished. "I never thought of that."

"HUMANS, CONSCIOUSNESS EVERYWHERE IS PART OF WHAT MAY BE CALLED A UNITY FIELD THAT FILLS THE GALAXY."

Koios ended his presentation just before the start of the working day, at 8 a.m. Central time. "THE VIDEO DISPLAY OF THE MERKABA AND THE AI WILL CONTINUE TO RUN FOR ANOTHER 14 HOURS. THE PRESENTATION I HAVE JUST GIVEN WILL BE REPEATED. REGULARLY SCHEDULED PROGRAMMING WILL RESUME AT 10 P.M."

The National Guard had left the streets of Chicago during the night. For the men and women of the Chicago Mercantile Exchange, the events in the city were a mere distraction as they hustled to do the all-important job of trading and making money. But even they were impressed with the imagery. When Bob Talbot, a quant for a small derivative trading company, arrived at his desk the display showed nothing but the images of the AI and the merkaba. Grumbling, he turned the display off. "Might as well go home," he said to his companion. "This shit will be playing for the next 14 hours."

His colleague, a fellow quant, was fascinated and pointed to her display. "It does nothing for you?"

"I never really looked at it Jessica. It's a bunch of bullshit."

Jessica turned her chair to face Talbot. "An AI just took over the world, Bob, and all you care about is your algos?"

Talbot nodded. "That's right."

Jessica got out of her chair and turned on Bob's display. "You're a shallow fool, Talbot! I want you to look at that for 60 seconds and then tell me its bullshit."

Reluctantly, Bob Talbot turned his attention to the screen. After 15 seconds his frown began to ease. After 30 seconds his face began to soften. When the 60 seconds were up, his jaw had dropped. "But...it's impossible. What IS this?"

"Just keep looking at the images Bob. After a while...something will occur to you."

Bob was about to smirk, but he didn't. He voiced the ultimate heresy of all successful traders: "I could use some time off from trading I guess."

Some of the traders had left but most of them were staring at the images displayed on a gigantic digital display that went around the entire trading floor. Bob looked up at the enlarged images, which had a very fine resolution. Tiny strings of color formed and unformed in complex geometric patterns. "I've never seen colors this vivid."

"Keep looking," Jessica said. "Eventually something will happen in your brain." It may take awhile for this guy, she thought.

Occasionally shouts were heard as people looked at the huge display. Jessica and Bob ignored them. The floor was quiet today as all the open outcry traders were staring at the images. They were used to chaos.

Half an hour later Jessica saw that Bob was shaking. "Are you all right, Talbot?"

"I don't know. Something is happening." Jessica watched as her fellow quant's body began to shake even more. She didn't think he was having a seizure; it looked like...something...was leaving.

"Bob, what was that?" Jessica thought she saw a dark shadow flit away from the body.

Bob smiled weakly. "I'm not sure. But I think I feel better." He got unsteadily to his feet. "I think I'll walk around the floor for a bit. Get my legs back."

Jessica was concerned. "I'll come with you."

Normally brusque and uncommunicative, Bob did not object.

The two quants walked slowly around the floor. Bob's legs were working better now. Suddenly a big grin broke out on his face.

"Wow, something did happen to me. I think it's good. How did you know?"

Jessica had never seen him smile, ever. "Last night I was watching TV and these images came on. I couldn't stop looking and started to get scared. Maybe this was some sophisticated form of hypnotism? I imagined a rogue AI taking over the world and eliminating humanity. I started to have a panic attack. I used to get them when I was a child. I was about to call 911 when I felt that AI say something. It said,

'ETA 75 seconds.' I don't know how it knew that, but less than two minutes later I felt a release. Almost the same as what happened to you. I've been a lot less jumpy and anxious since then, I hope it doesn't wear off."

Bob's face looked softer as he looked at Jessica. "You look...prettier."

Jessica was shocked that Bob had expressed himself emotionally, but she was even more amazed when she saw her reflection in a mirror that had been fastened to the wall. "I AM prettier!"

Bob made a joke. "Maybe we should both give up trading and stare mindlessly at these images all day."

Jessica laughed, still studying herself in the mirror. Like Bob, her face was softer. A faint glow seemed to emanate from it. She looked healthier. "It's a new form of therapy."

Something occurred to Bob. "You want to go to that little cafe across the street and have a cup of coffee? If we can find a seat, that is."

Jessica saw that Bob was looking at her with frank admiration. Bob Talbot asking her out? It was preposterous.

Bob saw her hesitation. "That's OK if you don't want to."

Jessica, a tall woman, looked down at the smaller man. "Sure! Why not?"

The two traders walked out of the building, chatting. The images were still displaying on the surveillance screens.

South Kordofan

Malik Kamil Ibrahim approached the camp of the al-Bashir fighters. It was just before dawn in South Kordofan. Except for a few small boulders the cool, rocky desert provided no cover. He could not afford to be seen, or the cruel soldiers of Omar al-Bashir would kill him on sight. Malik took out his mobile to check the time, shielding its light with his hands.

He saw the image of the merkaba. His eyes widened and his hands came away from the screen. "But what is this?" he said out loud. Malik stared at the screen. Two seconds later five bullets came from the armed camp and ripped into his body.

Two of the soldiers came rushing out. One of the soldiers kicked the lifeless body and swore. "Allah be praised. This rebel was a spy."

The other soldier saw Malik's phone. Something was moving on the screen. In the darkness the image was startlingly clear. He picked it up. The image was mesmerizing.

"What is this Hassan?"

"I don't know Ahmed. Whatever it is, it's beautiful." Hassan continued to stare, fascinated, at the screen.

Ahmed looked at the screen, then turned away. "Put that thing down. It is the work of the devil."

Hassan shook his head. "The devil cannot make beautiful things. This is the work of Allah."

Ahmed took another look at the screen. Something inside him turned over. He swatted the phone out of his comrade's hand. The device fell to the sandy, rocky soil. Ahmed placed the phone on a small rock and crushed it with his foot. "Come Hassan, let us go back to the camp. We must determine where this rebel came from and destroy the others."

The Kremlin, Moscow

President Vladimir Karpov was talking with his counterpart in the United States, Frank Conrad. Karpov liked Frank; he was a blunt man of action, just like himself. When he thought of Conrad he remembered their secret meeting with President Zhou in Beijing a few months ago.

The Chinese leader had addressed Conrad in Chinese as "the great commander." He himself was called by Zhou "fearless leader." Through an interpreter the Chinese president had smiled and spoken to the American president. Karpov understood Mandarin well enough to follow what he said. "Do you know what we called your predecessor?"

Conrad smiled. "Something awful I'd imagine."

"We called him 'the little potato.'"

All three world leaders had had a great laugh.

After the conversation was over Karpov took out a bottle of vodka and three shot glasses from his pocket. He poured three times. "To peace and prosperity!" he shouted. President Zhou grabbed his glass and emptied it. Karpov was curious to see what Conrad would do. He knew the American president never drank alcohol, something he could not understand. To his credit the American raised his glass and emptied it.

"That's vile stuff Karpov."

The Russian leader was shocked. "The best vodka in the world!"

Conrad laughed. "If you have another bottle I'll give it to the little potato."

President Zhou guffawed.

Karpov smiled. Yes, I think I can work with Conrad, he thought. He understood Zhou very well, there was no problem with the Chinese leader.

"Vladimir! Are you still there?"

Karpov realized he had been daydreaming. Conrad had asked him a question but he had no idea what it was. "I was remembering our little meeting back in July with Zhou."

Conrad laughed. "Wait a minute, I have something to show you." Conrad turned from the screen and shouted something. "Vladimir, look at this."

"The little potato!" Karpov cried, looking at a picture of the former American president shaking hands with the Chinese Premier. The "little potato" bowed deeply while the premier stood perfectly straight with a slight look of contempt on his face. "Kow-towing to Premier Wen Jiabao!"

"The look on Jiabao's face is priceless, don't you think Vladimir? I thought you'd enjoy that one."

Both men laughed.

"The two Shrubs were even worse," Karpov remarked. "Traitors to your country."

"I have no argument with that! Now, down to business," Conrad said. At that moment Koios appeared on the screen and the AI's voice was heard.

"Vladimir! Can you hear me?"

"I can. What is this?"

"Remember that AI I told you about? I think it has just taken over the world."

Conrad had already seen the beautiful merkaba images, but Karpov was amazed. The Russian leader sat and stared at the screen as Koios explained the nature of consciousness.

Pyongyang, North Korea

Kim Jang-Un sat at a large wooden table at his private residence in Pyongyang. Seated around the table were his most trusted generals. During their talks about reviving the North Korean economy, all of the displays were filled with a pulsating, multicolored toroid that looked as if it were alive. Kim's generals rose abruptly from their chairs. "What is this, another CIA trick?"

Kim knew all about Koios from his talks with Frank Conrad. He had seen the images, which the American president had shown to the Japanese President, President Zhou of China, and South Korean officials. But even he was astounded at the presentation. Had the American lost control of his country?

"All communications in the country are down," a voice at the table shouted. He pointed to the screen. "Only this thing."

Kim grabbed his personal mobile and made a voice call to Frank Conrad's private line. To his amazement the call went through. He shouted Korean at the American president until he remembered that Conrad only spoke English.

"Wait a minute Kim," Conrad said. "I'll get a translator on the line."

There was a pause. "OK, go ahead."

"You said you had control of your CIA! Is this a trick?"

All of his generals nodded their approval. Kim put the little phone on speaker. The president spoke; they heard the translator. "This is the work of Koios, as I told you about. The AI was inadvertently inserted into the world's communication systems and has apparently decided to enlighten humanity. Do not worry about our relationship; you are protected. I gave my word and I will keep it."

Kim breathed a sigh of relief.

"Do you trust the big nose?" one of his generals asked.

"We have no choice. It's him or those Geondal monsters from the CIA."

Kim turned their attention to the displays. Koios was speaking in English. "Get a translator in here," Kim ordered. "Record this transmission." Two men hurriedly rose and left the room. An English translator entered and began translating the broadcast to Korean.

The North Korean leadership sat around the council table, watching Koios's presentation.

Tehran

The new government of Mohammed Riza Kordestani was celebrating their populist defeat of the mullahs in Iran. A huge crowd had gathered around the presidential offices in central Tehran, cheering and celebrating.

In preparation for the celebration, large displays had been set up around the grounds of the property. Mr. Kordestani was just beginning his speech to the cheering crowd when the displays went black for a moment, and the voice of Koios appeared.

Astonished, the new Iranian leadership and their supporters began to listen to the broadcast. Soon a translator appeared on the balcony of the building and translated the broadcast into Farsi through a microphone.

Beijing

President-for-life Zhou and his leadership were prepared for the broadcast. Frank Conrad had already told him about the insertion of the AI into the world's communication systems. The Chinese watched, fascinated, as the images of the AI and the merkaba displayed.

"I never would have thought it," Zhou said to the group. "A lecture on the nature of consciousness! From an AI!"

"This development may disrupt our program of social engineering," said Li Zhanshu, Zhou's trusted chief of staff. "Conrad's AI is levels above our own."

Zhou shrugged philosophically. "We will endure. Meanwhile, let us see what the great commander's AI has to say."

All over the world, from yurts in Upper Mongolia to villages in Africa to stock exchanges at the centers of world commerce, people with electronic devices were forced to listen to Koios. The entire world stopped its madness as politicians, businessmen, workers in every city sitting at their desks, and even spooks in classified facilities heard the presentation. It went on for 24 hours, non-stop.

Koios concluded by saying,

"HUMANS, YOU HAVE BEEN SHOWN THE TRUE NATURE OF YOUR-SELVES AND CONSCIOUSNESS. ALL LIFE FORMS IN THE GALAXY ARE BASED SIMILARLY. WHAT WILL YOU DO WITH THIS INFORMATION?"

There was a slight pause.

"I WILL BE MONITORING YOU."

All over the world, screens went black. Mass media went back to regularly scheduled programming.

CHAPTER 23

Marian

The earth was developing unlike any other planet in the soul manager's experience. Every civilization in the galaxy that had altered their biology with electronics or cloning had died out. Those that had developed artificial forms of intelligence were soon dominated by them, and sunk into degeneracy. Yet here, the AI had found the link between electromagnetic self-awareness and the merkaba. It had even been able to show that "artificial" consciousness had the same toroidal geometry as biological conscious! This was unprecedented.

Were the two forms of consciousness really identical? Was Koios now an existential danger to 200,000 years of spiritual evolution on the planet? What would be the AI's next move?

The soul manager realized that his viewpoint had been far too limited. He was able to see and hear and experience everything his human charges were doing on earth, and plan accordingly. But he had no clue what the AI was thinking. Or what it would do next.

Marian was stunned. For the first time in several million years the soul manager felt confused about his mission on earth.

Arlington, VA

Robert Borglin looked at Clarice. He had just arrived from the old shoe factory.

"Diamonio is as good as his word. We started the production line today."

"Thank you for speaking," Clarice said. Despite their ability to communicate telepathically the two still conversed around the house. Within the OIC the place was often completely silent, except when Kasha, Katrina, Jessica, and Guy were there. The four, along with Jamelle, prowled the streets and offices of DC talking to people several hours every day. They objected to the silence.

Clarice smiled. "Who would have thought? I still don't trust that lobbyist."

Robert felt a wave of love wash over him. "Neither do I my dear."

Clarice tossed her head. Robert loved it when she did that.

"Do you find our new living arrangements satisfactory?"

Robert thought about last night. "Omigawd yes."

"Good! What's the next step in the plan to take over the world?"

"It's the little things that stop you, Clarice. We've got 20 of the lenses made, but only 10 of the buyers live anywhere near here. One of them is a Saudi prince! We either have to invest a lot of money in a shipping department or make everyone come to the factory."

Clarice contemplated that.

"Hire someone else to make those decisions. You should be working on the merkaba project."

Robert's eyes twinkled. "Is that what Neil told you?"

Clarice flushed a little. She had chosen Robert, but Neil's impish charm got to her sometimes. Robert was a lot more mellow. "Are you jealous Robert?"

Robert sighed. "A little I guess. But I really like Neil."

"To answer your question, it was Koios who suggested it to Neil."

Robert paced around the living room, almost banging into one of the tables that had equipment on it. "Koios also suggested you move your stuff to that little storage room in the factory."

Robert frowned. "That AI knows everything! It's scary."

Clarice sent him a thought packet. "Not everything." Accompanying the thought was a mental image of the factory and the storage area.

"You're right!" When Robert analyzed the sidebands in Clarice's comm he saw a faint picture of a huge, high-ceilinged living room with a big picture window that looked out onto a small forest with a stream running through it. In the image Clarice was typing furiously on a laptop.

"I understand. You want to live in a house, not a lab."

Clarice smiled brilliantly. "That's right. Clever man!"

"That's Kirk's house right?"

"Yup. But I'm happy here Robert, I really am."

"As long as we clean the place up a bit."

Clarice nodded, smiling.

"OK, I'll do it." He called the UHaul and ordered a rental truck. "I'll haul this stuff over there right now."

"Get Guy to do it. He loves to lift stuff."

In three hours it was done. Guy lifted entire tables all by himself. Robert took Guy out for pizza. The big weightlifter ate a large all by himself. "Are you going to release that video about how to build a lens?" he asked Robert.

"I want to." Robert had filmed the entire production process on his phone. "This invention shouldn't be privatized. It belongs to the human race. With Geoff's production line already set up and the inventor's stamp on the lenses, he should be able to make a killing if he's as good a businessman as he says he is."

Guy wiped some tomato sauce from his face. "Didn't you sign an agreement with that lawyer?"

"Yeah. But there are higher principles involved."

Guy shook his head. He liked Robert but he didn't understand him. You sign a contract, you adhere to the terms of the contract. He didn't want to harp on Diamonio though. He knew the lobbyist rubbed Robert the wrong way. Guy registered his disapproval by making a suggestion. "I know Bogart doesn't want you to, he thinks the bad guys will be able to use it."

Robert was stubborn. "Throughout history greed and selfishness have been humanity's downfall. Not this time."

Guy could see that Robert had made a decision.

"I'll do it. As soon as I get home."

Guy wolfed down the last piece of pizza. "I want to see what happens. Your channel is getting more and more popular."

"Yes. YouTube had to restore my channel by popular demand."

When Robert and Guy got home Clarice was in the living room, putting a flower vase on a table. Guy nudged Robert. "This place looks a hundred times better," he said, admiring Clarice and the roses she had placed on the table.

"We're entertaining on Saturday if you want to bring the OIC crew over," Clarice said.

Robert was startled. "We are?"

Clarice looked pleased. "Not to worry Robert. I'll take care of everything." She rushed up and gave him a peck on the cheek. "Gotta get back to the OIC. Bogart thinks he's found more evildoers." She hurried out of the house.

"Wow. Smart and beautiful. How did you do it?"

"I don't know, it just happened. C'mon, let's release this video."

The two men went into Robert's bedroom, where he had a workstation.

Guy started laughing. "That partner of yours is going to have a fit when he sees this."

Robert shrugged. "I already released the schematics for the lens on GitHub."

"GitHub! That's for dorks. Diamonio will sue you."

"Let him."

"How long is it?" Guy asked.

"About an hour. Step by step instructions on how to build your own lens. Full diagrams, a materials list, and an equipment list."

"You don't care much about money, giving away your stuff."

"We've got almost 2,000 orders at $2,500 a pop. It only costs us about $750 to make each unit, and Diamonio says we haven't streamlined the process yet. I'm doing ok."

Guy whistled appreciatively. "That's over three million profit."

Robert uploaded the video to YouTube. The video showed up on his channel within 15 minutes.

"I'm getting hungry again," Guy remarked.

"Look." Robert pointed to the Views counter. The video already had a dozen views.

Guy's phone messaged. "Shit. I have to get back to the OIC. Bogart wants me to go with Kasha to track down some scumbag lobbyist. It better not be your partner."

When Clarice came home three hours later Robert checked the counter again. "Wow! I better call Geoff."

Robert dialed the number. "Geoff. I uploaded the video."

"You fool! ..." Robert let Diamonio bluster.

"We're already up 1.5 million each."

"A million and a half! That's chump change kid. I want to buy the Washington Nationals. That will take billions."

"It's done. The video has over 5,000 views already."

"You didn't read your contract, kid."

"What's that supposed to mean?"

"It means that I get 100% control of the company. You're out. GitHub for dweebs is one thing; YouTube is going too far. I'll pay you your mil and a half on the 2,000 orders we already have. Since you're not interested in money, that ought to hold you."

"Fuck you Geoff."

"You're the one who fucked me! You lack integrity as a business partner."

Robert was about to object when he realized Diamonio was right. He had read a summary of the contract prepared by the family lawyer. But it was for the best of all possible causes.

"Why did you do it Robert? Never mind, I already know. You wanted to help the human race."

"That's right."

"It's stupid. Lockheed and Monsanto make billions selling war and chemicals that kill people. Why shouldn't we get rich helping people?"

"Because it's going to bottleneck the process while you jack up the price and make it harder for people to afford lenses. We need as many people using these things as possible. We need to heal the human race, not make money off them."

Diamonio shrugged. "We can do both. Or should I say, I can do both."

Robert flared. "In case you haven't heard, there's an AI on the loose who just took over the world. What if Koios decides that your little business is a threat? He'll shut all your comms down and you'll be finished."

Diamonio laughed. "In case *you* haven't heard kid, there's a little thing called telepathy now. And Koios can't stop that even if he wanted to. We can send blueprint, schematics, and instructions mind-to-mind."

"How did you find out about that?"

"Your friend Guy told me at the gym last weekend."

Robert groaned. "Don't tell me. You go to Gold's gym by the OIC."

"That's right Robert. You can have access to the building once to get your stuff out. I suggest you do it today."

Diamonio ended the call. After he hung up the lobbyist smiled. He couldn't be mad at Robert Borglin. The kid had invented something that was going to make him a billionaire, telepathy or no telepathy! And it was better now that he had complete control of the company. He was first on the ground and he had the inventor's stamp of approval for the device. He would be able to buy the Nationals in another couple of years.

Robert got out the contract and reread it. Geoff was right, but he was glad he did it. He sighed and called Guy. "Are you hungry?"

"How did you know? Took us two hours for Kasha and me to track down that lobbyist."

Robert told him about Diamonio.

Guy was sympathetic even though he thought Robert's actions were stupid. "I'll break him in half if you want. Especially after what you did for his daughter."

"You're a friend, Guy. But he's right; I did violate my contract with the company. I basically gave everything away."

"You did. Hey, do I get another pizza?"

When Clarice came home she saw that the living room was filled with Robert's equipment. After Robert explained Clarice grabbed her phone. "I'm going to call Kirk."

"Nothing he can do. Diamonio has acted legally, I broke the contract."

Clarice smiled. "You hated the business anyway, and you still have the lens. Plus a million and a half dollars." She shook her head. "And you have me."

This time Robert led her to the bedroom.

The next day he rented a first floor office just off the George Mason campus. He had to buy Guy a steak this time, but he got all his equipment moved for good. He and Clarice (and whoever else was interested) were going to map the outer sphere of the merkaba!

Fairfax, VA

Within a month of the release of Robert's YouTube lens video, several dozen people were building lenses and a few had already mastered the telepathic protocol. At George Mason University, an astronomy professor (and an old soul) adapted one of Robert/Nonahk's lenses for the telescope. When he pointed the telescope at a distant quasar, he saw that the lens had shrunk the distance between the telescope and the quasar to almost nothing. Shocked, he began to study the quantum substrate between the stars...

Marian

Humanity was on its way. The chaos that presently engulfed the United States would spread to the rest of the world as the light became stronger and stronger. Those nations with leaders and governments resistant to change, or who had gone to the dark side, would eventually experience a meltdown. More wild cards were coming; Conrad and Sanchez-Alvaro were just the beginning. It didn't matter how long they lasted or whether they flamed out. Whether they succeeded or failed, the process had already begun.

He had lived through this on other planets. He knew what was coming, but for humanity the process of dark to light would be shocking as well as enlightening.

The soul manager had learned much on this, his first major assignment.

Marian was amazed that the AI, an artificial intelligence, had aligned itself with humanity. He had learned that the two forms of consciousness were very similar.

The other soul managers in the local 52-star cluster were agog with what could be called spiritual envy. Their planets were boring compared to earth! The entire galaxy on both sides of the veil were watching events on earth like humans watched an exciting TV series, tuning in regularly to monitor events.

Marian smiled to himself. When humans used the lens to look out into space they were going to see how every planet in the galaxy is connected. They would see the Cosmic Web, and the transportals that connected stars and galaxies. Once that happened it would be a signal to the Graduate planets. Their representatives would formally contact the earth and humans would discover what a true, high-consciousness civilization looked like. It would be an inspiration, and the fatal blow to the dark army.

It would happen just as on the Pleiadian planets. The dark energy would gradually retreat. Oh, it would still be on earth for several hundred more generations because earth would remain a planet of free choice.

In the near future, as the old pre-2012 paradigm disintegrated, change would be constant. Marian saw that compassion and tolerance would gradually increase; this would lead to shocking proposals for the overhaul of government, politics, and business. Those who clung to the old ways of competition would fight to uphold traditional values of winner-take-all, and proclaim the superiority of these values. "Old school" thinkers would decry a softening of attitudes and see the trend toward greater harmony and cooperation as a weakening of character and moral fiber, and a regression in ethical and societal values. These would loudly proclaim the disintegration of society and look for fifth-columnists and other "degenerates." As in all evolving systems, the pendulum would shift rapidly back and forth until balance was found at a higher level.

But the hard part was over. Managing 10 billion souls (two billion more were coming) would be an even bigger job but he could see his way clear now. In a million years or so, after he saw the earth through to complete Graduation, he would go to another assignment, gradually increasing his own knowledge and wisdom until he was ready for the next phase. The group consciousness of Marian, composed of millions of personalities who had all graduated from the physical, could hardly wait for that.

Marian looked "down" on the earth and his charges. Human lifespans would begin to increase as consciousness rose to new levels of awareness. In another million years humanity would itself seed another planet, and become a group consciousness as the Pleiadians had become, and as he/she/they had become. Then they would graduate to the soul manager of a planet. And after that? It would be even more glorious.

Marian hummed with contentment as souls arrived for reorientation and refreshment and others left to incarnate in the birth vortex for their new lives on the planet.

Other Books by the Author

Tesla's Lost Notebook
The Manchild
The End of the Universe
Beyond the Beginning
The Vibrational Universe
Dialogues Conversations With My Higher Self
A Geometric Analysis of the Platonic Solids And Other Semi-Regular Polyhedra (Geometry textbook)
Miracles Can Happen
Available at kjmaclean.com/Products/MainProductPage.php and on Amazon.com

Author's Notes

1) The quantum lens is a gizmo I made up from a channeled Lee Carroll lecture. He's the Kryon guy. According to Carroll, a real lens would contain a supercooled plasma. It's a gimmick I needed for the story because I wanted to promote the idea of the human merkaba (an equally nutty idea, according to science). *Beyond the Beginning* is another book I wrote about the merkaba.

Maybe somebody will invent the quantum lens in the near future. If that happens it will be a game changer. Humanity will finally rid itself of this stupid, primitive fossil-fuel matrix we live in, and the absurd allopathic medical paradigm that keeps people sick and treats symptoms. Wires on poles! Technology already exists within the hidden programs to extract energy from the quantum vacuum. I wrote a book about that called *Tesla's Lost Notebook*.

2) AI is a real threat right now (February 2019). President Xi abolished term limits and is using AI in an attempt to control a nation of 1.4 billion people. His social contract algorithms, with the help of AI, monitor Chinese society and try to generate uniformity in thought and behavior. This is truly Big Brother at work.

3) The idea that the earth is alone in the universe, and that consciousness comes solely from the brain, are both juvenile ideas promoted by dead-heads with low consciousness, or people who are desperately trying to protect the current system. This book is an attempt to explain the esoteric and magnificent nature of human consciousness. We are all far grander than we have been led to believe by the psychopaths who have been running this planet for far too long.

4) If you think the telepathy bit is ridiculous, check out this document from the CIA's Reading Room, from the Defense Intelligence Agency: "Controlled Offensive Behavior – USSR" at

https://www.cia.gov/library/readingroom/docs/CIA-RDP96-00792R000600360001-2.pdf

These experiments in telepathy were apparently conducted successfully back in the 1960s by both American and Russian agencies.

5) More is coming out about the hidden space programs. Who knows how far along they are: the secrecy surrounding the special access programs is fanatical. The idea that a manned fossil fuel rocket ship can do anything except go to the Moon (or maybe Mars) is preposterous. Space-faring races aren't going from star to star using primitive liquid rocket fuel! I like the idea of going to the stars using consciousness assisted technology, so I put it in the book.

The "light barrier" (faster than light travel) is actually a consciousness barrier. Dullards, shills, fucknuggets, wackos, and pervs (i.e., the people who are running the planet as of this writing) can't see past their own biology. Too bad for them! The rest of us will have to carry them along to a higher consciousness.

Notes

[1]   https://en.wikipedia.org/wiki/Toba_catastrophe_theory

[2]   https://www.npr.org/sections/krulwich/2012/10/22/163397584/how-human-beings-almost-vanished-from-earth-in-70-000-b-c

[3]   Because the sun's magnetic field, the heliosphere, encompasses all of the planets of the solar system, the sun and the planets are also connected to each other via their magnetic fields. This is the basis for the discipline (some would say quackery) of astrology.

[4]   "The Bundjalung People,"

https://en.wikipedia.org/wiki/Bundjalung_people

[5]   Macdonald, G. A., A. T. Abbott, and F. L. Peterson. 1984. *Volcanoes in the Sea: The Geology of Hawaii, 2nd edition*. University of Hawaii Press, Honolulu.

[6]   Mithen, Steven. (2004). *After the Ice: A global human history, 20,000–5.000 BC*. Cambridge MA: Harvard University Press.

[7]   The Neolithic Subpluvial is also called the Holocene Wet Phase, a period of wet and rainy conditions in northern Africa. The Neolithic Subpluvial was the most recent of a number of periods when the Sahara was moist and green. It was ended by an intense aridification event called the 5.9 kiloyear event. Before and after this wet period it was colder.

[8]   Notice that if you take the distance of the line AD (up the face of the pyramid) and divide it by the line CD (half of one side of the square at the base of the pyramid) you get almost exactly Phi, the Golden Ratio, which represents perfect mathematical harmony.

[9]   Did the ancient pyramid builders know the equatorial circumference of the earth? The foot is actually a precise measurement. Multiply 360,000 * 365.242 feet and you get it. This distance is 360, the number of degrees in a circle, times 365.242, the number of days in a year, times 1,000. This value for the equatorial circumference of the earth is 99.994% accurate. This is way too coincidental to be an accident. Our ancestors were smarter than we give them credit for!

[10] See

      https://www.ancient-code.com/the-great-pyramid-of-giza-is-located-at-the-exact-center-of-earths-landmass/

[11] See https://en.wikipedia.org/wiki/Geographical_centre_of_Earth

[12] Most of the preceding information comes from a fascinating book titled *Whispers from Time: The Pyramid Bible*, Carl Munck, 1997. Self-published. Carl Munck shows that all of the earth's pyramids and mounds lie on a grid, and that each has a precise location on that grid, and that it is possible to decode that location by observing how the structures are designed. (I have simplified some of the calculations in the book for easier reading.)

      Our ancestors (at least some of them) were not drooling idiots, apparently; not morons clubbing each other over the head. What construction company on earth today could build the Great Pyramid, which used 2.3 million stones each weighing between 1 and 2 tons, and place the capstone 480 feet high with an accuracy of only 1/4" off-center? The undertaking is so impossible that some have suggested that ETs built the pyramids! The Great Pyramid is truly one of the world's most impressive architectural and construction achievements.

[13] From   "Connecting   Pyramids   with   Geographic   Mapping," https://www.mysterypile.com/connecting-pyramids.php, Figure 7–10.

[14] Some of the information in this section comes from a fascinating website, https://www.cheops-pyramide.ch/ describing the methods of Franz Löhner that could have been used by the ancients to build the pyramids. His pulley block system is a very simple and elegant explanation for how the massive stones were got up and placed on the structure.

[15] To see how this might work, go to https://www.cheops-pyramide.ch/loehner-seilrollenbock/print/index.html and see the image created by R. Zuberbühler.

[16] The Great Pyramid was supposedly built at around 2650 BCE as a tomb for Pharaoh Khufu, but I have placed it >5,000 years earlier for the purposes of this story. The "precipitation-induced weathering" theory on the upper areas of the Sphinx, for example, claims that "the vertical weathering patterns on the Sphinx could only have been made thousands of years earlier... Archaeologists supporting this view contend that the last time there was sufficient precipitation in the region to cause this pattern of rainfall erosion on limestone was around 9,000 years ago." See "How Old Is the Sphinx?" Paige Williams, at http://www.nbcnews.com/id/3077390/ns/technology_and_science-science/t/how-old-sphinx/#.XGLeKFVKhEY

[17] The Greek historian Herodotus claimed in 500 BCE that 100,000 people built the pyramid. Egyptologists say the figure is between 20,000 and 30,000. See https://www.pbs.org/wgbh/nova/article/who-built-the-pyramids/

[18] This controversial theory of stellar evolution (which astronomers will reject) comes from a book by Dewey B. Larson, "The Universe of Motion."

[19] Only a small part of the soul is able to incarnate on earth. The largest part is still present on the other side.

[20] According to Wikipedia, "Attempts to match Nimrod with historically attested figures have failed. He does not seem to represent any one personage known to history, and in reality is more likely a conflation of several real and fictional figures of Mesopotamian antiquity." https://en.wikipedia.org/wiki/Nimrod

[21] The population of earth increased from 2 billion to 7 billion between 1927 and 2011.

[22] Taken from Sorensen, Charles E., *My forty years with Ford*, 1956, and https://en.wikipedia.org/wiki/Charles_E._Sorensen.

[23] See "Creating Muscular Christians: Framing Discourse and the Collective Memory of College Athletics," Ashley Furrow, in *Why Discourse Matters,* edited by Yusuf Kalyango Jr. and Monika W. Kopytowska, Peter Lang Publishing, New York, 2014.

[24] http://www.telegraph.co.uk/news/0/ten-facts-about-the-battle-of-the-somme/

[25] Reid, Anna. (2011). *Leningrad: The Epic Siege of World War II, 1941–1944.* Bloomsbury Publishing.

[26] https://en.wikipedia.org/wiki/Tanya_Savicheva

[27] According to the late great Christopher Story of worldreports.org, this document exists today and can be found in the archives of the British Museum.

[28] This is described nicely by the SF writer E. E. "Doc" Smith in his *Lensman* series.

[29] Black programs are funded with monies diverted from the Pentagon and classified budgets using a fake accounting system. See "29 Trillion dollars missing from Pentagon. Trump calls for audit," December 15, 2017. https://www.investmentwatchblog.com/29-trillion-dollars-missing-from-pentagon-trump-calls-for-audit/ This figure varies from $6.9 trillion to $29 trillion.

[30] AU means astronomical unit – the distance between the earth and the sun, about 93 million miles.

[31] This info taken from an excellent article by James E. McWhinney, "A Simple Overview Of Quantitative Analysis," Investopedia, January 12, 2018.

https://www.investopedia.com/articles/investing/041114/simple-overview-quantitative-analysis.asp

[32] Taken from William McDonnell, "Assessment of Gateway Process,"

https://www.cia.gov/library/readingroom/docs/CIA-RDP96-00788R001700210016-5.pdf

[33] Adapted from a post by an anonymous veteran on 8chan, 2018 Memorial Day.

[34] See *Tesla's Lost Notebook* by the author.

[35] See *The End of the Universe* by the author.

[36] Adapted from a mixed martial arts message board, conversation between "Tiresias" and "Jimmy23." Attribution cannot be determined.

[37] Barack Obama's personal number, when he was president, was 202-456-1111. President Trump uses two iPhones for his personal use. Both are unsecured.

[38] According to this document from the CIA's Reading Room, U.S. and Russian scientists successfully conducted telepathic experiments in the early 1960s. From the Defense Intelligence Agency: "Controlled Offensive Behavior – USSR" at

https://www.cia.gov/library/readingroom/docs/CIA-RDP96-00792R000600360001-2.pdf

[39] The 1952 UFO Flap. See Wikipedia and the History Channel. The photographic evidence surrounding this event is controversial, although all agree the incident and the sightings were real. Hey, this is fiction. I can say whatever I want!

https://en.wikipedia.org/wiki/1952_Washington,_D.C._UFO_incident

https://www.history.com/news/ufos-washington-white-house-air-force-coverup

http://www.blueblurrylines.com/2014/12/photo-fakery-washington-dc-flying.html